*The
Finnsburg
Encounter*

The Finnsburg Encounter

Matthew T. Dickerson

3666

CROSSWAY BOOKS • WHEATON, ILLINOIS
A DIVISION OF GOOD NEWS PUBLISHERS

The Finnsburg Encounter.

Copyright © 1991 by Matthew T. Dickerson.

Published by Crossway Books, a division of
Good News Publishers, Wheaton, Illinois 60187.

Cover illustration: Chris Hopkins

Map illustration: Hugh Claycombe

First printing, 1991

Printed in the United States of America

Library of Congress Cataloging-in-Publication Data
Dickerson, Matthew, 1963-
      The Finnsburg encounter / Matthew Dickerson.
         p.   cm.
      1. Finn, King of the Frisians (Legendary character)—Fiction.
2. Fight at Finnsburg (Anglo-Saxon poem)—Adaptations.
3. Beowulf—Adaptations. I. Title.
PS3554.I316F56 1991   813'.54—dc20   90-15064
      ISBN 0-89107-604-2

99		98		97		96		95		94		93		92		91
15	14	13	12	11	10	9	8	7	6	5	4	3	2	1

For my wife Deborah,
the flower which heaven
has given to me

CONTENTS

AUTHOR'S NOTE

The tale here set forth of Finn and Hildeburh grew out of a small portion of the Old English heroic poem *Beowulf*. After Beowulf's victory over the monster Grendel, the hero and his brave companions gather together in Heorot, the famous hall of Danish king Hrothgar, to celebrate. In that portion of the poem, often called "The Finnsburg Episode of Beowulf" (lines 1064-1124), Hrothgar's poet sings a song about the famous battle of Finn and Hnaef. The tale is retold in brief by the *Beowulf* poet—a story within a story, as it were. At the time that *Beowulf* was composed, that tale of Finn and Hildeburh was probably well-known, and so the *Beowulf* poet needed only to give a brief summary of the events. Now, however, many centuries later, the full story of these events is long lost. All we know of the tragic tale of Finn is what we read in that small episode of *Beowulf*, and in a cryptic fragment of another poem which was discovered, transcribed by the scholar George Hickes, and then lost, but which seems to relate closely to the events told by the *Beowulf* poet.

Here then is given, as recreated in the imagination of the author, a fuller tale of Finn and Hildeburh, and of the events leading up to the fight at Finnsburg. No knowledge of *Beowulf* is necessary, but those who are familiar with that great poem may enjoy these speculations. In order to give a more realistic, historical flavor to the tale, I have placed the events during a particular period of history, namely the early seventh century. This proved to be a rather troublesome business, for it raised many difficult questions. Are the events of the Finn Episode based on a real battle? Did these people really exist in history? If so, when?

We don't know the answers to these questions. Thus in some sense this time frame is rather arbitrary. Historians, Old English scholars, and archaeologists have argued over the dating of the *Beowulf* poem for years. Some have dated the poem's composition as early as 500, and others as late as 1000. The closest one can come to a general consensus would be in the mid-800s, but that is really more of a compromise than a consensus. The tale of Finn, if already well-known by the time *Beowulf* was composed, must have taken place long before. If *Beowulf* was composed in 500, then the tale of Finn obviously could not have taken place after 600! My dating of the tale is as much for the sake of convenience as anything; there were some things about that period, such as the founding of Lindisfarne, that I wanted to include in my tale. But there are a few other good reasons for setting my story during that time. It has been suggested that the Hengest of this tale is one and the same as the Hengest who in the late sixth century finally defeated the remnant forces of the Britons under the famed British warleader, King Arthur. But once again, knowledge of these dates and events is not at all necessary to the enjoyment of the tale set forth here, which was written to stand on its own.

I would give my deepest thanks to Professor Robert Farrell of Cornell University. His expertise in medieval archaeology and Old English language and literature was invaluable to me. In addition to much enthusiastic encouragement, he also provided the critical eye that is so necessary to a novel like this. Considerable thanks are also due to Jan Dennis of Crossway Books for his encouragement and work with me on this project. There is no doubt that without the two of them, this would not have been written.

Matthew T. Dickerson
August 1990

The Finnsburg Encounter

A Map of
Friesland
and the
Surrounding
Kindgoms

N

Iona †•

† Lindisfarne

ANGLES

IRISH

SAXONS

JUTES

Cantbury •
Cantwara

FRANKS

† • Monastery

Miles 0   100   200   300
Kms   0   100   200   300   400

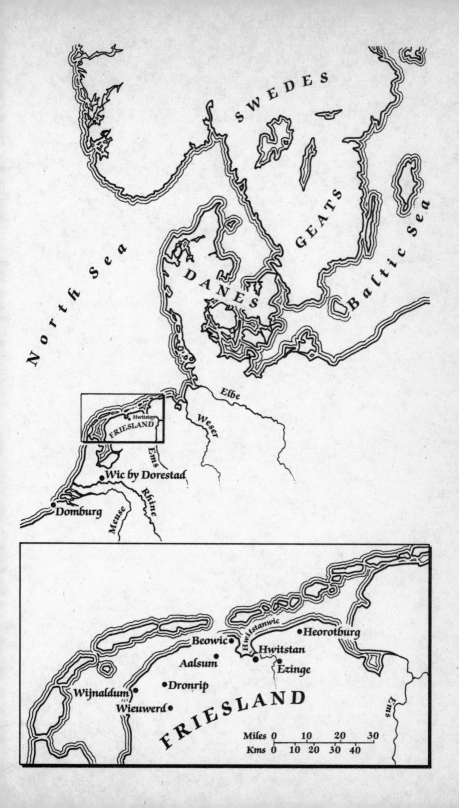

PART I

Hwitstan

I

Of Finn, Son of Folcwalda

Atop a small tower of stone overlooking the bay, as still and unmovable as the rock beneath him, stood Finn, the prince of Friesland. His unfaltering gaze scanned the far horizon for a sail upon the waters. Out across Hwitstanwic and beyond his eyes roamed, to the great North Sea from whence would come his heart's desire. He wore a red cloak of fine woven cloth, fastened at the waist with bright blue silk and decorated at the shoulders in green. Healfwyrhta, his mighty battle sword, hung from a loose strap over his back. An old treasure it was, proven times without count. In his left hand he held his great ash staff. And on a chain about the prince's neck was a polished ivory battle horn, new-made and not yet winded; richly decorated in silver by Deomaer the jeweler, it was a treasure worthy of a king.

Long had Finn waited for this day, and with no small labor had he prepared. This was his day. Many months of hope and longing would finally come to an end. It was Summer's Day, the day of the long sun. This was the day when Finn the strong, Folcwalda's son, wielder of Healfwyrhta, was to wed Hildeburh the fair, the jewel of the Danes, Hnaef-sister and Hoc-daughter, whose beauty was said to surpass even that of the empresses of the Fair Folk. It was for Hildeburh that Finn now waited, standing motionless upon his tower as he had for three long days. When she arrived, there would be a celebration and feast whose equal Hwitstan would not again see for many generations of men.

Before the sun had climbed halfway into the sky, the men and women of Hwitstan began to gather upon the hill overlooking Hwitstanwic to await the arrival of the Danes. Their work had been done; the preparations were complete. Never in their days had they seen such an abundance of fare as now awaited them in the village, and they were eager for it. More than a dozen wild boar had been killed and were already roasting over the fresh-dug fire pits back in the village. There would be pork for all—thanes, earls and commoners alike. Fish, too, they had in abundance; the weirs of Laguhunta and Lopystre had provided richly that spring. And of mead and beer, there was enough to quench the thirst of the entire village for a month and a day!

Deomaer, the jeweler and moneyer of King Folcwalda, stood among those waiting. As his eyes searched the horizon for a sight of the Danish ships, his thoughts drifted back, and he remembered the day when he had first heard of Finn's betrothal to the Danish princess. He had only recently returned to Hwitstan from the Jutish and Saxon lands on the Isle of the Britons. The last vestiges of winter were still upon Friesland . . .

●

Deomaer braced himself against the bitter chill in the air as he stepped out of his hut. The spring equinox was one week past, but the early morning still held the bite of winter. Ahead of him, a small circle of huts was beginning to emerge out of the slowly dissipating fog. There was yet no sign of life. He glanced up briefly and saw the first grey of dawn appearing in a clear sky, then turned his eyes downward, pulled his wool cloak tightly about him to protect his ears, and turned to head up the hill.

His hut was on the northern side of Hwitstan—the seaward side—so he had no need of crossing through the village to get to the sea. Like most of the huts in the village, his was a long, rectangular hole, three feet deep, with turf walls which rose a foot above ground and a sloping roof of timbers and skins. A heavy ox hide covered the doorway, which faced southward—away from the prevailing winter winds and into the village. Deomaer's hut was larger than some. It had two rooms. The front one was small and simple, containing only a short mat where Deomaer slept and a low table with two chairs. The back room was larger and contained the tools and devices of his trade. Deomaer was a jeweler, and soon, though he knew it not at the time, he was to be a moneyer as well.

Deomaer could feel the stiff breeze on his cheeks and ears as he walked around the back of his hut and started up the hill which separated village from sea. He trudged up it, keeping his head lowered to avoid the worst of the wind. A startled rabbit darted ahead a few yards, and then veered off to the right where it dove under a clump of grass. A flock of blackbirds rose from a bush to his left and flew as a group over the village and then down toward the pond. He lifted his head for a moment to watch them and then lowered it again. By the time he reached the summit there was a warm red glow filling the eastern horizon.

Standing atop the hill, surrounded by the first rays of the morning sun, stood a solitary silhouette. Deomaer recognized him at once; his size and stature were unmistakable. It was Finn, his prince.

Finn was a tall man, nearly a head taller than Deomaer; taller indeed than any in the village save only his father, King Folcwalda. He stood there still and silent, his left hand holding a sturdy ash staff and his right hanging casually at his side. His dark hair fell loosely to his shoulders, where it partially covered a long scar running across his collarbone from the base of his neck to his shoulder. From head to foot, every inch of Finn was a warrior and prince. Even through his heavy winter cloak, Deomaer could see Finn's finely tuned shoulders and the strength in his powerful arms. His hands and forearms were like tough leather shields—shields which had held steadfast through battle after battle and bore proudly the marks from all. And his legs were as sturdy as a young ash. A heavy broadsword, too long to hang at his side, was slung over the prince's back. And, though he couldn't see them then, Deomaer knew the prince's face as well, especially his dark green eyes. They were deep-set under a stern brow and seemed able to see right through whatever they were fixed upon. More than once Deomaer had felt that penetrating glance upon himself. It was a glance at once both fierce and compassionate. Finn was a prince whom one would be proud to serve. He was a prince for whom one would die.

As the jeweler stepped to the crest of the hill behind Finn, his eyes moved from the back of his prince to the magnificent view spread before him. The sparkling North Sea stretched out in three directions as far as the eye could see. He involuntarily held his breath for a moment and then let out a long sigh. He had seen the great sea a thousand times before, but it still filled him with awe.

The lone figure tensed at the sudden sound of Deomaer's sigh. His jaw jutted out slightly, and the grip on his staff tightened. Deomaer froze as he saw the muscles bunching up on the neck and shoulder of the prince. Finn's battle-hardened warrior's instincts had been aroused. In a moment of irrational fear Deomaer half-expected Finn's staff to come swinging around into his skull, or to see the sword loosed from off his prince's shoulders. But those things did not happen. Instead, the prince just as quickly relaxed his stance and turned to face the one who was intruding on his solitude.

"My lord," Deomaer said, kneeling before Finn. He knelt not only because Finn was his prince, which was reason enough, but because he was in awe of him. Such authority did he command that had Finn been a slave and not a prince, Deomaer might still have found himself kneeling before him.

"Rise and stand beside me, Deomaer, son of Dunlaf," Finn said. His voice was full and rich and laden with hidden power. But this morning it held the tone of invitation rather than of command. Deomaer rose. His awe of Finn increased his pride at the words his prince had spoken to him. "Stand beside me," he had said.

"Look across the sea, Dé," Finn began. Again Deomaer tingled with pride—Finn had addressed him with his familiar name. "To the north and west . . ." the prince began. Then he paused and gestured toward the sea with a broad sweep of his free arm. From the way the prince was casually addressing him, Deomaer might have thought his prince had been expecting him. Yet, he had seen a brief moment of surprise registered in Finn's muscles a few seconds earlier when he had walked up behind him and sighed.

"To the north and west of us, across the Swan Road, lies the land of the Britons where the Angles and Saxons now rule. To the north and east," he continued, adjusting his grip on his staff and pointing just north of the rising sun, "lies the land of the Danes.

And south of us," he finished, turning around and looking out over Hwitstan, "is the Merovingian kingdom—the land of the Franks. And beyond the Frankish kingdoms lie all of the great kingdoms of the continent. Our land stands at the center of these like a young sapling in the midst of a great oak forest."

Deomaer nodded mutely. He was trying his best to catch the import of the words spoken to him by his prince. Was Finn simply verbalizing his thoughts to the first person who happened by? Or had he wanted to speak to Deomaer in particular? Probably the former, Deomaer guessed. Nonetheless, Finn was speaking to him alone; he had used the word "our"; he had spoken of "our land"—the land of Finn and Deomaer. "Stand beside me," he had said. He had said that to Deomaer! Deomaer was standing beside his prince talking with him—or at least listening to him. The Jutish princes and thanes in Cantbury, or anywhere in Cantwara, never spoke with the commoners.

Finn glanced at Deomaer for a moment to ensure that he was listening and then continued. As he did, his voice began to grow slightly louder and took on a tone of urgency, or if not of urgency, then at least of importance. "The Frisian people have always been poor—our clan not the least among them. We are few in number and have no great power. Had not the Franks been so busy fighting amongst themselves, we would certainly have come under their dominion in your father's father's days. And now, reunited under the kinslayer Chlotar the younger, we have the greater reason to fear them. United by such treachery, they are all the more dangerous."

"We have spears . . ." Deomaer began to object, but Finn silenced him with a quick gesture.

"Spears will do nothing for us . . . or at least not yet. We stand now at a crossroads, Deomaer. The young sapling must grow or it will surely die. It cannot live in the shadows of the great trees forever. As I have said, we have great kingdoms on every side of us. This is a threat, yes; yet, we must remember that it is our one great advantage as well."

Deomaer looked puzzled.

"The wealth that we have, little though it may be now, has been gained from trade," the prince continued in answer to Deomaer's unasked question. "The best trade routes in northern Europe pass our shores, and the amount of trade continues to increase with each season. As the kingdoms around us grow, so does the trade."

"Folcwalda has used this trade to great advantage," Deomaer responded. "Have we not more wealth than ever before?"

"Yes," Finn answered proudly. "He is a good king." Between Folcwalda and his son Finn, there was none of the rivalry that so often separated a king from his princes. "He has established the beginnings of our wealth and the foundations of our kingdom. He is the first true king of our people. Never before have the Frisians been united in such as way as they are now."

He paused for a moment as if to honor his father, and then continued, "Nonetheless there is still much to be done." His voice gathered force. "Yes, there is much left to be done. We must act now. We must seize the opportunity given us." As he said the word "seize" his right hand swung around and gripped his staff, and he lifted it into the air. A sudden energy seemed to possess the prince. He straightened to his full stature and held his staff as if it were a weapon—the staff of power of Briton's Druid. For a moment he was a giant to Deomaer, like the great Eormenric returned from the dead. "Friesland is destined to rise and become a great kingdom . . ." He swung the staff high around his head. ". . . or to be crushed by the growing powers around it." The staff came crashing into the ground.

A shiver passed through Deomaer's spine, and he unconsciously pulled his cloak more tightly about his shoulder. Finn stood still for a moment, staring at the ground where his staff had put a small dent in the hard earth. Then he relaxed his stance, and the energy and passion which had possessed him slowly subsided to remain hidden in reserve, simmering below the surface. He began speaking once more, this time almost to himself. "We may yet become that great nation—like the Scyldings in the days of Beow—wielding such strength that others will bow down and pay tribute to us. But that day has not yet come; we have not the might to stand on our own against those who surround us. And so we must rely on trade and hope to survive. Trade has given us the wealth we have, and trade will make us stronger still. We must both protect and increase our trade. We must nurture what we have. We cannot survive great wars such as those which brought low the Britons and Geats, and even the mighty Rome. Yet neither may we afford to lose this land."

Deomaer nodded in agreement. He was still staring at Finn's staff, expecting at any moment for it to burst into flames under some spell from its wielder.

"In times past we have had little trouble. That is true," Finn said. "Weak though we were, and few in number, yet there were none who came against us in force. For apart from the trade which passes through our shores, our land seems barren and of little value. But do not be fooled! There are many now who envy our land and shores, for by them we control the trade routes. Hwitstan only exists because of Hwitstanwic. Without Hwitstanwic . . ." Finn continued, gesturing once again toward the coastlands and the sheltered beaches in front of them, "we have nothing. Because we rely on our trade, we must be able to defend our beaches and landings. I speak not merely for Hwitstan, but for all of the Frisian people—for all of Friesland. Our trade and our land are in peril."

"My lord," Deomaer objected, breaking out of his trance, "you know that your people will stand beside you in war."

Finn smiled. "I know you would. Who has ever had a more loyal hearthwerod? I do not doubt the valor of my people. But we are few, and war is ugly. When I speak of enemies, I speak not only of the Franks. Though they are the closest and strongest of the surrounding kingdoms, Chlotar their king is not the only threat to our people. You have seen Cantbury in Cantwara, the land of the Jutes. You know how rich and powerful they are. And Cantbury is but one of many Jutish cities, and the Jutes are but one of many tribes and kingdoms. They are as quick to unite as they are to fight amongst themselves. You know of Ethelfrith; his burial was a tribute to his greatness. At time of need, all of the Angles from Deira to Bernicia were united under his kingship to drive the last of the Britons out of their land. And to the south of them, the Saxons have been united by Ethelbert. Where will they go—the Angles, the Saxons, and the Jutes—when they have filled the land of the Britons? They will seek new land. It is their way. Surely you have not forgotten that Friesland itself was not always the land of the Frisians. Ten and five generations have our people dwelt on these shores, and yet others there were who were driven out before us. And if we are not careful, others there will be who will follow after."

Deomaer had forgotten. It was before the days even of his forefathers' forefathers when his people had settled the land. Yet who, he wondered, had been driven out before them?

"As I have said," Finn continued, "we are a small kingdom in the midst of many mightier ones. So what shall we do? We must be able to defend ourselves, and yet war must be a last resort. Our hope is in trade." Then, almost as if it were an afterthought, Finn added, "And were we the most powerful kingdom on either side of the seas, war would still remain but a last hope when all else had failed. War is always tragic no matter who the victor is."

War is tragic? Deomaer thought to himself. *Is not war glorious? Or so we have been told since the kings of old.* The chieftains were chieftains because they led their people in battle! What of Finn? Was he so different from the kings and chieftains of the north? Yet Deomaer himself was no warrior. What did he know of the clash of spears? "And if we must fight?" he said out loud. "If all else does fail?" It seemed to Deomaer that his prince was leading somewhere; that there was a riddle with the answer about to be revealed. What had Finn said? That they were not strong enough alone to survive a war against their neighbors, but that they must still defend their shores at need if they were to protect their trade. Then the question was how.

"What better way to prevent war," Finn answered, "or if war comes, what better way to win than to have a strong ally?"

Was this the answer to the riddle? Was Finn seeking allies? Among whom? Certainly not the Franks. Chlotar was treacherous. He could never be trusted, he who slew his own king. The Saxons? Possibly. They were kindred peoples. The Jutes as well. They would certainly be more faithful allies than the Franks. But they were far across the sea. Perhaps too far. Was Finn speaking of Rome? The emperor was even further away than the Saxon kings and had little contact with Friesland. Though once mighty, the Empire was now weak and unsteady, overrun and conquered every generation. Agiluf's rule had lasted only twenty-five years. A treaty with the South would bring no real benefit to Finn.

"Of what ally are you speaking, my lord?" Deomaer finally asked.

Finn answered his question with one of his own—something which in years to come Deomaer would realize was a favorite habit of his. "What ally is more sure than one which is bound by blood?"

"None, my lord," Deomaer answered, bowing his head. "But where do we find such an ally?"

"Where indeed, my friend Dé? Where indeed!" A broad smile slowly spread across the prince's face. "You know of the Danes."

It was a comment, not a question. Certainly Deomaer knew of the Danes. They were powerful, fierce, aggressive warriors. He had seen them sail on more than one occasion during his time in Cantwara. Even the proud Saxons sung of the Danes with fear and respect:

> *Shields make you ready,*
> *Round, hard, and fast,*
> *When ships of Spear-Danes sail to the bay!*
> *Swords boldly swing*
> *Swiftly and strong*
> *For gold and our treasure*
> *Must trade for our lives.*

For good reason the name of the Spear-Danes was well-known on every side of the great North Sea. Yes, Deomaer knew of them. He nodded his answer, and Finn continued.

"Ten weeks from now a Danish ship will arrive in this port. That ship will be carrying Hildeburh, sister of Hnaef, son of Hoc, the king of the Danes."

Was this what Finn was getting to? Did he want the Danes to come to Friesland? Few kings there were who desired to see Danish ships on their shores. "What of Hildeburh, my lord?" Deomaer asked.

"She is to be my wife," the prince replied. He could no longer contain his grin. It grew as broad as his face.

Deomaer remained silent for a moment as he considered this news. Then an answering smile spread across his face as well. A treaty with the Danes would gain instant respect for the Frisians, if not fear of them. There were few if any who would dare attack the Danes—or, he hoped, their allies. And even more importantly, the Frisians would be safe from the Spear-Danes themselves. What king would attack his own blood, particularly a sister! Finn was gaining the best treaty he possibly could with the Danes: the treaty of marriage.

Deomaer stared at his prince in admiration, seeking for appropriate words. The only thing he could think of was to drop to his knee again. This he did. "My lord," he said, turning his eyes downward. Like Folcwalda his father, Finn would make a good king someday. Deomaer was glad to serve him. More than that, he was honored.

Finn just laughed—a deep, full laugh—and then pulled Deomaer roughly to his feet. "The work is just beginning, Deomaer, son of Dunlaf, master jeweler of Hwitstan." His free hand came to rest lightly on Deomaer's shoulder. "It is time to put you to the test and see if my father sent you to apprentice in Cantbury for nothing. Are your hands now as skilled as the famous jewelers of Cantbury? What have you learned in your five years across the Swan Road? Will you make my land as famous as Cantbury of Cantwara?"

"We shall see, my lord." Deomaer bowed. "I am at your service."

"Yes, we shall see," Finn said. "For the next three months your new forges shall be blazing without ceasing. There will be a never-ending stream of gold and silver passing through your doors. I want rings for my thanes, wound gold for our necks, silver handles for our blades, and coins for our harbors—yes, a coin in honor of Folcwalda! And most importantly, Dé, the prize of your work, the heart of your labor, the treasure of my kingdom beside which all other treasures shall pale—I want jewels and necklaces for my wife which shall surpass all jewelry worn by any queen of the Angles, Saxons, Danes, Scyldings, Geats or any people anywhere. My queen is to be the crown of my head and the chief treasure of the Frisians. As she will be my crown, so too shall she have a crown beyond value."

There was a sparkle in Finn's eyes as he spoke of Hildeburh, and Deomaer wondered for the first time if there was more to the marriage than a convenient treaty between two kings. Why had Folcwalda—or was it Finn himself—chosen Hildeburh of the Danes? Deomaer wondered how much more was involved than simply the renown of the Danish spears. Folcwalda, it was said, thought and planned far beyond what even the most astute of his thanes could comprehend. And now Finn seemed to possess that trait as well. A treaty with the Spear-Danes was certainly good news.

But to the young jeweler all those thoughts paled beside the fact that Finn had put his hand on his shoulder and called him by his familiar name a second time.

"Return now to your home, Dé, and prepare for your work," Finn said, breaking into Deomaer's thoughts. "Keep this secret between us for just a short time. Very soon the whole village will know the joyous news, and then we will all celebrate together— a brief celebration now and a greater one soon!"

The prince had confided in him. "Keep this secret between us." He had used the word "us." With awe and admiration for Finn, and no little pride at having been held in his confidence, Deomaer turned and walked back down toward the village. He considered stopping at the first hut he passed and waking the inhabitants to announce that Finn had spoken to him in private. No, the first dwelling belonged to Folcwalda. Better not to awaken him. Instead, Deomaer returned to his own hut where he held back what would have been a very loud shout. He would do all he could to make Finn's name famous across the seas. Folcwalda was a good king. One day Finn would be too. Deomaer was determined to be his loyal follower.

II

The Gathering of the Hearthwerod

The same day that Finn had announced his betrothal to Hildeburh had also seen the beginning of the building of a great hall in Hwitstan. Though this was but a few months earlier, Hwitstan had been a much smaller village then, smaller than many in Friesland. When Deomaer had returned from Cantwara, Hwitstan had contained only twenty or so huts scattered around a small clearing. There had been a few livestock and rabbit pens on the west side of the village, and the small stream which flowed through Hwitstan had been dammed a few hundred paces before it tumbled down the hill and into the river after which the village took its name, there forming a little pond.

Yet though village and clan were small, it had gained much power in Friesland. This was due entirely to the strength and wisdom of its chieftain, Folcwalda. He had succeeded in uniting nearly all of Friesland into a single kingdom. Only a few Frisian clans still preferred their independence and resisted taking a High King.

But Folcwalda needed to be able to gather his thanes, earls and retainers before he could fully establish a high kingship in Friesland. Those who had pledged themselves to him, and their warbands with them, needed to be in one place with their king and war leader. And before Folcwalda and Finn could gather their warbands, they required a hall large enough to house them. They needed a hearth around which the people could gather with their treasure-giver. So they had begun the building of Hwitstanburg, as the great hall would be named. And much there was which had needed to be done. Some had begun at once cutting the timbers for the posts and roof, while others dug the fire pit at the center of the hall, and others worked at digging the holes for the wall's foundation. The timbers, once cut, had to be dragged into the village over rough, hard ground. Great flat stones, some as large as shields, were needed not only for the hearth, but also to place in the ground beneath the posts to prevent them from rotting or sinking. Those too had to be found and hauled in from the surrounding countryside. This was no small task. Yet despite the difficulties, the work had proceeded at a quick pace, and after only a few days the hall's outline and form had already begun to become visible. In a few weeks the walls had reached higher than Folcwalda's head. And then the smith had bound the timbers in place with iron, and the roof—the most difficult task of all—had finally been raised. When all that was done, the women did the wattle-work, weaving slender poplar branches in and out of the vertical stakes. The older children had finished the process by filling the gaps with a mud-and-grass daub which, when dried, left a hard, brick-like plaster.

Now, three months after it had been begun, the great hall was finally finished. And with it, atop the nearby hill, stood the new tower Finnweard which overlooked both village and bay alike: Hwitstan and Hwitstanwic.

When all was done, the villagers, many of whom had never traveled more than a day's walk outside Hwitstan, were in awe of the hall's size. It was over fifty paces long—not children's paces but the paces of a king! Even Deomaer, who had seen the great halls at Cantbury and Oxfordshire, was impressed. The village seemed suddenly more noble.

Nor was the hall the only addition to Hwitstan, for as the hall had grown, so had the village. Surrounding Hwitstanburg in every direction the eye looked, changes had taken place so quickly that few besides Folcwalda and Finn had been able to note or remember them all. The village had grown rapidly as men from the surrounding villages—Ezinge, Aalsum, Beowic, Heorotburg, and even as far as Dronrip, Wieuwerd and Wijnaldum—arrived in Hwitstan. New huts had appeared and were still appearing almost daily on the outskirts of the village.

Hwitstan was slowly becoming the center of a new kingdom.

And to Hwitstanburg, newly built, the warbands of Folcwalda and Finn had finally been gathered. Thanes brave and strong, hardy in battle and wise in counsel, came to serve the king whom they had proclaimed over Friesland and to receive treasure from his hand. And treasure they received from the first day they gathered around his hearth. Folcwalda's hearthwerod they were. Of their mighty deeds, tales would be told and lays sung.

●

Summer's Day was a day of celebration among the Frisians and Danes alike—the longest day of the year, the day that the life-giving sun was at the peak of her power. The celebration marked the time of warmth and growth, when animals could graze long and grow fat preparing for the hard winter months ahead, or for the table upon which they would appear. It marked the time when the hours of daylight came in abundance giving ample opportunity to labor and provide, to rebuild and remake, and to prepare for the darker, colder season. Summer's Day was a day of life. And for the war-tribes it was a time for battle and conquest, for raids and victories and spoils.

It was only fitting that the wedding of Finn, son of Folcwalda, and Hildeburh of the Danes should be on Summer's Day. It was a new beginning, not for Finn and Hildeburh only, but for all of Friesland.

And for Finn it was a day of proving as well, a day whose importance could not be overlooked. For though Folcwalda had nearly established a high kingship for himself, it would not necessarily be passed to Finn. A strong prince would receive the throne from his father; a weak prince would founder if there were strong chieftains to oppose him. If Finn could indeed marry, as he had promised to his people, the daughter of a powerful Danish king, none would dare oppose him; his claim to his father's throne would be established. If there were no queen, if the Danes did not sail to Friesland, then he would likely fall. Further, the high kingship would be dissolved.

And the Danes were already late. They were to have come three days before the celebration, but no sail had yet been seen and no word had been heard. Followers of the prince as well as those who jealously eyed the throne wondered at the promises of Finn.

The day of celebration had dawned sunny and warm. The last of the spring rains had finally blown over, and clear blue skies prevailed. Finn's tower had been completed only days before, and Finn had awakened long before dawn each of the past three days to take his stand atop it. For three mornings he had watched the dawn rise over the eastern hills and had waited alone for the first sign of the incoming ships. As Summer's Day progressed, more and more people ascended the hill and waited with him, standing in groups at the bottom of the tower while Finn silently kept his vigil above them. While the older villagers stood quietly waiting, eager for the coming celebration and curious about the wonderful Danes of whom they had heard much, the children of Hwitstan, patient and solemn at first, were soon playing down by the water's edge. The older brothers and sisters busied themselves searching for pieces of amber which had washed ashore during the recent storms, while the younger ran and played in the sand. An occasional shout of joy would erupt, and one or another child would come rushing up the hill carrying a smooth piece of sea-polished amber which they would present with pride to their parents.

Folcwalda, meanwhile, sat in council with his thanes. Soon after the completion of Hwitstanburg, they had joined him beneath its roof. And from that day forth they were blessed by their treasure-giver. Rings crafted by Deomaer, gold and silver alike, and battle-hardy weapons as well, that generous king did give in abundance to his thanes. And land too he gave to those who served him. Folcwalda's earls did not suffer any lack when they served their king within his hall. So as Prince Finn stood upon the tower waiting, Folcwalda's hearthwerod was gathered beneath the roof of Hwitstanburg. The benches had been set in place, and a fire was lit upon the great hearth.

In all of Hwitstan only the king's chefs and their apprentices labored still in preparation. They stood beside the roasting pits, turning the pigs on their spits and watching to see that they cooked evenly. Though some perhaps were jealous of those who sat at ease enjoying the day, they nonetheless approached their task with great care—and rightly so! A tale still circulated among them of a certain Jutish chef who, by neglect, had burned a cow while roasting it and had then served the vastly overcooked meat to the king. Livestock being as precious as it was, the king was greatly displeased. He sentenced the chef to the task of replacing the cow, a task at which the chef failed. The chef's death at the hands of that king was not at all pleasant. Folcwalda, though he was not wont to kill one of his servants, nonetheless encouraged the proliferation of that story among his cooks. He had Daelga, his poet, sing it to them at least once a year. Since Daelga had first told that tale among them, Folcwalda had not once been fed burned meat.

Mid-morning of Summer's Day came and passed, and so did midday. Finn kept his vigil, and Folcwalda remained in council with his thanes. The rest of the village watched and waited impatiently. They looked ever and again at Finn, hoping he would notice their impatience and begin the celebration. But the prince's eyes never dropped below the horizon. He stood in his familiar pose, one hand holding his staff, the other at his side, and his great sword draped across his back. His stance never faltered, nor did his watchfulness ever waver. There was no trace of doubt on his face.

Elsewhere upon the hill and down in the village, restlessness and impatience abounded. After a while even the older and more patient children tired of waiting and returned to the village to play games in the clearing near the great hall. Some of the men began to disperse back to their homes or farms. "In past years," Deomaer heard someone grumble, "the celebration would have started by now." The excitement which had been building until midday began to disappear. Many began to suspect that the Danes would not arrive that day. A few even hoped they would never arrive and that the marriage would not take place. Most, however, waited and hoped and trusted in the words of their king and prince.

Deomaer the jeweler was among those who believed in his prince and waited. And as he waited, his thoughts once more retraced the past few weeks.

●

The task he had been given had awed him at first. He was to mint the first Frisian coin—a coin in honor of Folcwalda. What design could he make for a coin to honor a king? He knew not. Nor was he sure of his ability to craft for Hildeburh, Finn's future queen, gifts of the beauty and splendor which Finn desired. He also knew the physical difficulty of his work, and that he alone was responsible for the task. In Cantbury the gathering of fuel for the fires had been the job, not of the masters, but of the youngest apprentices. Deomaer had no apprentices. He would need to do it himself, he had thought. But there he had been proven wrong in his fears. Finn had seen that the task was taken care of for him, giving him freedom to concentrate only on his craft.

The same day that work had begun on the hall, gold, silver and wood—all three in plentiful supply—had arrived for Deomaer. There were advantages to not being an apprentice any more! Deomaer had been able to begin immediately with the forging of some gold rings. It was a good task for him to start with. It was simple enough work, and would help to bring skill back into his hands which had spent weeks sitting idle. Furthermore, rings would be of immediate use to Folcwalda, who was generous in the giving of them to his thanes. For thanes had already begun arriving in Hwitstan even then, and would come in large numbers at the completion of the hall. When Deomaer's hands had relearned their trade through simple ring-making, he would begin his first task of real importance: the minting of a Frisian coin.

Yes, Deomaer had reminded himself, he was to be not only a jeweler, but a moneyer—*the* moneyer. Finn had not told him of this during their conversation upon the hill. Perhaps it had been Folcwalda's decision, one which Finn hadn't even known. Deomaer had felt both honored and afraid when he had been told a few days later by Folcwalda himself that he was to be his moneyer. Moneyer was a position of far greater importance than that of jeweler—though in Deomaer's mind one less interesting, for it allowed him less creativity. Jeweling was only a trade; moneying was an office! The coin he would mint would not only be the first Frisian coin, but the only Frisian coin. He would have to guarantee the constancy of the weight of all the coins he minted. Folcwalda's rune, and perhaps even his own, would be on each coin. As trade passed through Friesland, the coin would be carried throughout the continent and across the sea, perhaps even to his old master who would no doubt recognize the work of his former apprentice.

Deomaer laughed at the thoughts he had had. For a time he had envisioned poets singing in the same breath of Weland the smith and Deomaer the jeweler and moneyer. He laughed again. No, he would not become famous for the minting of a coin.

Once Deomaer had begun his work, gold and silver had come pouring through his doors in a steady stream. And he had known that as fast as it came in, his king had expected it out again in the form of rings. He had worked long, hard hours during those first few weeks. Where the precious metals were coming from, he did not know, nor could he guess, nor had he even time to wonder. There seemed to be a limitless supply. It was arriving faster than he could use it! Five years before, when he had first left the Frisian shores and sailed to Cantbury to be apprenticed to the master jeweler there, his village had been even smaller and poorer than it was when he returned. There was neither gold nor silver in great amounts. Why, he had wondered when he left, did Folcwalda even want a jeweler at all? But as a child of thirteen summers, he was not one to oppose the wishes of his chieftain—particularly not a chieftain of Folcwalda's might and stature! Furthermore, the winter before he had been sent away, both of his parents had died of the fever. Maybe Folcwalda had known that the two things Deomaer needed most were a change of scenery and something to keep him busy—a task to which he could devote himself. But later, when he saw the pounds of gold and silver coming through his door, it became obvious to Deomaer that Folcwalda had been acting on foresight. Folcwalda had known that there would soon be enough gold to warrant a jeweler, and he had planned for it.

Thinking of Folcwalda's great wisdom and insight, Deomaer had struck upon an idea: a coin that would be worthy of a king. He had been working in the heat of his forge, sweat pouring off his brow, his hands rapidly twisting the gold into elaborate serpentine arm bands, when he had a sudden, clear picture of exactly what he wanted to do. He had at once set aside his gold and tools and quickly grabbed a piece of char-blackened wood. With it, he began to draw the imagined coin on a piece of stone beside his hearth. He rushed to finish the drawing before the ideas faded from his mind. As soon as he had finished his drawing, he knew he had what he wanted. The coin he envisioned would bear the image of the great seabird riding the trade winds. It would symbolize both Folcwalda's love of the sea and the trade routes which established his kingdom. The great bird, with its piercing, far-seeing eyes, would also serve to remind Friesland and the world of the long-sighted vision of King Folcwalda, who had united all of Friesland into a single kingdom to stand against the Merovingians; who through marriage would gain the Spear-Danes as his allies; and who had had the foreknowledge to send a young clanchild, the son of his nephew, to apprentice with the master jewelers across the sea before his own kingdom even had any gold—in fact, before he even had a kingdom. King Folcwalda who had built the hall at Hwitstan which would stand until the poets sang of it. King Folcwalda, the long-sighted seabird riding the trades.

Deomaer had begun work on the coin at once, first carving out the mould that he would use to stamp the gold and silver, and then measuring the blanks of fixed weight. It took him many tries before he was satisfied with his mould.

III

Of Hildeburh Daughter of Hoc

As it had with the coin, inspiration for Hildeburh's jewelry had also eventually come to Deomaer, though not without some prompting from Finn. The prince had unexpectedly appeared at the jeweler's hut late one morning, startling him into dropping his work. The prince had looked tired, Deomaer remembered, but his expression had been eager—as if he thought that by helping Deomaer complete his work sooner he could shorten the days until the arrival of Hildeburh and the Danes. Deomaer still vividly remembered the conversation that had followed. Indeed, he remembered every word that the prince had ever spoken to him, such was his awe of Finn.

"Do I interrupt your work?" Finn had asked, gesturing at the tools in Deomaer's hand.

Deomaer shook his head no and put them down.

"Then come," Finn said. "Let us walk some distance and talk."

Deomaer nodded and followed Finn out the door, leaving the hot gold ring on the stone where it had fallen and bent.

Finn spoke casually to him as they passed southward through the village. "You have seen where we have cleared space for a tower?" At that time Finnweard had not yet been begun.

"The place seems well chosen, my lord. It is not the tallest hill, but it offers the best view of Hwitstanwic and the coastline."

"Indeed," Finn replied.

"Your father has much foresight."

"The tower was of my own planning," Finn said. It was a simple statement of fact and not a boast. "I have seen many towers along the Saxon and Danish shores, and each time I have thought of this hill."

"With a lantern on top," Deomaer said, "it could also act as a guide for ships." He was thinking of the few Jutish and Saxon burgs he had seen with towers rising from the corners. They somehow seemed better equipped for defense than did Hwitstan.

"Whose ships?" Finn replied, narrowing his eyes a bit and focusing them on Deomaer.

"What?" Deomaer asked, feeling a bit uncomfortable under Finn's scrutiny and forgetting for a second what he had just said. "Oh . . . Any ships, I suppose."

"Yes, any ships, or any person's ships. And when would a ship need a lantern to find the landing at Hwitstanwic?"

"At night . . . on dark nights . . . if they don't know the coast well."

"And who would want to land on our beaches at night?"

Enemies! The answer was obvious, so Deomaer left it unsaid. The tower had been built to help them guard Hwitstanwic, not to help others find it. Trading ships coming during the day could find Hwitstan easily and would have no need of such a light. It was Vikings and raiders who would benefit from such a lamp. The same sheltered beaches which made Friesland's coastal villages ideal trade locations also made them easy prey for quick raids. Hwitstanwic, as the cove, beaches, and islands beside the village of Hwitstan were called, stood at the mouth of a small river which wound its way north from the nearby village of Ezinge. The cove or small bay formed a natural shelter from the rough North Sea. In addition, the Frisian coast offered another natural protection. Long rows of barrier islands lined most of Friesland. Inside this row of narrow, sandy isles the seas remained relatively mild, even in the worst of storms. Ships carrying warbands as well as trade could pass up and down the calmer inner waters with little trouble.

Most trade routes from the continent passed through Friesland and out to the sea along its many rivers. The Hwitstan was among the smallest of these rivers. It carried only a tiny amount of trade coming down from Ezinge and some small Frisian settlements. The Ems and Weser Rivers to the east were larger and longer than the Hwitstan, and the Rhine and Meuse Rivers to the southwest were larger still. These larger rivers carried most of the trade that came from inland by ship. Would not Folcwalda have been wiser to have established his hall at one of these larger rivers? But who was Deomaer to question Folcwalda! For there were, to be sure, advantages to Hwitstanwic. Because of its natural bay, it was among the best landing sites in Friesland. Furthermore, the Hwitstan River was more centrally located than any of the larger rivers.

As they passed through the village, Deomaer listened while Finn explained his plans for two more towers. He planned to build them on the coast, one on each side of Hwitstanwic, far enough away to sight ships well before they reached the bay, but close enough to signal the tower at Hwitstanwic. And as he listened Deomaer began to think about Hildeburh. He had still not begun to craft anything for her though the day had drawn much closer.

"Tell me about Hildeburh," he had finally mustered the courage to say.

Finn smiled. That smile, too, Deomaer remembered. It was filled with a joy and mirth that shone often from the prince's face upon his people. To see Finn's smile was to desire to serve him. "That question has been written on your face for many days," the prince had answered. "I wondered when it would find utterance."

How was Finn able to read his thoughts? A wave of embarrassment flooded over him as he thought about that, but he pursued the question anyway. "Can you tell me about her?"

"There is nothing I would enjoy more than speaking of Hildeburh. I think there are few who could tolerate listening to me," the prince answered, and then was silent for a moment as the two walked on. Finally he closed his eyes and sighed. They had both stopped walking.

"What is Hildeburh like?" Finn had begun softly. "She is tall and graceful, thinner than her mother and sister, but somehow stronger. Her hair is long and blonde. Her smile is like the harbor on a quiet evening—peaceful and calm, both offering and providing comfort. And her anger? Her anger is like the North Sea in the winter months—fierce, wild and uncontrollable, but never out of control itself and always majestic. She has fifteen years now and possesses all the wisdom of a great queen."

Again Deomaer wondered how Finn knew so much about Hildeburh. Marriages of kings and princes were most often arranged for political reasons. It was not uncommon for the ceremony to begin with the bride and groom having seen each other only once, or perhaps not at all. This was more true of the larger kingdoms around them than it was of Friesland, but even among the Frisians it was very common for one chieftain to give a sister or daughter to another to seal a treaty. Yet Finn had been speaking of Hildeburh as though he had known her all his life—or all hers. Where had the prince gone, and what he had done while Deomaer was away? He had heard many allusions and rumors. Finn had often disappeared, taking with him, as was his wont, fourteen trusted warriors. He would return from places unknown laden with jewels and treasures uncountable, which he would lay as gifts at his father's feet. From what distant king he won such gifts, Deomaer did not know. Those who did know—Finn's thanes and companions—were those with whom Deomaer never had opportunity or reason to speak.

"She has never had a great love for the sea as do her kinsmen," the prince had continued. "She prefers rather the hills and quiet rivers. She loves the evenings more than mornings, fall more than spring, and the moonlight more than the sun. Her eyes themselves are like two great moons. They can grant you peace or trouble your heart."

"And which do they do for you?" Deomaer had asked.

"Until I am with her, they stir my heart to wakefulness. But when we finally come together, they will bring peace to my soul."

Then—whether spontaneously or not Deomaer did not know—Finn had begun to sing.

> *"Flower of heaven,*
> *Hildeburh fair,*
> *Crossing the sea*
> *In summer she came,*
> *Her hair like silver*
> *Softer than fleece,*
> *Her eyes like the moon*
> *On midwinter's night.*

> *By Finn was she found*
> > *Friesland's new queen,*
> *Hildeburh fair,*
> > *Flower of heaven."*

Finn had begun softly, but the song grew as he continued, until Deomaer stood transfixed by the beauty and power of the prince's voice. Then Finn was silent. There was now no doubt that this was no simple marriage for the sake of gaining a treaty with the Danes.

In the end Deomaer had crafted what Finn wanted—a treasure worthy of the greatest of queens. A brooch he had made, a brooch not of gold but of silver, silver for a woman who loved the moon. It bore upon its surface the image of the rising moon surrounding a great bird. It was no seabird, but a majestic land bird—a bird of the night, an owl. A silver brooch with a great, white, snowy owl like those in the far north; an owl with its large eyes capable of seeing on all but the darkest nights—capable of seeing and hunting. There were arm rings to match the brooch, all silver and all bearing the moon and the owl. And a special coin just for Hildeburh. On the one side it was the same as Folcwalda's: the seabird riding the trade winds. On the other side: the moon and the owl. The coin he set in an elaborate necklace—a coin with two sides, symbol of the union of Hildeburh with Finn, son of Folcwalda.

But would the union take place? He knew not. Three days they had waited for the Danes. Summer's Day was now upon them and indeed was quickly passing. Already midday had come and gone; in fact the third hour after midday was past.

IV

Waiting's End

"**F**inn!"

A loud voice caught Deomaer's attention. He turned around to see from whom it had come. Behind him stood a young man, richly dressed in the battle-dress of a Frisian lord. He was a chieftain, or perhaps a chieftain's son. Deomaer had not seen him before, but if his attire and voice did not deceive, he was no stranger to Friesland. Though no thane of Folcwalda's, he had Frisian blood within him. In his hand he held a naked blade, glinting in the sun. His shield was across his shoulder, ready at any moment to be taken in hand. Upon his head was a battle helm.

Behind him to the west, at the edge of the trees upon the crest of the hill, was a small warband, perhaps twenty-five men, all mounted. From whence had they come? Deomaer had neither seen nor heard them arrive.

"Finn, I challenge you!" the voice cried out.

Deomaer stepped backward away from the man. Had he heard the stranger correctly? Who was this who so boldly challenged the prince?

Finn made no reply.

"Finn, son of Folcwalda, I challenge you again. If you are not a coward, turn and speak to me."

For the first time that day Finn's eyes left the horizon. From atop the tall tower of stone, he turned and looked down upon the challenger. His eyes were firm and hard. He shifted his grip on his ash staff and held it with two hands. It was no meager weapon in the strong grip of a warrior. An ash staff could smash skulls as well as swords could split them.

43

"Speak your name, bold intruder," the prince said in a firm voice.

"You know well who I am," he replied.

"Well I do," Finn answered, "but that all my people may know the name of him who challenges their prince, I charge you now to make yourself known."

"Very well," the intruder replied. "I am Réadban, son of Ramlaf. And I speak not to you alone, but to all of your people. Let them hear me if they will. We have waited long enough, and for nothing."

To Deomaer's great surprise, there actually arose some murmur of assent. Some felt they had been kept waiting all too long for the feast and celebration.

"You make us wait in vain for your proud lies. There will be no marriage," Réadban continued. "Nor will there be a High King's torc for your neck. No claim does the tribe of Folcwalda have upon the throne of Friesland."

"Do you have greater claim?" Finn asked, his voice lowering dangerously. His hard eyes narrowed, and the grip upon his staff tightened. "If you do, then make it now."

"No claim does anyone have to rule our clan save our chieftain alone," the proud stranger answered. "We make no claim to rule over you, but we will have no High King for ourselves."

"So you may choose. But it remains still to be seen."

"No! It is not still to be seen. We have waited long enough. We wait no longer. You promise the support of Danish spears, but we see them not. And when we do, they will likely be piercing our shields." At these words a number of Finn's folk nodded. Many had feared the dreaded Danes for some time and had no desire to see them in their own village. Réadban was wisely playing on the villagers' fears as well as their impatience, seeking to gain their support. "If you will make claim, then make it now by facing my sword. He is a coward who trusts in the spears of others. Prove your worth with your own sword! Will you face me alone, or need I call upon my warband to bring you down from your feeble tower?"

Haughty words Réadban spoke, seeking to anger Finn into accepting his challenge. For many days he had watched and waited in hiding, hoping that the Danes would not arrive and that he would have opportunity of carrying out his plans. Many secret ambitions he harbored in his heart. Despite his words, he hoped one day to have the Frisian throne himself. He knew well that if the Danes arrived and Finn and Hildeburh were wed, he himself would have little hope of ever opposing them. And in truth, though he told the waiting people to the contrary, he suspected that the Danes would indeed come, and soon. That was why he was acting now and taking his chance. If Finn was dead, there could be no marriage. Even if afterwards Réadban had to flee for his life to escape the vengeance of Finn's kin, he would survive and return to power later. All the better if Friesland was in turmoil and had no prince. But he needed to provoke Finn to a fight if his plan was to succeed. Further, he needed to defeat him.

"Fool," Finn spoke, "you contradict yourself even as you speak. You say that my promises are false and the Danes will not come, and then you warn us that the Danes will come and will be our enemies. You cannot have both! And you are twice a fool if you think to threaten me with your warband." In one swift move he pulled his horn to his lips, and Réadban stepped back suddenly as if the ivory were a strung bow. But Finn did not wind it. "If this horn were sounded, in but little more time than it would take me to kill you, the warband of Folcwalda would be upon this hill and not one of your men would ride from Hwitstan alive. If a single man takes but one step closer, none shall live to see tomorrow."

"Are you a coward then?" Réadban shouted. But he knew at once that his plan was failing. He knew Finn was right. If he could not anger the prince, then he could not defeat him. And his warband could not fight against Folcwalda's. Even now, men in the village were looking up at them and wondering. Some were picking up their spears and swords. He shouted again in desperation, "Come down. I challenge you again. Come and prove your own sword." But with his neck craned up to see Finn, he felt much less threatening than he would have liked.

"Your challenge I will accept," Finn answered clearly and without hesitation.

Réadban's face revealed his surprise at the prince's response. And then it showed his fear. For as much as he had hoped that his plan to provoke Finn would succeed, he hoped also that it would fail. He had seen Finn wield a sword and was afraid to meet him in battle. Had he truly thought his plan would succeed, he might have been less willing to try.

But Réadban's surprise and fear were the next moment replaced with rage when Finn continued, "If you persist in being a fool, I will accept your challenge, but you will wait until your head has cooled. Seven days hence you may appear before me and face my sword if you will. Then shall nobody stand between us. This day I will raise no weapon, for it is the day of my wedding."

"Seven days I will not wait," Réadban began to reply, but Finn interrupted him.

"Seven days you will wait. For when you see the Danes arrive according to my word, you may yet repent of your accusations. On that day you may bow and swear fealty to the king, or face judgment for the offense given me this day. For I account the offense of your insults to be great! Until that day I will hear no more. But in this I warn you: move not one man from where they stand or you shall all be struck down and your bodies sent to the pit!"

So fiercely spoken were Finn's words that his challenger stepped back as if struck. He glared angrily up at the prince, but either he could think of nothing to say or he thought better of saying it. A long silence followed in which neither Finn nor Réadban spoke. Réadban stood seething, but did not move. Those around watched in stunned amazement at what had taken place.

Very slowly Finn turned back to face the sea. His people followed his example, each making a conscious effort not to look at Réadban, though all were curious what he would do next. The angered young chieftain lowered his sword to the ground and fumed, but he made to move either to leave or to call his warband. He joined those waiting, hoping furiously that the Danes would not come and that Finn would be humbled.

Moments later the clear tone of Finn's ivory horn sounded forth from the top of the hill and was heard for the first time in Friesland: a long, beautifully clear sound ringing from the tower overhead. In later years the mighty horn of Finn would be heard many times, bringing joy to the ears of his followers and fear to his enemies. But now it brought fear to Deomaer, for the moment he heard it and realized what it was he thought the worst—that Réadban's warband was sweeping down upon the unarmed villagers and Finn was signaling for help. Little did it matter that Folcwalda would soon be there to avenge them. Deomaer would be dead within seconds. But when he turned to look, neither Réadban nor his warband had moved. Then why had the horn been winded?

There could be only one other reason: the Danish ship had been sighted.

Before Finn's horn had finished ringing, Folcwalda appeared from out of Hwitstanburg followed by his thanes. His long strides carried him quickly up the hill, and in a few short moments he was standing beside the tower atop the hill with his thanes beside him. Ulestan stood on his right and the brothers Eormen and Edmen on his left. They were flanked closely by Aelfer, Beow, Froda and Hereric the Geat. Some others stood beside these on both sides or followed at a little distance. There were twenty thanes in all; twenty-two mighty Frisians, each with their own warbands and retinue. They were a fearsome band, armed and war ready, veterans all of many battles. And as mighty as his thanes appeared, Folcwalda was greater than all, both in strength and stature. Seeing him, it was clear how Folcwalda had been so quickly accepted as king. His kingship was visible in him. He was a chieftain among chieftains! And Finn also.

At their appearance, Réadban's followers, who until then had remained astride their horses, dismounted and backed away nervously. Folcwalda glanced briefly at them once, and then longer at Réadban, but said nothing.

In the bright sun of the later afternoon Folcwalda, with his brazen boar's-head helm and his bare sword which dangled at his side, glittered as much as the sea before him. His blade was chipped, scraped and scratched in a dozen places. And as badly battle-scarred as his sword was, the boar's-head helmet was worse! What those blows which had so dented that metal would have done to Folcwalda's head had he not been wearing the helmet, none would desire to guess. The king's arms too were bare and as covered with scars as the blade which they held. Both hands were missing parts of fingers. Many who saw him were amazed that so many scars could appear on a man who was still alive. But the dents on the helmet and sword were testimony to the blows which had missed him.

Then Finn strode forth from the tower to stand at the side

of his father. He appeared quite in contrast to Folcwalda. His sword was wrapped tightly in leather and was still draped over his back. He wore no helmet upon his head, but his hair flowed freely down over his neck and shoulders. Rather than a leather breastplate as his father wore, he had his red, sleeveless tunic with green patches on the shoulders and a blue silk belt. Only the covered sword gave hint to the warrior that Finn was. But even unarmed he looked nearly as formidable as his father. Surely these two would daunt the mightiest of warriors. Even the Danes would have to respect twenty-two Frisians such as those collected here!

Deomaer the jeweler looked again at the thanes collected behind the king. Eormen and Edmen, the strong and impetuous duo, had been the first to stand beside Folcwalda in his early days. These brothers were rash and adventurous, but loyal to the bone. They were hardy in battle, so Deomaer was told. In their youth they had acquired much fame and many enemies. Aelfer and his cousin Beow were the quiet ones. They carried spears—an idea they had borrowed from the Danes—and Roman short swords rather than the traditional broadswords of the Frisians. Froda was the youngest of Folcwalda's thanes, and but a little older than Finn. He was no chieftain himself, but a cousin of Lynd, the chieftain of a large clan in the far southwest. Only five men and six horses were counted in his warband. Nonetheless, though he was not as powerful as the others and commanded no large host, Froda was a good friend of Finn and would likely prove to be his strongest supporter when the time came for the passing of the kingship. The two had traveled much together. Froda had only recently returned from wars in the east between the Geats and Swedes, where he had won much glory and was given noble gifts. To Folcwalda in turn he gave those gifts, including four tall war horses, pledging his allegiance once again with humble words to his king. He was a good thane who sought not for his independence.

Hereric the Geat was the enigma of Folcwalda's hearth-werod. He had pledged himself to Folcwalda only two years ago after fleeing the land of the Geats for a reason none but he himself knew. Some rumored that he was a descendant of the evil Heremod the Dane. Heremod had sought refuge among the Jutes many years ago after slaying his own kinsmen. The Jutes had not only refused his request for refuge, but had killed him and sent his body back to the Danes. That was little more than rumor now, a tale told by poets around the mead benches. If there was any resemblance between Hereric and Heremod, nobody was alive to know. To Deomaer, Hereric didn't seem like a kinslayer. He was calm and quiet, almost meek. He never spoke of fighting, nor did he even take place in the wild boar hunts. He carried himself about Hwitstan with great humility for one so close to the king. Only in battle did he show himself to be bold. Yet battle was something rarely seen in Friesland, aside from occasional small skirmishes and raids along the southwestern and eastern borders. Most of Folcwalda's thanes who had seen battle had seen it elsewhere.

Of all Folcwalda's thanes, Ulestan the Wise was the most honored. He bore the family emblem of an owl on his shield and helm, and was called "The Owl" because of his great wisdom. The king knew and trusted that wisdom. It was rare to see Folcwalda anywhere without Ulestan at his right side. The two were like brothers. In his youth Ulestan had married Folcwalda's younger sister Fealla. A year later she had miscarried and died. Though their time together was short, Ulestan's love for Fealla had been so great that he had never taken another wife for himself, though Folcwalda's other sister Ingwa had been offered to him. Deomaer knew nothing of Ulestan's kinship, but he knew it to be noble since both Fealla and Ingwa had been offered to him.

Ulestan, Aelfer, Eormen, Edmen, Beow, Froda and Hereric stood with Folcwalda now—the closest and most trusted of Folcwalda's thanes. Following these thanes up the hill were many of their retinue, the members of their warbands. Last came Daelga the poet. His jubilant laughter could be heard by all as he ascended the hill. As eager was he to witness great events as to sing of them. In his lifetime he had already seen much and would bear witness to much more—tales both of joy and of sorrow.

"Eormen," Folcwalda said when the Danish ship had come into full view and moved toward the landing.

"Yes, lord," the thane answered with a slight bow and bend of his knee.

"Extend to our guests the hospitality of this land. See that they are treated well."

"Your wish," he responded with a smile and a nod.

"Ulestan," Folcwalda continued, the edges of his lip curling slightly in a concealed smile as he did so, "accompany Eormen to see that he doesn't start a war with our future allies."

Eormen's answering smile was unconcealed. "You underestimate me, Lord Folcwalda. There are too few of them. I would wait until we were outnumbered by fifty or two fifties before I tried to begin a war."

Folcwalda laughed. His thane was probably not very far from the truth. "Yes, you are quite right. Nonetheless, Ulestan will accompany you and see that our guests receive a proper welcome."

Ulestan nodded, and the two proceeded down the slope to the beach followed by ten other armed warriors who stood close by. The children had all retreated back to the village long before Finn's horn sounded, and the beach was almost empty when the Danish ship began to ride the low surf up to the sand.

"Aelfer and Edmen . . ."

"Yes," they responded in unison.

"Remain with Finn. The rest of us will return to the hall."

"My lord?" Finn asked in surprise.

"It is fitting for a king to greet his guests from his hall," Folcwalda answered. "You may remain here to greet your future bride and escort the Danes to the hall which will someday be yours." He looked his son squarely in the eyes as he continued, "Bear yourself with pride today, Prince of Friesland. This marks the beginning of a great kingdom which will soon be yours."

"Not too soon," Finn said smiling in return. Then he turned to watch the incoming ship. "What have we here?" he suddenly exclaimed.

Folcwalda turned and gazed upon the beach to see what had caught his son's attention. A second and third Danish ship had just come around the point and were now rowing into the cove.

"Two more Danish ships?" Finn asked rhetorically. "They must have sixty warriors with them. Is this a wedding or an attack?"

A brief look of surprise and perhaps even doubt crossed Folcwalda's visage. It remained there only a second, and then the look of resolute calm which was much more familiar was restored. "Froda, Hereric and Beow," he commanded, "join Ulestan and Eormen on the beach. The rest of you return with me to the hall where we will greet our honored guests as a king should." He turned and began down the hill back toward Hwitstanburg. As if nothing more than a parting thought, he added to Finn, "You have your horn should you for any reason need me." Then he disappeared over the crest, followed by the few thanes not assigned to other tasks.

Finn turned again to face the Danes. The first ship had slid neatly onto the beach. There was a brief interchange between Ulestan and one of the Danes as they stepped forth. Deomaer did not know for sure who they were, but his guess was verified a second later as he overheard Finn talking to Edmen and Aelfer. "That is Hnaef, son of Hoc, a good prince . . . and Hengest, his loyal thane, after him. Oslaf the Jute follows next. Though he is no Dane, he holds some kinship with Hnaef. For more than a lifetime Jutland and his folk have been ruled by the Danes. There is some enmity between Jutish and Danish blood. I do not recognize the two who follow Oslaf, but they bear the same shield boss and helm. I would guess them to be Oslaf's brothers—Guthlaf the elder and Hunlaf the younger."

Then Finn's voice faded in the wind, and Deomaer couldn't hear what was said next. Two more armed Danes stepped from the ship and were followed immediately by an older Dane who, from his stature and bearing and from the way he was treated by both Ulestan and the other Danes, could only have been Hoc himself. Hoc was tall and broad, old, wise, proud; a king if Deomaer had ever seen one. He alone of all the Danes, save his daughter, wore no helmet. His white hair flowed out in a single braid reaching halfway down his back. If his appearance from afar was not utterly deceiving, he was taller even than Finn or Folcwalda. He towered even over his own son Hnaef. Stepping from the ship, he reached behind him and, to the joy of Finn, offered his hand to a waiting Hildeburh, who rose from her seat and stepped onto Frisian soil for the first time.

Deomaer could almost feel the ground shake from the great leap which Finn's heart took as his future bride stepped ashore. Her beauty was no less than Finn himself had described it. She was certainly a treasure. For the first time Deomaer doubted the worth of the gifts he had made for her. As she ascended the hill to the waiting Finn, her beauty seemed to grow with each step. Deomaer stood transfixed by her eyes, as did Edmen and Aelfer.

Only Finn was able to step forth. It was to him that her loving gaze was directed. Even as Finn moved to greet her, Hoc and Hnaef stepped ahead of her and intercepted him.

"Peace, Finn," the Danish king said, raising his hand in greeting.

"Welcome, Hoc, king of the Danes," Finn replied, pulling his gaze off his beloved only with great difficulty. "Your presence honors us and is much awaited." He avoided the temptation to look past the king at his daughter, though he knew her eyes were on him.

"We welcome you also, Hnaef, son of Hoc," Finn continued, addressing the other prince. He extended his hand, and they grasped each other by the wrists.

"It has been long," Hnaef replied.

"Too long," Finn said, smiling.

"Where is Folcwalda?" Hoc asked.

"He awaits you in his hall," Finn answered. He wondered how they would respond to Hwitstanburg.

"Friesland is graced with a new hall?" came a voice from behind Hnaef. It was the one Finn had identified as Oslaf. From this close Deomaer had a much better view of him. He was about the same height as Deomaer, but broader and sturdier. He held a single spear in his right hand, and his left was hooked on a small purse hanging at his side. From head to foot he was decorated with silk. A red silk band was wrapped around each arm and another around his waist. A purple silk ribbon hung from his spear, and another was braided in his hair. There was even green silk on his leggings. How proud he must be, Deomaer thought, that he wears more silk than his king. Hoc wore only a single, thin strand of the precious material around the bottom of his braid. Oslaf's brothers Hunlaf and Guthlaf were dressed in fashion similar to Oslaf. "And will there be treasure-giving at this hall?" Oslaf asked. Deomaer thought there was a great deal of arrogance in his voice. Perhaps Hnaef thought so as well because he quickly motioned Oslaf to silence.

Finn said nothing for some time, apparently wondering whether he should answer Oslaf or address only the king and the prince. He kept his eyes fixed on Hoc. When neither he nor Hnaef said anything, Finn chose to answer Oslaf. "As you shall soon see, Folcwalda is a generous king. Rings are given freely in

Hwitstan." As he said this, he glanced past Oslaf down to the beach. The two other Danish ships had pulled ashore, and there seemed to be some trouble between the Danes and the Frisian guards. "Ulestan, see to welcoming the rest of the Danes," Finn said, nodding toward the beach.

Ulestan had already noticed the situation and was whispering something in Eormen's ear. "Yes, lord," he replied. "I will provide shelter for them in the outlying homes and see that their ships and weapons are well looked after while they are our guests."

"Wisely done," Finn said catching the meaning behind Ulestan's words. He turned back to address Hoc, and his glance once again caught Hildeburh's. They held one another's gaze for a brief moment, and then Finn motioned to Hoc and Hnaef. "The day is late, and the pigs are on the spit. This is Summer's Day. Mead and beer flow freely. Come and enjoy the hospitality of Hwitstan and all of Friesland."

"We are honored," Hoc replied and motioned to his own thanes to follow him.

Deomaer watched as Finn, Hoc, Hnaef and Hildeburh started down the hill toward the hall at Hwitstan. Aelfer and Edmen followed closely behind Finn. Hengest remained close behind Hnaef. Guthlaf, Oslaf and Hunlaf followed at a distance and talked quietly among themselves, occasionally pointing toward something they saw off to one side or another. The jeweler then turned back toward the beach. The turmoil seemed to have subsided as soon as Ulestan arrived, and he and Eormen were now leading a small company of Danes up the hill. The remainder of the Danes, some thirty or so men, stayed with the Danish ships under the watchful eye of the ten Frisian guards who remained behind.

Deomaer walked briskly and entered the hall only a few paces behind the last of the Danes. Most of the village was gathered outside, wandering about and trying to look busy while hoping to catch a glimpse of what was taking place inside. To them this hall was the symbol of the new importance of Hwitstan. When work on the hall had begun, the village had suddenly grown to almost three times its normal size. This growth could only be attributed to the hall, they thought. And from the moment it had been completed, chieftains and thanes from across Friesland had not ceased entering and leaving its doors. And now the Danish king himself, a giant in their eyes, had entered the hall. Imaginations ran wild with pictures of kings conjuring spirits and casting spells or performing elaborate rituals; or of fights to the death between the Frisians and Danes over the treasures given by the two kings. The truth, Deomaer knew, would be much more mundane. He already had a good guess what would happen: there would a be a rather long ceremonial greeting followed by some giving of gifts—mostly gold and silver rings and pendants crafted by Deomaer himself. If Folcwalda were gathered with his own thanes only, the gifts would have included ancient and proven swords, spears, and all forms of war gear. But these gifts of time-honored weapons would not be likely today. It would be foolish to give a trusted sword to someone who might someday use it against you. Following the gift giving, there would probably be a more private interchange between the kings and princes. Then the wedding and Summer's Day celebration would begin.

Despite the villagers' imaginations of the glories of a mighty king inside his hall, in the best of times a hall was more of a home—a place for shared story and drink, for friendship and comradeship among the loyal followers of a chieftain—than it was a place where great plans were laid and daring challenges issued. It was true that in times of war a king would gather his thanes in a hall and fill them with brave words of noble deeds, would speak of life and death, of fear and courage. But a hall was also the place where warriors would return after a war to find peace—a warm fire, a mug of mead and fellowship—the things most worth going to war for and the things which made returning most worthwhile. The mystery surrounding a hall added to the awe the villagers had of those who entered, but little of that mystery was grounded in truth.

Nonetheless, as Deomaer strode past the villagers he felt a certain pride that he was among those who were allowed to enter. Inside were gathered the Danes and those whom Deomaer called the "important" Frisians: the thanes and retainers of Finn and Folcwalda and a few others, such as Deomaer himself and the poet Daelga—those who had some special position of honor within the village. Deomaer wasn't sure if he had been given a place within the hall because of his work as jeweler and moneyer or because of his common, though distant, ancestry with the king. He hoped it was because of his work.

"Warriors all, save us alone," Daelga whispered in his ear, catching him by surprise and making him jump. "Common men we, with kings to dine." Before Deomaer could respond, the poet was gone. Was his awe that visible as he looked around him? Or was Daelga, too, able to read his thoughts?

The jeweler slid onto a bench near the door and watched as Hoc approached Folcwalda's bench. He had appeared merely tall while standing outside. Inside the hall he was a veritable giant. Some of Folcwalda's mightiest armed men looked puny in comparison. On one side of Hoc walked the smaller Hnaef, still a large man by any measure. On Hoc's other side came Hildeburh, holding firmly to his extended arm. Her face revealed her timidity and modesty, but there was no fear in her expression. Hengest, Oslaf, Guthlaf and Hunlaf walked a few paces behind their king, and the rest of the Danes dispersed into the hall in groups of three or four, making room for themselves among the Frisians. Hoc held everyone's attention. As he approached Folcwalda's throne, the Frisian king rose to greet him.

"Hail Hoc, son of Heort, descendant of the gods. Welcome to Hwitstan and Friesland. May your journey have started in peace, and may it end in peace. Hail Hnaef, son of Hoc. May your name one day be as honored as your father's, and may your hand be as generous. Hail Hildeburh. May your name be forever praised among the Frisians as was your mother's among the Danes. May you be a fruitful vine," he continued with a wink, "growing in fertile soil. Welcome to our family."

So saying, Folcwalda extended his arm in greeting. His bearing was strong and confident. For some reason Hoc's stature did not dominate Folcwalda's as it had the others'. Though the Danish king was taller even than Folcwalda, something about the Frisian king—his manner perhaps, or his strength, or the way he held his arms or shoulders, or simply his air of confidence—enabled him to stand undaunted beside the giant of a Danish king. They stood as equals. Deomaer found this very reassuring. He was intimidated by the Danes, but Folcwalda's bearing and manner gave him courage. A good king inspired hope in the hearts of his people.

During this greeting, Finn had stepped to the side of his

father. His gaze was now freely fixed upon Hildeburh, and she returned it openly.

"Greetings, Folcwalda, son of Folgar," Hoc replied. "May your kingdom last forever. Your welcome does us great honor. May we return that welcome in our halls. Peace to you and your hall. May we leave with the same peace that we brought."

Folcwalda bowed his head slightly and removed from his neck a magnificent gold torc decorated with garnets and surrounded by a twisting silver wire. Deomaer beamed with pride at his own workmanship as his king placed the gift in the hands of Hoc. "May this always be light upon your neck, and may the head that wears it never be cloven."

"May the hands of the giver be as blessed as those of him who received," Hoc returned, bending the torc around his own neck.

Then Finn stepped forward and approached Hnaef. "May your reign be as mighty and long-lasting as your father's." He removed the golden boar's head from the top of his staff and presented it to the prince. "May your staff never break," he concluded.

Hnaef likewise clasped the hand of Finn. "May our nations as well as their princes be as brothers, and may your staff once again suffer from the weight of too much gold."

Then Oslaf coughed rather loudly and took a slight step forward. Deomaer noticed that both he and his brothers had their hands resting lightly on the hilts of their swords. *Are they expecting gifts as well?* he wondered. At the same time that Oslaf was seeking attention, Ulestan entered the hall leading a large group of Danes from the second and third ships. The Danes proceeded to disperse into the hall. There was no small bit of elbowing and pushing as they made room for themselves. Neither of the kings or princes seemed to notice either Oslaf or the new disturbance, and Deomaer wondered if they would. Ulestan quietly made his way to the front of the hall, where he stood a few paces behind Folcwalda. The dialogue between the kings continued, and the hall soon settled as all eyes and ears focused on them once again.

"In return," Hoc continued, "we bring to you the greatest treasure in the land of the Danes." Taking a step forward, he placed his daughter's hand on the arm of Finn. She squeezed it gently, and Finn placed his free hand on top of hers. "It is not without sorrow that our land parts with its chief source of beauty," Hoc continued. "May you treat her well and preserve the peace that is now between us. It would not go well for an ill hand to touch a daughter of the Danes."

"Nor would it go well," Folcwalda answered sternly, "for an ill hand to touch the wife of a Frisian king."

"Finn, son of Folcwalda . . ." Hoc began to say, turning toward the Frisian prince. But whatever he was going to say he never finished. A deep, lighthearted laugh bellowed from the old king as soon as he looked at his daughter. She had already slid under Finn's arm and was gazing longingly at him, oblivious to the situation around them.

Folcwalda and Hnaef both caught Hoc's laughter, and it soon spread throughout the hall. Though most of those present didn't know the reason for the sudden outburst of gaiety, they were quick to join. The tension which had been building suddenly eased out of the room like a receding tide. Finn and Hildeburh both looked up and blushed, but joined in the laughter.

"Enough," Folcwalda finally bellowed. "Let the feast begin. We have much to celebrate this Summer's Day, not the least of which is the joining of Finn and Hildeburh. Let them lead the way."

Finn grabbed Hildeburh's hand tightly and almost whisked her out of the hall through a mob of Frisians and Danes who parted to make room for them and cheered them on as they went. When they stepped out of the hall, a huge roar of applause and greeting arose from the village. Those who were waiting outside joined the cheering for the prince and his bride-to-be. Hildeburh held to the prince, and he never let go of her but once for the rest of the day and night.

Then began the feasting all had waited for. Though the boars were still roasting, there was a great enough abundance of other fare to make men happy.

The hall soon began to empty, though the two kings remained. A second bench had been placed next to Folcwalda's as a place of honor for Hoc. The two now sat side by side as if they were old friends—and maybe they were for all Deomaer knew.

"Why three ships and such a large warband?" Deomaer

heard Folcwalda ask as the jeweler tarried just a moment behind the throng.

"Ah, that is nothing," Hoc replied. "It was only at the urging of Oslaf and his brothers. They thought it would be safer in the case of unforeseen events."

"Unforeseen events?" Folcwalda laughed. "Since when has anything ever taken Hoc by surprise? And who would dare to attack any Danish band, no matter how small?"

"Yes, I know." The Danish king sighed. "But as I grow older, I am afraid I grow more easily swayed by my thanes. Hunlaf can be very persistent. Let us not allow that to be a thorn between us. We have much else to discuss, not the least of which are the kingdoms which are gaining power in the south."

"The Merovingians!" Folcwalda spat.

V

The Lay of Folcwalda

Deomaer turned and walked out of the hall. The sight outside was almost overwhelming. The mead was already flowing freely, and the Danes and Frisians were laughing and hugging as if they were brothers. Children ran in and out everywhere, for the most part ignored by their parents and older siblings. Most of the celebration took place in the large clearing to the north of the hall, on the seaward side of the village. Scattered about the edges of the clearing, many of the younger warriors took part in a myriad of athletic contests. There were sword fights played with mock swords of leather-covered wood, stone-throwing events, wrestling contests, and many other games of skill and strength. All this went on for some time.

Then once more Finn's horn was sounded. All the village turned to look toward the hall from whence the sound had come. There beside the great ash stump stood Folcwalda's poet. In a single, twisting leap Daelga was atop the stump, harp in hand. With eyes greener than the leaves of the ash beside him, and light curly hair that fell to his shoulders, he could have been a boy of fifteen summers. But he was ageless. His thin frame belied the strength in his wiry muscles. And his eyes, green and alive in the summer sunlight, could turn suddenly grey beside the winter hearth fire and pass through a man like the fell north wind. Two generations of kings he had served already, and a third would follow. Bard, scop, poet—whatever one would call him, he sang and men listened.

"With strength of twelve,
    Of twenty, the mighty,
Wise Folcwalda,
    Friesland's good lord.
To Swedeland's shores
    He sailed alone,
The Swan Road crossed,
    Sea's icy waves.
With courage bold
    There brave deeds did;
A prince he left,
    Returned a king."

So began Daelga to sing a tale of the mighty deeds of the king. "Folcwalda the Fair" this king was called—the son of Folgar, the lord of his folk, the hawk. Many brave deeds and feats did Folcwalda accomplish to win his throne, but none earned him more glory than the recapture of his father's golden torc. This tale Daelga now told, and men and women drew near to listen. Though all but a few in Friesland had heard the tale before, yet such was Folcwalda's fame and Daelga's gift that they listened readily. And there were others besides, king and thanes from many kingdoms who had come to celebrate the wedding of Folcwalda's son Finn. They would do well to hear of the wisdom and strength of the new Frisian king.

Folcwalda had been a young prince, not yet able to sit astride a horse, when the Swedes led by Ongintheo had come raiding along Friesland's coast. Six and ten ships, fifteen spears each, sought the plunder of war. As swift as birds' flight, they appeared seemingly from nowhere and were gone, and none could stand against them. Villages were burned which would not pay the ransom, and Frisian women and children were killed or taken as slaves. When the rumor of these raids reached Folgar, and the smoke from surrounding villages clouded the sky, he raised what small warband he could to stand against the Swedes. For though his clan was small he was a proud king, and he would pay no ransom. It was not many days before they came, and when they did a battle was waged. The king and his small Frisian clan fought valiantly to defend their village, but the fight was in vain. The Swedish warband was far too great. Though he stood and fought until the end, Folgar was finally killed and the golden torc taken from his neck by Ongintheo himself. However, Folcwalda his son was neither killed nor taken captive. At the command of Folgar, an old and wise thane had hidden the prince in the hills. There, from his vantage atop a rocky slope, Folcwalda watched the entire battle. With the eyes of a hawk he saw all that took place, and in the hour his father fell he swore he would one day recover the torc.

Tall and strong grew Folcwalda, and fair to gaze upon, but grim was his mood and fiercely determined his spirit. Weak was the old thane who had saved him, barely able even to walk in his old age, but no greater warrior had ever lived in the lands of the Frisians. He taught Folcwalda well. No sooner could he hold a sword, but Folcwalda was swinging it mightily. No sooner could he hold a spear, but he was already wielding it like the veteran of many wars. Like a wild boar he was, and none could restrain him or dissuade him from his purposes. When the old thane died, Folcwalda would wait no longer. With spear, sword and shield he set out alone for the land of the Swedes, seeking to reconquer his father's torc and avenge his father's blood. Many were they who would have traveled with him had he asked. Sons and brothers they were of the thanes who had fallen with Folgar, and they desired vengeance upon the Swedes. But Folcwalda knew it not.

For one man to attempt the seas alone was no small feat itself. But neither wild winds, nor high waves, nor the icy waters of the bight daunted him, for fate led him on. He sailed northward to the lands of the Angles. When his food gave out and his sail tore, he abandoned his ship and turned inland. He crossed the Angles' land to the great Baltic Sea and the burg of Schleswig, where the name of his father was known among the people. They gave him a new ship and provisions for many new days, and he pressed on eastward.

Shelter he found in the lands of the Danes, and fast friendship was quick made with Hoc, their young king. Many promises and vows they exchanged, and they swore to uphold each other in war should Folcwalda ever become king. But despite Hoc's words to dissuade him, Folcwalda would not stay. His voyage was soon resumed, and none of the people of the Danes thought to see him again. Yet one gift Hoc gave him at his parting, and that served him well. A proud and hard helm was forged for him in the Danish smithies, and ever after, to the end of his days, Folcwalda wore that helm whenever he rode to battle.

Onward he traveled. Northward from the land of the Danes he sailed to the Geatish shores. A home he could have found there too had he desired, for their king was old and he looked upon Folcwalda as a son. And the Geatish people loved him as well and gladly would have had him for a prince, for he was tall and fair to look upon. Nor did they have any great love for the Swedes who had done them as great harm as they had done to Folcwalda. The Battle-Scyldings they called the Swedes, and they were bitter enemies. There in the Geatish hall of King Hrethmond, another treasure was given to Folcwalda of greater value than countless rings or jewels: an old war sword of wound steel, worn by the Geatish king in the days of his youth. Proven in battle times without count, it would not fail a steady hand. Folcwalda received it gratefully and laid his own blade aside. But he sought not a treasure-giver, nor did he desire a home. He sought only the golden torc that had been his father's. A few days only he remained among the Geats, gathering his strength and readying for what lay ahead. Brave words he heard at his parting, and proud rings and treasure he was promised if he returned. Then the wind filled his sails once again.

It was no weary sailor who arrived in Swedeland, but rather a prince strengthened by his long journey and hardened by his days at sea. The determination which kindled his spirit had risen to a roaring flame. He cared not if he died in his quest, but he would live not a day longer without his father's torc. He set helm on head and shield on arm and strode confidently to the hall of the king. Such was the fierceness in Folcwalda's glance and the strength in his muscles, and so great his stature, that though he had never swung blade in battle he appeared to those who saw him a mighty warrior. Men fell away before him.

Now, the time of his arrival was early summer when the Swedish kings were gathering at their summer halls beside the sea from where they could carry on their wars and raids more easily. Ongintheo had once more gathered his warband about him and was preparing to set sail. Had Folcwalda arrived with his own warband, he would never have seen the inside of Ongintheo's hall, for the Swedish king's warband would have met him on the beach and a battle would have been waged there. But Ongintheo sat outside his hall and, seeing Folcwalda approaching alone, thought him no threat. When the young Frisian prince placed his helm on his head, the Swedish king laughed aloud. "Does this one come alone seeking war?" he jeered.

But the laughter died in his throat when Folcwalda spoke. "I am Folcwalda, son of Folgar and rightful owner of the torc about your neck. Will Ongintheo, the honored king of the Battle-Scyldings, fight with me, or will he hide like a Swedish dog?"

Dead silence fell upon those who heard these words. Venom dripped from Folcwalda's mouth. Long had he pondered how he might challenge Ongintheo, and he had chosen well. His words cut a deep wound and then poisoned it.

A look of fear crossed Ongintheo's face. He knew nothing of Folcwalda, but could see that the boy had the strength of a giant. He had no desire to fight him. But neither was Ongintheo a coward, and strong words had been spoken. Kings did not come by their kingship easily, and many a Swedish throne had been lost because a bold thane saw a weakness in their treasure-giver. Ongintheo could not allow his thanes to see him refuse so bold a challenge. And that was Folcwalda's only hope, for he could not face Ongintheo's entire warband alone.

"Come, take the torc," Ongintheo replied as he rose to his feet. "Cut it from my neck if you will."

The words were hardly from his mouth before his sword was whirring down on Folcwalda's head. The Frisian prince was unprepared. He was no battle-hardened warrior, and though he had been taught well he was untried. Only at the last moment did he raise his own blade to counter his enemy's blow. Ongintheo's blade caught his own, knocked it back, and then came down upon his head. Had Folcwalda not been wearing the Danish helm, the battle would have ended at that moment. But the helm held strong, and Ongintheo's blow, to the astonishment of both of them, glanced off.

Ongintheo, seeing Folcwalda's youth and inexperience, pressed the attack. Folcwalda staggered backward, and Ongintheo swung his sword again. Folcwalda caught the blade on his shield. He tried to raise his own blade, but had no time. Another blow and then another he took with his shield. The blade bit deeply into the hard wood. Folcwalda managed a weak swipe at Ongintheo's legs, but the Swede brushed it aside with his own sword and swung again.

For a long time the battle raged such. It went ill for Folcwalda, but he kept himself alive. Nor did his strength diminish, for he was in the prime of his youth, and many days at sea had taught him a stamina which Ongintheo did not understand. Still, the Frisian prince could land no blow, and his shield was battered sorely. All the time he was forced backward. With each blow landed upon him, Ongintheo's thanes cheered.

Then came the fiercest blow that Folcwalda had yet felt. It rattled his bones and jarred his arm. When he looked down, his shield was no more. A look of triumph filled Ongintheo's face. But Folcwalda as yet knew no fear, for if he could not recover his father's torc he preferred death. He cast aside the splinters and gripped his sword with two hands. Now every blow of his enemy meant his life, for if he failed to counter just one, it would surely finish him.

But Ongintheo was winded. And as Folcwalda continued to frustrate the attacks against him, a brief hint of fear appeared in his enemy's face. The prince saw that fear, and for the first time he felt hope. A blow was dealt at his head. He stopped it and returned one. Ongintheo fell backward, and suddenly Folcwalda was on the attack. He advanced and swung his blade more fiercely. The Swede blocked the blow and staggered. The prince swung again with all his might, leveling a great two-handed swing. The blades met in midair. Only one held. The Geatish work did not fail; the blade of Ongintheo shattered.

A look of horror crossed the Swedish king's face. Folcwalda paused for a moment. Ongintheo's thanes saw all and started forward to protect their king. But they knew they would not be in time. Folcwalda's blade was too quick.

Yet, the Frisian warrior did not swing. For at the same moment that the Swedish king's blade shattered, a young child stepped forward among the ring of onlookers, and the unexpected movement caught Folcwalda's eye. So much did the child look like the king that he could not have been other than his son. A vision flashed in Folcwalda's mind of a young Frisian prince standing atop a rocky hill watching his father die.

Mercy stayed his hand. He lowered his blade and stepped back. Little understanding did Ongintheo have of Folcwalda's actions, but relief and thankfulness filled his heart. That night the torc of Folgar was placed on Folcwalda's neck by Ongintheo himself.

Daelga's tale ended there after the recovery of the torc, but Folcwalda's great feats had not. The king was known far and wide. With that act of mercy shown to the Swedish king wisdom had come to the young prince. Or perhaps wisdom had always been his and his mercy had been its first revelation. With his father's torc about his neck, Folcwalda had returned from Swedeland to Friesland to begin an even greater work, one that would last his lifetime. He began to build a kingdom.

From the very first, when Folcwalda had gathered the chieftains of Friesland to be his thanes and united the villages under his rule, he had known what he was doing. It was no simple desire for power which prompted him to act. Folcwalda had understood that if the rest of the chieftains didn't unite, Friesland could not stand against the Merovingians long. The other chieftains knew this as well, and though most were slow to act, Folcwalda was persistent and persuasive, and his arguments finally found ears. As a single kingdom, he told the chieftains, they could act as a unified force. And more important than their increased military might was the centralization of the trade customs and fees which were the source of income for most of Friesland. As a unified kingdom, the individual villages would stop competing against one another and would thus increase the profits of all the Frisian villages. At first only a few chieftains joined with Folcwalda. But each one who did added to the momentum and swayed others until there was a large following behind the future king. Those who were not easily persuaded by Folcwalda's arguments were occasionally won by force. For among those who had early pledged themselves to Folcwalda were chieftains of the most powerful clans of Friesland. The brothers Eormen and Edmen, strong, mighty, hardheaded, and loyal, had alone persuaded many to follow a single king. Little use had those two chieftains for words. However, their swords spoke loudly.

Eventually all but a few villages in the more remote parts of the land had taken Folcwalda as their king. The Half-Franks, clans of mixed Frisian and Frankish blood dwelling at Wic by Dorestad on the Rhine and at Domburg at the mouth of the Meuse River, were the last major clans to bow to the king. And Lyndlaf, the son of Lynd, the chieftain of the Half-Franks at Dorestad, had already promised his allegiance in secret. He had asked only that his father be left alone to rule the village until his days ended. Folcwalda needed only wait until the death of Lynd, who was already quite old, and Wic by Dorestad would be part of the kingdom.

VI

The Winning of the Bride

When the Lay of Folcwalda had been finished, it came time for the chief event of the entire celebration: the winning of the bride. A high fenced pen had been erected on the west side of Hwitstanburg, and roaming about within was a wild boar. Angry at its captivity, it charged madly at any who came too close. Though a sturdy fence separated them from the beast, mighty warriors backed away quickly from its charges. They had too often seen what damage such a creature could do, even when caged.

While some taunted and further angered the boar, Finn was ushered to the far side of the pen where Hunlaf the Jute, familiar with the custom, handed him a cruel hooked spear. The prince knew what was required. A large crowd had gathered to watch. While the boar was kept occupied at the other end of the enclosure, the prince climbed over the wall and entered the arena where his right to manhood would be tested.

To the great distress of the women of Friesland, the challenge of the boar was a traditional rite of the wedding day. A few days before a wedding a wild boar would be captured and caged. It would be fed well for a day or two, but then left hungry the morning of the wedding to increase its aggressiveness. Of course, no boar needed to be left hungry to be dangerous. They were vicious creatures by birth. A single enraged boar could wreak havoc among an entire village before being captured or killed. With one lunge their powerful necks and knife-sharp tusks could rip a hole from a man's knee all the way to his belly. No wolf pack or even a bear would fight the wild boar. It was a mighty beast, the bane of many lesser animals and of not few hunters. On more than one occasion victory had been won by a boar against a potential groom and the wedding celebration had been brought quickly and gloomily to an end. The wiser young men of the village would not drink the mead cup on their wedding day until after their encounter with the boar. Those who drank of the cup too soon did not usually fare well.

As Finn was a great warrior and the son of a chieftain, the village had found and captured a particularly ferocious boar. Two men had been injured caging it.

And now Finn was within its enclosure. Its hackles were raised as it turned to face him. Finally it had an opportunity to vent its fury, for an enemy had come within the cruel fence which encaged it. The mighty boar wasted no time. It lowered its tusks and charged with blood in its eyes—Finn's blood.

Finn took a step forward, planted his feet firmly, lowered his spear, and braced himself. Seeing the spear, the boar veered at the last second and rushed past Finn, crashing into the fence behind him. Finn took a swipe as it passed and drew the first blood.

The boar felt the pain, and its anger increased. Circling to the far end of the pen, it charged a second time. Once again Finn leveled the spear-point at the creature's heart. This time it did not turn away. The full force of the boar's charge exploded into the point. The spear given him by Hunlaf proved too weak. The shaft shattered, and Finn tumbled over backwards, holding only splinters. Hildeburh shouted and started toward him, but was held back. Some thought the boar had been killed, others that Finn had been hurt by his fall. Neither was true. The prince appeared stunned, but he was uninjured. And though the spear-point had impaled itself deeply into the boar's front leg, the beast was by no means finished. Finn rolled quickly to his feet as the boar approached him again.

The boar's third approach was slower and more deliberate. Blood spilled from the wound in its leg, where the end of the spear was still protruding. Its eyes were fixed cruelly on its enemy's belly. Finn unsheathed the great broadsword which hung on his back and lowered the point until it stood two inches from the boar's snout. They stood for a few moments looking at each other. The boar's huge nostrils flared in and out in time with its heavy breathing. Finn's visage was grim and determined. A sword was generally not a good weapon to use against a boar; it was too short, and there was no good way to brace it between yourself and your opponent. The boar seemed to sense Finn's vulnerability as it lowered its head and stepped forward.

In the wink of an eye Finn raised his great blade a few feet and brought it down with all of his strength. The stroke went clean through the target, and the contest was over. The animal's head rolled to the side. Its lifeblood pulsed forth in streams onto the ground. A few of the women who had already partaken of one too many cups of mead fainted. The rest of the crowd cheered.

Finn wiped off his blade, raised it high into the air in victory, and then resheathed it. Hildeburh was already running across the pen. She reached Finn and leapt into his arms. The crowd cheered again.

The cooks entered the pen and dragged the boar out behind the hall where the roasting pits were. A few seconds later, following tradition, they emerged again, carrying a boar that had been roasting all day. The cooked boar was brought to Finn as if it were the wild boar he had just killed. Finn was handed a knife, and he cut a large hunk of the meat. There were more cheers as he ripped off a huge bite with his teeth. Then, to the amusement of the onlookers, as the hot juices dripped down Finn's chin, Hildeburh grabbed the knife from his hands and cut an equally large piece of the meat for herself. She bit into it even more savagely than Finn had. Though she didn't know it at the time, she had just begun a new tradition in Friesland.

Once Finn had taken his bite, the feasting began in earnest. Three more of the roasts were carried out and set on huge wooden blocks outside the hall. From that point on, every man, woman and child ate as much as desired when desired.

From out of nowhere the poet Daelga suddenly appeared once more and jumped again onto the stump in the center of the clearing.

"Come, listen, and drink," he proclaimed laughing as he strummed on his lyre. The commotion quieted quickly as more and more people noticed him. His reputation throughout

Friesland was high, and his earlier singing of Folcwalda's Lay had raised it.

"Come, hear, and enjoy," he sang louder, still strumming. A few more gathered around the stump. Those closest to him sat down.

"Come, open your ears, and see what enters," he said more quietly. Then, when he had a crowd large enough for his liking, he changed the strumming on his lyre and began to sing.

> *"Of dragons and demons*
>> *Daelga will sing;*
> *Of ents, armies, edges,*
>> *Endings and death;*
> *Of Saxons and Scyldings,*
>> *And Spear-Danes and Jutes;*
> *Of battles and beasts,*
>> *Of beer, mead, and wine.*
> *Now lays shall be lifted*
>> *With lyre and with voice;*
> *Tales will be told;*
>> *Times past relived.*
> *Your ears open wide*
>> *These words you will hear;*
> *Of princes and pride*
>> *Poems will tell.*
> *Of doubt, courage, duty*
>> *Daelga will sing."*

Without hesitation the poet once again changed his strum and immediately started into a whole series of poems and songs. He sang first of the creation of Middle-earth and of the wars between the ice giants and the gods. He followed with a song of Weland the smith, half-god and half-man; how he was imprisoned by the evil king Niphad who had him hamstrung to prevent his escape, and of how Weland gained his revenge by first killing Niphad's two sons and then ravaging his daughter Beaduhild before flying away on man-made wings, leaving the evil king to die in anguish. He finished with the tale of how Weland finally returned to take Beaduhild for his wife and of the birth of their son, Widia the adventurer. Daelga continued with more tales of

Friesland and Folcwalda. Then, to the delight of the gathered Danes, he sang of the legendary Danish king Scyld Scefing and the glory of the Spear-Danes of old. Their princes did brave deeds, and far and wide many tribes paid tribute to Scyld. His son Beow was famous as well, and his glory also spread quickly. Very few, if any, left before the tale was finished. Continuing in this vein and taking only a few breaks to refill his mead cup, the poet Daelga was able to continue entertaining until long after the sun had set.

Finn and Hildeburh listened long enough to hear the first part of a new poem about Folcwalda, which Daelga promised to continue the following night. Then the couple danced and drank until the last red of the sun dipped below the horizon. In accordance with the tradition, Finn then swept Hildeburh up in his arms and carried her around the entire village, ending at the new home he had built for her with his own hands. "The young princeling brags of the growth of the Hwitstan," Deomaer overheard Hunlaf saying to his brothers as Finn turned the first corner, "but he will soon be cursing these ugly new huts when Hildeburh grows heavy in his arms."

"You do not know our prince," Deomaer replied under his breath. The jeweler was right. Finn began to sing and almost ran the final stretch, with Hildeburh holding on tightly and singing with him. Then, without a word, Finn swung into the hut, pulled the skins tightly over the entrance behind him, and was not seen again for two days.

VII

Farewells

The absence of Finn and Hildeburh did not lessen the enthusiasm of the celebration, which continued unabated late into the night until one by one the warriors sank into unconsciousness. Though most managed to find their way into Hwitstanburg where they collapsed on a bench or beside the hearth at the foot of their chieftain, more than a few spent the night outside on the ground.

Yet the mead was still plentiful, and the celebration of summer continued the following day and the day after as well. The Danes and Frisians were soon joined by many hale warriors from lands far and wide as numerous ships, proud and full, sailed into Hwitstanwic from across the Swan Road. They came bearing kings, princes, chieftains, thanes, earls and warriors alike. By Folcwalda's invitation they had come to join the celebration and to witness the alliance of Danes and Frisians. Nor did those present lack opportunity to form alliances and treaties with other war leaders and clan chieftains who had also come. For that reason alone, many great chieftains had come or sent their princes and earls. And even those who had no wish or need for new alliances were drawn to the celebration for fear that if they were not present, they might find, in their absence, that their enemies had suddenly allied against them. Folcwalda, in his wisdom and cunning, had preyed upon these very motivations to gather together those powers whom he desired to witness his new bond with Hoc. Each king or prince whom he greeted was let to see very clearly the bench of the Danish king beside that of his own.

On the first night, Saxon and Swedish princes with their small warbands had arrived from opposite directions at the same time. Each eager to be first into the village, they had nearly run up the hill. The Saxons and Swedes were followed shortly by a band of English thanes with their young prince, no more than ten summers old. And early the following morning a ship bearing a grey and battle-hardened chieftain of a small Jutish tribe arrived. His battle-axe in hand, he stepped ashore appearing ready at any moment to enter into battle. He had no love for the Swedes, nor for the Danes, who ruled too much Jutish land. Only with great difficulty was he convinced there was no trap waiting to be sprung.

And so it continued throughout the celebration and for many days afterward. The Frisian guards at Hwitstanwic were kept busy that week. Fortunately for those in the village, the warbands were so concerned about the danger from each other that many of their men were left on the beach to guard their ships. Small camps spread out all along Hwitstanwic.

The chieftains, however, all found their way to Hwitstan, where they entered the new hall and were greeted warmly by Folcwalda and Hoc, who spent the greater portion of those three days sitting side by side on their new thrones. Neither king partook of the mead cup to any great extent, but neither did they discourage their followers from enjoying its pleasures.

Folcwalda took special interest in the arrival of Ecgwalda, the ruler of the Half-Franks of Domburg. Ecgwalda's people were the only remaining Frisians not to accept Folcwalda's kingship, save for the powerful clan at Wic by Dorestad. (But Lyndlaf, soon to be the chieftain at Dorestad, had already promised his allegiance. It was only a matter of time—months or maybe even days—until his father would die and pass on the crown.) Ecgwalda was the last obstacle to a completely unified Friesland. His small village of Domburg in the southwest was on a long peninsula near the mouth of the Meuse River, not far south of the Rhine. For most of its great length, the Meuse was deep and wide. It flowed into the North Sea from deep in the heart of the continent, making it one of the best trade routes in the north. Many goods destined for or coming from the English, Jutish and Saxon cities passed through Domburg, due east of Cantwara and not far from the narrowest point of crossing—a journey of no more than twenty miles. Thus, though Ecgwalda's tribe was small, it was strong and wealthy. Furthermore, Domburg was easily defended.

Its position on the end of the peninsula left only one narrow approach by land.

The village's main weakness lay in the number of small islands scattered about the bay at the mouth of the Meuse. The islands could act as shelters for invading armies which might hide there, waiting to attack. Landings on most of these isles were fairly easy, leaving Domburg vulnerable to quick raids from the sea. Yet even the islands could be used to Domburg's advantage if the clan's chieftain planned well. Small outposts scattered about them would serve to give warning of attacks and could also be used to harry the ships of an invading army. Domburg could be built, by either Folcwalda or his enemies, into more than just the largest of Friesland's trade centers. It could become a strong city as well. It was vital to the unity of Friesland to gain Ecgwalda's allegiance, and to do so quickly and without shedding Frisian blood.

If forced to it, Folcwalda had the military might to conquer Ecgwalda and seize Domburg by force. Many of his thanes had suggested such more than once. In fact, a plan for doing so had been brewing in his mind for over a year. He refrained only because the growing Merovingian kingdom watched his every move closely. A war within Friesland would surely invite raids from the outside; if not from the Merovingians, then from overseas. Furthermore, Folcwalda loathed to shed the blood of his men unless it was necessary. Even so, he knew that failure to add Domburg to the kingdom soon would severely weaken Friesland's dominance of the best trade routes.

Ulestan, too, was aware of the importance of Domburg and thus of Ecgwalda. When he saw the chieftain arrive, he made a point of gathering the best of the Frisian knights—those that could be found sober—to stand in the hall beside Folcwalda. Deomaer, from the back of the hall, watched with interest as Ulestan made every effort to display the might of his king to the visiting chieftain from Domburg. He noticed as well the way Ecgwalda looked upon Hoc with fear and respect. The new allegiance with the Danes was having its desired effect—at least upon Ecgwalda. Late on the second day of feasting, Ecgwalda approached Folcwalda and said a few words which only Ulestan and Hoc were close enough to hear. Folcwalda rose to his feet, and the two stared at each other for a few moments and then smiled as they extended hands and grasped each other by the wrists. Whatever had transpired bode well for Friesland. Ulestan disappeared shortly after that, satisfied that his efforts had succeeded.

Deomaer left the hall as well. He wandered around the village enjoying the festivities and the great feast provided by his king. The jeweler also took advantage of the many merchants who seemed to have appeared out of nowhere. Thinking ahead to the winter months, he bought himself a new fur-lined robe. The pouch of gold coins which had been given him by Folcwalda and which now hung at his side gave him a certain power he had never before experienced. It also made him the focus of attention of any merchants who happened to discover his new wealth. Though this was at first a boon, it soon became a nuisance. Before long, Deomaer found himself seeking less visible places from which to enjoy the celebration and avoid the merchants. It was only then that he began to notice the frequent disruptions around the village. Princes and their thanes, full of mead, would bump into their counterparts from other tribes and kingdoms, and tempers would flash as if the small collision of two bodies was enough to begin a war—and perhaps it was; Deomaer did not know. At other times seamen would come to blows arguing over the purchase of a piece of cloth or the last pair of leather sandals.

But each and every time there was an outbreak of tempers, just as the situation was about to veer out of control, Ulestan would appear out of nowhere and the disruption would cease as quickly as it had erupted. Or if it wasn't Ulestan, it was Aelfer or Beow, both of whom the jeweler frequently saw conferring with the elder thane. And as Deomaer watched more closely, he saw something else as well—something which disturbed him greatly. Each time there was a particularly hostile or violent incident, there would be Hunlaf, Oslaf or Guthlaf quietly slipping away from the scene like dogs caught stealing meat. Deomaer wondered if Ulestan saw them too. But he said nothing, for it was not the place of a jeweler to involve himself in the making of treaties or the governing of people. Nonetheless, he shuddered to think what the days would have been like had not Ulestan been at hand and had he not had the wisdom to require all of the arriving bands to leave their weapons in their ships or with their horses in camps outside the village. But Ulestan was there, and the situation never did get out of hand, and Deomaer was able to sleep in peace those nights—or at least in as much peace as could be expected in the midst of such a big celebration in such a small village.

When Finn and Hildeburh emerged sheepishly from their hut near midday on the third day of feasting, Hwitstan was in shambles. Drunk warriors lay scattered at odd angles all across the village; wine and mead cups lay broken and spilled across the grounds; there were more than a few bruised and bloody warriors—victims of overenthusiasm in some of the rougher sporting events; and on the south side of the village ashes still smouldered from a fire which had consumed one hut in the middle of the second night. Surprisingly enough, however, there had not been any fatalities, and there were still enough sober villagers and warriors, both Frisian and alien, to raise a loud cheer for the new couple as they emerged.

"Long live Finn," the Frisians shouted.

"Long live Hildeburh," echoed the Danes.

"Long live Finn and Hildeburh! Long live Finn and Hildeburh!" everybody joined in.

All arms were raised in salute as the two walked through the clearing and entered the great hall. Hoc and Folcwalda sat watching as if they had been expecting them.

"You return so soon?" Folcwalda asked in jest.

Both Finn and Hildeburh blushed. "The feasting is over," Finn replied.

"You look well, my daughter," Hoc said with a smile.

"I am well, Father. More well than I have ever been."

"Would that I could say the same about all my men," Folcwalda laughed.

"And I," Hoc said. "This could be the longest sea voyage any of them have ever taken. I fear the ground is already swaying beneath them."

"Perhaps you should remain with us for another week," Folcwalda suggested. Hildeburh gazed at her father and asked the same question with her eyes.

"Another day perhaps." Hoc smiled back at his daughter. "But not another week. I'm afraid that the new blood bond between our kingdoms might quickly be broken if our men are together much longer."

"Is that a prophecy?" Hnaef laughed. With his thane Hengest he had stepped up behind his sister and now kissed her on the cheek.

Folcwalda glared. For the first time in three days the smile dropped from his expression. Hnaef didn't notice. He kept smiling at his sister and new brother.

"Not as long as we rule our people," Finn replied, returning his smile and extending his arm at the same time.

They grasped each other firmly by the wrists. "Not as long as we rule our people," Hnaef echoed.

"Then let us share the mead cup and drink to peace. I have grown thirsty, and I'm afraid I've missed the best of the celebration."

"No," Hnaef laughed. "We've missed the best of the celebration. But we did the best we could. There might not be any mead left."

"No mead? For the prince and his bride?"

"You underestimate your father," Hoc said. "If I know him at all, the best of the mead still remains. Am I right?" the Dane asked, turning to the Frisian.

"You know me too well, my friend." Folcwalda smiled. He raised his hand and gestured to a servant, who returned a moment later with a companion. They were carrying six full cups. A small amount of remaining mead was quickly passed around the hall, and some to the village as well.

The two kings rose and stood facing the two princes and the bride.

"We drink to peace between our people," Folcwalda said.

"We drink to the happiness of the daughter of the Danes," Hoc added.

"We drink to the bond of blood," Finn said. Whether he was referring to the bond between himself and Hildeburh or between the Frisians and the Danes, nobody knew and nobody asked.

"We drink to many trips across the sea," Hnaef finished.

"In both directions," Hengest added.

Tears came to Hildeburh's eyes, but she said nothing. Six cups were lifted and drained. Throughout the hall and in the village every hand which held a cup, save for three, was lifted in salute, and every cup which still held mead, save for three, was drained. Only Guthlaf, Oslaf and Hunlaf refrained from drinking, though each held a full cup. Deomaer alone noticed the three cups which tipped slightly to pour a few drops onto the Frisian soil.

●

Summer's Day celebration was over.

In the end, King Hoc remained more than one day. In fact, he remained another ten as his ships were repaired and his stores resupplied. The work probably could have been done in two or three days, but the king was intent on conversations with Folcwalda. Most of these talks concerned the Merovingians and their king, Chlotar the Younger—or Chlotar Kinslayer as he was called by Folcwalda. But they also spoke of trade rights, customs, and harboring rights for Danish ships. Many agreements were sealed with drink. During that time Finn also had to deal with Réadban as he had promised. But when the Danes had arrived, Réadban had lost heart. He knew his plan had failed, and he was all too eager to receive Finn's mercy when it was offered. He swore fealty to Folcwalda and Finn and promised tribute to the high kingship.

When Hoc finally left, many more tears were shed—as many by the departing king and prince as by the Danish princess who was left behind. Finn and Hildeburh remained atop the tower long after the Danish ships were out of sight, and then, shortly after the sun disappeared, they slowly walked back to Hwitstan, hand in hand, and entered their new home.

PART II

The Thane

The wedding celebration of Finn, son of Folcwalda and Hildeburh of the Danes was long remembered by the poets of Friesland. Yet many of the events which followed them in their later years were fated to be remembered far longer, for it is oft the way in this world that tales of sorrow are longer lived than those of joy, and trials of woe may make better song than days of happiness.

Such was the saga of Finn and Hildeburh.

VIII

Deeds Remembered

wo winters had passed since the wedding of Finn and Hildeburh, and summer was coming upon Friesland once again.

Early one morning late in the spring, as Ulestan the thane strode back toward the great hall of Hwitstanburg from his watch above Finnweard, and as the red of dawn was fading to blue, two men rode into Hwitstan. Tall thanes they were, and no simple messengers. Their proud horses, though sorely tired, bore well the travel-weary men. Their dark green cloaks, covered with mud from hard riding, were torn and tattered in many places. Yet these thanes held their heads high. Beneath the worn green cloaks, bright red garments and precious metals still glittered. Their shields were utter black with but a simple silver device: an upturned sword. It was the device of Ecgwalda. When one of them spoke, it was with the distinct accent of Domburg.

"I come to speak with your king," he said to the men who had gathered in front of him.

Eormen stepped forth boldly and stood before the proud strangers who, from astride their great mounts, towered over the thane. Edmen stepped up beside his brother. The other thanes of Folcwalda formed a loose half-circle around the riders as Eormen spoke. "We would have your name, bold warrior, before you would ride freely through Hwitstan."

"I come to speak to your king," the stranger repeated simply.

"Then you have come none too early if you are who you seem to be," Folcwalda replied, stepping forth from the great door of his hall where he had been watching the riders approach.

He appeared tall and strong, even beside the mounted warriors, as he drew near and stepped through the tight circle of his thanes. Finn followed a moment later, but remained at the edge of the circle and said nothing.

"I am Elfwine of Domburg," the rider said, steadying his horse, which at the approach of Folcwalda had suddenly sidestepped and grown skittish. "This is my brother Elfhere. We are thanes of Ecgwalda. If we seem other than we are, we give apology." Folcwalda did not reply, and the messengers looked nervously from face to face before continuing. "We come with a message from Ecgwalda to Folcwalda." He pulled a cloth wrapping from a pouch at his side and, unwrapping it, produced a small gold object which he handed to Folcwalda. The object was a Frisian coin which bore a curious device. Piercing the coin from edge to edge across its diameter was an intricately filigreed, miniature silver sword with a single, small green jewel set in its hilt. It was the work of Deomaer the jeweler and moneyer, and had been given by Folcwalda to Ecgwalda to acknowledge him as a thane.

Folcwalda examined the coin and nodded his approval. "You may speak," he said.

"Our message would be better said under the great roof." The rider gestured toward the hall.

The king nodded, and two of his servants came forward immediately to take the messengers' horses as they dismounted. Along with his thanes, the visitors followed Folcwalda into the hall and stood before him as he took his great seat by the hearth. At another word from the king, two chalices of wine were produced for the messengers, and Folcwalda's own great drinking horn was also filled. With a look of gratitude the messengers gladly accepted the wine, and each took a great drink before looking again at Folcwalda, eager, it seemed, to have their message heard.

"You have come far, and so I would offer you rest from your labors," the king addressed the strangers. "Yet you come, it seems, with no little urgency. I will hear your message, and then you may accept the hospitality of our hall."

Elfwine bowed his head and then began formally. "Domburg and the surrounding villages under the care of Ecgwalda are suffering from the blades of raiders." Folcwalda looked vaguely surprised but did not interrupt, and Elfwine continued, "Our message is simple and comes from the mouth of Ecgwalda. The token of the silver sword was given that you would know from whose mouth these words are spoken." He looked questioningly at Folcwalda, who only nodded for him to continue. With a hint of nervousness in his voice, he went on. "Then these words I will speak: In defense of the Frisian people against the attacks of the Franks, Ecgwalda requests the aid of he who would call himself a king."

At these last words Ulestan saw the hands of every warrior in the hall go quickly to his sword. And he himself was no exception. Forty men were ready at that moment to fight the one who so boldly challenged their king. But Folcwalda gave no hint of taking offense. "Is there more?" he asked, holding first Elfwine and then Elfhere in his gaze until they faltered and looked away.

After a moment Elfwine continued, "We have lost, in addition to the lives of our men, a good steel plough with share and coulter. Its value to our people is immeasurable, and it will not easily be replaced."

Folcwalda nodded in agreement. He knew the value of good steel. Domburg had been fortunate to have such a plough, and he knew that it was well guarded. With it, four oxen had been able to do the work of eight! It would be missed by all of the villages under Ecgwalda's care.

Elfhere then stepped forward and spoke for the first time. "The raids have come both by land and by sea, but in this we have no doubt: it is the work of the Franks."

Folcwalda tightened his grip upon his sword, and his eyes narrowed at the mention of the Franks. But neither he nor any of his thanes were surprised. They had little love for the Merovingians or for Chlotar their king and were quick to expect evil from them.

"Did riders from Hwitstan arrive in Domburg this past autumn?" Folcwalda asked, once again holding the eyes of Elfwine as if to gauge his honesty.

"No, they did not come," Elfwine replied. "But for that there may be answer." A look of anger swelled to his face. "When we left Domburg we were four."

"Robbers?" Ulestan asked.

"It may be," the Half-Frank from Domburg replied. "There

were twelve or thirteen in the attack. When we rode off, their were six less of them. Yet the cost to us was great as well. Our companions who fell were two counted highly among our people. They gave their lives that our message would make it safely to Hwitstan, and they will now receive no proper burial for their brave deeds, for we deemed it ill-advised to stop. Whether or not the villains were simple robbers, I will let you judge. They bore no devices on either cloak or shield—only three even had shields—and their attack was ill planned and poorly carried out. And yet," he said with pride, "it is not the way for robbers to attack well-armed men such as us. And they fought long after common cutthroats are wont to fight, even to the death of six of them. And consider also that it is in the interests of Chlotar that our message never come to your ears."

"Your words are well taken, Elfwine," Folcwalda replied. "May the death of your companions not be in vain." Elfwine and Elfhere bowed. "And now," Folcwalda continued, "I bid you leave this hall and accept the safety of this village until I may decide better how to act on these words. When you have rested from your journey, I may call on you with more questions."

The men dropped to one knee and bowed, then rose quickly to depart.

"What words of wisdom do you have for your king?" Folcwalda asked when the Half-Franks had been led from the hall by servants.

"Let Domburg fend for itself," Eormen said at once. "They were loath to join the other chieftains of Friesland. Let them taste their independence."

"What if they intended to keep their agreement but were distracted by the raids?" Hereric asked.

"For two years? Surely they could have sent a message sooner," Eormen replied.

"They are slow to offer help but quick to ask it," Edmen added to his brother's plea.

"Perhaps they sent earlier messengers who met the same fate as ours," Hereric suggested.

"Would not these recent messengers have spoken of it had an earlier message been sent and failed?" Edmen asked.

"They almost surely would have," Aelfer interceded, "but that is not the important question before us now. Let us assume the worst of Ecgwalda, that this is the first message he has sought to send, that he has made no move until now to honor his pledge to our king. But now he has acted, and less than two years have passed. Two years is not so long of a time, is it? And consider further that Ecgwalda has appealed to 'him who would call himself king.' Pardon, my liege," Aelfer said in apology to Folcwalda, and then continued, "It is a just appeal. The Frisian people have never had a king. Will they grant the high kingship so easily? We have been seeking the allegiance of Domburg for many years. How better to gain their allegiance than to offer our support to them now? Eormen says to give them a taste of their independence; I say we give them a taste of a united kingdom, answer their need. We have forty men ready to leave. Gratitude makes better allies than fear."

"You treat him as an honored thane to be defended and not a disloyal chieftain to be punished." Eormen's voice rose. Edmen sat beside his brother nodding and scowling, and the hall grew silent for a moment.

"Aelfer's words are very wise." Ulestan broke the silence after a few moments. "And it would seem well to heed them. Yet something I do not understand bothers me."

Folcwalda turned toward Ulestan and nodded for him to continue. Carefully did he heed the words of that thane.

"There is something in this message from Ecgwalda that is to me greatly disturbing. Chlotar has gained much power in his life, but he is now growing old. Why would he suddenly and openly attack the Half-Franks? Have not his enemies more often fallen by poison and assassination rather than through open war? Nor has he ever sought to add Friesland to his kingdom. He has already many enemies and powerful foes to his south. Would he seek even now to expand his kingdom? Or would he rather strive to preserve that which is so frail and tenuous?"

"Chlotar needs no reason for his actions," Folcwalda answered. "He is a kinslayer and a coward and deals always in treachery and deceit."

"Does pirating for treasure ever need any explanation but the treasure itself?" Hereric added.

"Nor have these been open attacks," Aelfer continued. "If I understand the words of Elfwine, they seem more like small raids at night, concealed by darkness—acts for which Chlotar has always been known."

"Then you trust the word of Ecgwalda? His story has the ring of truth?" Ulestan asked of Folcwalda, ignoring for the minute the words of Hereric and Aelfer.

"I trust his word," Folcwalda replied with an assured manner that left no room for that question to be raised again.

Ulestan bowed his head and said nothing else. The messengers, he agreed, had spoken with sincerity. They were not men of deceit. And yet there was something about Franks raiding Domburg that did not seem credible. As he pondered how best to counsel his king, thoughts and memories of the past two years swept through his mind—memories of other events cloaked in deception.

Folcwalda's thane found his thoughts drifting back to the wedding of his prince. Throughout Hwitstan and all of Friesland—for chieftain, thane, warrior and peasant alike—Summer's Day and the wedding of Finn had been a time of feasting and of celebration. But it had not been so for Ulestan. Angles, Danes, Frisians, Jutes, Saxons and Swedes had been present together in Hwitstan, and among them were many kings and chieftains whose people were at war with one another. As a thane of Folcwalda, and not the least among them, Ulestan's was the task of keeping peace and a semblance of order between them all. In the fulfilling of that task he found himself sorely tried. For gathered in Hwitstan were many strong and brash men of war for whom the clash of blades was a way of life. And among these, of particular challenge were three Jutish brothers upon whom Ulestan laid the chief blame for his troubles. The names of these brothers were Guthlaf, Oslaf and Hunlaf, and they would surely play some part in the events that followed.

Long after the days of feasting were over, memory of the deeds of these brothers haunted Ulestan like a bad dream. Nearly every time he had turned his head, some new trouble was erupting somewhere in the village. To his dismay, it always seemed somehow to involve the three brothers. They were constantly starting arguments and causing disruptions. Wherever they went, tempers suddenly flared. Around some corner or behind some hut the thane would hear first one voice and then others rising in anger. Hurrying toward the sounds in an effort to quell the disturbance before it could grow, Ulestan would find a small crowd on the verge of blows. And there, a few steps to the side, would be Guthlaf, Oslaf and Hunlaf, arms folded across their chests, wearing wicked grins. At the sight of Ulestan their smiles would change to frowns and they would disappear, leaving him to settle the affair as best he could.

At first Ulestan assumed that the involvement of one of the Jutish brothers in each of the disturbances was merely a coincidence—too much mead and too many proud warriors in a small village. Yet the outbreaks grew both more frequent and more violent, and their continued presence at each became too much to be taken as coincidence. Slowly Ulestan grew suspect. Yet what could he have done? They were clever and never gave any clear cause for Ulestan to even as much as speak with them. He needed first to discover their purpose—for some evil plot or purpose they must clearly have had! It was almost as if the Jutish brothers wanted a war with the Frisians, or to start a war between the Frisians and some other tribe or kingdom. As to why, Ulestan could not guess. He knew very little about the young brothers save that they held some distant kinship with Hoc. Of these brothers, only Guthlaf was yet proven in battle. Yet they were all three brash.

Ulestan, however, had had too many other concerns to be constantly watching any of the brothers, no less all three of them, nor had he the time to be guessing at their plots. Even without their help, there would have been some amount of trouble with that many warriors from different tribes together in one village with much wine. And Ulestan had other duties as well and needed, at times, to be at the side of his king. Furthermore, even had he the time and desire to do so, there was little he could have done to stop the mischief of the Jutish brothers, or so he thought. It was not that he feared them—in the swinging of blades and the clash of arms Ulestan was as skilled as any and could well have defeated any of the three. Rather, he didn't want to give the Danes cause to break the new and fragile bond between their peoples. A fight with Guthlaf would quickly have ended his troublesome behavior, had a fight been provoked, but the brothers were too wary and never once themselves lifted a hand in anger. Ulestan knew too well that to have raised his own edge against the Jute would have seemed unjust to all and would have been ill for the newfound unity between their peoples.

Nonetheless, had Ulestan known what wickedness Guthlaf, Hunlaf and Oslaf would later accomplish, he may have quickly put an end to their lives regardless of the immediate consequences. But he did not know, and so he did what he thought wisest, and that was to keep one watchful eye on the brothers. To this end he enlisted the aid of Beow and Aelfer. Between Ulestan, Beow and Aelfer, they succeeded in maintaining as much order as could be expected.

Neither Folcwalda nor Finn ever heard from their thane what deeds the three Jutes had done during the feast, though in later days, when he remembered those deeds and saw what came to pass, Ulestan wished with all his heart that he had told his king. But during the celebration Folcwalda had been busy with other dealings, and Finn—well, Finn was in a whole new world. Still, Ulestan had it in his mind to tell his king all that he had seen. But that was not the way it would be, for shortly after the wedding, with the swiftness and fury of a winter storm, came the illness. Alas, *illness* is too small a word to describe what struck Hwitstan. For nearly a moon Ulestan had lain in bed with a fever that raged through his body even as it raged through the entire village. The thane lay upon what seemed to be the bed of his death, and the days of the wedding feast—and indeed all such memories of joy and health—seemed as distant as the edge of the seas where the waters fall off the world. Ulestan passed back and forth between waking agony and terrible nightmares which plagued his fitful sleep. In his illness, time itself seemed to meander like the winter nights in the lands of the north—to drag like a laden sled through heavy snows. When the fever was at his worst, in a brief moment of consciousness he who had avoided death in more battles than he remembered cried out to the gods to grant him a place with his fathers. The gods had listened not to his request. Though twenty and two men, as well as many women and children, had died in Hwitstan that summer, Ulestan was not one of them. For some other fate or purpose he was spared.

After more than a moon, the fever finally broke. If the illness was like winter, his healing was like spring, bringing back life where it seemed to have vanished. Yet even spring takes time before it is summer. It took nearly another full moon for Ulestan to fully recover his strength. To him this seemed especially slow. At first he could not even sit, no less stand, without the aid of another. Yet as his strength returned, many came to keep him company. And when he had guests, his spirits were lifted. Folcwalda himself came to him frequently in between his journeys around Friesland. And when the king himself wasn't in Hwitstan, he made sure that someone else was always there to take care of his chief thane. Much has been said of the loyalty of many a thane for his treasure-giver, but rarely has more love been shown by a good king for a trusted thane than was shown by Folcwalda to Ulestan. Many hours did he spend at the side of his sick thane, and great care did he take to see to the knight's recovery. Yet of all his visitors, Hildeburh his new queen was the dearest to Ulestan. She came frequently to sit beside him, and there she would talk for hours, telling stories about her land or her people—especially her brother. And with no one, save her own husband, had she a more willing ear to speak to than she found in Ulestan.

By autumn Ulestan was once again traveling at the side of his king. Yet ever afterwards, to the end of his life, the swinging of a sword brought a dull pain to his right shoulder.

During the summer, fall and spring that followed the wedding, Hwitstan herself underwent many changes. The mood throughout the village was one of quiet excitement. New buildings were occasionally appearing here and there, but not nearly as fast as they had during the few moons before the wedding. Nonetheless, Ulestan knew the importance of this growth, slow and steady as it was, and he was not deceived by the quiet. Folcwalda's hearthwerod continued to increase in size as more Frisian chieftains kept their bargains and sent troops to his command. His number of thanes had increased to nearly forty, with twelve forties of armed men under the command of those thanes. His claim to the high kingship was now virtually unopposed.

And with this growth in Hwitstan came a change in the character of the village. No longer was Hwitstan the quiet, unobtrusive Frisian village it had been since its birth. It was the home of the High King. The very presence of Folcwalda and his thanes meant the presence of wealth. And where there was wealth, there were traders. Hwitstan became a frequent stop for trading ships traveling along the coast—ships that until recently would have passed by without a second thought about the lonely village, perhaps without even knowing of its existence. Now, however, the presence of the High King Folcwalda and his hearthwerod all but ensured that Hwitstan was a safe haven from robbers, and that alone was an inviting enough reason to attract traders! The gold and silver were an added invitation.

During the warm months of the previous summer, a marketplace of sorts had actually sprung up in the clearing near the center of the village. It was something of a wild place, with chickens running underfoot and the squeals of lambs and pigs echoing through the streets—yes, there were even streets in Hwitstan now—and pushy traders hawking their wares. The increased noise and commotion of the village and of the market in particular was what drove Ulestan to the tower Finnweard more and more often. Atop the tower was one of the few places he could find peace.

For more than traders came to Hwitstan now. Chieftains and kings of other tribes made frequent visits to Hwitstanburg to deal with Folcwalda. To these chieftains and their bands, the hall was a place of welcome with men of kindred heart and spirit.

Despite the growth and change in Hwitstan, much had not changed and perhaps never would. Men, women and children still needed to eat, sleep and stay warm. Regardless of the size and import of the village, survival was still the main concern for the majority of the villagers, who were not princes, kings or thanes. Survival was a demanding master requiring much and leaving little time or effort for any other pursuits. So after the Summer's Day celebration and the wedding of Finn and Hildeburh, the men and women of Hwitstan had quickly settled back to their quiet routines and labors—the fields they worked and the livestock they tended.

At times, when he tired of the days of traveling cold, damp and crowded across an icy sea or riding tired and sore for leagues on end across an unfriendly terrain—at times like those Ulestan almost envied the simple lives of the peasants. Their work was hard and their lives difficult; they never thrilled at the excitement of the rush of spears. But neither had they ever known the dread of a falling axe or felt the pain and sorrow of seeing a sword brother fall in battle at one's side. Their pains, fears and sorrows were of a whole other sort. Yes, he envied them at times. And they, he knew, envied him. Perhaps if either knew as much about the hardships of the other, they would be more content with who they were.

So the following summer came and Ulestan was well again, save for the oft returning pain in his shoulder. Though his memory was restored, the whole series of incidents with the Jutish brothers somehow felt too far in the past to worry about. After a time it slipped from his mind. The allegiance of Domburg was more pressing business. During the wedding celebration, Ecgwalda, the chieftain of the Half-Franks who dwelt at Domburg, had finally pledged his people to Friesland and to Folcwalda. With the pledge came a promise to send a warband of twenty men with ten proud horses and a sturdy ship. Two years had passed, and neither men, nor horses nor ship had arrived.

Folcwalda had sent three riders the previous autumn, but none had returned. Whether they had reached Domburg or not none knew, but Folcwalda was greatly displeased, and he brooded for many weeks pondering his course of action. The following spring approached, the second since Finn's marriage, and the king began to prepare a warband for a voyage to Domburg. He gathered forty men, thanes and warriors alike, and two great ships were made ready with stores of goods for travel. They would only await the thaw.

But the thaw had come and passed, and the warband had not gone to Domburg. Folcwalda had been delayed by news from the north: Hoc was ill and dying. The warband bound for Domburg turned instead toward the land of the Danes to honor the passing of a king.

Ulestan, for a reason never explained to him, had not traveled with Folcwalda, and it was many days before the king returned to Hwitstan. When he did, it was only briefly. Of Hoc's funeral he said nothing save that it was the way all kings would one day go, to be with their fathers and to await the great battle. "Though few," Folcwalda added, "would make the journey with the strength and grace of Hoc." After that, Folcwalda would speak of that Danish king no more.

Once again he prepared his warband for the voyage to Domburg. The ships were resupplied with food, and a few days later Folcwalda was again ready to depart, Ulestan with him. On the very day they were to leave, the messengers arrived.

It was Finn's voice which finally broke the silence and brought Ulestan's thoughts back to the present. "If Ecgwalda's word can be trusted and his people have truly suffered the edge from bandits," the prince said pensively, "then perhaps we can sever two heads with one swing of the blade." He looked about the hall at the faces of those present. His cryptic comment had aroused their curiosity.

"Speak on," Folcwalda urged.

"Surely we wish to secure Domburg as part of Friesland. As Aelfer has said, this has been our goal for some time now. Friesland with Domburg is a much greater nation than a Friesland without Domburg," he said as if it were a clear fact with which none might disagree. Eormen started to object, but the rest of the heads were nodding, so he wisely remained silent. Finn looked at him and then continued, "It is also to our advantage to end any raids on or near Frisian soil. If robbers and raiders see that our villages are easy prey, it will not be long before Hwitstan itself is suffering that plague."

"You are suggesting that we spill our own blood in defense of Domburg when they are so slow to bow to the Frisian king?" Eormen finally said with indignation.

"No," Finn answered to everyone's surprise, save perhaps his father's.

"But you said . . ."

"I said we could sever two heads with one swing of a blade." Finn stood up as he spoke and began to walk around the benches. What two heads was Finn speaking of? Ulestan wondered. From the looks on the faces of the other thanes, the same question was running through their minds.

"Ecgwalda pledged himself to our king," Finn began when he had placed himself at the right of Folcwalda. "Twenty fighting men, ten horses, and a ship of war were his promise. Yet two winters have passed with no word. Perhaps Ecgwalda began to think again of the great distance between Hwitstan and Domburg and of his own strength. Perhaps he reconsidered his words. Or perhaps he only moves slowly, in no great hurry to part with twenty men from his own hearthwerod. Again he considers the long distance to Hwitstan and ponders how long Folcwalda will wait and whether or not he will cross the distance and when.

"But suddenly Ecgwalda finds himself on the wrong end of a falling blade." The prince clenched his left fist while his right arm swung down in a chopping motion, and three thanes lurched backward, almost falling off their benches. "Raiders pillage his villages. His servants are killed in their sleep. His plough is stolen and his winter stores ransacked. His people look to their lord for protection, and he finds himself unable to give it. The thought of a High King—a more powerful army—gives him hope. Yet the distance to Hwitstan, which previously could not have been long enough, is suddenly too long. Can a king in Hwitstan help his people?

"The answer is yes. It must be yes if Domburg is to be part of Friesland. Ecgwalda must be made to know that Hwitstan is close enough to give him aid if needed—and close enough to threaten him if necessary. We shall heed his call for help—but not the help he might be expecting. This is where we may sever two heads with one but one blow if we are swift enough, bold enough, and wise enough. We can put an end to the raids on our shores and redeem Ecgwalda's pledge with one move. I propose that I go to Domburg with a warband. But it will not be the forty men Aelfer has suggested. I will go with only twenty men. Ecgwalda will do better than fulfill his word to Folcwalda. He will place two twenties of his own men under my command. With three twenties of men I will defeat the raiders. And when the Frankish thieves have been laid in their graves, I will keep half of the Domburg warhost that went with me in fulfillment of Ecgwalda's pledge. I will go to Domburg with twenty men but will return with forty. Thus we will have gained our pledge from Ecgwalda and defeated our enemies at the same time, and Domburg will be Frisian not from fear but from gratitude."

For the third time the hall was silent. Yet such bold confidence did Finn show in his own plan, and so great was the trust of the thanes in their prince, that all, even Edmen and Eormen, were already firmly convinced it would succeed. They needed only a word and they were ready to act.

Ulestan alone seemed to have doubts. *Is Finn so sure he can defeat these raiders with a warhost of only sixty armed men?* he thought to himself. But he said nothing out loud.

"There is much wisdom in your plan," Folcwalda finally said when nobody else responded. "Yet, you have forgotten one thing," he added with a smile.

"Have I?" Finn asked.

"This journey is likely to take much of the summer."

"By ship even at a light pace we can reach Domburg in but a few days," Finn objected.

"Yes, and then you must sway Ecgwalda to your plan," the king answered. "Perhaps he may be persuaded easily, perhaps not. Yet even if he is persuaded easily, you must still defeat this enemy. Before you can do that, you must find him. Surely you have considered that."

"Yes."

"And will you leave your wife this close to the birth of your heir?"

All eyes turned toward Finn, who at first appeared embarrassed but then quickly swelled with considerable pride. It was clear that the other thanes were as surprised by this news as Ulestan was.

"When?" Ulestan asked.

"Soon, she tells me," Finn answered so all could hear. "Not more than three more months, perhaps only two."

"Is she well?" came a voice. Ulestan wondered the same thing. He thought it strange that he had not seen Hildeburh in more than three months—not since the heavy snows. But it was not his place to ask. So she had been with child all this time?

"Her back is very sore, so she walks little. She will be fine though. I think she is more shy of the size of her stomach." He laughed. "She is strong. She tells me I will have a big son."

"A son?" many voices asked at once.

"A son," Finn answered definitively. "Finnlaf, son of Finn, son of Folcwalda, son of Folgar, descendant of Friesc and the gods."

"And so, Finn, father of Finnlaf," Folcwalda said firmly but with no little mirth, "you will remain in Hwitstan while I lead this band to Domburg to deal first with Ecgwalda and then with the Frankish swine who harry our people."

"As you deem best," Finn replied, taking his seat. He looked both disappointed and relieved.

"Lord?" Ulestan asked.

". . . and Ulestan shall accompany me," Folcwalda continued, answering the thane's question before it was even asked. "The rest of our warband shall be chosen from among the forty now ready to depart. We will leave tomorrow."

The voyage, however, didn't begin the next day, nor even the day after. The spring rains began that very night, and by the next morning the winds were howling across the seas and the village was ankle-deep in mud. The wind didn't abate for nearly a week, and it was not until then that Ulestan received Folcwalda's summons to the tower.

So it was that thane Ulestan came to be standing atop Finnweard at the side of King Folcwalda and Prince Finn. Aelfer and Beow soon joined them, and the five gazed silently across the sandy cove. The morning sun was dancing in bright diamonds and pearls on the gentle waves rolling onto the beaches of Hwitstanwic below. Though he knew their voyage must soon begin, Ulestan was in no hurry to leave the peace of the tower.

The spring rains had come to Friesland early that year, and the last of those showers had blown over during the night. For the first time in many days they awoke to a bright, clear sky. Even the low, dense fog which almost perpetually covered the seas and coastal lands during that time of year had lifted, briefly giving respite from their oppression. It was the type of day that inspired courageous men to seek adventure, that conjured in the imagination pictures of far-off lands; for those whose traveling days were over, it brought memories of voyages past; and for those who were already far from home, it was a day that renewed their strength and provided the courage to continue on for just one more day or one more season. The air held a promise of summer, and Ulestan breathed it deeply.

Down below, on the beaches of Hwitstanwic, a small Saxon trading ship full of goods to be brought to the Isle was sliding off the sand onto the outgoing surf. In his younger days, before he had loved and lost Fealla Folgar-daughter, Ulestan had been on many such a ship setting out for distant lands and anticipated adventure. Yet now he watched only with detached interest— curious about the craft's destination, but with no desire to go himself. He was content with the relative peace and quiet of his new home in Hwitstan.

"We will leave tomorrow," the king finally said, breaking

the silence atop the tower where the five men still stood. "I will take Ulestan, Edmen and Eormen with seven and ten seamen. Aelfer and Beow, you are to journey by horse to Wic by Dorestad with a command of twenty mounted warriors. See if Dorestad has encountered the same problem with raids. Let them know also that Domburg is now Frisian and that we tire of waiting for their pledge. Make that message very clear to Lyndlaf. He is their chieftain now. When you have accomplished this, return to Hwitstan. Finn may need your help before we return."

Aelfer and Beow left immediately to make preparations. When they were gone, Ulestan turned to Folcwalda. "I have many misgivings about this voyage, my king." Questions had been growing on his mind ever since the messengers had arrived from Domburg.

"Speak of them," Folcwalda answered.

"Is it wise to travel with such a small warband?"

"What danger do you foresee, friend Ulestan? Our journey is along the Frisian coast. We, if anyone, are surely safe there."

"It is not the sea voyage that I fear. We know nothing of these Frankish warbands that are raiding Domburg."

"If the warbands were of great size," Folcwalda responded, "the raids would not be so secretive."

"But if they are Franks, then it matters little how large the raiding bands are. There are many more Franks in the Merovingian kingdom. Surely this small band is only a token."

"Chlotar works by treachery and assassination. He will not risk an open war with us and the Danes. He has too many other concerns to his south."

"Are you so sure the Danes would fight as our allies?" Ulestan asked. "Is our blood-bond so strong?" He intentionally avoided looking at Finn as he said this. He meant no injustice to Hildeburh or her people. Finn's expression, however, gave no indication of offense at Ulestan's comment.

"No," Folcwalda answered coolly, "I have no such belief. But it is not important whether the Danes will fight at our side or not. What matters is that Chlotar is not sure they won't. He is not deaf. He may not fear the Danes, but he will not provoke them needlessly, and he has surely heard of Finn's wedding."

"Do you know Chlotar so well?"

"It is a small problem." Folcwalda sighed, avoiding Ulestan's question. "Do you doubt your king? Fear not. Though we need them not, we will have a warhost of forty Half-Franks at our sides."

"That is my other fear, my lord," Ulestan continued. "In Domburg we will be outnumbered by the Half-Franks. Though they have pledged themselves to you, we have seen no evidence of this pledge. Needn't we fear the Half-Franks of Domburg at least as much as the Franks themselves? Ecgwalda could easily preserve his independence by killing you."

"Is Folcwalda so easily killed?" The king laughed heartily. Then his eyes narrowed. "Ecgwalda would not find my life readily taken from my body. Nonetheless, you are wise in fearing him. He is a powerful chieftain and not easily swayed from his own purposes. Yet he is also faithful to his word. He will not fight against us—not in hiding as a thief anyway. He also knows that killing me would not destroy Friesland. Do you think my son would not avenge my death?" He smiled at Finn as he said this, but Finn's expression remained somber. Folcwalda's voice took an even more serious tone. "Perhaps my life will be taken— though not, I believe, by Ecgwalda. But whoever ends my life will find that Finn is a more dangerous adversary than I ever was."

"One more question, my lord," Ulestan persisted.

"Only one?" Folcwalda smiled. "The day that Ulestan has but one question is a great day indeed."

Ulestan smiled at the jest and directed his question at Finn. "Does Finn have a plan for defeating this raiding band—or bands?"

"I have none," Finn answered. "But as I have been shorn of this duty . . ." he said with a stiff glance toward Folcwalda and a sharp tone that only Finn could have safely used toward the king. ". . . as I have been shorn of this duty, it is no longer my responsibility."

"Had you any when you first proposed this journey?"

Finn only smiled and said nothing.

"We are only lacking information." Folcwalda spoke in defense of his son's plan. "If we can find these raiders, we can surely defeat them. To this end, perhaps I know even more than Ecgwalda. I have eyes and ears overlooking Domburg which even Ecgwalda does not have—or does not use. I think perhaps these might have seen and heard much since last I spoke with them."

"What eyes and ears are these?" Ulestan asked.

"You shall see," Folcwalda said with a grin, "but you shall have to wait. You have used your last question." So saying, the king spun and climbed down from the tower. Ulestan waited a moment and then followed. He would let his king concern himself with such plans and mysteries. It was the thane's glorious task only to follow and obey. This Ulestan did.

The ship was quickly made ready, and Folcwalda, Ulestan, Eormen and Edmen departed as planned in the first light of pre-dawn the following morning with seventeen Frisian seamen and warriors and a sea-wise veteran named Swanfolgan. Though Swanfolgan held no rank and was not counted among the thanes, his knowledge of the ways of the seas was unequalled, and Folcwalda relied heavily on his wisdom. In name Folcwalda was king, but on the seas he would rarely overrule a decision of Swanfolgan.

Even as Folcwalda and his small warband marched out of the village toward the beach, Aelfer and Beow were busy readying their band to depart on their journey toward Dorestad, where they would speak with Lyndlaf. As the ship pushed off the beach and rowed out of Hwitstanwic, the mighty horn of Finn could be heard blowing farewell from atop the tower. The kingdom of Folcwalda was being solidified at last!

IX

Toward Domburg

The voyage to Domburg was begun in good spirits on a bright day late in the spring. With three thanes and seventeen warriors Folcwalda sailed, seeking both to bring Ecgwalda into the fold of Friesland and to rid the Frisian borders of a pillaging warband. It was the first time in some years that Ulestan had started on such a quest—a quest which would surely lead to the clash of peoples. As they rounded the point and sailed out of Hwitstanwic, the veteran thane felt his heart pumping with excitement and no little anxiety, though of these emotions he revealed little. The craft plunged through the still-icy water and passed quickly out of the sight of Finn, who stood atop Finnweard. The plan, as Ulestan understood it, was to travel a mile or so from shore but well inside of the Frisian islands. There they could make good progress not having to turn with every contour of the land and yet avoiding the rougher waters beyond the islands. If the water grew too difficult, they would move closer to shore and, forsaking the oars, push along with long poles.

Eormen and Edmen, the other thanes accompanying their king, showed their anticipation and excitement more than did Ulestan. Though the ship kept a good pace, thanks to the energetic work of sixteen oars, the two brothers seemed impatient right from the start and looked as though they were ready to jump into the sea and pull the ship to Domburg with their teeth. Ulestan saw more than a little of himself in the two thanes. Such was their zeal and impetuousness that it was difficult for Ulestan to remember that they were but a year and two younger than himself. As opposed as they had been to aiding Ecgwalda at first, they were now eager to act and fully bent on ridding Domburg of its plague. That much could be said about them—they did nothing halfheartedly. As advisors, Ulestan doubted their wisdom; as comrades in battle, there were few better. Either would quickly lay down his own life for that of his king or fellow thane. Ulestan found himself traveling with these two brothers and talking with them—or rather listening to them—for the first time in many years.

"What is our plan for finding these Frankish pirates?" Eormen asked impatiently when they were barely out of sight of Hwitstan.

Ulestan tried to hide his smile at the question and waited for Folcwalda to answer—or to avoid giving answer.

"We travel to Domburg," Folcwalda began with a answering smile to Ulestan's, "and we redeem our pledge of twenty warriors from Ecgwalda. Then we find this band of Frankish raiders and defeat them."

Eormen and Edmen smiled and nodded as if they understood the plan perfectly. Folcwalda said nothing else, and the two thanes remained quiet for a time. Then Eormen suddenly had a very puzzled look on his face. "How will we find this band?" he asked.

"By keeping our eyes and ears open," Folcwalda responded. "We will lay a trap for them, and they will fall into it as surely as a fish falls into a weir."

Ulestan waited for Eormen to ask the next question, but he didn't. Once again the younger thane seemed satisfied with Folcwalda's response. Ulestan could not resist and asked the question himself. "And what is this trap we have devised?"

"It is not yet devised, my friend. Can you set a net without first coming to the pond?" The king's voice held a lighthearted challenge for Ulestan to continue questioning him.

This time Ulestan resisted the challenge and turned his attention to Eormen and Edmen. They had already forgotten about traps and raiders and were busy reliving past battles. Such was their zeal for speaking of adventure that Ulestan spent the remainder of the day listening to them tell of their exploits. It was as though this was their preparation for the battles in the days ahead. And perhaps it was. Ulestan knew well enough that it was no easy thing to ready oneself to enter battle and face death. If speaking of past battles gave them the courage to continue on, so be it. Their tales were certainly ones of courage and bravery. Had Ulestan not fought at their sides and did he not know of their strength and skill, he would have thought them greatly exaggerating. Despite any embellishments of their glorious victories—and embellishments there were—yet there was also truth in all they said.

Eormen and Edmen were strong brothers, and Ulestan would not have wanted to stand against them blade to blade. Both had fought at the side of Ethelbert in his wars to unite the Saxons. They had returned with much treasure for their king and well-known names for themselves—and more than a few enemies. Eormen carried a blade given him, as he frequently pointed out, by Ethelbert himself. Cleofend that blade was called, and it was said to have been crafted by the hand of Weland himself. After his victory over Niphad, the works of Weland were ever unequalled by any human smith, for it was said by some that he was given the gift of his craft by the gods. Others said he was himself half-god and half-man.

Ulestan looked the blade over closely. It was certainly well-crafted. The marks of many battles were but faint scratches on its hard surface. Whether Cleofend was the work of Weland Ulestan did not know, but it was a mighty weapon and was indeed a worthy gift from Ethelbert. A blade which stood the strength of Eormen was a blade indeed!

Ulestan returned the blade to Eormen, and the brothers continued their tales. At the death of their father Edweard, Eormen had returned to Friesland to assume the rule of his clan and to serve Folcwalda, who was just coming to power. Edmen had remained on the island, where he traveled to Northumbria to fight at the side of Ethelfrith against the Britons. Ulestan and Edmen met for the first time shortly after that.

Ulestan had traveled to the Isle only months before Edmen. Both were seeking a king to serve—a treasure-giver with hearth and hall—and both had found one. But they had chosen different kings. Alone of all the Frisians, Ulestan had fought at the side of the Britons who sought to defend their lands against the invading Saxons. Those were the days of Ulestan's youth. Though he spoke of them only rarely, he thought of them often. The Britons were a noble race in every respect, and their Celtic traditions were rich and mysterious. Only in trusting too long to the strength of the Roman Empire to protect their shores did the Britons err. In the end that error proved fatal. For many lives of men the Roman armies had protected the borders of the British Isle, leaving the British tribes at peace and undisturbed. By and large most tribes were unaffected by the Romans save that they grew lazy, relying on the Roman armies to guard their borders, leaving them in peace—or to fight and quarrel among themselves.

But even the greatest nations fall into ruin. Slowly it seemed—yet, in the scheme of nations and histories it was fast enough—the Romans disappeared from the isle of the Britons, leaving behind as they went empty villages and unguarded shores, both of which the Saxons found inviting. They left as well their new religion, which had found favor in the eyes of many chieftains and villages. By the time a great king rose among the Britons and took the place of the departed Roman rule, the Saxons' hold on their land was too strong to be shaken. Perhaps even then, had the Saxons been the only enemy, the Britons might have held much of the island, eventually even repelling the Saxons. But there were invasions from the Picts to the north as well as the Irish, and those, coupled with the invading Angles, Saxons, and Jutes, proved too much. Despite their proud effort, the Britons eventually fell and were driven back for the last time. The Isle of the Britons was overrun.

Ulestan had fought a losing war at the side of the Britons. Yet even in defeat they were a noble race who never once dealt unfairly with enemy or friend. Myrthen was the name of their battle-chief. A king among kings he was, a generous giver of treasure. Though defeat he suffered and lands he lost, yet his kingdom was still glorious. Thrice Myrthen had saved Ulestan's life. Twice he had stepped in front of the young thane when he fell and guarded him with his own life until he was able once more to rise. A third time an Anglish battle-axe had missed Ulestan's head only because the arm wielding it was severed by the sword swing of Myrthen. Ulestan returned that favor only once and saved the life of Myrthen's son. For that act, Ulestan had been rewarded with the sword he now bore, and he counted himself the richer for it. Though it had not come from Weland, it was a proud blade and had never yet failed that thane. The unnamed edge still hung at his side.

It was in one of these last battles that Ulestan had seen Edmen amidst the overwhelming Anglish horde bearing down upon the outnumbered Britons. The design on Edmen's helm and shield were unmistakably from a powerful Frisian clan. Many Frisians had fought as paid soldiers of the Anglish war-chiefs, but Edmen stood out among them. He was no simple paid soldier, but a future war-chief fighting as a thane beside a great king whom he had chosen to serve. Ulestan and Edmen had come close to the clash of blades that day, but it was not ordained. As they drew nearer and nearer, a sudden rush from a band of Jutes carrying short spears pushed them apart. When they next met, they were serving the same king and their tales had come together.

The voyage toward Domburg continued through the day. The weather remained sunny and calm, and in the afternoon, at Swanfolgan's suggestion, the steersman ventured the ship further out into the offing where it could gain a fairer trim. Folcwalda, who was deep in thought, appeared unaware of Swanfolgan's command. The ship continued to travel smoothly on the calm seas and late in the day began to swing southward with the coast-line. As the sun set, it was no longer in front of them but far off to starboard. It had dropped burning below the water before Folcwalda called a halt to their travels. They had made it past the mouth of the great bay and were now journeying southward along its east shore. It had been a good day's journey. They had nearly reached the point where they would leave the shore and cut westward across the bay. They would wait until morning for that. Commanding the seamen to put the ship ashore were the first words Folcwalda had spoken since shortly after departure. The seamen steering the craft gladly obliged, and the ship swung toward the port. In a few minutes it had slid neatly onto the beach.

A fire was started, and a stew was made with some well-salted pork and a generous amount of barley from the past autumn's harvest. When they had finished the meal, the warriors, including Folcwalda, Ulestan, Eormen and Edmen, quickly found places to lay their heads.

X

The Crossing

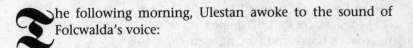he following morning, Ulestan awoke to the sound of
Folcwalda's voice:

> *"Wind from the west,*
> > *Waves we may cross;*
> *Bay is still blue*
> > *With breeze from the east;*
> *Stay in the shallow*
> > *When south wind blows hard;*
> *When north wind comes*
> > *Cross not at all."*

The thane laughed to hear his king singing. Many times in
the past he had heard wise veterans of the sea—hoary old warriors and wanderers—singing that song, but he had never heard
it from the mouth of his king. Folcwalda's voice gave new meaning to those words by which many lived and without which
many died. Indeed when the west wind blew, the bay could be
crossed directly, saving as much as two days of travel. The same
was true with an east wind. When the south wind blew, it was
better to travel further into the bay to avoid the crosswinds.
When the north wind blew, it was best not to voyage at all, but
to stay on shore. The bay was treacherous in the north wind, and
many ships seeking to cross in it had been lost against the islands
and reefs that dotted the bay. "Oft," Ulestan remembered his
father telling him as a child, "there is wisdom in the tales told by

old wives and the songs sung at the hearth." His father had been filled with much good advice.

On this day the wind was from the east, and the sun rose once again into a clear sky. Following the words of the song, they would attempt to cut straight across the bay. "If the weather continues like this, we could reach Domburg on the eve of the morrow," Swanfolgan proclaimed. Folcwalda nodded but said nothing. His mood, after reciting the gnomic lines, was once again somber.

The small warband broke their fast hurriedly and then entered the long craft for the second time, and the voyage continued. They had not long been in the ship traveling southward before Folcwalda pointed to a familiar jut of land on the port side—a low, rocky hill shaped by wind and time to vaguely resemble a boar's head facing west.

Swanfolgan nodded in recognition. "There is the boar facing west where we journey. Shall we follow his gaze, my king?"

"We have the east wind," Folcwalda replied.

Swanfolgan barked the commands, and the ship swung around to starboard until it was facing westward with the wind. Then the men let out a long sigh of relief and pulled the huge long-oars in from the icy water. The heavy woolen sail was opened and lifted onto the short mast. Immediately afterwards, seventeen wine flagons were simultaneously opened, and after long and much enjoyed drinks of the precious beverage as many pairs of hands were quickly wrapped in furs, and the wind was left to do her will. A quick gust coming off the hill filled the woolen cloth, and the vessel began to move with the wind and waves. She quickly gathered speed and was soon gaining on the low swells moving west with her. Up the slow rise of one and then down the other side, the bow would first rise up and then dip back down, and a light spray would blow over the stern as they cut into the next low hill. Save for the slow rising and falling, and the occasional light spray, the craft glided smoothly across the water, leaving the warband fairly warm and dry—a condition much appreciated but not very common in the north seas.

The remainder of the morning was bright and sunny, and the wind kept at their backs. With no oarwork required, the band remained in exceptionally good spirits. Those who had taken the longest shifts the previous day quickly dozed off, and the others lapsed into idle conversation with each other. Edmen and Eormen, who seemingly never tired of telling tales of adventure, entertained the seamen sitting closest to them with more tales of Saxon war victories.

Ulestan, tired of the brothers' stories, turned to Folcwalda. But the High King had his mind elsewhere and was not of a mood to talk idly. "The shallower waters will warm rapidly in this sun," he remarked cryptically and was then silent. Despite the fine weather and the ship's swift progress, he seemed wrapped in a dark fog, and Ulestan, unsettled by his king's silence, himself sat quietly gazing at the horizon.

As the late morning passed into early afternoon, the steady breeze shifted just slightly from the east to the north. Atop the larger westward-rolling waves little choppy whitecaps began to skitter across the surface, and the sail was quickly adjusted. In the contrary seas they began to ship some more water, and, amidst stifled grumbles, a few hands were set to bailing. More time passed, and the wind shifted even more to the north. The few seamen who were still asleep woke quickly, or were awakened, and the bailing continued. The icy spray worsened. Still, there was no cause for concern as the ship was not in any danger of being overwhelmed. All on board expected the west shore of the bay to be appearing very soon.

Yet as the day progressed and the ship continued on her course, there began to rise all about her a low fog. This appeared out of nowhere and rapidly thickened. The dark water was absorbing light and was warming in the early-afternoon sun. On the coast of Friesland, late in the spring, when the sun had begun to rise high in the sky but summer had yet warmed neither air, water, nor land, there frequently arose a fog which could become very dense in a matter of little time. It was not an uncommon occurrence to those who lived on those seas; it was glum and eerie nonetheless. The air darkened swiftly, and within a few minutes the fog had risen above their heads. Then came a low moan from one of the seamen who had been watching the stern, and an even darker fog suddenly came in with the wind. The craft was now completely enveloped.

The change was immediate. Visibility dropped sharply to almost nothing. Those in the stern could no longer see the bow, nor those in the bow the stern. Even Folcwalda, as large as he was, was but a dim, dark form rising from the middle of the ship. The water around them had all but disappeared. It made its presence known only by the rise and fall of the ship and by the sudden icy slaps which caught men's faces unawares. A dark blanket had suddenly been thrown across the seas—a damp and icy blanket of stillness. Every man in the ship felt the sudden grasp of hundreds of cold, clammy hands taking hold of them. All voices ceased as suddenly as the fog had come. Ulestan barely dared to breathe. Twenty imaginations simultaneously pictured rocks looming out of the water ahead and great sea monsters rising from behind. Nobody moved for many heartbeats.

"The breeze still holds, and the sail is yet full." Folcwalda's voice rose loudly above the chilling silence. It was true. The wind was not yet abeam, and they could still make good use of it. "We shall reach the far shore in good time and with little effort."

"Well spoken," Ulestan answered, though in his heart he was not so sure. Fog was nothing new or unexpected—not to the Frisians. Ulestan had been in the grip of many an icy cloud in his years of travel, and these seamen were well-tested for the tasks at hand. Even so, the fog was dangerous, and it always affected the mood of seamen for the worse. For good reason Ulestan was ever fearful of the great waters. His home was the solid ground, and no number of sea voyages would ever make him at ease in a ship. Yet it was a thane's job to serve his king and to lead the king's warhost. That good thane knew there was more to leading a warhost than swinging a blade. Ten bold men in good spirits could defeat forty if the forty had lost heart.

"This is an easy day for the oarsmen," Ulestan said, pointing with one hand to the sail full of wind and with his other to an oar lying unused on the side of the ship. Only those closest to him could see his mirthful expression, but most could make out his hand gestures.

"Easy indeed," laughed an unsteady voice from behind the thane. "But who did the labor yesterday?"

Ulestan's hand, it was true, had not touched an oar, and the jest was well taken. "Perhaps this will redeem your grudge," he said, and he pulled from the bag beside him a large wine flagon. He handed it to the seamen behind him. Edmen and Eormen followed Ulestan's lead, and three large flagons were passed around the ship until each man had had a healthy swallow or two.

"I would that the wine were hot," the man answered, "but nevertheless I consider my grudge redeemed—until the morrow, that is, when my hand returns to the oar."

"So be it," Ulestan laughed. "Until the morrow." A few other voices laughed with him, and the seamen continued in light conversation for some time after that. But the change in the wind some time earlier had finally found its effect on the waves, and they were now rolling from starboard to port. With each swell the ship rocked and dipped its side frighteningly close to the blackness beneath. The tops of many waves were breaking with the wind and splashing onto the sail and into the ship. The woolen sails were soon soaked and heavy, and most of the men were busy bailing.

After his initial brief words of encouragement Folcwalda took no more notice of the ship and left its governing to Swanfolgan. Content at least that the spirits of his men were lifted sufficiently, the king remained quiet and gazed intently into the water beside and in front of the ship. Silence seemed to have pervaded his mood since the voyage had begun, or even before that. But a High King Folcwalda was, a king among kings, and it was not Ulestan's place to question him. If he chose silence, then silence he desired and silence he would have. Ulestan well knew the uselessness of trying to drag words from him when he wasn't ready to speak. The thane therefore also remained silent and kept his eyes on the seas, though he knew not for what he was searching.

The ship continued dipping, rolling and rising again—sailing now with the wind and waves nearly abeam—and the seamen busily bailed or sat nervously waiting for some stony island or reef to suddenly appear in the water before them. The wind abated somewhat, but its direction, as much as Swanfolgan could perceive, remained constant from the north. With the heavy wet sail and the lighter breeze, the ship with its small warband traveled now more slowly than they might have been able to with oars, but Folcwalda and Swanfolgan agreed to let the men rest, for they would likely be needed later. So progress continued, but at a slower pace than in the morning. The men watched and waited, but there was nothing much that could be done.

Knowing this, they continued to talk amongst themselves in hushed and nervous tones. Conversations grew less frequent and subjects changed rapidly, leaving many thoughts cut off in mid-sentence.

A few hours passed, and Folcwalda began to look more intently ahead into the mist. It seemed, if anything, to be thickening. A loud, hacking cough erupted from somewhere near the front of the ship, and every man on board looked up nervously. The few remaining vestiges of conversation came to an abrupt halt and were not continued.

"Lord Folcwalda . . ." Swanfolgan said into the stillness some time later.

Folcwalda didn't answer immediately. His gaze was fixed on a point somewhere off to the port side of the ship.

The seaman waited a moment and spoke again, in a slightly firmer but obviously nervous voice. "Lord Folcwalda?"

"Speak, friend," Folcwalda answered. His voice showed only a little strain.

"By my guess we should be at the western shore shortly. If we have gauged the winds correctly, the land should be appearing ahead or a bit to the port very soon," Swanfolgan said, pointing. As the chief seaman said this, everyone close enough to hear him turned and looked where he was pointing.

"That is my thought as well, Swanfolgan," Folcwalda replied. "It is good to hear it from you."

"Then perhaps," the seaman continued, "a few men should prepare the long-oars and the poles should we come upon shore suddenly."

"That is wise," was all Folcwalda said. His mind still seemed focused elsewhere.

Swanfolgan waited for his king to say more. When he didn't, the seaman gave the orders himself. Reluctantly four of the men near the front and another four in the back pulled their hands from out of their wools and readied their long-oars. Others continued bailing to keep up with the slow shipping of water. Two more picked up poles should the need or opportunity arise to pole along the bottom.

Still nothing happened, and no land came into sight. The wind picked up even more. As it did, the fog thinned slightly—or was it just Ulestan's imagination? Another hour or more passed. Every voice was silent. All eyes looked eagerly across the port side of the craft anticipating the sudden appearance of land—or fearing that it would not appear.

In the midst of the eerie fog and strange silence, Ulestan found his memory drifting back to a tale he had first heard as a young man in the hall of a British warlord. In his mind swirled a vision of a beautiful young maiden from a powerful northern tribe.

●

In the ages long past, when the gods still walked the earth like men and fire-breathing wyrms still crawled forth from their lairs, there lived a mighty chieftain of the north. Great was he, and many were the clans who paid him tribute. In strength, might and riches there were none to surpass him. To this mighty one in the days of his glory was born a single child—a daughter. Ywänna he named her, and she grew up to be tall, stern, proud and wise. It was said that Ywänna's beauty was so very great that even from her youth the poets sang of her and men dreamed of her. Such grace, beauty and strength were hers that the love a tribe will often give to a great prince was instead given to her. And such was her father's love for Ywänna and so great was her wisdom that though he had no male heir to inherit his kingdom, he never begrudged his wife for bearing him a daughter rather than a son.

Now when Ywänna grew older and came of the age when she might freely choose and act of her own accord, she grew to love a young chieftain from another, smaller tribe. His name was Beow, and he loved her as well. Though his tribe was small, Beow was a great chieftain among men, and his strength was the strength of twenty, and his wisdom was like the wisdom of Oden. The love between the two became great indeed, and, as Ywänna's father approved of Beow, it was laid on their hearts to wed.

As it happened, however, one of the lesser half-gods was on one occasion walking the earth in the evening of a long summer day. Passing through a narrow valley, he saw Ywänna bathing in a mountain stream. At that very instant, he conceived in his heart a desire to have her for his own. But when he approached her, she fled. The god let her go for the time, thinking he would follow her and find where she lived. That he did.

Now Ywänna reached her village safely with the god following her in secret, and when she arrived there, Beow was waiting for her. Though they were not yet betrothed, the arrangements were being made even then between him and her father. When the god heard of the arranged betrothal, he grew very angry and swore in his heart that if he could not have Ywänna nobody could. In all of his might and splendor, he approached the clan chieftain. In front of both Ywänna and Beow he made his demands known. Yet Ywänna was strong-willed, and despite all of the might, power and wealth of the god she would not have anyone other than Beow.

"So be it," the god declared with the anger of hatred. "Your doom is fated." He disappeared and was gone. Instantly a huge cloud filled the sky, and the winds roared savagely though moments before there had been still air. And as Beow looked into the sky, he trembled, for great pieces of ice were falling from above like boulders upon the village. Valiant warriors were struck with death blows, and the very buildings themselves were laid to waste. Women wailed and tried to hide, but there was no place to flee the devastation. All the while, the god's ruthless laughter could be heard lingering in the air among the screams of the dying.

Ywänna, meanwhile, suddenly found herself in total darkness, bound by unseen chains. For a long time she could neither move nor see. Yet she did not despair. Rather than crying, she sang a powerful song of love for her Beow. So beautiful and heartfelt was her song that stars fell from the sky that night in order that they might hear her song more clearly. But the song only infuriated the half-god, for it was not sung for him. Ywänna's bonds grew tighter and the darkness blacker, but she continued singing. When she could sing no longer, she dropped into a deep sleep. When she awoke, she had been released from the chains. But where she was she knew not. She knew only that she was alone on a small island, with nothing to be seen in any direction save for a dense fog hanging over the seas. She was lost with no hope for help.

Beow, meanwhile, was struck to the ground with a piece of

ice which pounded into his shoulder with the force of a charging boar. Yet due to his mighty strength his shoulder did not break, and he retained enough of his senses to raise his great warshield over his head. Beneath the protection of that shield, which had aided him so often before in battle, he sat and waited. For three days and nights the storm vent its fury upon the helpless village. When the storm ended, broken and battered bodies lay everywhere. There was not a living soul to be found. Among the whole tribe, only Beow had survived.

For three days Beow searched for the body of his beloved, burying the bodies of those slain as he found them. With great honor he put Ywänna's father to rest at sea along with the weapons of many foes whom he had vanquished in his lifetime. But nowhere among the ruins of the village could Beow find Ywänna's broken and crushed body.

His heart verging on despair, and knowing not what else he might do, Beow cried out the name of his beloved with all his might. His voice sang out to the heavens and resounded upon the face of the earth. "Ywänna," he called three times, full of distress at her loss, yet hoping she still lived.

When he stopped, he thought he heard her replying to him in song. Listening to that sweet, clear voice, his heart was once again lifted, and his strength returned. So great were the deeds of Beow which followed that they could not be told in seven times seven tales without repetition. The mighty warrior spent seven long years following the sound of Ywänna's voice. Through many trials and hardships his path finally led him to the edge of a distant sea. There, at the shore, Beow could hear Ywänna's voice coming to him clearly across the ocean. Looking more closely, he saw a small island of clouds rising up from the middle of the waters and knew where he needed to go.

Beow labored day and night for many days building himself a small sturdy ship to take him on his voyage. Knowing not how long the journey would last, and expecting some evil against him, he filled the ship with great stores of all kinds of foods which he could hunt or discover. While he labored, he made his home in a nearby village, which treated him well and with honor and supplied him with much of what he lacked. There he learned from villagers that the mysterious cloud had risen in the sea seven years ago and had, since that day, neither moved nor diminished. On calm days a sad and beautiful voice drifted across the waves and into the village. Many powerful kings had sought to penetrate the mists, thinking that surely the voice was that of a great queen in dire distress. Yet so great was the enchantment protecting the island that their attempts had been in vain. Only a few had even returned with their lives, and those with only a remnant of their warhost. To this end, the villagers warned Beow not to attempt the feat, asking him instead to stay and become their king.

But Beow was not daunted, nor would he set aside his love for Ywänna. He prepared all the more vigorously until he finally felt ready to set out.

For seven more years he strove against dangers, powers and enchantments of every kind, seeking to come at last to the lonely isle. Each time he encountered a new trial, he persevered and survived. Yet to his dismay, he never found himself closer to his goal. Finally, as his strength began to wane from the long years of struggle, a terrible and unnatural storm, more ferocious than any he had yet encountered, raged against him. Though the heavy fog stirred not at all, the water grew so violent that Beow's ship was torn apart, and the mighty prince found himself in the midst of the raging seas. He struggled to stay afloat, and though many times he was pulled under, by means of his strength he managed to stay afloat or to surface for a quick breath before being pulled under again. On and on he struggled until the last of his strength left him. He gave himself up to death, thinking that he had failed his beloved . . .

Beow awoke to the taste of cool fresh water being poured gently into his mouth. Still clinging tightly to his great warsword, he opened his eyes to see Ywänna kneeling beside him where he had washed up on the beach of the enchanted island. On that very day, after fourteen years of waiting, they became man and wife.

But the moment Beow washed ashore, the god knew what had happened and that his enchantment had been broken. In his rage he came down like a storm intent on destroying them both. Yet so great was the enchantment around and about the island that not even he could come through it. For if the truth be known, the other gods had pitied poor Beow and Ywänna. In the middle of the night, after Beow lost consciousness, they had carried him ashore alive. Then, with their combined might, they had so increased the power binding and protecting the island that none even of their own kind could ever go there again unaided.

Thus Beow and Ywänna began a kingdom which many say lasts to this day. Neither were ever seen again, though some say that Beow's sword was returned to the world as a sign that he and Ywänna were finally united and that the sword was no longer needed by them. It was also said that whoever possessed that sword would carry with him the blessing of Ywänna and the strength and wisdom of Beow.

●

Ulestan let his eyes close, and for a moment he imagined himself lost in the mist and enchantment woven around Beow and Ywänna. Had he somehow drifted into their story? Or had their story grown to encompass his?

"We should have reached the west shore some time past." Swanfolgan's voice broke the stillness. Though he intended his words for the king's ears only, every man in the ship heard them.

"Have we misread the wind or the seas?" Folcwalda asked.

"In this mist I could well have done that," the seaman confessed, "but it is still my thought that we have kept a straight course."

"Perhaps we have come too far to the north and, missing the western peninsula, have passed into the North Sea itself."

Swanfolgan laughed unconvincingly. "Then we too shall soon be invading the Isle of the Britons."

"Yet that is unlikely with this wind from the north." Folcwalda finished his thought.

Swanfolgan nodded his agreement, but added another discomforting thought. "Are we sure this is still a north wind? We have little bearing in this fog, and the waves and tides are uncertain around this bay."

Folcwalda turned to face Swanfolgan, and those few who were close enough to see their eyes in the fog caught a hint of an unspoken conversation passing between them. The king's words, when they came, were spoken slowly and clearly. "Many years have I trusted your knowledge of the seas and your wisdom in the ways of the waves."

"And the wisest sailor alive will tell you that the seas are wilder than the meanest boar and less predictable than any woman," Swanfolgan replied. "Any man who says of the seas, 'I know all her ways' is but a great fool. No less I than any other."

"And the wisest among the wise will know the most ways to deny knowledge without confessing ignorance," Folcwalda said more sternly. But then a sudden mood change came over him, and for no apparent reason he began to laugh loudly and fully. Every heart that heard that laugh was at once lifted and strengthened. "So be it." The king's voice rang out firmly. "When the knowledge of the wise fails, we follow their guesses."

No sooner had those words been spoken when a dim shape loomed up out of the water just a few feet from the starboard side of the ship where Ulestan was staring. The thane took a deep, sharp breath which nobody else noticed. He alone was looking to the starboard. He alone had seen . . . had seen what?

"My king," he said, pointing where he had been looking. But by the time he had Folcwalda's attention, the thing had passed and he was pointing at nothing. Folcwalda looked at him in amusement. Not more than a few seconds later, however, another low shape appeared. This time Folcwalda was watching also. No sooner had he seen the shape when he started to bark commands.

But the commands came too late.

There was a soft thud near the bow of the ship. The thud was followed by a slow skid as the craft slid onto a low sandbar and came to a sudden halt. For a long moment everyone just sat and stared. Folcwalda said nothing. Swanfolgan said nothing. Everyone in the ship knew what had happened: they were grounded. It was not the first time this had happened to any of them. Everyone in the ship also knew what needed to be done, and it was not pleasant. But they were, all of them, experienced seamen, and as soon as one stood to the task the rest followed. Ten and five pairs of legs slowly lifted over the low sides of the ship and stepped into the water beside them. Though each knew what to expect, the icy seas came nonetheless as a shock upon their legs. With grimaces of pain and discomfort and more than a few words of anger spoken toward the gods, they set to work.

The draft of their ship was quite shallow, and so the water was just above their ankles where the ship had grounded. But with each passing wave there was an icy splash, often rising over their knees. And an unlucky few were caught by the occasional odd wave—every seventh one, some said—as they were bending to their task. These found themselves wet to the teeth.

Despite the cold and wet, the ship was pushed, lifted and dragged until it finally slid free. The same fifteen pairs of feet, now numb with cold, stepped back into the ship. Then the unavoidable coughing and shivering began. Perhaps there were some who were too cold and wet to consider how fortunate they were to have found, in the midst of the fog, ground—or rather shallows, for real ground they had not yet reached. Though the shore may have been quite close, in the dense fog the ground could have been in any direction except behind them. But the ship was underway again with the sail still up. They knew that the crossing was now nearly finished.

"We must be near a small island in the west of the bay, somewhere north of the mainland," Swanfolgan said with relief. "We should veer to the port soon and come upon land. Shall we turn to the port now?"

Folcwalda shook his head no. "Continue on," was all he said. His silence was echoed by every man in his warband. For a short time the ship sailed on, and every eye was searching eagerly for land. But so dense was the fog that there was little chance of seeing shore unless they passed within a spear-thrust.

The wind slowly lessened and seemed to shift back to the east, and the waves settled to a low roll. The men grew hopeful of landing soon and peered all the more eagerly over the port side of the vessel. A short time passed before there came once again the sounds that all dreaded—the soft thump and the slow, skidding halt. The members of Folcwalda's warband looked at each other and groaned. They had not even begun to dry off.

Ulestan joined this time as the warband stepped once more into the cold water and experienced the sudden, painful shock followed by the slow numbness. Though they were no more eager than before to step into the icy water, they were more ready this time than last, and the task was completed swiftly. Ulestan shared with the others the dull ache in his legs as he stepped back into the ship. He had no hope of dryness for some time to come.

"To the port?" Swanfolgan asked again and again. Folcwalda shook his head no without giving any explanation. A few men grumbled, but none spoke out loud. Swanfolgan shook his head in disbelief. The sails caught wind, and though the breeze had died even further, the ship moved on.

This time they slid onto a third sandbar almost at once. And the fourth followed soon after that. Each time the men were forced out of the ship, the cold penetrated that much deeper into their bodies and their leggings soaked up that much more icy water. Neither Folcwalda nor Swanfolgan were blind to the danger. Many a good thane and soldier were lost, not to blade and battle, but to cold and sickness from wet sea voyages. With each time they stepped back into the water, the chance that one of them would not return to Hwitstan increased. But each time the ship slid upon another sandbar, they had no choice but to get out and free themselves.

"By the gods, we are blind!" Folcwalda shouted suddenly, and his hand came slapping down against the flat of his sword.

"What is it, my lord?" Swanfolgan asked, startled.

"These are no islands around us. We have turned south too soon. This accursed wind and fog have deceived us! We are traveling southward, not westward, and down the inside of the bay, very close, it seems, to its western shores, though east of them and not north."

"Lower the sail," Swanfolgan ordered at once. More clearly than the rest, he saw the implications of what Folcwalda had said.

Ulestan, too, understood what his king was inferring. His mental picture of the bay was clear enough to understand. They had sought to sail westward across the bay, around the northern end of the peninsula, and then south along the outer coastline. Instead, if what Folcwalda now said was so, they had turned southward too soon and were now sailing down the inside of the bay. They would need to turn the ship around and sail straight north, in the opposite direction. Then another thought struck the thane. Swanfolgan had wanted to turn to the port some time earlier. But if Folcwalda was right, then turning to the port would have led them back into the middle of the great bay. If they had listened to Swanfolgan, they would be sailing in circles.

The other seamen must also have understood at least the first implication of what Folcwalda had said, that they would now need to turn completely about and sail in the opposite direction. A few were now cursing, while others were coughing harshly. But as Swanfolgan had commanded, the sail was lowered. It took four men to lower the heavy wool, laden as it was with water, and those who took the task were drenched in the process. The ship drifted slowly to a halt.

"If you are right," Swanfolgan said, his head sagging and his voice low, not doubting his king's assertion, "the shore will not be far off our starboard."

"We will land here and rest for the night," Folcwalda replied. "A fire would do us well."

Swanfolgan nodded and ordered the seamen to man their oars. The craft turned to the starboard and had not traveled far at all when from the fog in front of them the dim forms of trees loomed darkly, and the ship slid suddenly and neatly onto a solid beach.

Folcwalda had been right.

XI

Eyes and Ears

The fog persisted through the evening like a bad cough. Swanfolgan finally managed to start a fire from bits of deadwood found in the bushes along the beach, and a few of the men gathered around it. But the fire, low and sputtering, shed little warmth and gave off much smoke. In the end these men joined their fellow companions, wrapped themselves in their furs and skins, and dropped off to sleep knowing that the next morning would likely bring more of the same.

It did. When Ulestan awoke, it was to an even denser fog than they had encountered the previous day. There was no dawn to speak of, only a vague brightening of the grey around them. It looked to be an unpleasant day. And the prospect of returning over the same seaways they had covered the afternoon before was disheartening.

After a small hunk of tasteless bread, Ulestan joined the men as they stepped wordlessly back into the ship garbed in clothes and boots still damp from the previous day. Their progress was painfully slow. Working against a steady wind, they rowed and poled northward in shallow waters near the shore. Now and again they ran aground on sandbars hidden just below the surface and were forced, as they had been the day before, to get out into the cold water and slide the ship free. Each time the numbness penetrated more deeply into their hands and legs, draining valuable energy and making it that much more difficult to power the ship. Had the fog not been so dense, Folcwalda would certainly have steered through deeper water to avoid the groundings. Yet on a day like this, such a strategy would have been far too perilous. Many a ship and its warband had ventured boldly into such a fog only to vanish and not return.

On this day Folcwalda himself took many turns with an oar, and often, with words of encouragement, himself stepped into the icy water to help free a beached ship. Such was a good king! Ulestan, and, with some reluctance, Eormen and Edmen followed their king's example. Slowly the land passed beside them, dim shadows behind the fog. It was past midday when the ship finally reached the northern point of the peninsula. Finally they were able to turn west and then south again. As soon as the wind was behind them, the heavy wool sail, still wet from the day before, was raised. It caught the breeze at once, shaking water over two of the four men who lifted it, and the ship started to move without the oars. The men were too exhausted to say a word as they pulled their oars in and wrapped themselves in their furs. The rest of that day they traveled only with the aid of the wind. At least a day had been lost from the error, but they were now again on course.

At dark, a gloomy and tired warband turned into shore for the third night. With some dry wood and his tinder, Swanfolgan was this time able to produce a warm blaze. The mood of the company lightened somewhat as they sat beside the bright fire and ate healthy portions of the stewed mixture of salted pork and barley. Even those in good spirits, however, were tired, and more than a few were sick. Without delay they wrapped their thoughts in sleep.

The fog cleared somewhat on the fourth day, and late afternoon found them passing the mouth of the Rhine River, where they stopped in a small fishing village to spend the night. The villagers were quite surprised to find a warband in their midst and were more than eager to aid Folcwalda however he asked. The king made sure his men were well provided for from the village before he disappeared into the large house of the village chieftain. Ulestan and the rest of Folcwalda's men made themselves comfortable in and around the large house and were there when Folcwalda emerged the following morning wearing a rather determined smile.

"What have you learned?" Ulestan asked once the ship had slid quietly off the beach and out of hearing of the village.

"Perhaps very little . . ." He paused.

"But perhaps much," Ulestan finished. He had served Folcwalda long enough to make some guesses as to the king's thoughts.

"Perhaps," Folcwalda said, and then stopped as if he would say nothing more. After a moment, however, he continued, "The raiders have not traveled this far along the coast. It is thus likely that they are coming from the south—from among the Franks, just as Ecgwalda guessed."

"Or maybe they have just passed by this village. There is little to be taken in a raid."

"Yes, there is little to be taken. And there are also very few to guard what little there is to be taken. These are just fishermen who move inland in the winter. Their allegiance is given to Lyndlaf at Wic by Dorestad, which is just a short distance up the Rhine. If the raiders were looking for greater riches, Wic by Dorestad would surely have been their easiest target. The river would lead a warband right to the walls of the city and would offer a fast escape as well."

"And they have not done this?"

"No . . . Or at least not yet, according to the chieftain here. Warbands have not traveled up the Rhine."

"But others have?" Ulestan asked, catching the intonation in Folcwalda's voice.

"Yes, others have," Folcwalda replied. "Danish ships have begun to make frequent journeys up the Rhine."

"Danish warbands?" Ulestan was appalled at the thought of Danish warbands on Frisian soil. He, too, knew of the ferocity of the Spear-Danes.

"No, not warbands . . . Not according to the fishermen. The Danish ships are carrying traders."

"That is not uncommon."

"No," Folcwalda said. "Not if they returned bearing merchandise. But they always return with empty ships." The king fell silent for a few moments.

Ulestan wondered if there was any connection between the Danes and the Frankish raiders. Or perhaps the raiders weren't Franks at all, and it was the Danes themselves raiding Friesland. But why would they do that? Certainly King Hoc would not have desired war with his own daughter—or Hnaef with his sister. And why would the Danes pass by Wic by Dorestad to raid Domburg?

Unless for some reason the Danes wished for the Franks to take the blame for the raids. Or unless Wic by Dorestad was buying its freedom. But if so, then the Danish ships would not be returning down the Rhine empty.

Ulestan let those thoughts pass. It was more likely that the Danish trade ships had nothing to do with the Frankish war parties. Yet, he could not shake from his mind the thoughts of Hunlaf and his wicked deeds.

By mid-morning, with a strong breeze at their backs, Folcwalda's small warband was making good headway through the islands north of Domburg. Looking about him, Ulestan knew they were getting close. The islands about were growing familiar. They would reach Domburg not much later than midday, he thought. It would be good to be on land again.

To Ulestan's surprise, however, while they were still many miles from their destination, Folcwalda barked a quick order to Swanfolgan, and the ship suddenly veered toward the northern beach of a small wooded island off the port side of the ship. Before Ulestan had a chance to ask why, they had slid onto shore. Looking about in confusion, the men slowly disembarked and dragged the ship onto the beach, waiting to hear why they had stopped. Ulestan looked about as well, but there was nothing to be seen save for beach, sea and trees. Folcwalda conferred softly with Swanfolgan, but said nothing yet to explain his actions. Instead he told Swanfolgan and Edmen to stay with the warband while he took a short journey. Ulestan and Eormen were to join him. Without a further word, Folcwalda turned and trudged off the beach, disappearing through a stand of low, scraggly pines. Ulestan and Eormen looked first at each other and then at Swanfolgan and Edmen, who merely returned their blank stares. Then they started off in their king's footsteps.

"Where do you take us?" Ulestan asked once he had caught up to Folcwalda. He was glad to be on solid ground for a time, but curious as to why the voyage had stopped short of Domburg.

"We go to see with my other eyes and to hear with my other ears," Folcwalda replied enigmatically.

Eormen said nothing, but labored to keep pace with his king's long strides as they made their way across the island. He, too, seemed happy to be out of the ship and eager to use his legs for a change. "Men," he said, "were meant for the land and not for the sea." He said nothing about Folcwalda's cryptic comments.

As they walked further into the island, Ulestan began to glimpse the lay of the land around him. The whole of the island seemed to be one low, wooded hill which sloped gently down to a meadow near the northern end of the island and dropped off steeply to the south. A peaceful quiet pervaded the scene—not an eerie silence such as they had felt in the fog, but a pleasant calm. A few small birds chirped here and there and flitted from tree to tree, and an occasional gull could be heard not far away. Leaves and needles rustled high in the sky atop tall trees which swayed in the breeze, creaking as they did so. But there were no man sounds, nor was their any game to be seen. The three quickly traversed the meadow and made their way up the small wooded hill, sweating only slightly in the cool of the late morning.

When they reached the summit of the hill and looked down the other side, Ulestan finally understood what Folcwalda had been speaking of, if not who. Just over the top of the hill, nestled against the rocks below the crown on the steep south side, stood a low hut. The side of the hill formed two sides of it, and the other two were built of odd pieces of driftwood. At first glance it seemed hastily and poorly constructed, a primitive hut that one might expect children to build. But as Ulestan approached and examined it, his impression began to change. Before long he was staring at the building in astonishment. What had first appeared to be hasty construction was surprisingly careful and intricate craftsmanship. The pieces of driftwood that first looked lazily thrown together were so tightly twisted, woven and interlocked that it was difficult to determine where one stopped and the next started. Indeed, it looked as though the walls were as wind- and weather-proof as the wattle-work walls in Hwitstan. The hut had a low entrance across which a heavy piece of boarskin hung loosely. And with what must have been painstaking care, a small translucent window had been made by stretching scraped sealskin across another small opening. The posts supporting the walls were so firmly planted in the ground—in the very rock, it seemed—that they appeared as solid as the hillside. Even the location was perfect; the hut was exposed to the south where it could absorb the sun's heat year round, but was protected from the north, from whence came the coldest winds. To the right of the hut, a small cave opened into the hillside, and from the rock wall beside that, a fresh spring trickled down into a basin carved in the rock below it. A well-worn path curved steeply down from the summit of the hill to the small level space in front of the dwelling.

As they descended the path and came around to the front of the hut, Ulestan saw the boarskin slowly pulled aside and wondered what or who was about to emerge. Strange indeed did he expect the one who lived here to be. And how had a hermit such as this ever come to know Folcwalda? He watched and waited. From the entrance of that small dwelling, out stepped the eyes and ears of which Folcwalda had spoken. He was a tall man, with light grey eyes, once blue. Hair as white as old bone was pulled in a tail behind him. His leathery skin, in contrast with his hair, was tanned to a deep brown and was stretched taught across his tough, slender frame. Fine, wiry muscles and sinews lined his bare arms and accentuated each movement and gesture. A heavy, loose-fitting wolfskin was draped across his shoulders, and he wore well-used trousers whose color was now undiscernible but was something akin to green.

"Folcwalda, my son," he exclaimed joyfully.

"Wulfanwod," Folcwalda replied, and the two embraced as though they really were father and son.

"The sight of you brings joy," the old man said after they had released each other.

Folcwalda grinned broadly. Ulestan had not remembered seeing his king this happy in a long span of time. "You bear yourself proudly," he said with great conviction. "Your blood does not lie. You are still a king."

"Behold my kingdom!" the stranger responded, gesturing toward the entire island with a broad sweep of his hand.

"A kingdom indeed!" Folcwalda answered.

"With no chieftains to oppose me," Wulfanwod added with a hidden smile, as if he knew the reason for Folcwalda's visit. Then he looked at Ulestan and Eormen and abruptly changed the subject. "You surely prosper, O people's king, if you have many other thanes such as these."

"I wish that I had twenty thanes such as Ulestan the Wise and Eormen the Bold," Folcwalda replied. Ulestan and Eormen stepped forward and bowed. "They have served me well. Such should a thane be."

"But you did not visit me to boast of the strength of your hearth companions," Wulfanwod concluded. "Ever is the mind of Folcwalda planning and plotting."

"You know me well," the Frisian king laughed. "Even so, I would talk for a time. I desire your wisdom."

"The wisdom of a madman? Then you are mad yourself."

"Never was Wulfanwod a madman," Folcwalda said sternly. "But if your tongue needs loosening before you will speak with a friend, then loosening shall it have." So saying, he unslung from his back a leather bag which Ulestan had not before noticed and handed it to the old man. Wulfanwod untied the leather straps and removed the contents. He held in his hands a heavy fur cloak and two leather flasks of mead. "May you be warm on the coldest of nights," Folcwalda said in blessing.

A broad smile spread across Wulfanwod's thin face, and he gestured his visitors to follow him into his small hut. They did and found it more spacious than they had expected. There was room for all four of them, though there were only two short stools, which he and Folcwalda took, leaving the two thanes to sit on the floor. The hermit reached behind him and produced a single, large drinking horn with which to share the mead. "Too many days of fish," he said as he filled the cup. "It has been long since I have tasted mead."

He took a long draught, and then the mead cup was passed among the four of them. As they drank, Folcwalda and Wulfanwod spoke casually of the passing of time and times passed, of news and tidings of the world, and of the rise and fall of kings and tribes, speaking always as if these things were but matters of little import. And perhaps to Wulfanwod they were. Not until some time after one of the flasks had been emptied did their conversation end and Wulfanwod agree that he had been brought to knowledge of the events in the world around him. Wulfanwod had been the son of a Jutish chieftain during the days of Folcwalda's father's father. Small fragments of his tale emerged during their talk, and the rest was shared later by Folcwalda after he, Ulestan and Eormen left Wulfanwod and returned to their warband. When Folcwalda had returned from his victory over Ongintheo, still only a young prince but now wearing his father's torc, he had been sent by his kin to the house of Wulfanwod to be taught the use of the sword and the ways of a chieftain. Wulfanwod took this task to heart. For many years he treated Folcwalda like his own son—or more, like a younger brother. Together they roamed the nearby forests hunting wild boar and occasionally wolves or bear. When Folcwalda grew old enough, they left their own kingdoms and journeyed together far and wide across the north seas seeking always to learn—"to grow in wisdom, might and knowledge," as Folcwalda claimed, but Wulfanwod laughed and said they did it only for treasure and fame.

Early one spring, when the snows were melting, the two went hunting deep into the forest. For three days and two nights they followed the trail of a mighty boar. It was a great chase, and when they caught the beast it took both of them to kill it. They feasted on some of the meat that very night and then packed the rest to return to the village. But when they returned three days later, it was only to find the village in smoke and ruins. A savage warband had raided Wulfanwod's clan, showing no mercy. Both of his parents and his two sisters had been brutally murdered; his father's skull had been cloven by an axe, and both of his sister's bodies had been savagely rent. All around them lay their dead companions; the thanes of the king had made a circle around him where they had died in futility in his defense.

Wulfanwod gaped in dismay at the scene for a time, wandering aimlessly about the carnage, eyes wide open in an appalled stare as he looked at those he loved lying here and there, some almost unrecognizable in death. Then he went mad with fury. A horrible cry tore loose from his throat, and he conceived in that moment what he would do: he would avenge the death of his family and clan upon their brutal murderers—alone, he thought, though the young Folcwalda was still with him. Wulfanwod kept a ship hidden by the shores of a nearby river, and he thought of it at once. Heedless of any danger, he ran to where it lay, slid the ship into the water, and set out in pursuit of his foe.

Folcwalda only just managed to get into the ship as it slid into the river. Wulfanwod, intent on his pursuit, did not even notice him. But where was the pursuit to take them? Folcwalda wondered. The attackers had left no trace. For days the two of them traveled west and south with no sight of their unknown foe. It was a miracle that they survived in the small ship for as long as they did, but a strong wind had propelled them on, and the sun shone brightly day after day.

Four days passed, and they came upon another burned village. Flames still licked at the sides of many of the houses. Wulfanwod's eyes narrowed and brightened. The raiders were not long gone. Folcwalda and Wulfanwod pressed onward for two more days, traveling day and night without food or rest. But then the pursuit failed. The wind shifted to the northwest and brought with it torrential rains. On the seventh day, their ship was battered ferociously. For the first time Folcwalda sought to dissuade his friend from traveling further, arguing that the two of them alone would not be able to stand against a warband that had destroyed his entire village. But Wulfanwod would not be persuaded and still pursued his foe. Such was his mood that he gave no more thought to the strength of his enemy than he did to his safety on the seas.

On the eighth day the ship struck a sandbar extending out from a small island. Moments later the craft was lost in the wind and waves. Wulfanwod and Folcwalda barely made it to shore with their lives. They were stranded, and the pursuit was ended. Wulfanwod had no hope of vengeance. So great was his grief and anger at that time, and so impotent was he to assuage either, that he finally became entirely mad. Yet Folcwalda kept them both alive. And after a time the madness subsided. Folcwalda built a small boat and escaped the island to eventually find his own people again.

Wulfanwod had no more people to find. He stayed alone on that very island, making it his home for the remainder of his days. As a hermit he lived, eating whatever he might grow, dig or catch. In the years that followed, Folcwalda returned many times to visit his friend, and they remained as close as brothers. When he came to visit, Folcwalda would bring such gifts as he thought fitting, and they would relive stories and tales of days past. Wulfanwod would ask about the world outside, and Folcwalda would seek Wulfanwod's wisdom on whatever matters were troubling him. And it seemed that the light in both men's eyes would brighten for a time.

Now Folcwalda sought a favor. "I need your eyes and ears," he finally said.

"It has been said that the eyes of Folcwalda are far-seeing like the eyes of a hawk. Is this not so?"

"They do not see far enough," Folcwalda replied. "I need rather the eyes of a wolf."

"What is it you wish to see, brother hawk?"

"In truth, many things. But I will content myself with just two, friend wolf."

"If it is mine to give, it is already given," Wulfanwod replied.

"I seek tidings of Ecgwalda and of raiders."

Wulfanwod's eyes narrowed. "Of Ecgwalda I can tell you little. He is a cunning king, boastful, proud, ambitious and secretive. Yet in his dealings I do not doubt his honesty."

"He knows of your existence?"

"How could he not? I live but a short gull flight from his hall, and I do not seek to be hidden. Smoke rises from my island. Fishing nets are cast from my shores. Yes, Ecgwalda knows of me and speaks with me when it meets his desires. I trade with him for a few things I need—some fish for an occasional taste of boar or a drink of wine. And the Frisian gold you brought me from . . ." He hesitated for a moment. "The hidden gold from the ruins of our village still holds me in good stead and encourages occasional visits from passing traders. Yet Ecgwalda sees me little for one who lives so close. With each passing season his visits are shorter and less frequent. And in that I do not complain. He thinks me crazy—am I not, in many ways?—and I do nothing to sway his mind the other way. I am happy now to avoid the world of ambitious kings."

"Does he deal also with the Franks?"

"With the Franks? No! He despises them. His people are called the Half-Franks, but in truth there is little Frankish blood in them. Ecgwalda's father's father's mother was a Frank, but the love between her and her husband was never great. There is, perhaps, some dealing with Frankish traders. I see their ships passing along the coast time and again. When Ecgwalda speaks of Chlotar it is with great disdain but also with some fear.

"But then," Wulfanwod added in a tone of warning, "neither does Ecgwalda have much love for any Frisian who calls himself king. Were it not for his fear of the Franks, he would surely have very few dealings with the Frisians."

Folcwalda laughed. "You know much for one who claims to know little."

"What I have told you is nothing," Wulfanwod said. "It is not difficult to read Ecgwalda's ambitions. His actions are harder to predict. I could have told you as much if I had spoken to him but once in my life. He is little different in his desires and fears from any chieftain anywhere, save but a small bit wiser and perhaps slightly more trustworthy. Surely I am telling you nothing that you have not already guessed."

"Perhaps not," Folcwalda agreed. "But of the raiders I know nothing."

"Now there is a mystery. I have heard something of these raids from a trader who stopped here this spring. Of the extent of the raids I can tell you nothing, but there was a curious thing."

"Speak of it," Folcwalda asked, his eyes showing sudden interest.

"There was a day, more than a summer ago, when a strange ship landed on my island. At first I thought the men to be traders and went to meet them. But it seemed they were not looking for me, so I approached warily. I did not recognize them; yet from their costume and hair it was not difficult to see that they were Franks. Their ship was long, holding thirty or more, and they were armed more like a warband than traders. I thought it wiser to remain hidden, and I watched and waited. The men stayed on the beach all night, but lit no fire. Then late the next morning another ship appeared from the north. It too landed on the island. Whether it was a trade ship or a warband, I could not tell, but commanding that ship were two chieftains richly dressed in Danish fashion. They were haughty and proud and well-armed with old swords. These two certainly were not common traders. A long meeting took place between them and the Frankish warlord, but of that discussion I could discern nothing from my place of hiding. In the end some gold passed from the Danes to the Franks and they parted ways. Only after I heard of the raids did I remember again that strange meeting."

"What do you think of it?" Folcwalda pursued.

"I think nothing of it," Wulfanwod laughed. "It is for the hawk to make his conclusions. I will have nothing of the dealings of the outside world."

"And this is all you know of the raids?"

"This is all I know of the raids, yes. I do not venture off this island and, as you can see," he continued, gesturing toward his barely furnished surroundings, "there is nothing here of interest to a raiding warband. I can tell you nothing of the raids."

The faces of Folcwalda and Eormen echoed the disappointment that Ulestan felt, but they said nothing.

Then a slow, rather sly smile spread across Wulfanwod's visage. "I could tell no tale of these raids . . . but of the raiders themselves, perhaps I could tell you something."

Folcwalda's interest was rekindled instantly.

"There is a small island not far from here in the direction of the summer sunrise. When you leave here, I will point it out to you. A healthy man could swim there from here. I have seen a Frankish warship land on that island many times in the past year. They always land on the seaward side so they cannot be seen from the coast—but of course I can see them—and they always go in and out late at night or early in the morning. Their ship they keep well hidden. They light no fires and rarely stay for long."

"You know this to be a Frankish warship?" Eormen asked. He could not conceal his excitement.

"It is a warband, no doubt. The way they hide, they could be naught else. As to its Frankish origin, that is only a guess."

"Are these the same that landed here?" Ulestan joined the conversation.

"I have the eyes of a wolf, not those of a hawk," Wulfanwod answered, rolling back his eyes and baring his teeth. For a moment Ulestan could see how he had gained the reputation of being mad. Then he regained his kingly appearance and looked at Folcwalda as if he were tired of the questions.

"Have you told Ecgwalda of this warband?" Folcwalda asked sharply, ignoring Wulfanwod's glance.

"He has not asked."

"And there is but one ship?"

"I have seen but one. Yet there are many such islands, and I cannot see them all. Nor do I care to," he added as an afterthought.

Folcwalda nodded his head and sat still for a moment. Then he rose to his feet and addressed the two thanes. "It is time to pay a visit to Ecgwalda of Domburg."

The four of them rose together and departed, heading over the top of the hill and back toward the beach.

When they had come across the meadow and were approaching Folcwalda's waiting warband, Wulfanwod stopped. "I will go no further. I have no desire to be among too many men again. Yet it was good to see you, son of my heart." He pointed through the trees toward a nearby island. "There is the land I spoke of. That is where these raiders may be found."

Folcwalda made his thanks known to Wulfanwod as they clasped each other by the shoulder and embraced as brothers. Then farewell was said, and Folcwalda turned to go. But as he did, Wulfanwod suddenly grabbed him by the shoulders. Folcwalda turned back.

"Beware, old hawk," the hermit said in a strong voice, his penetrating eyes fixed more firmly on Folcwalda than they had all that day. "Our time is coming quickly to an end, you and I. The old ways are passing. Slowly perhaps, but they are passing."

"Death claims us all," Folcwalda replied lightly. "We go to the hall of warriors to join our fathers. Even the proud Hoc has fought his last battle. I too will someday join him."

"I speak not just of death," Wulfanwod said more slowly, his eyes still fixed on the king. "I speak of our *ways*. They are passing. Like a duck in fall, or an arrow off the string, time flies a straight path and turns neither left nor right. Change will overtake us."

"As always, you speak in riddles."

"Do I, friend?" He laughed. "Yet now I will speak plainly. The many gods are dying; the One is coming. I have seen it. This new God is strong. His messengers are few but bold, and He sends them to the corners of the earth. Change will come if death does not first take us."

Folcwalda's eyes narrowed, and his muscles tensed. He pulled slightly away from his old friend, and his voice grew suddenly cold. "Of what do you speak? Do you follow this new god?"

Wulfanwod tilted his head back and cackled. His eyes rolled back in his head, and he once more appeared the crazy hermit. "Nay," he said. "I am no believer, but a prophet only. Go and do what you will."

With Ulestan and Eormen at his side, Folcwalda turned abruptly and walked at a brisk pace back to the waiting ship. He spoke not another word, and neither of his thanes was willing to break the sudden heavy silence. But none of them could forget Wulfanwod's last words, and Ulestan dwelt long upon them.

Tales of sorrow, it has been said, may indeed outlive those of joy. And yet it is also said by the wise that amid the tales of greatest sorrow and ruin there is often joy, and amid deepest darkness Light that endures. That Light was long in coming, but its arrival was foretold. The darkness grew, but the flame was already burning which would pierce that darkness. Past ways perish; new times come. Old kings depart to make room for the young. And many gods die to prepare for the One.

XII

Domburg

Edmen leapt to his feet when he saw Folcwalda walking back down the beach toward him. The thane caught his brother's eye, but Eormen's glance told him nothing. Ulestan laughed to himself when he saw the look of anguished curiosity on Edmen's face. That one did not like to be left out of anything. To have to remain behind was the worst thing that could have happened to him. Swanfolgan, on the other hand, was content to be with his ship, and he rose more slowly. The rest of the warband, weary from four days of travel at sea, sat where they were and waited.

It did not take Folcwalda long to convey to Swanfolgan and Edmen what he had learned from Wulfanwod of the Frankish raiders, which he did with no mention of the hermit himself. Such keen excitement did they have at the prospect of catching their enemy unawares in their place of hiding that none thought to ask from whom Folcwalda had gathered his information—or if they did, they thought better than to probe their king with questions. When he was done, Folcwalda donned his battle-gear for the first time on the voyage. The warband greeted him with a loud war cry. Beating their swords upon their shields and shouting more chants, they returned the ship again to sea for the final leg of their voyage.

A short time later they were sliding onto another beach. This one was clearly inhabited. A dozen or so ships similar to theirs lay on shore in one direction, and in the other tools, fishing nets, and other signs of habitation were strewn about haphazardly. The skin roofs of a few buildings could be seen peering over the top of a low hillock just a short distance away. The village of Domburg lay nestled there. Half a dozen village fishermen stopped their work to watch Folcwalda's warband arrive. As the company started to pull the ship onto the beach, four armed guards emerged from behind a low tree where they had taken some shelter from the noonday sun. Their eyes raised at the sight of Folcwalda, and they looked upon him in admiration.

"We greet you," Folcwalda said, not waiting for the guards to issue their warning or welcome.

"We greet you in the name of our king," the foremost of the guards replied, looking first at Folcwalda and then at Eormen, Edmen and Ulestan, who stood proudly beside their king. They, too, were in their battle armor—sword at side, shield on shoulder, helm upon head. Few there were who could stand against those four in battle. The guard bowed to each of them and then continued, "Who are such proud manner of men as to bear sword and shield across the great Swan Road to enter the domain of Ecgwalda? Speak your purpose, men of renown. If you seek welcome, welcome will be granted. If you seek war, war will be granted. Yet be warned that we are wary of warbands and men bearing armor onto our shores. In the name of Ecgwalda, I Aeltar, son of Aelman adjure you by the gods and by your honor to speak the truth."

"By the gods, by my honor, and by the edge of my sword I will answer you," Folcwalda began, rising to his full stature and placing his hands on the hilt of his battle-hardened blade. All four guards involuntarily took a step back. "I am Folcwalda, son of Folgar, High King over all Friesland. I come by right and by my own authority to stand on these shores. Bring message to Ecgwalda that his king has arrived to visit his subjects and those under his protection. Tell him to prepare a welcome befitting me." As he finished, his thanes stepped up beside him, and the rest of the warband formed a tight wall to his right.

To the honor of the four guards, they held their ground and did no disservice to their own chieftain; if they were daunted, it did not show in their manner or voice. Bowing and showing his respect to Folcwalda, Aeltar spoke again. "Folcwalda, son of Folgar and those who stand beside him I welcome to Domburg and to the land of the Half-Franks," he said with clarity. "I will speak your message to Ecgwalda. Until that time, your band must remain on the beach or remove their weapons if they have wish to follow." He gave the order as if he had the power to enforce it.

"We will wait," Folcwalda replied, "but not for long. Ulestan and Eormen will accompany you." The latter was clearly a statement and not a question.

The guard glanced at the thanes as they stepped forward and then nodded his approval. He looked as though he were about to say something about their weapons, but then he thought the better of it and remained silent. Ulestan and Eormen followed Aeltar and one of the other guards up the long slope and into the village of Domburg. The other two guards stayed behind and waited nervously among the Frisian warband.

The village of Domburg was much as Ulestan had remembered it from his voyages many years earlier. There was a single, tight circle of huts—no more than a stone throw across—facing inward. In the center was a small, low-ceilinged hall. A meager marketplace had sprung up on the near side of the hall, and a group of merchants and buyers gathered there in the mid-afternoon sun. Two strangely dressed Saxons were dealing in brightly dyed wool, and beside them Ulestan recognized three Frisian slave traders whom he had recently seen in Hwitstan. A poor peasant dressed in tattered rags was holding two chickens and bargaining—unsuccessfully, it seemed—for some wool. Ulestan was aware of the purse at his side and had a sudden urge to make the purchase for the man. But even as he had that thought, the wool trader nodded and handed the peasant a heavy woolen cloak. The peasant bowed and smiled warmly as he parted with one of his prizes.

On the far side of the village, through the gaps between huts, could be seen the village land. Even now men stooped over freshly tilled earth and laid the seed that would be their lifeblood in the coming winter. In fact, in every direction he looked Ulestan saw men and women hard at work, much as they were in Hwitstan at that time of day. Only the emblems on the shields and helms of their lords distinguished them from peasants in Hwitstan.

As he approached Domburg's hall, Ulestan forgot these thoughts and became acutely aware of the circle of huts now enclosing him. He felt like a fish caught in a weir, swimming toward the net. Quite a few eyes now turned in their direction and watched the two strangers as they crossed the clearing and passed the marketplace. The market grew suddenly quiet. Without any words passing between them, Ulestan's and Eormen's hands both fell casually to the hilts of their swords. Aeltar, on the other hand, was clearly more at ease than he had been on the beach just a few moments ago. His head was held high, and his gait was confident.

Ulestan and Eormen followed Aeltar to the door of the hall, where they were asked to wait as he spoke with Ecgwalda. Aeltar emerged just moments later and, with a look of satisfaction, ushered them inside. Moments later he disappeared again, leaving the two Frisian thanes to face the chieftain.

The hall was small and warm. A low blaze glowed on the hearthstone. A group of warriors, no more than fifteen, were gathered around the hearth in the middle of the hall. Ulestan quickly spotted Ecgwalda amongst them. The chieftain of Domburg was motioning them to join him.

Ulestan and Eormen looked momentarily at each other and then obeyed the summons. As they approached, Ecgwalda rose to greet them. First raising his right hand in peace, he then extended it in welcome. It was a friendly greeting used often by warriors in the north and not at all what Ulestan was expecting. Nor was this the Ecgwalda whom they had thought to see. Always before, they had seen Ecgwalda as a hardened warrior, grim and battle-weary, trusting few, speaking little, sharp of tongue. Here in the safety of his hall he appeared instead a kind and gentle lord, a father to his people. The genuine warmth of his greeting put Ulestan immediately at ease—though he felt somehow that he shouldn't be—and he extended his own hand to accept Ecgwalda's greeting.

"I hope your king comes on a journey of peace," Ecgwalda proclaimed. Was there a subtle emphasis on the word "your"? Ulestan couldn't quite tell. Ecgwalda's person seemed to exude warmth and comfort. The thane felt it difficult to mistrust him.

"Folcwalda is never eager for war," Ulestan replied. "Nor is his servant Ulestan, who is also at your service."

Ecgwalda smiled and released Ulestan's wrist. But as he did, he held Ulestan's gaze for a moment longer. Ulestan, bold and confident, did not waver under scrutiny. He returned Ecgwalda's penetrating stare. And he was surprised at what he saw. The chieftain's eyes were moist and red—or was that just a reflection from the fire?—and his cheeks sagged sadly. When Ulestan finally looked down, he noticed the nearly empty mead vessel in Ecgwalda's left hand. It was a great glass drinking horn with many arms and claws reaching out from all sides, some of which still held remnants of the golden liquid. If that had been full of mead before he had drained it, then Ecgwalda's eyes would now be very red indeed. Suddenly self-conscious, Ulestan looked away from the mug and glanced around the hall. Every eye in the hall was closely examining him. That, he thought, was to be expected of this chieftain's hearthwerod.

"And are you, too, at my service?" Ulestan heard Ecgwalda asking Eormen. The question surprised Ulestan as much as it did Eormen.

Eormen appeared a bit nervous, but he bowed. "Eormen, thane of Folcwalda," he replied. "As Ulestan, I serve first and always the High King. But while I am in your hall I humbly seek your pleasure." At the word "humbly" Ulestan caught a twist of sarcasm in Eormen's voice.

"It is my pleasure that you be warm and accept my hospitality," Ecgwalda answered, ignoring, if he heard it, the sarcasm. A nearby servant quickly filled two mead cups and handed them to Ulestan and Eormen. Ulestan was surprised to find it warm. "Will you speak of your purpose among us?" Ecgwalda asked casually.

"We have come . . ." Eormen started to reply, but Ulestan cut him off, afraid of what he might say. Despite his age, Eormen was still impetuous and was not the best of spokesmen or diplomats.

"We have heard word of your troubles," Ulestan said tentatively. How much should he say, he wondered. Hopefully Folcwalda would arrive soon. To say too much might give away something Folcwalda didn't want revealed.

"Word has reached the High King that his subjects have suffered from raids," Eormen stated when Ulestan did not continue. In his overboldness, he had no fear of saying too much.

"Ah, yes," Ecgwalda replied, again either oblivious to Eormen's emphasis or not caring.

"Of Folcwalda's brave deeds you have no doubt heard," Eormen went on, unprompted. "Your affairs have been made known to us by the messengers whom you yourself have sent, that your people lie in fear each night suffering pain and affliction at the hands of the Franks. Far and wide across the sea men know that your hall has now no peace. Folcwalda seeks you that you may know what his hand may accomplish."

To the proud words of Eormen, Ecgwalda responded with a sullen silence. Nothing more did he say until Folcwalda himself entered the hall a few minutes later. But though the chieftain's face feigned a calm indifference, a grim and angry storm brooded within.

Folcwalda was followed by his entire warband. They filed into the small hall looking nervously about them as if expecting a trap. But Ecgwalda's hearthwerod, suddenly finding themselves outnumbered by the warband from Hwitstan, appeared at least as nervous. When Folcwalda's men realized they were in the majority, they were immediately more at ease. They followed their king as he strode straightaway to the hearthstone beside which sat Ecgwalda.

Ecgwalda, meanwhile, seemed to take no notice of anything that was taking place around him. He remained on his bench drinking from his now refilled horn and gazed blankly into the fire. Only when Folcwalda had stopped just half a pace away did Ecgwalda look up. For the second time the thought struck Ulestan that this was a very different chieftain of Domburg than he had been expecting. Folcwalda had spoken again and again of Ecgwalda as being cunning and dangerous yet honorable. The war-chief in front of him looked neither cunning nor dangerous, but simply tired. Were it not for the clarity in his eyes, Ulestan might have thought him drunk. Or was this all a charade—a carefully plotted illusion? Was it his intent to disarm his opponents? To make them less wary? Did he even perceive Folcwalda as an opponent?

A few more warriors from Domburg stepped quietly through the doorway and took benches near the walls. Were there four more of them or five? Ulestan could not tell because the hall was dark, and most of Folcwalda's men stood between him and the door.

Ecgwalda finally rose to greet his guest. "Welcome in peace," he stated simply. It was quite a change from the way the guard had greeted them on the beach.

"Your welcome is received in the peace in which it was given," Folcwalda replied carefully.

Ecgwalda laughed. "Your brave-hearted men have traveled far over the sea swells. Yet still you wear your war-dress and battle helmets. Will you not rest?" He gestured toward the seats surrounding the fire. "There is mead for you and your men. Or beer if you prefer. We are not without our comforts."

Ulestan sensed that there was a great deal more going on between these two chieftains than that which was spoken. But it was difficult to identify exactly what. Each and every word bore tremendous weight, but it was a weight unmeasurable.

Folcwalda gazed intently at Ecgwalda. One hand rested firmly on his sheathed sword, the other held his helm, which he had removed upon entering the hall. Ecgwalda returned his gaze casually, with an almost intentional lack of intensity.

Two more of Ecgwalda's men entered the hall through the main door. Ulestan tried to draw Folcwalda's attention to the newcomers, but the king's gaze was focused on Ecgwalda. Folcwalda's men were now looking eagerly upon the great urns of mead and beer which had been brought to Ecgwalda and now sat at his side. Their journey had been tiresome, and they were all too glad for it to be over.

"Our purpose carries with it great importance," Folcwalda said after a moment's silence. Nonetheless he accepted the mead that was offered to him in a large glass mug with small silver plates on the sides and bottoms, presumably where the precious glass had been broken and repaired. "The urgency is no less than you yourself made it to be in the message delivered with the token of the silver blade." Reaching into a small pouch at his side, Folcwalda returned the coin and blade to Ecgwalda.

"Is it not said that undue haste foils the plans of the urgent? If your purpose is both urgent and important, then it surely deserves thought and discussion." Ecgwalda took his seat as he said this. If nothing else, he was confident. There were few men who did not seek to stand their tallest in the presence of Folcwalda if for no other reason than a desire not to be daunted by his physical size and might.

Folcwalda motioned his men to sit and then took the bench opposite Ecgwalda. The wine was passed around, and the voyagers wasted no time quenching the thirst brought on by four days of harsh travel.

"You speak wisely," Folcwalda said. His manner seemed to relax somewhat. "But those who wait while a blade falls on them will feel the sharpness of the edge."

"Is this blade falling upon me now? Yet I know already how sharp an Ecg may be." Only then did Ulestan notice the battle sword which leaned unsheathed against the chieftain's bench. At that moment ten more warriors from Domburg entered the hall. These made their way closer to the hearth and sat down quietly. Aeltar was among them, his eyes looking questioningly at his leader, who nodded enigmatically back.

"Has not the blade been falling upon you?" Folcwalda replied.

Ulestan finally got his king's attention and indicated with his eyes that more of Ecgwalda's men had entered the hall. It was now Folcwalda's band that was outnumbered. Folcwalda saw and understood, but he gave no indication for his thanes to take any action. Eormen and Edmen sat toying with their swords.

"To what do you refer?" Ecgwalda asked. The intent of his question was clear: was Folcwalda speaking of his own warband or of the Frankish raiders? Ulestan found that he himself did not know.

"I speak of the Franks," Folcwalda said bluntly. "Or have your messengers lied when they spoke of raids?" His voice cut through the tension sharply. Some of his men, looking around and seeing for the first time that they were no longer in the majority, started to grow nervous again.

"The message was true." Ecgwalda's reply was disarming. He seemed to take no offense at Folcwalda's questioning his honesty.

"What damage has been done?" the High King asked, suddenly changing the direction of the conversation.

Ecgwalda leaned back and sighed. He thought for a moment, either trying to calculate in his mind the extent of the harm done to his people, or trying to decide how much to tell his guest—or perhaps both. It was unwise, Ulestan knew, to speak to other chieftains too much of your own losses, particularly of men, for if other chieftains know too much of your weaknesses those weaknesses will likely be exploited.

In a moment Ecgwalda came to a decision and replied,

"They have been significant but bearable. Our first loss was our metal plough. With it, we could prepare a field with but four oxen—or two if the field was soft and flat. Now we must use a team of eight and heavy wooden shares." Eormen started to interrupt, but Ecgwalda silenced him with a hand before the thane could say anything. "If you think it was one of our own villagers, you are mistaken. A metal plough is something to be prized, and we guarded it with care. Every evening we made sure it was returned by those working the village land. A life was lost vainly defending the plough. And the later raids have been more costly. Much livestock has been taken, perhaps one third of the village stock."

"They have come by land?" Folcwalda asked. Ulestan understood his king's reasoning. Raiders would not try to steal cows or even pigs by driving them into their ships. It would prove not only too difficult but too noisy as well.

"The animals were slaughtered silently on our own land and hastily and carelessly carved. Only the meat was carried off," Ecgwalda answered, also perceiving the reason behind Folcwalda's question. "We were able to salvage some of what remained, but that did little for us through the winter."

"Has there been a clash of blades?"

A mist gathered in Ecgwalda's eyes. "Thrice they have come upon our guards, and thrice our guards have not lived to see morning. It is sorrow to me to think of what they have done in their hatred. Fate has swept away many good thanes. No more will they drink ale in the hall. Their lifeblood lies spilt upon our soil."

"And the enemy they opposed?"

Ecgwalda shook his head. "Perhaps the enemies' lives were spilled as well. But if so, they leave no witness to the success of our guards. They carry their dead and dying with them."

Folcwalda glanced around him and then back at Ecgwalda. "Your son Ecglaf?" he asked with sudden intuition.

"Nine days past . . ." Ecgwalda replied. Anger, grief or both edged his voice.

"How?" Folcwalda asked in pity, thinking perhaps of his own son.

"We do not know. He was on a hunt and returned late. Perhaps he came upon the raiding band and sought to dissuade their purposes. Or perhaps it was they who came upon him unawares." As he spoke, Ecgwalda pulled his sword from where it leaned against the bench and rested it on his lap. "His body was found near our beach. A spear protruded from his gut, and his arm dangled limply from his side, half severed. Aelthulf, my friend, lay at his side, still breathing. His left hand held the broken haft of his shattered blade. His right was clutching a cloven Frankish shield. He had not the strength or breath to speak, but when I arrived he held the broken shield for me to see. He wanted me to know that he had died as a warrior." Rather suddenly Ecgwalda rose to his feet. "And so you can see, King Folcwalda, that my people are eager to fight a foe we can find."

Ulestan looked about him. Some fifty of Ecgwalda's warriors had risen as well and were now standing around their chieftain with their hands on their swords, glaring intently at the intruders. The hall was full. More must have slipped in while Ecgwalda was telling his story. Eormen and Edmen were already on their feet with their blades drawn. The rest of Folcwalda's men were rising, but made no move to their swords. Ulestan rose too. Every man in the hall now looked at one or the other of the chieftains, awaiting a word or signal. Every man stood ready to fight and die at the command of his king. Loyal earls and thanes were they who would serve their treasure-giver with such loyalty.

Of all those gathered in the hall, Folcwalda alone remained seated. Such was the intensity in that room and so jealous were all for the honor of their kings that a battle might well have begun that very moment without any order being given had Folcwalda stood suddenly to oppose Ecgwalda. And Ulestan knew that not one of his companions would ever return to Hwitstan alive were that to happen. He thought of Finn and Hildeburh and wondered if he would ever see their child.

But Folcwalda remained calm, as a king should. He well knew the consequence of his actions. Slowly and firmly he motioned Ecgwalda to sit. And for what seemed like forever to Ulestan, Ecgwalda defiantly resisted Folcwalda's authority. But in wisdom, submission or perhaps both he eventually complied with the High King's stern command. When he did, the two sat facing one another while the rest of the hall waited.

"Do you desire that I give you an enemy you can see?" Folcwalda inquired.

"Do you speak of Franks?" Ecgwalda asked in response.

"Are the Franks your enemies, or are we?"

Ecgwalda had no more questions, so he gave an answer instead. "The Franks at least I know are my enemies."

"Then perhaps I can give you an enemy you can see and fight," Folcwalda answered.

With a casual hand motion Ecgwalda told his followers to sit. They obeyed reluctantly, and Folcwalda's band followed. "Speak to me of this enemy," the chieftain demanded. The memory of his son's death still burned in his mind.

"I will gladly speak of this enemy. In this, if in nothing else, we seek the same end. And perhaps I know more about this enemy even than you."

Ecgwalda's eyes glimmered as Folcwalda said this. A hope lit up his face as he imagined a means of ridding his people of their plight. Or perhaps it was a hope simply of avenging his son's death. Ulestan could only guess. Ecgwalda was a difficult man to comprehend. "Speak of this knowledge that is hidden from me, yet visible to the eyes of the hawk." The tone of his voice was dangerous and full of sarcasm. And Ulestan knew that the danger was not for the host but for his guests.

"Of this knowledge I may soon speak. Perhaps toward our common goal I can hope to succeed where you have failed." At the word "failed" a new, darker gleam appeared in Ecgwalda's eyes. A number of his men again placed their hands upon their swords. Yet Ecgwalda said nothing and made no motion.

"I have no love of the Franks and would gladly end their raids. Yet there are other matters of greater importance," Folcwalda continued. "I must first speak of something else."

Ecgwalda glared at Folcwalda as if the delay were a personal affront to him. Yet he held his sword impatiently and still said nothing.

Folcwalda looked back at him closely, as if trying to measure his stature and judge how he would respond. "It is now two years since you pledged yourself and your people to Friesland and to its High King."

Ecgwalda winced. His relaxed and casual manner had disappeared at the mention of his son, and now every muscle in his body was tense and drawn. Still he said nothing. Ulestan found that he too was tense, and he consciously forced himself to relax.

"You made a pledge to me, and yet naught has been done since then," Folcwalda continued. "Two years is a long time."

"The lands under my rule and care have had their own worries and concerns," Ecgwalda replied, struggling, Ulestan thought, to regain his indifferent composure. He paused for a few seconds more and then continued, "Enough of my men have been killed by these raiders without me sending more away myself." With a deliberate effort he took his hand off his sword and took a long draught from his horn. His face relaxed, and the tight grimace faded to a sarcastic grin. "Hwitstan is a long distance from here. What have I to do with the troubles of Hwitstan?"

"And what does Hwitstan have to do with the troubles of Domburg?" Folcwalda finished the thought.

"We understand one another well," Ecgwalda answered.

"Then understand me now." Folcwalda rose suddenly to his full height and stature. His voice boomed, and the hall resounded with echoes. "I mean for every village, every man, and every chieftain in the land to be united. I mean for Friesland to be one kingdom. And I mean to see this accomplished by whatever manner and means it takes to bring it about. I will not rest until this is achieved." Tall and straight did he stand as he spoke. His helmet in hand and his proud head bared, Folcwalda towered over every man in the hall. The High King of Friesland was revealed in all his might and glory. Power and authority were his. He commanded them as he spoke, and there could be no refusing. His thanes looked up in awe and admiration while the men of Domburg cowered and trembled and those closest to him backed away. Mighty indeed was the king of Friesland, like the kings of old, and those who met him in battle before or after would not testify otherwise.

Ecgwalda started to speak, but Folcwalda was not finished. "This is the only means for the survival of our people. Even now our land is being invaded. Only a united Friesland can hope to stand against the adversaries around her. I do not mean to fail. We will conquer. There will be a High King. If not me, then it shall be my son after me. The alternative is slavery and death. That I will not have!"

If Frisian blood must be spilled that more Frisian blood may be saved, Folcwalda might as well have said, then that is a price we will pay. The echoes of his voice faded into the wooden walls, and the room fell deathly silent.

Ulestan waited anxiously for Ecgwalda's response. If the chieftain perceived Folcwalda's speech as a threat, which in many ways it was, why should he allow Folcwalda and his war-band to leave Domburg alive? He would not. He would kill them all now, Ulestan thought morosely, while they were outnumbered two men to one. Then Folcwalda's words would lie useless on the ground, as would Ulestan's body. Yet Ulestan was a warrior. He had faced death for his king before and would do so again. Never was a treasure-giver more worthy of the lives of his servants and thanes. The king who had revealed himself today was the king to whom Ulestan had pledged his life in service. Folcwalda was willing to die for his belief in Friesland. Ulestan was willing to die for his belief in Folcwalda.

If he was called to do so, Ulestan would face death once more. But there was authority in Folcwalda's voice, authority which perhaps Ecgwalda could not refuse. And wisdom as well, wisdom which Ecgwalda maybe had heard.

Ecgwalda's response surprised all—all save Folcwalda. Was Folcwalda ever surprised? "I ask again," Ecgwalda said, "what has Domburg to do with the troubles of Hwitstan, and what has Hwitstan to do with the troubles of Domburg?"

"Nothing . . . And everything," Folcwalda replied without hesitation. "We are here, are we not?" he said, as if that were an answer to the second question. Then he sat down and continued in a quieter voice so that those toward the edges of the hall were barely able to hear. "Do you require a demonstration? Then a demonstration you will have. This shall be our pledge: we will rid Domburg of the raiders which plague your lands and people, and we will see that you are freed." He hesitated intentionally and then continued very slowly, "But there is a price."

Ecgwalda matched the tone of Folcwalda's voice nearly perfectly as he articulated equally slowly, "There is always a price." Whether he was referring to Folcwalda or to life in general, Ulestan did not know.

Folcwalda laughed. "There is always a price," he repeated. "And I will name that price. The price is your allegiance."

"You are predictable," Ecgwalda said, drinking another large swallow of his liquid, "but I desire to hear more." The eagerness in that chieftain's eyes belied the calm and easy tone with which he spoke.

Now the two great leaders were smiling at each other like old friends. The tension was easing out of the room like water off the beach. Folcwalda told Ecgwalda of his plan with both his warband and Ecgwalda's hearthwerod listening intently. He laid the plan out in greater detail than even Ulestan himself had heard it, and the plan seemed good. "I will lead this warband," Folcwalda concluded a few minutes later, "and grapple with the enemy, foe against foe. Twenty good thanes and warriors have I with me, and forty more trusted sword-bearers shall you provide from your own hearthwerod. We will defeat the Frankish swine who pillage our shores. Unafraid, we will accomplish this deed and purge the evil from our land. And when the victory is complete I will return to Domburg and redeem your pledge. Twenty warriors from Domburg shall return with me to Hwitstan. What do Domburg and Hwitstan have to do with one another? Everything if that is what we choose."

Ecgwalda said nothing for a long time. When he finally responded, it was softly and slowly. "For this decision I will need some time to consult my thanes. Until the decision is made I extend to you the hospitality of my hall and my people." Without another word he rose and strode from the hall. Five of his thanes, including Aeltar, followed him.

XIII

A Clash of Blades

The decision did not take as long as Ulestan feared. Late the next day Ecgwalda returned to his hall astride a great black stallion. Mud and sweat soaked his garments, and his horse labored from hard riding. He had gone to visit some of the smaller villages under his rule to confer with the clan chieftains who owed him allegiance and looked to him for protection. From his appearance, he had traveled far on that errand. When he entered the hall, he strode right to where Folcwalda was sitting surrounded by his men.

"One of my villages was raided early this morning," he said, his eyes smouldering. "They are growing more bold. They burned down the house of one of my chieftains. Further, they killed both him and his wife as they sought to escape."

Folcwalda's eyes narrowed as well. "Did you think they would grow less bold with success?"

Ecgwalda did not hear him. "Forty men are waiting for you outside. When you return to me the spears and shields of these Franks, twenty of those men are in your service."

As they left the hall, Ulestan turned once more to look inside. Ecgwalda had resumed his place beside the fire with his drinking horn in his hand. His features were once again dispassionate save for his eyes, which alone revealed the passion within him. Even from a distance Ulestan could see the anger burning within the oppressed ruler. The thane stepped outside with his king.

Folcwalda was already ordering the men. Aeltar seemed to be in charge of the Half-Frankish part of the warband, and he passed the orders on as if they didn't matter until they came from

151

him. All sixty men were quickly armed and on their way to the beach. Ulestan knew where they would be going.

Accompanied by the shouting and clamor of sixty armed men going to war, three warships pushed away from the beach. With oars in the water, they headed out of the cove, around the point, and then straight north. By the time the sun started sinking to the port side, all three ships were pulling onto the seaward side of Wulfanwod's island. Folcwalda ordered the men to bring the ships into hiding on the shore and to remain out of sight. Then he, Ulestan, Eormen, Edmen, Aeltar and Swanfolgan started across the island. It was a short walk to the other side, and they arrived with enough daylight left to see clearly the island where Wulfanwod said the raiders had been landing.

To their disappointment, the beach looked empty. There were no ships to be seen anywhere, nor were there any fires or signs of activity. But raiders might not light fires, and ships could well be hidden. The island was too far away to see marks that would be left in the sand if a ship had been dragged onto shore. There could be a warband there . . . or it could be empty. Their hopes might be in vain. They simply had to wait and watch. From a hiding place off the beach, they stood silently and observed.

"Perhaps Wulfanwod has seen something," Ulestan said.

Aeltar's eyes lifted in sudden comprehension. "So that is how Folcwalda knows so much. I have heard of the crazed hermit but have never seen him. I had begun to believe him mere legend. I can see I was wrong."

In the fading light Ulestan couldn't tell whether Folcwalda was grinning or frowning, but whichever it was, it was savage. Yet he made no move to look for Wulfanwod. Perhaps he knew how the hermit would have responded to the invasion of his island. "We will wait," he said.

For a long time they did only that. Ulestan sat down, as did Aeltar. Folcwalda remained standing. Eormen and Edmen began to fidget impatiently, and Swanfolgan looked nervously over his shoulder in the direction of his ship. Then, just as the last bit of red was about to disappear over the horizon, both Ulestan and Folcwalda caught a glimpse of movement. A red glitter, like the sun reflecting off armor, appeared on the island's shoreline. It moved down the beach to the water for a moment, and then back into the woods.

"They are here," Aeltar hissed, "and Ecglaf will be avenged."

Folcwalda looked at Aeltar and nodded. "He will be avenged." Then he turned to the brothers. "Edmen and Eormen, remain here out of sight and keep an eye on that island. The moon is full tonight, and the sky is clear. You should see well enough. If there is any movement, notify us at once. Return at first light. We return now to prepare the warband."

Leaving Edmen and Eormen behind, Folcwalda led Ulestan, Swanfolgan and Aeltar back to the camp.

As Folcwalda had said, the night was bright—so bright that Ulestan was unable to sleep. At least he blamed his unrest on the brightness of the moon. Yet he knew that it was truly his own uneasiness that kept him awake. No number of battles could fully prepare him to enter another without some amount of fear. But the fear didn't bother him. What bothered him was that his fear kept him awake. Glancing around him, he noticed that many others of the warband were also awake, staring at the sky or tossing and turning. When he tired of pretending sleep, Ulestan rose and began to walk. He had no particular thought about where to go except that he desired to be away from the rest of the band. It grieved him to sleep in the company of men before a battle and to know that the next time some of them slept it would be the long sleep from which they would not awake. His walk therefore carried him away from the beach and the other men and into the middle of the island. A slight breeze was blowing from the south, and it seemed to carry with it a soft sound like conversation. Ulestan turned into the breeze and followed the sound as if it were more than just the wind.

He took only a few score steps across a clearing and up a slight rise and then came to an abrupt halt. Not fifty feet in front of him two men were standing in the middle of the clearing, gazing up at the stars. The wind blew gently down the slope, and the voices carried to him once more. They were indeed voices, he thought. He tried to discern the words but could not. He took a few steps forward. A twig snapped under his feet, and the two men turned to face him. Seeing him, one of the men turned immediately and headed in the other direction at a quick walk.

The taller of the two drew his sword with one quick motion and started down the hill toward Ulestan.

Ulestan stepped back and reached for his own blade. Only then did he realize that it still lay beside his blanket. He took another step backward as the stranger approached, brandishing a blade. A number of thoughts raced through Ulestan's mind. How had the raiders come unnoticed to the island? How could he warn Folcwalda? How could he escape? What was death like?

But another step revealed that it was Folcwalda himself approaching. Ulestan breathed a sigh of relief. "It is I, King Folcwalda," he said out loud.

Folcwalda recognized the voice and lowered his blade. "What brings you away from our camp?" he said more softly than Ulestan expected.

"I could not sleep, my lord," Ulestan replied.

Folcwalda nodded as if he understood. He turned and started walking back in the direction of the camp, motioning Ulestan to follow.

"You were with Wulfanwod?" Ulestan asked when he had matched his king's stride. He felt an uneasy silence and desired conversation.

"It was none other," Folcwalda answered. "I desired to speak with him 'ere the battle on the morrow."

"Why here in the meadow?"

"Wulfanwod also desired to speak with me. Unplanned, this is where we met."

Ulestan was not used to having Folcwalda answer questions so easily. "Did you learn what you wanted?"

Folcwalda breathed deeply. It was as close to a sigh as Ulestan had ever heard from him. "Yes and no. Rarely with Wulfanwod are his answers as direct as the questions asked of him. Yet, there is much wisdom to be gained from his words. This time, however, I did not come with many questions but simply to talk. You see, I too could not sleep. Are you surprised? Wulfanwod and I are old friends, and sometimes an old friend can accomplish what nothing or no one else can."

Ulestan nodded in agreement, though at the time he could not think of any old friends. "Do you fear tomorrow's battle?" he asked.

"Any battle is to be feared. He is a fool who does not fear

war." But a second later the High King continued, "Yet tomorrow I think we will have victory with little cost. Wulfanwod confirmed that there is but one ship on that island. Unless there are more Franks in other ships close at hand, we will have the enemy outnumbered with no place to flee."

They were almost back to the camp when Ulestan asked one more question. "When the battle is finished will we return home? If so, the voyage will be shorter than we had hoped."

"You will return home soon, yes," Folcwalda answered, "though it may not be tomorrow. We must still return to Domburg bearing the tidings of our victory. Yet in seven days' time you should be standing in Hwitstan."

"'We,' my king," Ulestan corrected, but Folcwalda had already turned aside to find his blanket.

Ulestan awoke as the first grey of dawn lit the sky above him. The rest of the warband was rising and silently making their preparations—girding their armor, testing the straps on their shields, strapping on helmets—and Eormen and Edmen were just now returning through the woods.

"There is no movement yet," Eormen announced loudly as he entered camp.

Folcwalda smiled, but gestured for them to lower their voices. When the warband was ready to depart, he gathered the men around him, both Frisians and Half-Franks. More than a few of them appeared scared, but Folcwalda's stature and voice drew them together. When they were together, he began to speak to them with bold words.

"Today will the death of Ecglaf, son of Ecgwalda be avenged, and not his death only but the death of all from Domburg who have fallen to the sword of the Franks. Today we will put an end to the raids which have spilled Frisian blood on the soil of Friesland. No more shall the Franks exact a toll on our people. The victory will be ours indeed. We shall show the strength and courage of Frisians in battle. But any victory, no matter how sure, must still be won. As the clash of blades draws near, let your soul grow stronger. Do not faint or fear, but let your swords be firm and your heart hardened for battle. We are brothers. Stand beside one another, and let us neither fall nor fail. Then we may return to the mead hall glad of heart to see the sun rise on another day. This blow we strike for Domburg, Hwitstan, and all of Friesland."

As one, sixty men raised their swords high in the air and let out a soundless shout. Without saying a word, they turned and headed to their warships. All three were soon off the beach and gliding through the water. Aeltar led one ship of Half-Franks, Edmen and Eormen led a second ship of the men from Domburg, and Folcwalda led his own warband with Swanfolgan and Ulestan. It would now be only a short passing of time, a score of scores of heartbeats, until swords would clash. Ulestan stiffened in anticipation.

Folcwalda's ship rounded the point first and came into full view of the beach where the Franks had landed. It was followed within seconds by the other two. Ulestan sat close to the front of the ship so he would be able to get out quickly. There was still no sight of enemy guards. That was good. Their hope was to come as close to the island as they could without being seen. Once on shore, they should have an easy victory.

The oars dug into the water, and the craft moved swiftly. Ulestan could hear the clear hiss of the bow shearing smoothly through the low waves. One third of the distance was crossed, and Ulestan watched the approaching shore expectantly. They could be seen at any time, and the Franks would begin mustering to prevent the ships' landing.

Halfway to the shore, there was still no sign of movement in the Frankish camp. Hope rose in Ulestan's chest. Perhaps they would come by surprise and their landing would not be opposed. They were swiftly crossing the distance.

Just then a lone man appeared out of the trees at the edge of the beach. He didn't see them as he walked along the edge of the trees for a few steps and then started toward the water. The sun was rising directly over the island, and its rays were just touching the heads of the taller men in the ship. Sailing into the sun, it was difficult for Ulestan to see ahead. But he could see well enough. The Frankish warrior on the beach lifted his head. He saw the approaching ships, but for a split second he hesitated, not knowing what to do.

"That is good," Folcwalda said softly. "He doesn't know our purpose. He is waiting to see if we see him. He knows that if he yells, he will only call attention to himself."

Another thirty heartbeats, Ulestan was thinking. They would be there in just a few short oar strokes. The men near the front of the ship pulled their oars in and drew their blades, preparing to jump as soon as they reached the shallow water. The sun caught the metal blades and sent a bright reflection back to the beach.

"Beware," the lone man on the beach shouted to his comrades as he ran toward the woods. "To arms! We are discovered." His call came too late.

Three ships slid neatly onto shore just as the first Franks emerged from the woods carrying their spears and swords. Four of them rushed down the beach without waiting for the others. Edmen and Eormen strode up to meet them, flanked on either side by five Half-Franks. The leading Frank was off-balance as he met Eormen's blade. He threw his shield up in defense, but Eormen caught it and pushed it aside long enough for his sword to pierce the enemy's neck. Edmen deflected two furious blows with his shield and then countered. One blow and his opponent staggered backward. A second blow and he was on his knees. Their swords met and clashed. Only Edmen's held. His enemy's shattered, and the momentum of Edmen's blow carried his blade deep into the side of his foe's neck. The other two Franks fared no better. Outnumbered five to one, they fell quickly. One spear missed its mark, and its wielder had no second chance. The last Frankish spear found a target. But even as a Frisian warrior fell pierced, four more jumped forward and avenged their friend.

The rest of the Franks were not so foolish. They gathered in the trees at the edge of the beach but did not advance. There were at least twenty of them, but not many more. They would not be cut down one at a time.

The rest of the Frisian army gathered as well. For a few long seconds the two armies faced one another. Folcwalda's men were all out of their ships now, and they began to move slowly up the beach, forming three wedge-shaped walls with their shields held in front of them. While they were on the beach and their enemy was in the woods they were vulnerable—though not as vulnerable as if they had had to attack from the water. Even as Ulestan thought this, five Franks stepped forward, and a loud *twang* announced the release of arrows. One flew high, and three were caught in the shields. One found a mark, and a second of Aeltar's men fell with an arrow in his leg. Another volley was fired, but found no gaps in the shields. Then, at a word from Folcwalda, the attack began. The Franks didn't have time to shoot again as sixty men ran the last few steps up the beach.

Instantly the sound of sword on sword hammered through the woods. Ulestan was able to watch for just a moment, and then he was in the fray. A large Frankish warrior decided to make Ulestan his target and managed to plant himself in front of the thane's charge. He was slightly taller than Ulestan and a bit younger, and the way he held his shield and sword indicated more than a little strength. Not waiting for Ulestan to strike the first blow, his sword hammered down a hard blow which Ulestan took squarely on his shield as he staggered back a step. And the enemy didn't relent. Blow after blow was levied, causing Ulestan to retreat a step at a time until he found himself having to keep his footing in soft sand while fighting uphill against a taller opponent who had firm soil beneath him. The Franks may have been outnumbered, but at the moment there was no help in sight for Ulestan. Yet he was a battle-hardened warrior. He had fought with the Britons against the Saxons, had dealt blows to Franks and Jutes, and had more than once faced the battle-axes of the northern tribes. Shifting his weight to his left foot, he pushed forward with all the strength of his legs and, using his shield as an offensive weapon, thrust it up underneath his enemy's shield, knocking his enemy's shield into his face. With his remaining strength and balance, he swung his sword underneath his shield and felt it hit home. It was not a great swing because the main thrust of Ulestan's strength had been thrown into his shield, but it was enough to cut through his enemy's leather leg protection and to draw blood.

The Frank, however, recovered quickly and threw his own weight back down on top of Ulestan. He seemed not even to notice his wound. Ulestan staggered back for a minute, and they were separated. Blood flowed from a deep cut under the enemy's eye where his own shield had caught him in the face. Ulestan was still unscathed. Then the battle was rejoined, and the Frisian warrior was parrying another blow with his sword. His opponent attacked fiercely, and Ulestan had to fight completely defensively. He had no chance to return any blows. One of the enemy blows was bound to catch him soon if he did not prevent it. But he was having a hard time moving and keeping his balance in the soft sand. The advantage was not his. He must either gain more solid ground or lure the enemy onto the sand with him.

Ulestan took three sudden steps backward, being careful not to lose his own footing. Thinking that Ulestan was retreating, a look of triumph spread across the Frank's face. He advanced to fill the gap. As soon as his feet sunk into the sand, however, he lost some of his balance and stumbled. Ulestan used the opportunity to level a heavy blow at his enemy's head. Off-balance, the Frank's shield came up instinctively to block the blow. As it did, his vision was momentarily cut off. Ulestan stepped quickly to the side. The Frank swung his blade wildly toward where Ulestan had stood when he had last looked. But Ulestan was no longer there, and the Frankish blade cut through the empty air. The warrior stumbled forward, and as he did he felt Ulestan's blade stabbing through his left side.

XIV

Pledge Redeemed

The remainder of the battle did not last long. The host from Domburg fought as men who remembered each raid and every life they had lost to the hated Franks. They fought with vengeance and determination, not wont to show pity.

And the Franks were outnumbered from the start. They were a raiding party and did not expect open confrontation. There were three men to their every one. With little hope did they begin the battle. Yet even when their ranks were reduced to ten and then five and finally only one, they did not surrender. To the last man they fought, and his parting blade stroke took one of Folcwalda's men with him to the grave. They did not sue for mercy.

That Ulestan did not understand. Why hadn't the Franks surrendered when their defeat was so sure? If the Franks had been fighting on their own soil to defend their native lands, they would have had reason to fight to the death. But they were raiders fighting for spoil, not a king's hearthwerod defending his hall. Did they fight on only because they had no hope for mercy? Or did they have some other hope? The questions troubled the thane.

Though the fighting had ended before mid-morning, it was late in the day before Folcwalda's warhost was ready to leave the island and return to Domburg. The injured were attended to and the slain counted. In all, the king's host had suffered only seven deaths, six of which were men of Domburg. Swanfolgan had received a cracked rib, but was able to walk. Many others had suffered injuries as well—injuries which would cause some pain for a time but would eventually heal. These were common losses in battle, small compared to the damage done to the enemy. And Ulestan was unscathed. If a battle could ever be successful, surely this one had been, he thought.

That this was the same warband which had raided the outlying village the day before was proven a short time after the battle. A store of the spoils from that raid was discovered near the Frankish ship hidden in the bushes by the shore. "A small recompense for the lives lost," Aeltar said when the treasure was returned to him. "Yet Ecgwalda shall be glad of its return. No doubt is there now that these were the enemy."

Added to the spoils were many jewels and treasures taken from the Franks. Many Danish coins were found among the Frankish warhoard in their ships, and good weapons as well, hard swords tested in battle. These Folcwalda claimed for his own by his right as High King.

In all of the treasure found only one thing was missing. Nowhere was found among the fallen a chieftain's torc. This too Ulestan thought odd, and he said so to Folcwalda.

"It may be that their chieftain wore no torc;" Edmen said. "A torc marks the neck for a sword."

"Or it may be that their chieftain was not present," Ulestan replied. "Where might he have been?"

"Or there may have been no great chieftain among them. These are raiders seeking plunder, not an honored warband of Chlotar's," Folcwalda said, ending the conversation.

That evening three ships returned to Domburg to celebrate the victory over their oppressors. There was laughter of warriors, shared mead, and cheerful song as Folcwalda's warband joined with Ecgwalda's thanes beside the hearth. Many stout-hearted warriors gathered in the hall that night to hear the tale told by Eormen of the victory over the Franks and of Folcwalda's might in battle.

Ecgwalda spoke after he had heard of the avenging of his son's death. He praised his own men highly, and none missed the words he spoke of Folcwalda's conquest of the enemy. "Long have I endured hardship from this hateful foe. Many griefs have been laid upon me. No longer does my son walk the world beside me. I have been deprived of my heir. Now by great deeds and acts of courage have we been delivered. By the wisdom of Folcwalda—wisdom given by the gods themselves—strife has ended. My son is avenged. Let none now doubt that Folcwalda is High King indeed." And before all his men Ecgwalda knelt before Folcwalda.

Folcwalda then laid upon the lap of his new servant the greatest of war-swords taken from the hoard gained from the Franks. Addressing king and people, he announced, "Indeed we have achieved works of courage and gone boldly against the strength of our enemy. Let peace now reign in your land. As you are a faithful servant to your king, so shall your king be to his people."

Then Ecgwalda rose and praised his men further and gave gifts freely and generously to his thanes and earls. None of his servants could complain about their chieftain that night. Yet Ulestan could not help but notice, nor did he wonder why, that even in the midst of the victory celebration there was no joy in Ecgwalda's eyes. The ruler acted dutifully as a good chieftain, yet in his heart knew that no victory could return his son to him. Nor was he alone in his grief. Four young wives and twice as many children mourned that night the loss of their husbands and fathers in battle. Ulestan had no heart for a celebration that night. He was a warrior, and as a warrior he knew that to return from battle alive was reason enough for joy. Yet a dark foreboding filled the good thane's thoughts. He had seen enough battles in his life to be tired of them. To fight for his king was noble. Yet, to celebrate the loss of lives, even those of enemies, did not lift his spirits. Ulestan stayed in the hall that night, not in joy, but dutifully as a good thane should, at the side of his king.

Folcwalda, the good king, made his presence known that night and was generous in the giving of gifts both to his own thanes and warriors and to those of Domburg. Though the hall was not his, he assumed for himself the role of High King, and Ecgwalda did not contest this. In that one thing Ulestan rejoiced—that honor was now given to Folcwalda. No longer was he an enemy in Domburg, but a king instead. Far and wide had he journeyed, and his wisdom and courage were long known to all. But now his might had come to the aid of these men, and they would not quickly forget.

When the tales had been told and gifts given, then Ecgwalda's poet rose and began to sing. He sang first of the day's victory, which he had already put into song, as Daelga himself might have done. Then he continued with other tales until long after dark while the wine and mead flowed freely.

The following morning, to Ulestan's disappointment, they did not begin the return voyage to Hwitstan. Nor did they the following day. Folcwalda had decided instead to remain in Domburg for a time. He would travel with Ecgwalda and give his own men a chance to recover from their battle wounds and travel weariness. Accompanied by Eormen, Edmen, Ulestan, Aeltar, and one of Ecgwalda's older thanes named Ulfhere, Folcwalda and Ecgwalda spent the next fortnight traveling the lands under Ecgwalda's care. The village of Domburg was situated on a long peninsula on the southern part of the bay at the mouth of the Meuse River. The company traveled by horseback all the way up the peninsula, stopping at various smaller villages as they went, and then to the north side of the bay. When they had seen those lands and spoken to many of Ecgwalda's earls and clan chieftains, they explored the bay itself and the multitude of small islands which dotted it.

As they traveled, Folcwalda's eyes scanned the land like a hawk's. At certain places he would call for a halt and ride up hillsides, or he would dismount and pace the ground. All the time he was making comments to Ecgwalda about the defense of Domburg and how it could be changed into a much greater trading center. "A watchtower should be built here," he would say, or "A series of signal towers atop these hills would help you watch your villages and aid them in the event of further raids."

By the time they returned to the village of Domburg, Ecgwalda and Folcwalda had become great friends. So also had Ulestan and Aeltar. Though neither spoke often, when they did they understood one another well—almost intuitively. Aeltar, too, had been married once. His wife had died during the cold winter four years ago, leaving a young son in Aeltar's care. Aelfin was now entering his tenth year. "Already he handles a sword well," Aeltar claimed with pride, "not like a toy, but with strength like a man!"

While they had been gone, Swanfolgan had seen to the reprovisioning of their ship. Long before Folcwalda's return, those who remained were ready to depart. But Folcwalda's warband would not leave Domburg alone, for Ecgwalda proved true to his word, even going beyond his pledge of twenty warriors.

Twenty and five warriors and a sound ship were provisioned from Ecgwalda's purse. They would join Folcwalda in Hwitstan. The warband of the High King would grow by twenty-five shield bearers and a good and noble thane. Aeltar himself was being sent to serve Folcwalda and to command the host from Domburg. Twenty and four warriors would travel with him. The remaining one would journey with Folcwalda, filling the seat left vacant by means of a Frankish sword.

Along with the thane and warriors there traveled a young child. Seeing Aeltar's reluctance to leave Aelfin behind, Ulestan had spoken a good word in the ear of his king. By the invitation of Folcwalda himself, Aeltar was to bring his son. Aelfin would be raised and trained in the house of Folcwalda. No greater news could the brave Aeltar have heard, and that much more did it increase his loyalty to his new king.

So the plan for departure was laid. Two mornings after Folcwalda's return to Domburg, his warband made ready to sail to Hwitstan. Their ship was to leave first so Folcwalda could stop and speak with Wulfanwod as he had promised. Aeltar would come a short time later with the host from Domburg. They would meet at Wulfanwod's northern beach and afterward sail together.

It was in high spirits that Folcwalda's men left the hall at Domburg. Parting words had already been spoken, and a second feast had been held by the hearth. More treasure was given by the kings, and their thanes were richer for it. Ecgwalda had blessed the parting with a great gift-giving. Gold rings as well as swords were given in abundance to those who had gained the victory, and especially to those in his warband who were now going to serve Folcwalda in Hwitstan.

"We have far to go and desire to see our home once again," spoke Folcwalda to his new thane Ecgwalda when the evening waned. "Much we have accomplished. The kingdom of Friesland grows stronger each day, not the least from the good men who sail with me on the morrow. And you have the token of the sword and coin. If on earth the High King may once more help his servant, let the coin be your sign. It shall not go unheeded. Nor shall I forget your pledge. These twenty and six warriors are but a symbol. Shall Friesland need more, then must Domburg answer the call, be Ecgwalda their chieftain or not."

"Great is your strength and wise your words," Ecgwalda replied. "If spear or sword shall take you from us, then Friesland has lost a good king indeed. No better could we choose as guardian, as you have proved by your noble actions, saving my people from the hand of our oppressors. You have brought peace. As long as I rule the kingdom, my sword is yours."

Folcwalda's warband had won a victory, had feasted at Domburg, and had rested well from their wounds. Now they were eager for their homes. The band of brave ones came to the beach where their ship was waiting. Never had Folcwalda seemed more confident to the eyes of Ulestan than he did now as their ship slid into the sea. With Domburg's allegiance having finally been given, Friesland was one.

A cold wind was blowing down from the north as they rowed out of the small cove and turned toward home. Then the reality of the coming sea voyage became once more clear to all. More than a few sighs of protest were heard as the oars were put into the water to work against the wind. "If you wish to journey south and visit the lands of the Franks," Swanfolgan yelled at those whose protests were loudest, "then we can surely pull in the oars and raise our sail." That was the only comment required to stifle the complaints. None were eager to travel any farther south, for all thoughts were of home. Slowly, for the wind against them was strong, progress was made. They reached Wic by Wulfanwod by midday.

Folcwalda once more left his small warband with the ship and went to visit his friend. He took with him Ulestan, Eormen and Edmen, who was eager to see the hermit's dwelling of which he had heard.

"It is quiet today," Ulestan commented a few moments after they had left the beach. Edmen and Eormen were talking too loudly among themselves to notice, but Folcwalda nodded his head in agreement. The birds that had filled the woods on their first visit were strangely absent.

"I am still curious about the battle," Ulestan said, trying to begin a conversation with his king. When he mentioned the battle, Edmen and Eormen stopped their own talk and listened.

"What troubles you?" Folcwalda asked, though his thoughts seemed to be elsewhere.

"Why didn't the Franks surrender? What did they hope to gain from fighting to the death?"

"Their honor," Eormen and Edmen answered in unison as if the answer were obvious.

"Yet, these were servants of Chlotar, were they not? Were they men of honor? And we saw no chieftain's torc among their fallen," Ulestan reminded them. "You have spoken of Chlotar as a kinslayer, murderer and thief. Isn't he more likely to deal in subtle deceit and treachery than in open battle?"

"Perhaps so," Folcwalda said. Ulestan could tell he had the king's attention now. "So what conclusion do you draw?"

Ulestan thought for a moment and shrugged. He could not take his reasoning any farther. "Only that it seems to me strange," he finally answered.

Folcwalda nodded, and the four of them continued walking. The conversation ceased, and a sullen silence took hold of them all as they crossed the meadow and ascended the long slope. Before long they were at the top of the hill, looking down from above at Wulfanwod's little dwelling. The island's sole human inhabitant had not yet appeared.

Folcwalda and his thanes walked unhurriedly down the path. When they reached the hut, the king called for Wulfanwod. There was no answer. For the first time that day, his look of confidence and joy faded. Where was his friend? With clear concern showing on his face, he strode to the entrance of the hut and pushed aside the skins. The king took one step inside, then froze.

Ulestan, Edmen and Eormen pressed forward at once and looked past their king. The sight brought grief to all, though to none more than to Folcwalda.

Lying on the stone floor in a puddle of his own blood was Wulfanwod the hermit. Sword wounds covered the body of the once-mighty king. His left arm had been nearly severed at the shoulder. Blood still dribbled from a gaping wound in the side of his skull. His right hand clutched futilely at his ash staff—a gift from Folcwalda himself years earlier. A staff! Wulfanwod had no sword to defend himself. His body was still warm, the blood still wet. The remains of his left hand yet held the wool cloak Folcwalda had given him just a fortnight earlier, now slashed to pieces. Wulfanwod had used a cloak for a shield. Futility against swords!

Ulestan's heart rose to his mouth, and he turned his head away. Though he had seen death and dying times without count, his stomach rose to his mouth. Were the birds in mourning too? Was that why they were so silent today?

Folcwalda fell to his knees beside his old friend. Tears were already streaming down his face as he pulled the tattered remains of the wool cloak from Wulfanwod's hand and placed it over his body. Ulestan had never seen his king cry. Tears were streaming from his own eyes as well. Eormen and Edmen turned around quickly and stepped out into the fresh air while Folcwalda knelt with his face hanging over the body of his friend. His tears fell to the floor and mingled with Wulfanwod's spilt blood. Ulestan stood beside his king and wept with him.

For a long time nobody moved or spoke.

Then, very gently Folcwalda picked up his old friend in his arms and carried him outside. He bore him as if he weighed nothing. Ulestan picked up the staff, still whole, and followed his king. Weeping, Folcwalda set his friend on a raised rock beside his hut. He carefully folded Wulfanwod's right arm across his chest. Ulestan set the staff gently across his body, while Folcwalda knelt beside him holding his maimed left arm.

Eormen and Edmen began to gather rocks for a mound. A sudden thought struck Ulestan . "Lord Folcwalda . . ." he said as gently as he could. Folcwalda did not look up.

"Lord Folcwalda," Ulestan said again, more urgently, "his body is still warm. The blood is wet."

Now Folcwalda looked back at his thane. A fierce fire began to smoulder in his eyes.

An answering light arose in Ulestan's eyes—a glimmer not of loss or revenge, but of knowledge. "My lord Folcwalda," he said a third time, "there is but one reason the Frankish warhost did not surrender."

Folcwalda's eyes phrased the question more clearly than his voice. *Why?*

"They were expecting companions—a greater warband to fight beside them. They must have been expecting them soon, or they would not have risked their lives. And it must have been a large warband, large enough to have turned the tide of the battle." Ulestan finally understood. "The Franks we defeated were not alone—at least, they were not meant to be."

"Swanfolgan," Folcwalda whispered as he rose to his feet. Not another word was spoken. At once the king and his thanes were racing over the top of the rise and back down the hill toward the beach where they had left the warband. The trip seemed to take forever. None doubted that battle awaited them. Ulestan was short of breath and stumbling before he was halfway across the meadow. He ran on anyway, trying to keep pace with Folcwalda.

They heard the sounds of battle many heartbeats before they came in sight of the beach. When he heard the first clash of swords, Ulestan's mind raced ahead of his feet. How large was the enemy host? What would Folcwalda do when he reached the beach? Was Swanfolgan still alive? Was there any hope? He had little time to think, but in the time he had, his imagination bordered on panic. What would they find?

When he stepped upon the beach and saw the scene before him, his fears were realized. Folcwalda's warband, led by Swanfolgan, had formed a tight circle with their backs to each other. They were surrounded by at least forty Franks who formed an impassable barrier around them. And the Franks were slowly but surely bringing the wall down on the outnumbered Frisians. Already five of Folcwalda's men lay slain. Only twelve remained fighting. One of these was Swanfolgan, whose ribs were still so tender from the previous fight he could barely swing his sword. Yet he valiantly defended himself while shouting orders and encouragement to his men.

Ulestan had no more time to think. Without slowing his pace, Folcwalda charged down the beach with three thanes in his wake. He drew his sword as he ran, and only at the last second did he shout his battle cry. At that fearsome sound the closest Franks turned in fear to see the Frisian High King and three of his mightiest thanes bearing down on them in wrath. Nine fell quickly to the swords of Folcwalda, Ulestan, Eormen and Edmen in their first assault. The rest fell away like water. The king was quickly through their ranks and rejoined with his men. A loud cheer broke forth from their midst. Hope was theirs again.

But no sooner had Folcwalda and his thanes broken through the wall but it closed behind them with fresh men. The entire Frisian warhost was surrounded!

"Well timed, my lord," Swanfolgan wheezed. "I am sorry I have failed you so."

"You have done well, my friend," Folcwalda said loudly enough that all would hear. "Now let us turn the tide against these swine."

And for a time it appeared that they would. Pulling his injured sea-chief into the center of the circle, Folcwalda stepped forward to fill the gap. With Ulestan on his left and Edmen and Eormen at his back, he faced his foe unafraid. Anger and blood-lust burned within him as he thought of his fallen friend. He fought with the strength of ten, raining down blows of such power that none could stand against him. His very presence gave his men renewed courage and might to turn back the blades of their enemies—enemies who perhaps felt fear for the first time that day. Hard and well fought the warband of Folcwalda against overpowering odds. None could find fault in their courage and bravery.

Angered at the sudden appearance of Folcwalda, the Franks redoubled their attack. On they came with greater intensity, seeking the blood of their enemy. Some, careless and foolish, threw themselves immediately against the mighty Folcwalda. And these fell quickly. From then until the battle was over, Ulestan saw nothing but the flash of swords just in front of them. He turned aside thrust after thrust, felling two Frankish attackers while gravely wounding a third. And for every sword thrust that Ulestan gave, it seemed to him that his king gave two—and with greater strength. Franks were falling away from him as if they were clothes he was shedding. Five lay at his feet within minutes. And yet the Frisians were still outnumbered at least two men to one, and the circle was beginning to collapse on all sides. He and Folcwalda were forced to take steps backward, not to retreat from their own opponents, but to keep the circle tight, for three more of their companions had fallen.

Further, more Franks kept coming. They, too, were avenging the loss of kinsmen. Ulestan knew in his heart that they would offer no mercy. He knew this from the way they had slaughtered Wulfanwod, defenseless though he was. The entire warband knew that the Franks they had defeated had not sought mercy, and these would not offer it. So, despite their weariness and their small hope for victory, the Frisians fought on with no thought of surrender. But Ulestan, too, was growing tired. Every enemy he cut down was replaced by a fresh new body. He had not even regained his breath after racing across the island.

Then, out of the corner of his eye, Ulestan saw Folcwalda stagger. Sudden fear came over him for his king. Blood appeared on Folcwalda's shoulder, and his sword tip dropped suddenly. This could not be! Sensing victory, the Frank who had inflicted the injury pressed ahead. He did not see Ulestan's sword rise in his king's defense until it was too late and Ulestan's blade pierced his neck. Yet the thane's defense of his king was not without cost to himself. As his eye left his own enemy, that warrior took advantage and aimed a blow at Ulestan's unprotected left side. The thane lifted his shield too slowly. He deflected the blow well enough to save his life, but felt the keen edge of the blade cutting deeply into his thigh as it glanced off his shield. Then Ulestan's sword slid out of the Frank's neck and he was defending himself again, ignoring the pain. The warrior jabbed suddenly. Ulestan let his enemy's blade slide harmlessly into the edge of his own wooden shield. It was an old trick. He wrenched his shield back and pulled his enemy's sword and arm with it. With one swing the arm was severed at the elbow, and the man fell away with a scream.

Ulestan looked back the other way in concern for the High King, but Folcwalda had recovered. He was once more fighting furiously despite the blood spilling from his wounded shoulder. Another cut opened on his forearm, but he ignored it, and yet another attacker collapsed before him. The circle closed some more, and Ulestan noticed another of his companions fallen on his left. Swanfolgan left the relative protection of the center of the ring to fill the open gap. *He will not last long, injured as he is*, Ulestan remembered thinking later.

Then, as it had in the past, Folcwalda's voice rose loud among the clash of blades. In the midst of battle the king's soul was felt among his men, and their courage was renewed by the brave words of their proud battlechief:

> *"Courage shall be harder,*
> *Heart shall be keener,*
> *Mind shall be stronger,*
> *As your strength lessens."*

Every man among Folcwalda's followers hearkened to those words, and their strength if not their hope was renewed. For a time the Franks found themselves beaten slowly back. Folcwalda's warband would make their enemy pay dearly for seeking the death of their king. Yet though their courage was great, their strength and energy could not be maintained.

Ulestan took the flat of a shield against the knuckle of his sword hand. Pain shot up his arm, and he almost lost his grip. The strength in his hand suddenly vanished. There was nothing to be done. He adjusted his grip and fought on, once more ignoring the pain. He looked about him and saw that his companions were once again pressed to their limits.

Folcwalda staggered again. This time he fell to his knee. The Franks cheered. *What is happening?* Ulestan wondered. *Is this not the great Folcwalda? Is he defeated so?* Only Ulestan's quick response saved his king's life. He literally threw himself in the way as a sword swung toward the king's unprotected neck. The enemy screamed to find his fallen prey taken away from him. The blow would have severed head from body had not Ulestan caught it on his shield. The force of the blow sent Ulestan, who was already off-balance, lurching to the side. When he looked up, Folcwalda was on his feet again, and the Frank was on his back with his skull cracked. But Folcwalda's leg was bleeding profusely, and his shield hung limply from his side.

He will not last long, was Ulestan's last thought before a blow caught the side of his head. Suddenly it was night, and he was unconscious before he hit the ground.

Folcwalda saw his thane fallen, and a new fury came upon him. Ulestan did not see the mighty sword-swing of his renowned king, the swing that severed head from body of the one who had struck his thane down. Nor did he see the enemy sword stroke which shattered the blade of the High King. The old sword which had served Folcwalda well in the past failed him now. Ulestan did not see Folcwalda fight on with a shattered hilt.

Ulestan also did not see Aeltar landing with his warband a few moments later. He missed the surprise on the faces of the Franks as they suddenly found themselves surrounded. Folcwalda's warband had exacted such a cost on them that they had not the strength to face the fresh warriors from Domburg. The Franks' numbers had dwindled. Only ten and five of the once large Frankish host remained, many of whom were injured. Of the Frisians, only five were still standing with Folcwalda when Aeltar arrived. Edmen and Eormen still stood almost unscathed. Swanfolgan had taken Ulestan's place beside his king. He no longer held his shield, but grasped his sword in both hands and swung it in crossing circles just well enough to preserve his life. And the lone seaman from Domburg who had been sent by Ecgwalda stood on Folcwalda's other side.

XV

Home at Last

Ulestan awoke late that night. Consciousness came to him slowly—like the dawn, but infinitely more painful. His head pounded. Thousands of swords were piercing his skull. And all was black. When he gained enough awareness to realize he was still alive, his eyes were slow to focus. He thought he had been blinded. He gasped for breath. Pain shot through his leg, through his eyes, through his entire body. Points of light began to appear . . . Blurred images. It was night—dark, cloudy, moonless. A fire burned somewhere off to the left—a few feet, or was it a few miles away? He could not tell. His eyes would not focus, but he could hear. The groans of wounded men filled the air. So he was not alone. That was good. Or was it? Who was about him? The Franks?

Fear filled his thoughts. Folcwalda? Eormen? Edmen? Were they still alive? He tried to sit, but pain shot up his spine like an arrow.

He lost consciousness again.

When he awoke next, it was morning. The tide was high. The surf was pulling him under. He was drowning but could not move. He spat water from his mouth and gasped for air . . .

Ulestan opened his eyes and dimly saw the form of Aeltar kneeling beside him with a cup of water. Aeltar's expression was determined but not unkind. Ulestan stared back at him blankly. It took him another moment to realize that he was on solid ground and could stop struggling.

"You are fortunate to be alive, my friend," Aeltar said. Ulestan did not feel at all fortunate. His grimaces reflected his discomfort. "When I arrived, I thought you were dead. You nearly were. A Frank was standing over you with a swordpoint not far from your neck. Fortunately my men are good bowmen."

Ulestan tried to nod his thanks. He wondered if his communication succeeded. His stomach had risen to his throat, and he felt too nauseous to talk.

"Here . . ." Aeltar gave him the cup of water. Ulestan finished it quickly and hoped for more. "That was quite a blow that put you out," Aeltar continued, reaching up toward the back of Ulestan's skull. He touched a tender lump, and Ulestan winced.

"Folcwalda?" Ulestan finally asked. "Is he alive?"

"Alive," Aeltar answered, but he was shaking his head sadly. "Yes, he still lives, but only barely. This battle did not go well with him. He bears injuries which would have killed five lesser men. And yet he breathes still. But if truth be known," he added in a barely audible voice, "he will be lucky if he lives to see Hwitstan again."

Ulestan was filled with dismay. "Who is with him?" he asked quickly.

"Eormen is with him now."

"Only Eormen?" Ulestan asked, wondering if Edmen had been killed.

"And Edmen as well," Aeltar added. "They are both well. Folcwalda himself is conscious and eager to be going."

"Why are we waiting?" Ulestan asked as he struggled to get to his feet. The effort was beyond him, and he collapsed grimacing. For a moment everything went black. "Why are we waiting?" he asked again, more softly.

Aeltar looked back at him as if the answer were obvious in Ulestan's own weakness. But mercy moved him, and he said nothing of Ulestan's condition. "We wait while our dead are buried and the wounded tended," he answered.

And while the wounded and dying breathe their last, Ulestan thought. He had been in battle before. He remembered well the horrible deaths of the injured, though he often tried to forget. None who had ever watched perish the victim of sword or axe could ever claim that war was glorious.

Then Ulestan examined his own body, wondering what awful wounds he himself had received. The pain in his head made him fear the worst. For a horrible moment, while he struggled to rise, he could not feel his legs. What had happened to them? He was relieved to find that except for the cruel lump on his head and a deep gash above his left knee he was unharmed. The wounds had already been washed and bound. He tenderly felt his leg and slowly bent it to test its strength. Movement was painful, but the muscle still worked.

"Take me to Folcwalda," Ulestan demanded. "I need to see my king before he dies."

Aeltar was a thane himself; they understood each other well. He helped Ulestan, who fought back the nausea as he struggled to his feet. Half supporting himself and half leaning on his companion, the thane went to see his dying king. The sight was worse than Ulestan imagined. Folcwalda was sitting up, leaning against a rock with a pile of cloaks for a cushion. He was covered head to foot with wounds, some almost as deep as his bones. The worst had been tended, but there were so many that the king seemed to be bleeding everywhere. His visage was grim and determined. It was obvious that by sheer force of will the king was suppressing the pain and keeping himself alive. Edmen and Eormen were not there anymore.

"Ulestan, my friend," Folcwalda said before his thane had a chance to speak. "It is good to see you well!" His left arm hung limply at his side, but his right made weak gestures as he spoke. Tears came to Ulestan's eyes. "Twice in this battle you saved my life that I might live to command but a time longer—to avenge the death of Wulfanwod on yet one more enemy." *For naught*, Ulestan thought to himself. "I am thankful, my good friend. No better thane could a king ask for. It caused me great pain to see you fall. I am glad you are on your feet again." The king coughed uncontrollably for a minute. Blood trickled out his mouth and down his chin.

"My king, I would gladly have died for you!" Ulestan said. With all his heart he meant it.

"You may still have the chance," Folcwalda smiled weakly. He coughed again, and more blood came out. "I fear, however, that I will not be fighting again." Ulestan did not argue. His king was too noble for Ulestan to deny the truth.

"Thus I have a favor to ask of you," Folcwalda continued.

"You are my king," Ulestan argued. "You need only command!" To see his king so humbled distressed the thane deeply.

A great king need not ask favors of his thanes. It was his to grant favor to them. The king was the treasure-giver.

"This I ask as a friend and not as your king," he said kindly.

Tears flowed freely down Ulestan's face. "It is already given," was all he could say.

"You have served me well," Folcwalda said. "Serve my son. His burden will be great."

Ulestan nodded his answer as Edmen and Eormen came striding up the beach.

"All is as you commanded, my king," Eormen reported, bowing. "The ships are ready to depart."

"How many of us?" Folcwalda asked.

"We are eight," Edmen replied. "Aeltar still commands his full host."

"Aeltar's men will sail both ships," Eormen added. "Though it will be slow with so few men to man the oars for two ships, the wounded will need too much room for us to attempt the journey in one."

"Then let us depart," Folcwalda commanded. Even as he was dying, his voice held great authority.

"My lord king," Aeltar said, "the bodies of the fallen have been lain in the ships."

"Put them to sea in honor."

"And the Franks?"

"Set them to flame." Folcwalda spit blood. "See that their foul carcasses do not despoil the kingdom of Wulfanwod."

Aeltar nodded and turned away. Ulestan was left to support himself while the once-proud king was half carried and half dragged down to the water's edge. To see his king carried so . . . Ulestan bit his lip. After the torch had been set to the funeral pyres of the Franks and the Frisians had been put to rest in honor, the two ships and the remainder of the warband slid out to sea.

The voyage to Hwitstan was slow and arduous. The wind blew strong against them throughout the journey. Eormen had been right; there were too few men to effectively man the oars on two ships. Yet they had no choice.

By the end of the third day, Folcwalda was on the verge of delirium. They had barely covered half the distance to Hwitstan. Only the mounds of furs stacked on top of the dying king kept the chills away, and even that only partially. As they traveled, the

High King drifted in and out of consciousness. When conscious, he spoke little or not at all, asking only how much longer the voyage was. He was only barely able to eat the small morsels of food given to him. And he could not assuage his thirst. When he was unconscious, he spoke in a fevered dream. At times his dreams were simple delirium—unintelligible ravings which his loyal followers tried not to hear. At other times he seemed almost lucid, speaking clearly and coherently to his son Finn, who was not there. "Treat your thanes well," he kept saying. "They are your heart and soul."

Toward the end of the fourth day, a huge storm blew up from the east. The ships were forced to the shore. The gale raged all the next day and into the morning of the day after—the sixth since the battle. Eormen and Edmen and two of the Half-Franks were able to hunt some rabbit. Though it was appreciated, it did little to raise the spirits of the men. Folcwalda grew progressively worse. Ulestan didn't know how the king continued to breathe, but he did. The storm passed over and continued on into the west, and the journey continued at midday on the sixth day. Only the faint rise and fall of Folcwalda's chest showed that he was still alive as they placed him back on the ship. When he was awakened to be fed or given water, he took what was given him but said nothing. The dreams and illusions were gone; he had ceased talking with Finn. Now he looked like a man already dead.

The long-absent ship arrived on the beaches of Hwitstanwic on the evening of the eighth day after the battle. More than a month after he left, the great king had returned to his home. His task had been accomplished. His lifelong vision was complete. His duty was fulfilled.

The two ships were spotted from the tower as they rowed back into the bay. Folcwalda's great war-shield hung from the bow of his vessel. Next to it and on the bow of the other ship were hung the shields of Ulestan, Edmen, Eormen and Aeltar. From atop Finnweard the guards recognized all but one. At once a messenger was dispatched to the village to proclaim the good tidings. The other watchman came down to the beach to greet his king. When he saw Folcwalda he almost fainted. He looked in turn from Ulestan to Eormen to Edmen and then back to Ulestan. None of them spoke a word. The guard looked about him. The other men getting out of the ships were Half-Franks. This was not the same warband that had set out. He knew not what to do.

Then Folcwalda regained his consciousness. He wondered why the rocking of the ship had stopped. He opened his eyes on Hwitstanwic . . . and did not recognize it.

Ulestan saw his king's vacant stare. "You have returned," he said quietly.

A look of comprehension returned to Folcwalda's eyes, and he smiled. For the final time was granted him the chance to think clearly. "Carry me to the shade, that I may look upon the sea."

With all honor and respect his command was carried out. "Where is Finn?" he asked the guard after he had been set down on some grass near the beach. His voice was no more than a whisper, but he spoke with dignity.

The guard's answer caught in his throat. "He comes even now," he finally said. Even as he spoke, Finn topped the hill and started down the back side. He was surrounded by a half dozen of his and Folcwalda's thanes.

He still doesn't know, Ulestan thought. But Finn must have guessed something of the truth. Halfway down the hill he broke into a run.

"Father!" he cried when he saw the king.

"Son," Folcwalda replied in a whisper as Finn fell at his feet. Their hands held each other tightly as Finn comprehended his father's condition. "We must get you back to Hwitstanburg."

"To Finnsburg." Folcwalda smiled. It was a beautiful smile, one that Ulestan never forgot. "It is Finnsburg now. But no," the king continued, "it is too late."

"Why do you say that?" Finn pleaded.

"I will not be dragged and carried into my own home," Folcwalda said. He knew that he had lived out his life's time on earth, that his number of days was over. "My time has come. This wound is mortal. You are king now."

Of all the battle-hardened warriors present, not one was without tears in his eyes.

"Serve your people well and they will serve you well," Folcwalda continued, and Finn could only nod in reply. "You are all witnesses," he proclaimed clearly. "I have passed my kingship to Finn. Serve him well as you have done for me."

Ulestan dropped to his knee. Whether he was bowing to

Folcwalda or Finn, he did not know. The rest of the company followed suit, and all present knelt before their kings, the new and the old.

"Friesland is one kingdom now." Folcwalda addressed everyone with a hoarse, barely audible whisper. A sudden shaft of red light from the setting sun broke through the clouds and fell on Folcwalda's face as he lay propped there. An illusion of color returned to his pale face.

"You are one people. Finn is your king," he said. He began to speak as one who had spent the last eight days preparing this speech. But he coughed weakly, and his voice was nearly spent. "For many years have I ruled our people. You have served me well. I could not have asked for more loyalty or courage from my followers. So should hearth companions be! For that service I thank you . . . But I do not release you." He coughed again. Blood began once more to trickle out the side of his mouth. Ulestan tried to wipe it away, but it grew to a steady stream. "I hold you to your service and call you to serve Finn. Finn is me and I am Finn."

Then the passing king's thoughts changed completely, and his eyes lost their focus. "Finnsburg," he said suddenly. "From this day forth the hall at Hwitstan shall be called Finnsburg. By my son's hand it was built, and by his hand it shall be ruled. That should be said in its name. So I decree and so it is." Then he fell silent, and his eyes closed for the last time. The red sun disappeared again behind a cloud, and his face was white once more.

"You have a grandson," Finn whispered.

A calm smile spread across Folcwalda's face, and he passed into death.

The following morning Folcwalda, son of Folgar was given back to the sea. He was laid to rest in a great ship, surrounded by the weapons of those he had slain in his last fight. A bright gold wreath was set on his head, and many other marvelous treasures were added as well. His gold torc Finn took as his own, as Folcwalda had wished. With the torc passed the kingship of Friesland. Ulestan bent it around Finn's neck even as the tide took Folcwalda on one more journey.

Daelga's voice rose in a last lament:

"Gone is our king,
    Cold now in death.
Felled by his foes,
    Folcwalda was.
One journey too many,
    Made he, our king.
Sailed from these shores,
    Ship bore him off,
To Domburg far,
    To free her lands,
And Friesland gather,
    One folk, one king.

"Gone is our king,
    Cold now in death.
Felled by his foes,
    Folcwalda was.
Yet victory won,
    Wise our great king,
Though never to hall
    Or hearth will return.
Great is our grief!
    Was good, whom was lost.
For Hwitstan, Alas!
    Long shall we mourn."

The last battle of Folcwalda was made into a great and sad song which was sung in honor in many mighty halls for many years to come. For those who had dwelt for a time in his presence, there was yet some joy in its hearing—joy and sorrow mixed in measure. Such was a good king.

PART III

The Monk

XVI

The Mission

Willimond of Lindisfarne tucked his head closer to his chest. The young monk's eyes were shut tightly, but he was much too cold to sleep. With numb hands he pulled his heavy, wool cloak closer about his lean body. Wet through from the constant splash and spray, his well-worn garments now felt altogether inadequate against the icy wind. One more wave would hardly make a difference; there was not a dry spot left anywhere on him. The cold had penetrated his bones quite thoroughly.

As the last rays of the evening sun sank into the sea far behind, another icy wave lashed against the side of the ship, and the cold spray caught Willimond in the face. His body stiffened involuntarily with shock as the water ran down the front of his neck in a thin stream and settled on his belly. He ignored it as best he could. Both of the monk's hands tightly gripped the precious parchments in the leather pouch at his waist. With one hand he let go of the pouch and hugged his knees, coughing harshly as he did.

As he had for ten of the past fourteen days, Willimond sat huddled, cold, stiff, and cramped, in the bottom of a trading ship bound for Hwitstanwic. His aching body now seemed incapable of any movement other than his furious shivering. But that mattered little, for there was no room for him to move even if he could. Standing on shore looking into the boat fourteen days earlier, Willimond would not have thought there was space for him among all the goods. Yet when the gold coins appeared, the traders assured him they would find room. They had—but not much.

With Willimond on board, the twenty seamen, under the orders of two rich traders, had sailed the trading ship southward from the small island monastery of Lindisfarne along the eastern coastline of the great Isle of the Britons. They had journeyed along the shores of the Angles and Saxons to the southern point of the isle and then had crossed the channel to the continent. From there they turned northeastward along the coast of Friesland. During the nights, which had seemed all too short, they stopped for lodging in coastal villages and occasionally traded with the inhabitants. These were but brief rests, and Willimond remembered little of them. Only in Cantwara, Eoforwic, Lundenwic and Wic by Dorestad had they stayed for two successive nights to take advantage of the wealth in those larger trading villages. After a stay in Hwitstanwic, the ship would continue on to the lands of the Danes. Willimond would be happy, he thought, if he never set foot on any ship again. He now knew every plank and curve of that vessel. Each successive day on the sea had seemed colder and wetter than the one before. Whether the air had actually grown colder or whether he simply began each day with wetter garments, Willimond did not know. It did not matter. What mattered was that now, finally, they were approaching their destination. Though he himself had little concept of distances at sea, he had been told that the ship would not stop again until it had reached Hwitstanwic and that that would not now be long.

Willimond once again found himself wondering what Friesland would be like. How would he be accepted in Hwitstan? How would the king treat him? What was he to do when he arrived? Would the barbarian chieftains listen to a new religion? Would his mission succeed? Willimond did not know the answers to these questions. Nor, though they themselves had sent him on this mission, did the fathers at Lindisfarne. All they had been able to tell him was that all things were in the hands of the Father. "The answers," they had said cryptically, "will only come in time. It is not your duty to know the outcome, only to obey." Only to obey . . . to obey and have faith.

Willimond had been called by the Holy One, and so he must go. That much, at least, should have been simple.

During the winter, when his "calling" had come, he had been very sure of it. He had known then that he was to leave

Lindisfarne and go south—that he had been entrusted to bring, to any who would hear, the message to which he and all those of the order at Lindisfarne had given their lives. The fathers themselves had confirmed the calling and blessed him with many blessings. And with that call had come an excitement to serve the God, a confidence in the importance of his work—of His work. Only a few months ago, Willimond thought, he had been so sure of that call.

Then spring had come and with it trade ships. When passage to Hwitstanwic had actually been purchased, suddenly he was not so sure. He did not doubt his God, only that he had been called to leave Lindisfarne. Had he been deceived? What was he really doing? Do men change the course of their lives because of dreams and visions in the night? It was true that the fathers had confirmed his calling. But had they done so only because of his dream, or had the Holy One spoken to them as well? Was his dream just a dream, or had God really spoken?

Willimond did not doubt God. He doubted himself. He doubted his vision. He doubted his calling.

Yet he was acting. He was bringing the good news to those who had not heard. He was obeying the great order, going into all of the world and making followers for the true King. That was more than his duty; it was his life. There was no higher calling to which he could give himself. He needed no dream to remind him of the necessity and import of that command. And with the command was a promise. The One who died and rose again was with him always, even unto the end of the age. Or the end of the earth? Yes, to the end of the earth as well. He needed no special calling beyond that. Or did he? There was so much he did not know.

And yet, carrying his doubts with him, he had left Lindisfarne a fortnight ago. He had purchased passage on the first trade ship of spring, wondering if he would ever return.

Leaving Lindisfarne was the most difficult decision Willimond had ever made. Twice in the past he had left his home, but it had been different then. The first time had not been by his own choice. He still remembered the day when his father had brought him to the monastery at Iona to give him to the order there. He never saw his father again. Aidan, a kind and energetic monk who had been taught by Columba himself, had taken Willimond into his care. He had poured out on Willimond the fatherly love which Willimond had never known from his real father. And there had been food at the monastery. How many days had his own father not been able to provide? His mother had given to Willimond her own meager shares of what they did have. Her very life she gave him. When she died, his father lost hope. Perhaps the wisest thing he had ever done—the only great thing he did—was to bring Willimond to Iona. There at least he would be cared for and fed. Life in the monastery at Iona had not by any means been easy; much was expected of him. Yet there was a shared joy in that labor that even a boy of nine summers could feel and understand. And with the work came teaching as well. In less than two years he was able to read from the Holy Writings himself. He loved his life there, especially the learning. That much, at least, his father had done for him.

As Willimond grew older, Aidan had begun his own labors in earnest. Leaving Iona for long periods of time, he had journeyed among the Northumbrian peoples, in the region between the Forth and the Humber Rivers, where the Angles were responding in great numbers to his message. Willimond was but fourteen when he first joined Aidan on one of his journeys. There he saw in practice what he had heard the fathers preaching from the manuscripts: "Having thus a fond affection for you, we were well-pleased to impart to you not only the Gospel of God but also our own lives, because you had become very dear to us." Aidan poured his very life into his work, and the people responded. It was thus with greatest joy that Aidan had received the summons from Oswald, the king of Northumbria, to begin a church there. When word came to Iona from Oswald's castle in Bamborough, the monks had fallen on their knees in unison to sing praises and thanksgiving to God the Father. The door had finally been opened among the Angles for the church in Northumbria!

Thus at the age of eighteen Willimond had joyfully left his second home, along with many of the monks of Iona, eager to accompany Aidan to Lindisfarne where they would establish a new church among the Angles. The journey there was long—longer than when Willimond and Aidan had traveled alone. The band of monks, eager though they were, traveled slowly, carrying with them many parchments and manuscripts of the Holy Writings, and stopping often at villages to preach as they went.

But there was great anticipation for the new work that would begin. Willimond was not leaving his home. His home was coming with him—Aidan, the writings, his teaching, his friends—all the things Willimond counted dear.

He had been in Lindisfarne but two years when he had received his calling to leave and go south to the lands of the Frisians. Only two years! So much was still to be done. The building was only just taking shape. And unlike Aidan, he was not going with the invitation of the king. He knew not what to expect.

The monk opened his eyes as the first star of night was appearing in the darkening sky. Within moments other stars followed, tiny points of light appearing here and there without any discernible order. But Willimond knew there was an order. As he watched, a larger point of light suddenly appeared to the starboard a short height above the water. An older seaman saw it too and barked a quick order. Almost at once the ship swung sharply toward the new light. The oars pulled swiftly through the water as the seamen rowed with renewed energy, knowing, as Willimond did not, that their voyage was almost at an end. As they drew closer, the light—a low watchfire—seemed to rise higher in the sky. Willimond was able to see beneath it the faint silhouette of a tower, and beneath that a low, dark hill sloping down to the sea. One moment the ship was hissing through the water with the wind and waves behind it. The next moment it was sliding to a halt on a narrow beach.

Willimond's heart leapt with sudden anticipation. The chill in his bones was momentarily forgotten. He had reached Hwitstan.

As the seamen rose slowly and stepped out from the ship, an escort of six armed men emerged from the shadows to greet them. The two traders, dressed in rich furs decorated with silks, stepped between the hired seamen and bowed to the guards. Willimond rose stiffly behind them and stepped onto the beaches of Hwitstanwic.

"In the name of Finn, son of Folcwalda, lord of Hwitstan and High King over Friesland, we greet you who come in peace. Who is it that seeks shelter on our shores? For what purpose do you come?"

The Frisian accent and dialect still sounded strange to

Willimond, but he had already begun to grow accustomed to it during his brief stays in Domburg and Wic by Dorestad. The Frisian language was for the most part the same as that spoken among the Angles, though there were some few words here and there which he did not know and others that were spoken somewhat differently. Still, he understood the guards fairly well.

The two traders seemed to have no difficulty at all understanding the accent and immediately were able to shift their speech to mimic that of the guards. "We come laden with wool and skins from the Great Isle. We are seeking trade in the market of Hwitstan." Their calm, imitated Frisian dialect succeeded at once in putting the guards at ease.

"From what regions have you come and to which do you travel?" the guards now asked.

"We journey from the lands of the Irish through the lands of the Angles and Saxons and on northward to the home of the Danes."

The questions continued for a few moments, and then the traders removed a few coins from their bags and delivered them to the guards. Willimond began to shiver again and looked eagerly toward the tower where the fire burned brightly. Then the traders, followed by their hired band, were following two of the guards up the hill straight toward the fire. Willimond fell in step, unnoticed among the seamen. They crested the hill and walked past the tower Finnweard, where Finn the king stood watching, staff and sword in hand. They started down the far side of the hill into the village of Hwitstan.

The trail and village were dark, but Willimond was fortunate that the path was smoothly worn. It required all of his efforts simply to cause his cramped, cold limbs to work as intended. He could little have walked on a rough path. Even as it was, he stumbled more than once. Though he could see nothing, he kept his eyes fixed on the ground in front of him. All he saw through the corners of his eyes as he descended into the dark village were the lights of fires shining through windows and doorways. What was the village like? he wondered. Were they being watched? But he was too afraid to look. He must wait until morning light—wait and trust the Mighty One.

The small band of seamen walked to the edge of a circle of huts and turned toward a rather large building to the left. More money was paid by the traders to a short man standing by the doorway. After receiving his coins, he limped off into the darkness. Then they were inside. And to Willimond's pleasure, a great fire roared in a hearth set against the far wall. Before long the whole band was gathered on benches around the fire.

Willimond was already almost asleep when the short man returned with food just a few moments later. He was accompanied by a woman about his same age and height. Her eyes were bright and her smile was quite cheery, despite being nearly toothless. In the light of the fire the monk noticed that the man's right hand was badly mangled, as if many years ago all of his fingers had been broken and never set. The couple carried with them numerous loaves of bread, two great jugs of wine, and a pot of stew that the man had hooked over the wrist of his damaged hand. From the conversation between the old man and the traders, Willimond discovered that the small hall was a bedding house for the crews of trading ships. These traders had been there many times before, and while spending a day trading in Wic by Dorestad they had sent a message ahead with another ship telling of their arrival on the following day. Thus they had been expected in Hwitstan that evening. A few coins were given to the old man in payment for the food and lodging, and the man seemed especially appreciative.

The two traders and the old couple disappeared. As none of the seamen took notice of his presence, Willimond availed himself of the food and drink. Before long, he was out of his wet garments and fast asleep close to the fire.

It was long after dawn when Willimond was disturbed by the slow stirrings of the seamen. An accidental kick in his ribs from an old traveler stretched out beside him startled Willimond into wakefulness and sent him into a fit of violent coughs. The cold which he had caught on the voyage had now settled deep into his lungs. He slowly sat up and looked around. The men about him were turning, rolling and grumbling. None of them were eager to start the day. Some few of them never rose at all, knowing that they would not be leaving again for a few days. Others began to stir along with Willimond. A kind, young sailor who had on occasion thrown an extra blanket to Willimond and had frequently asked him about his life in Iona and Lindisfarne looked over at him and smiled. Willimond returned the smile as he pulled on his long robe, which the fire had partly dried during the night.

"Tell me more . . ." the young man started to say. Just then the older of the two traders stepped through the doors and saw Willimond standing there.

"You still here?" the older one barked, his Frisian accent dropped. The young sailor turned away quickly. Willimond suddenly remembered where he was—and why he had come. "If you want a second night, it will come from your own purse," the trader grumbled. "You are on your own now. You only paid for the voyage."

"Now, if you want work . . ." the younger one said, a shrewd smile spreading on his face as he stepped up behind his fellow.

Willimond shook his head. *I already have work*, he thought. He walked to the door and reached for his cloak, which hung on a peg. His hand pulled back quickly. The cloak was still cold and soaked through with seawater. For a brief moment he looked with envy at the stack of rich fur and wool cloaks that belonged to the traders. He weighed his purse, which he had been given by the fathers upon his departure, and then looked at his own dark, coarse robe and his worn, wool cloak.

After weighing his purse again, he decided it would be unwise to make a rash purchase only to alleviate a temporary discomfort. The fathers would not have approved. There was little enough in the purse as it was, and he would likely need it later. He would need to eat, if nothing else. There was no telling how or when or even if he would be received by Finn. The few coins he possessed felt like very few to him indeed! He wondered how many days he might have before they were gone. Not many, he thought. He would need to gain the king's favor soon!

But thankfully, he reminded himself, he was not under the power of the Frisian king, but under the mercy of the Great King. A sudden wave of peace swept over him, and he tossed the purse back into his pouch alongside the carefully rolled parchments. With much discomfort he donned his old, wet garments and his cloak, heavy with water, and stepped out into the village.

The first thing to meet Willimond's eye was Finnsburg, the great hall of Finn, which rose directly in front of him in a clearing in the middle of the village. It was much larger, he guessed, even than the holy meeting house at Lindisfarne, though that had not yet been finished when he left. The sturdy beams of Finnsburg seemed solid proof against wind and storm, if not against sword or flame. Surrounding the hall on all sides was a double ring of low wattle huts, most of which were facing to his left, away from the sea. To his right, beyond the huts, rose a gentle slope which was topped by a small tower—the same tower, he guessed, that he had passed the night before. To the left, past a few more huts, was a small pond. On the other side of that pond was a second group of huts set in somewhat random fashion with a small clearing on the far side. A stream flowed out of the pond, down behind the hut he had stayed in—one of the largest in the village he now noticed—and into a river some distance behind him. Down at the river men were pulling fish from a newly built weir.

All this Willimond took in under the clear skies and bright sun of a warm spring day. "God gives strength and grace enough," he had been told by the fathers, "for us to endure those trials which He allows upon us." That was good, for the monk did not think he could have lived through another day at sea. Never had he been more thankful for sunshine and solid ground.

XVII

An Audience with the King

As he gazed about him and breathed the air deeply, Willimond wondered where he should begin. There was much that needed to be done. And now he was all alone. No one had come with him. Not even one. He felt a twinge of anxiety. *If only Aidan were here*, he thought. But he was not.

So the monk stood there looking at the village, at the great hall of Finnsburg and the many smaller huts about it, at the people moving about carrying on life's work. He listened to the sounds of daily activity around him. Animals squeaked and squealed in their pens. Hoes dug into the ground. Willimond tried to envision a church rising in the clearing beyond the pond—a church in which to worship the living God. His imagination took hold of the idea. Yes, he would build a great church. It would rival the hall of Finnsburg itself, with wide stone pillars and tall gates. He pictured baptisms in the pond in front of him. King and peasant alike from all across Friesland would come to be submersed and to give their lives to the Holy God. He saw himself preaching a mighty sermon to the gathered peoples. All listened as he taught them the Word of God.

The monk was caught up in sudden excitement. It would be a great work he would do, no less than what Aidan himself had done at Lindisfarne, or Columba at Iona, or even Colubanus at Luxeuil and Bobbio (though Willimond had only heard of Luxeuil and Bobbio and had never actually been there). His calling—his vision—would not be in vain. His mind raced ahead thinking of all that he had to do, of the great burden on his shoulder.

And then the excitement was replaced by a wave of anxiety which was no less shocking than the cold North Sea that had splashed him so mercilessly for the past many days.

He must find the king soon; the work must begin at once. If it was to be accomplished, he needed to act. Yet, his purse was so small. How would he accomplish such a great work? It was too much. He would fail.

A rush came upon him—a rush as close to panic as Willimond had ever felt. The young monk turned and almost ran toward the great hall of Finnsburg in the center of the village. But being clumsy—he always had been—he had taken but five steps when he tripped over something unseen and sprawled headfirst and ungraciously into the well-trampled mud of Hwitstan. His right hand landed firmly in the warm remains left by some animal just moments earlier. His left hand landed in a cold puddle, remnant from the previous night's rain.

He lifted his head from the dirt in front of him only to hear laughter erupting from the two traders who still stood behind him. Their words were not kind. Willimond let his head fall back down. He suppressed a response and tried not to listen. He did not want to move. He lay there until he heard them walk away.

Then anger and frustration welled in his chest. He rose to his knees. Unintentionally, he wiped his face with his right hand. Then in sudden disgust he wiped with his left instead. Was this his reward? Did God treat his servants thus? Was it a sign that he should not be there? Blood trickled from his nose. His hands and face were repulsive. What was he to do now?

Cease striving and know that I am God. The words Willimond had heard many times as the monks at Iona read the Psalms now echoed through his mind. *Cease striving . . .*

Willimond paused. It was not his own work he had come to do, but the work of the Father. . . . *and know that I am God.*

But so much needed to be done . . .

Unless the Lord builds the house, they labor in vain, he heard Aidan saying. Aidan, who had been like a father.

But Willimond was all alone. Aidan was not with him.

Unless the Lord guards the city, the watchmen stay awake in vain, the voice said clearly.

Cease striving!

Pray, Willimond said to himself. *Though you be not with them anymore, remember the words of the fathers—of Aidan. What have they taught you? Have you forgotten in so few days? Stop acting and pray. Be not a fool. Trust in God's power and His timing. Remember whose work it is that you do!*

Still on his knees, Willimond lowered his head and prayed silently, "Father, I thank Thee that Thou has brought me here safely. I am Thy servant. Now, in Thy time and according to Thy will, wilt Thou grant me an audience with the king and accomplish the work for which Thou has brought me. Thou art God, and Thy kingdom is forever."

Slowly Willimond rose to his feet. He lifted his eyes and looked again at the great hall in front of him. This time he made no move to approach. He looked around at the village again and saw it as it really was. It was no more glorious and no less needy. The traders were gone. Everybody else seemed too busy to have noticed him. For that he was thankful.

As he stood there silently, there emerged from Finnsburg a tall man of kingly appearance dressed in a bright red cloak with a sturdy blade hung loosely at his side. His manner was regal and confident, and those whom he passed lowered their heads in respect.

Surely this is Finn, Willimond thought, and he made up his mind to approach him immediately. *The God has answered my prayer already!* To Willimond's joy, the king looked right at him and started walking that way. The monk took a few steps forward and then, as the king drew near, dropped to one knee, as he knew was the custom from his dealings with Oswald.

The king stopped walking. Willimond looked up to see him staring down with a look of mirth. Before the monk could say anything, a small child, perhaps of eight years, ran out from a nearby hut. Seeing the king, the child went to him at once.

"Uncle," he shouted and jumped into his arms.

"Young Finnlaf," the man replied, throwing the younger one into the air.

As he landed, Finnlaf turned and looked at Willimond, who still knelt a few steps away. "Uncle Ulestan, who is this man with the funny hair?"

My hood, Willimond thought. He had forgotten to put it on.

Now he remembered how those who were not accustomed to monks reacted to tonsuring. A wave of embarrassment swept over him as he thought of the large half-moon which was shaved from the center of his head. But that was the least of his concerns with his appearance. His whole front was still covered with mud and manure.

"We shall see," Ulestan replied to Finnlaf.

"Uncle Ulestan," the young man had said. So this was not the king. Yet how noble was his appearance. A thane perhaps? But the lad—Finnlaf was his name?—surely this boy was the son of Finn.

"Rise," Ulestan said to Willimond. "You need not kneel before me, nor before this young man, though someday perhaps you shall," he added with a wink at the younger one.

Willimond rose awkwardly. "Forgive me," he began, struggling to remember what he had learned of Frisian customs. He continued haltingly, "I am new to this land . . . Such was your appearance that I mistook you for the king."

"That you are new to this land does not surprise me," Ulestan said, looking at Willimond appraisingly. "That much I determined from afar. Yet had I not, your voice surely would disclose as much."

The monk dropped his eyes for a moment and examined his muddy cloak. Already he was disadvantaged. *Not by my appearance will I now receive an audience with the king,* he thought to himself. *Yet I will not despair.* "Where then," he asked, "would I find your king?"

"Ah," Ulestan answered. "If you had seen him, there would be no doubt as to his kingship." Finnlaf stepped away from Ulestan and also began to examine Willimond closely. "For what reason do you seek Finn?" Ulestan asked.

"I bring him news of the God." The words sounded odd to Willimond in this strange land.

"News of the god?" The slight lifting of Ulestan's eyes revealed surprise. "Of which god? There are many."

"My father knows about the gods," Finnlaf said boldly. "He is descended from the gods."

"Of 'the gods' I do not speak, but only of One God, the true God." Willimond could feel his boldness growing.

"This 'one god' that you speak of, is he mighty?" Ulestan asked, fingering the hilt of his sword.

"Mighty?" Willimond answered. "He is mightier than all kings, mightier even than the great emperors to the south. He is mightier by far than all of the other gods. With a word, this God stills the very seas!"

"How is it, then, if your new god is so mighty that we have not heard of him?" Ulestan asked, forcing a slight mocking smile that ill concealed his growing curiosity.

Finnlaf, meanwhile, losing interest in the conversation, disappeared in the direction of the pond.

"God is not a new god," Willimond replied, watching, with disappointment as Finn's son departed. He turned his attention back to Ulestan. "The One God is before all the gods. It is He who brought the world into being. He formed the sun and moon and stars. He set mighty Orion in the skies. And He is unlike the other gods in another way too—this God cares about men."

"A god who cares about men?" Ulestan asked thoughtfully, the half-mocking smile now gone. "That would be different indeed. What is the name of this god?"

"The One God has no name. He is."

"Then how can one know this god who has no name?"

"This God sent his only Son to become a man and to live the life of a man, that those who desire to know Him may know Him through His Son," Willimond answered, amazed at the wisdom of the questions being asked him and eager to answer them rightly.

"This is interesting teaching indeed!" Ulestan replied. "And your god has a message for our king?"

"He has a message for any who would hear Him, be he king, thane or peasant."

"I would hear that message," Ulestan said slowly.

Willimond could barely contain a shout of joy as Ulestan left, promising to seek for him an audience with the king. Though there would be many times in the years to come when Willimond would again doubt his calling, no such doubts plagued him now. *Surely I have been brought here with a purpose*, his thoughts sang. *So quickly is the hand of God at work!* He fell once again to his knees, this time to lift his voice in thanksgiving to the living God. If any other than God Himself had been close enough to hear him, they might have thought it strange to see a man kneeling in the mud speaking to the air. But Willimond's concerns were far from that thought.

Rising from his knees a short time later, Willimond determined that he would make the most of the opportunity God had provided him. His thoughts returned again to his appearance. It would certainly not do for him to stand before the king as he was. He looked around for a place to wash and make himself presentable. The pond seemed the obvious solution, but Willimond decided against it. It was too visible to the entire village and not, at least as far as he now knew, appropriate to their customs. The river? The thought of entering into that cold water did not at all please him, but he could think of no better answer. At least the sun was warm today. And it would not help matters to wait; the sooner washed, the sooner dried. Turning at once, he followed the small stream a few hundred yards down a hill to the mouth of the River Hwitstan where it flowed into Hwitstanwic. Three men were working the weirs, checking the nets as the tide flowed quickly out. Their work was met with great success.

"It is a bountiful day," Willimond heard a voice proclaim joyfully. It came from a handsome, brightly dressed man who sat astride a richly decorated brown and white stallion, watching the work proceeding in the river below him. He would later learn that this was Froda, a thane and close companion of Finn.

"It is indeed!" came the response from a stocky man with bright red hair, a short, stout neck, and lean, muscular arms. He was standing waist-deep in the water, struggling to pull in a large net laden with silver fish which were flopping ignorantly about in a vain attempt to free themselves.

Though he did not remember making a decision to move that way, Willimond suddenly found himself carefully laying his pouch aside and wading into the water to help the man. Though the man gave Willimond a rather curious glance, and was obviously quite surprised to find a stranger entering the cold water to offer aid unasked for, he did not refuse the offer.

Froda also watched with curiosity for a moment and then turned his mount and disappeared over the hill.

Willimond was thoroughly drenched by the time he had finished helping this man and two others empty the weirs. Before they were half finished, he had removed his robe and was wading, like the others, in his short undercloak. Though the water was icy, the sun was directly overhead, and the air was exceptionally warm for spring. As the tide began to return, the men stepped onto shore with their tasks completed. Willimond then found to his surprise that his robe and cloak were completely dry for the first time in days. And his cough had, at least for the time, disappeared.

The three keepers of the weir nets now stepped toward Willimond. The foremost, to whom Willimond had first offered his help, bowed his head in greeting. "You are not from this village," he began slowly. His words were careful, though not distrustful. "It is not common for strangers to offer aid. For yours we are grateful. I am Lopystre."

"I am Willimond of Lindisfarne," the monk replied. "I am grateful for the opportunity to help. I have seen and worked weirs similar to this, though not as well made. We had none at Lindisfarne. These are sturdy and well crafted."

The man bowed again. A look of pride crossed his face. "These are Lindlaf, my son, and Lawyrke, my brother." The other two bowed their heads as well. Watching them, Willimond noticed the great resemblance between the three—especially between Lopystre and his son Lindlaf with their matching locks of bright red hair. Lindlaf was already quite strong, though Willimond guessed him to be no more than fourteen summers.

"Are these your weirs?" Willimond asked.

"They belong to Finn," Lopystre replied. "But it was my father who built them and we who keep them." As he answered, he appeared to be examining for the first time the strange, long, loose-fitting robe and peculiar tonsure of Willimond.

"I know nothing of Lindisfarne," Lawyrke said with a clean, high voice that surprised Finn.

"It is far to the north, in the lands of the Angles," Willimond responded. "Our land is known as Northumbria. It is the land north of the Humber River and extends as far as the Forth River. Oswald the king rules fairly and with a just hand. Lindisfarne is but a small island."

Of King Oswald, these three had heard on occasion some tales from the mouths of various thanes. Of Northumbria and Lindisfarne, however, they had never heard mention. As some do when hearing of vague, faraway places to which they will never travel or even desire to travel, the two elder fishermen simply smiled and nodded. "Are you a trader?" Lopystre asked, his curiosity aroused only slightly by the strange names.

"No, not I," Willimond replied. "I am a servant of the living God and of Jesus, His Son . . . though my voyage across the sea was on a trading ship," he added as an afterthought.

"You have been across the sea?" Lindlaf asked. His eyes widened with sudden interest, though to Willimond's disappointment it was obviously interest in his voyage and not in his vocation. "I have never been on the sea."

"Yes, I have crossed the sea," the monk replied slowly. He envied the child for not having suffered through a sea voyage, and had no wish to recall his own. But it was too late. Lindlaf was already assaulting him with a steady stream of questions, many of which he asked before the previous ones were even answered. That was how Willimond found himself slowly walking back toward the village telling his three new companions about the island of Lindisfarne and the monks who dwelt there. Before long he was sitting at a table with Lopystre's wife and young daughter, enjoying a small but much appreciated noonday meal and telling eager listeners about his purpose for coming to Hwitstan.

The three fishermen were soon his friends. *In this too,* Willimond thought, *is the hand of God at work.*

Willimond spent the rest of the afternoon working with his three new friends, repairing and resetting the nets for the next catch—a task as difficult, time-consuming and important as hauling the heavy nets in once they were full. They didn't stop their labors until the sun was nearly down.

Lopystre and his son were preparing to return to their home and had just offered a second meal to Willimond when Ulestan came striding down the hill from the village. He cast a long shadow across the river as he approached.

"I heard that you would be here," the thane said. "It is good that I found you. Finn desires that you join him in the hall and speak of your new god."

Lindlaf, who already admired Willimond for having been across the sea, now looked at him in sudden awe for having so soon been invited, by none other than Ulestan, to sup with Finn in the great hall. His eyes wide and his mouth ajar, he stared at Willimond.

The monk bowed to Ulestan, but before following him he turned to the three fishermen. "I hope to see you again. I am grateful for your generous hospitality. I know not what this meeting will bring, but I know I have already found friends in this new land."

"May your God be with you," Lopystre replied.

Willimond smiled. *He will be*, he thought as he turned to follow Ulestan up the hill.

●

It took a few moments for Willimond's eyes to adjust to the darkness as he stepped into Finnsburg for the first time to meet the High King of Friesland. Though the evening air was cool, his forehead had already begun to sweat with anticipation. Exactly what he expected to find, Willimond was not sure; perchance something rather grand—something far more impressive than the crude rock buildings at Iona, or the hall in which he had spent his first night in Hwitstan. But what he saw when his eyes finally adjusted to the dim surroundings surprised him by its very lack of grandeur, for Finnsburg was unexpectedly simple. In the center of the hall a low fire burned on a large, flat hearthstone. Surrounding the hearth, a number of crude benches were set in a circle. The rest of the hall was dark, plain and empty. A high-raftered ceiling full of smoke and shadows gave the place an ominous mood, not at all like the spacious courtyards and windowed halls at Lindisfarne. Twenty or so sturdy thanes sat about the fire, holding large mugs and staring rather darkly at the stranger entering their midst.

Willimond looked across the fire and finally saw him whom he sought. There, through the flickering tongues of flame, sat a tall, stern figure on a bench higher than the rest. Surely this was the king! His right hand grasped the hilt of a sword which lay across his lap. His left held a large drinking horn. A sturdy ash staff with a golden boar's head leaned against the bench beside him. Encircling the king's neck and glittering brightly behind the dancing flames was a wide gold torc. Many other gold and silver rings were wrapped around his wrists or hung loosely from his neck. Dark hair, almost invisible against the dim, smoky background, hung below his shoulders. Stern and proud was the face beneath. Had Willimond been closer and at a different angle, he would have seen a rough scar running across the back of the king's neck along his right shoulder.

Willimond paused for a moment and offered another silent prayer as Ulestan left his side and took his place beside the king. With all eyes upon him, the monk slowly and nervously made his way forward across the hall and around the huge hearth. No one spoke as he approached. When he was but two strides away, he stopped and dropped to one knee.

"Lord," Ulestan said, "this is Willimond of Lindisfarne."

"Rise and be seated," Finn said. Willimond obeyed, but he remained silent, waiting for some sign to speak. The thanes who were gathered around the hall scrutinized him carefully. Willimond glanced quickly to the side and noticed the face of Froda among those present. No others save Ulestan had he ever seen before. Then he returned his focus to the king.

"Willimond brings word of a new god that walks among men," Ulestan said.

"Does this god eat among men as well?" Finn asked.

"He did," Willimond replied.

"Then let us eat as well, that we may have a full stomach to hear these new tidings." The king raised his right hand, and almost at once four men and two women came forward from near the back wall bringing with them plates laden with cheeses, smoked meats, loaves of dark bread, and a pot of warm stew made from barley and some tubrous roots. A mug of wine was given to Willimond.

Finn at once began eating from the various foods set before him, and his thanes followed him. Willimond watched Ulestan for a moment and then followed his example, all the while wondering when and what he should say. Nobody spoke while the food was being consumed. Was it always that way? Or was the silence due to his presence?

All too soon for the nervous monk, the feasting ended. The thanes leaned back and began silently drinking their wine. They were waiting for something. Was it for him? He felt not the least bit bold. Yet he knew not when he might have another audience with Finn. On sudden inspiration he held up the piece of bread in his hand and began to speak.

"The God I serve gives to His followers living bread," Willimond began. The words came as much of a surprise to him as to the others. "Those who eat His bread never hunger again." Lifting his wine mug, he continued, "To those who thirst, He gives living water, that they may never thirst again."

Without looking around him, Willimond could tell from the sudden deepening of silence that he had the attention of every man in the hall, except perhaps the king, who seemed preoccupied.

"What is the name of this god you serve?" Finn asked suddenly.

"His god has no name," Ulestan answered before Willimond had the chance.

"Does he speak?" Finn asked Ulestan. Whether the king was referring to Willimond or to God was not clear.

"He has spoken in many ways," Willimond replied. "To those who will listen, He still speaks."

"How does one hear this god speaking? Does he talk with you?"

Willimond thought at once of the vision that brought him there, but he said nothing about that. "He has spoken through His people. His words have been collected and written down." So saying, he carefully pulled from the pouch at his side a bundle of parchments which he unrolled to show to Finn.

Finn took the parchments and examined them. He had learned some symbols and runes, but the ones on the parchment were strange to him. "Did your god write these words?" he asked, pointing to the rolls.

"He spoke to His servants, and His servants wrote these words."

"Are you the servant that has written these words?"

"Yes," Willimond answered at once, thinking of the long weeks and months he had spent copying the scrolls from the manuscripts at Iona and Lindisfarne. Then, realizing what Finn meant, he corrected himself. "No, I am not. These words were spoken to other servants many years ago. We make many copies that others might see and hear the words of God for themselves. This which I have made is but a copy."

"Then the words of your god will not be destroyed with these rolls," Finn said, and he tossed one of Willimond's scrolls—

Willimond didn't see which—into the fire, where it disappeared in seconds.

Willimond started to leap up and then stopped himself as he saw Finn tighten his grip on his sword. He released a silent moan. He had probably spent a day on that scroll alone in preparation for his mission to Hwitstan. In but a few breaths it was gone. There was no way to replace it—at least not for some time. And yet, for some reason he was not angry. *This was but my work,* he told himself, *destined to perish.* Then a new thought entered his head.

"The writings of these servants are but one way God has spoken to us."

"How else has he spoken?" Finn asked, holding another parchment loosely in his hand as if to toss it into the fire as well.

Willimond paused for a moment. On a sudden whim he began a story, wondering, even as he did, how it would be received. "There was once a mighty king," he began, "who planted for himself a great vineyard. He also built a high wall around the vineyard and raised a house where the grapes could be pressed and wine made. This king then called upon a group of his servants to work the vineyard and, when the time came, to harvest the grapes for him. He then returned to his castle. When the time of the harvest finally came, the king sent one of his thanes to collect his rent from these servants. But the servants had taken it into their heart to keep the wine for themselves, so they beat the thane and sent him away."

Willimond looked around him and noticed that all gathered were listening eagerly, some gripping their swords which lay close at hand. He had their attention, he thought, and continued, "The king was not pleased with this treatment, so he sent another thane. This thane they also beat and sent away. So the king sent a third thane. This time the servants killed the thane and sent his body back to the king. The king was greatly displeased. 'I will send my own son,' he said. 'Surely these wicked servants will honor my son.' But when the king's son arrived, the servants said to themselves, 'We will kill the king's son, and then the vineyard will be ours.' This they did. What do you think that this king will do?" Willimond asked.

"He will send an army and destroy those servants," Finn answered at once. A loud roar of approval rose from his thanes.

"My God is like that king," Willimond said. "He has sent many servants with messages, but these servants were ignored by most and sometimes killed. So God sent His only Son to bring the message Himself. God has not spoken through other servants alone, but has spoken through His Son, who is exactly like Him."

"And did the wicked servants kill the god's son also?" Finn asked, his eyes narrowing and his hand dropping again to the hilt of his sword.

Willimond suddenly thought of young Finnlaf playing by the pond that morning. He knew that Finn was moved by the tale. Was Finnlaf an only son as well? But the monk had intended the story only to illustrate how God had spoken through His Son and not how the Son had been killed. Could it be that God had purposed him to tell that tale for a very different purpose?

"Yes," Willimond answered, watching to see how Finn would respond. "The servants have killed the God's Son as well. But God is stronger even than death, and His Son rose again from the dead."

"I would hear more of this god who would not spare his only son to save the lives even of his wicked servants," the king said as if in judgment. He released his sword and set Willimond's parchments down on his lap.

"Gladly would I tell you all I know," the monk answered, excited at Finn's response and eager to begin at once.

"Then you shall return to me in seven days," Finn said.

Willimond's heart sank to his feet. Seven days? Seven days seemed like forever. Why not now? His second thought, one for which he was later ashamed because of his lack of faith, was, *What shall I eat? My purse will not last forever.*

In answer to two unspoken prayers, Finn handed the parchments back to Willimond, who immediately placed them in his pouch. Then the king said for all to hear, "Until you come before me again, you are my guest. I have been told that you have found a useful place in our village tending to the nets and weirs. So you shall continue until I call upon you again. My servants shall see that you are fed as are the other weir-tenders. You shall make your home with them."

"I am greatly honored by your generosity," Willimond replied, rising to leave. As he did, he noticed for the first time a beautiful woman seated a few feet behind Finn. She was concealed in the shadows where only a few occasional flickers of light from the fire reached her. But though she sat in the dark behind the others, her expression showed that she was indeed intent on the conversation. Further, neither the darkness nor her loose-fitting robe could conceal the fact that she was soon expecting a child.

Willimond turned and departed from his first audience with Finn, the High King of Friesland.

XVIII

Judgment

The next seven days passed much more quickly than Willimond could have hoped. He rose well before dawn each day so he would have time to read his scrolls and pray before the work began. Then he spent the remainder of the day giving what aid he could to Lopystre and his kin. The monk proved a fast and eager learner and soon mastered the various tasks of maintaining and harvesting the weirs. Each weir—there were three smaller ones rather than one large one as Willimond had seen in various places in Northumbria—consisted of two low walls angling inward toward a net on the downstream or seaward side. As the tide went out, fish which had come in with the tide were funneled along those walls and into the waiting nets. The walls were built of logs and smaller branches tied and woven onto solid posts which had been planted firmly in the bottom of the river. Though well built, the weirs faced a difficult labor of fighting the tides day in and day out and required constant maintenance. The weir-keepers were often rebuilding damaged walls, repairing nets, and resetting the deep poles, the hardest of their tasks.

Willimond did not notice when, on his third day in Hwitstan, the traders with whom he had come reloaded their ship and departed for northern lands. He smiled broadly on the fourth day of his labors when the friendly and talkative Lawyrke placed a hand firmly on his back and told him that he was a great help.

Lopystre also made it known, though more subtly than Lawyrke had, that he was pleased to have the help of two more hands to work his weirs. From the day of his meeting with Finn,

Willimond had been taken into Lopystre's family and treated like a brother. It was not an easy chore to provide food even for one's own household, Willimond knew, but he noticed that the weir-keeper's table did not seem to lack for having an extra body to feed. He wondered if Finn had seen to it that Lopystre's pay was increased to take care of Willimond. Whatever the case, Lopystre's family continued to be quite hospitable to the monk, and they made for him a small sleeping mat in the front corner of the hut. He was welcome to stay, they told him, as long as he desired. As he had no possessions of his own save his scrolls, the space was sufficient. In fact, it seemed quite large compared to the sleeping quarters of the monks at Lindisfarne—and just as private. The rest of the family slept in one small back room.

In the evenings, when the day's labor had been finished and Lawyrke had gone to his own home to be with his wife, Willimond enjoyed his first taste of family life. Lindlaf, who was about the age Willimond had been when he first left Iona to travel with Aidan, proved to be an eager listener to all he might tell him about Lindisfarne and about being a monk. In fact, the boy's questions usually far exceeded Willimond's knowledge and ability to answer. He looked with great interest at the fascinating dark scratchings that Willimond called "writing." Again and again he asked the monk to read the scrolls. Before long the lad was able to recite many of the passages himself, though he was doing it from memory and was not actually reading the scrolls.

Lopystre and his wife Berigyldan also listened with interest as Willimond spoke to them of the God and His ways. Though they asked him few questions, they seemed eager to learn more. It was Blostma, however, their daughter of five summers, who took the greatest liking to Willimond. Whenever she could, she sat upon the monk's lap, playing with the funny hair around his shaved crown and giggling. This pleased Willimond to no end, though he invariably blushed whenever she kissed him on the cheek.

On the eve of the seventh day Willimond hardly slept. Long before his usual early hour, he rose, donned his cloak, and stepped outside. The air was crisp and cold, and the moon, nearly full, still shone brightly as it settled partway down the western sky. Willimond walked up the hill toward Finnweard. The moonlight revealed a lone watchman atop the tower where he stood guard over the village. The guard looked down at him as he approached, but made no sign of acknowledgment.

Unless the Lord watches the city . . ., the monk thought as he reached the top of the hill and looked out over the seas. Far to the north, faint red and green streaks rose into the sky and faded eerily in and out of one another. Willimond had not seen the Northern Dawn in many months. It was a welcome sight, one he missed. As he watched the magnificent display in the heavens, his thoughts returned to Aidan and Lindisfarne and to the many who had gone there with him to begin the work in Northumbria. A low star appeared in the northwestern sky, somewhere close to where Willimond imagined Lindisfarne to be.

"Father, bless their work, even as Thou hast already blessed mine this past week," Willimond began. He walked the beaches of Hwitstanwic and prayed for the rest of the night until the sun rose into a cloudless sky.

That day was filled, as the past six had been, with hard work. Willimond put himself to it knowing that difficult labor speeds the passing of time. As he stood out in the river gathering fish and repairing nets, he noticed that Ulestan and Froda rode by many times, both separately and together. Yet though they watched him from a distance, neither spoke to him nor approached. *Perhaps*, Willimond hoped, *these two desire to hear more!* But if they did, they were content, it seemed, to wait until he brought his message before Finn.

Aside from Ulestan and Froda, Willimond did not meet or even see any other of Finn's thanes; yet he heard much about them from Lopystre. Aelfer, Beow, Froda and Ulestan, once thanes of Finn's father, looked now to Finn as their treasure-giver. These, along with his younger thanes Aeltar of Domburg, and the brothers Guthman and Guthric from Dorestad, were the king's closest and most trusted earls and advisors.

Hereric the Geat, the oldest living of Folcwalda's thanes and a thane now of Finn, was also still seen in Hwitstan now and then, but he spent much of his time traveling with Edmen. Since the death of his brother Eormen, Edmen had grown restless. Oft these two warriors, Edmen and Hereric, found battle in faraway lands and brought treasure to their king. Though still loyal to Finn, Edmen had not found an outlet for his grief. Rarely did he sleep in Finnsburg by hearth and king longer than a few nights.

Nor did Finn restrain these two. A good and wise king, he allowed them leave him for long periods, and often sent their swords about Friesland to do his will, maintaining the loyalty of his chieftains and collecting what tribute was due him.

The other members of Finn's hearthwerod were lesser known than these nine, and none were spoken of as much or as highly as they.

Late that afternoon Ulestan came on foot to summon Willimond. When the thane arrived at the river, the monk was resetting a heavy timber that had slid out of place, leaving a large gap on one wall of the middlemost weir. The thane stood watching for a moment as Willimond and Lindlaf together slid the beam back into place and lashed it securely. Willimond, who had not seen the thane arrive, was startled to hear Ulestan's voice speaking loudly from so close. "The king requests your presence," was all the thane said. He hesitated for a moment, then turned and walked away.

Willimond hurriedly retrieved his cloak and parchments, turned and waved to his new companions, and then followed Ulestan up the hill. Ulestan kept the pace quick, and Willimond was not able to catch up to him until they had passed between two huts and were in the center of the village, almost at the door of the hall. He wanted to ask the thane what Finn had thought—what Ulestan himself had thought—but the thane's silence daunted the monk. He would have to wait.

When Willimond entered Finnsburg for the second time, the scene was vastly different than it had been the previous week. No more was the mood dark and somber, but bright, joyous and festive. A lively feast had already begun, and the benches were laden with trays of fresh fish, cheese and bread. It was as hearth and hall should be in the presence of a good gift-giver. The noise of so many joyous thanes talking and laughing filled the hall with such mirth and excitement that Willimond's spirits were lifted at once. Was it an illusion, or was the hall more brightly lit this evening? As Willimond walked toward the fire, nobody but Finn took notice of him. The king, however, watched him intently, almost eagerly, and nodded to him as he approached. Willimond bowed before Finn, who acknowledged his bow with another nod and then pointed toward the wine and food. The monk sat beside a bench a short distance from the fire and partook of the fare. Then he watched and waited. There were a number of new faces he had not seen before. Some were more richly dressed than others—perhaps chieftains under Finn. Others were clearly men of war, members of the king's hearthwerod; burly and scarred, they looked out of dark eyes that spoke of fearlessness.

A tall, thin fellow whose grey eyes and curly black hair seemed to defy any guess at his age sat the closest to the fire and listened to all that was said by the thanes, occasionally repeating it in verse or telling riddles. He held a small harp which he would occasionally strum, and his voice was so rich that it resembled singing even when he wasn't. Whereas Lawyrke's voice was high and crisp, this man's was full and resonant. More so even than Finn, he seemed to hold the attention of all those gathered. Daelga the poet, he was, though the monk did not learn that until later. Ulestan kept silent and took for himself the seat at Finn's right hand, a seat he had held since the passing of Folcwalda. A few seats behind Finn sat the same woman whom Willimond had seen before. In the brighter light she was undeniably pregnant, though she dressed in a way that minimized her large womb. Beside her sat a slightly younger man and a woman who was also with child, though not as far progressed. At one point the man began fitting her with some bright green gems which he placed in a stunning gold circlet low around her neck. She spoke a few words to him, and he nodded and took the gems back. Surely this woman was none other than the queen. And the two beside her? Perhaps the king's jeweler and a serving woman of the queen.

There was still some food left when Finn rose to his feet and held his sword aloft above him. Immediately the entire gathered company except for the queen rose as well. Willimond followed their example.

"We will hear a song," Finn declared and sat again.

As the rest of the company settled back to their benches, Daelga jumped up on his. Running nimbly around the edge of the hearthstone, so that the fire did not singe his clothing, he took his place across the fire from Finn.

"Hear, then, the tale of Weland's revenge," the poet began. "Weland, by hindrances, experienced persecutions; he knew hardship, that noble-minded earl!" Gathering energy from the strumming of his harp, he burst into a song that lasted nearly half an hour before he ran out of breath and returned to his seat, drenched in sweat but exulting in the excitement of his own tale.

All gathered lifted their mugs in appreciation, and as one voice they sang in response, "To hearth, to home, to song in the hall. To king and queen and prince." This they repeated again and again, louder each time, until Finn raised his sword once more. Removing a silver ring from his right wrist, he cast it toward the poet, who caught it, flashed it around in his hand, and then made it disappear so deftly that none saw where he hid it. The poet bowed to the king, who pointed toward the bench with his sword, thus indicating there should be yet another song.

Daelga smiled and rose once again to his feet. As if he had not exerted himself in the slightest, he stepped again onto the bench with fresh energy. This time, however, he sang slowly and softly, enchanting the crowd with the tale of Friesc and the settling of Friesland; of the time when wolves and bears ruled the land north of the Rhine and how Friesc had won Friesland from the mighty black boar.

By the time he finished, Willimond found that even he had been enchanted by the power of Daelga's voice and tale. He could have listened all evening. Almost he envied the life of the thanes, so joyous was their celebration. To hear Daelga was a privilege. If such a voice could but sing the gospel, he thought! Then he thought, *How will any here deign to listen to me now?*

Even as Willimond thought this, Finn turned to him abruptly. "You have heard the tales of Friesland. What new tale do you now bring among us of strange and powerful gods?"

Certainly I am being tested. That is why he had the poet sing, that I must follow after him in my weakness. His mind shook with sudden fear and trepidation. His knees began to tremble, and he found that he could not stand. He opened his mouth, but no sound came. He looked from eye to eye and found not one that looked upon him with pity. He sat there speechless for what seemed like ages with every eye upon him. Time itself seemed to be standing still.

Then, as his eyes returned to meet Finn's, and despair had almost swallowed him, a calming voice suddenly filled his mind with reassurance. *No, My child, this is not your testing, but Mine.*

He looked around. Had the others heard that voice?

Ulestan was watching him intently. Behind Finn, the queen sat silently listening as well.

Speak, My child, not with the wisdom of men, but in the power of the living God.

Willimond rose slowly to his feet, his legs finally supporting him. Could others see him trembling? He opened his mouth. And when he did, to his great surprise his voice came out calm and bold. So calm, in fact, that he was not sure it was he himself speaking.

"Much have I heard of the gods of Friesland whom you fear and honor." His eyes were upon Finn, but he knew that every man in the hall was listening. "Do your gods care about men? Can you speak with them? Do they listen to your prayers? Or are your gods concerned more with their own doings than with the affairs of men?

"The God who made the world and all things in it is Lord of the heavens and the earth. It is He who created the seas and the dry land. He sets the times in motion. By the will and word of the One God did Friesc establish the borders of your land. According to His plan did the great boar fall at the hands of that mighty one. He establishes kings and kingdoms. He is mightier than all the kings of men, mightier than the gods made by men. He is mightier than the very seas!

"And yet, He cares about men. He Himself gives life and breath to all things. He made every nation of mankind to live on the face of the earth and set their boundaries about them. He desires that we seek Him, and seeking, He promises that we will find, for He is not far from each one of us. In Him we live and move and exist."

When Willimond finished, Finnsburg was silent. Ulestan stared blankly into the fire. Daelga sat idly fingering his harp. The queen's eyes were wet with tears. The thanes and fighting men sat with eyes downcast. The richest of the chieftains looked idly about, casting their eyes from here to there, but avoiding the glance of Willimond.

Only Finn still met his gaze. "What sign or token does your God give that he cares about men?"

"He gave the greatest sign for which any could ask. He gave His only Son as a gift that we might know life."

"Again you speak of a mighty god who would sacrifice his own son to save the lives of his people. Of this I would hear more."

"On the scroll which you burned were written the following words: 'For while we were still helpless, at the right time, Christ died for the ungodly.' This thing God did, not because we deserved it, but because He loved us. Though we knew Him not and had turned away from following Him, He called us back to Himself with His only Son."

For many long hours after that, Willimond sat beside the fire answering questions and telling Finn of the One God and of Jesus, His Son. He continued until well after the moon had begun her descent and all but Finn, Ulestan, Froda, Daelga and Hildeburh had turned away and ceased to listen. Only when Hildeburh's eyes had also fallen shut did Finn turn Willimond away.

"But two more questions I would ask," Finn said.

"You know I will answer if I am able," Willimond replied. He felt that sometime during the night a barrier had been torn down between himself and the king.

"Why have you come?"

Willimond sighed. He, too, was tired. "There are many reasons why I have come. Or rather, many reasons why I have been sent, for I did not just come—I was sent with a purpose. God desires that all might know Him. 'To as many as received Him, to them He gave the right to become children of God, even to those who believe in His name.'

"I came to bring you news of a God who cares about you, that you too and any who desire it might become His children. I came also because I thought God called me to come. I still think He has called me." As an afterthought he added, "It is my hope to begin a church here where all who desire might worship the living God."

"And what of those who do not believe?" Finn asked.

"My message is a message of hope," Willimond replied. "It is for all who would hear it." He paused before continuing. "For those who do not believe, the Bible speaks of judgment. It is as you yourself have said of the king who planted the vineyard. He will bring an army and destroy those who killed His Son."

XIX

The Church

Willimond awoke late the following morning. Hurrying to the river, he found Lopystre, Lawyrke and Lindlaf already at work.

"For once," Lopystre laughed, seeing Willimond approaching, "we have risen before the monk!"

Willimond laughed with him as he stripped off his outer garments and waded into the stream to help with the work. He had much to laugh about that day.

"You are in bright spirits, my friend," Lawyrke commented in his high voice. "I take it that Finn treated you kindly."

"You, too, have treated me well," Willimond replied. "You have taught me to fish. But last night I was a fisher of men."

Willimond had meant that in fun, but Lopystre set down his net and turned to him. "What do you mean?" he asked quite seriously. "How can one be a 'fisher of men'?"

And so for the second time in two days Willimond found himself speaking of God and His promises to all who seek Him. All that day as they worked under the warm spring sun, the monk explained how God calls His followers to bring the truth to others. "Have I not related to you," he told them, a great smile spreading across his face, "that among Jesus' first followers many were themselves fishermen—James, John, Andrew and Simon. In fact, Jesus, the Son of God Himself, oft went fishing among them." At this the eyes of Lindlaf lit up. He had grown to love the stories Willimond was telling him about Jesus, but he had not before heard that Jesus was a fisherman.

"Early one morning, after a long night of fishing, Jesus was in a boat with Simon the fisherman," Willimond began the tale.

"'Put out into the deep water and let down your nets for a catch,' Jesus said to Simon.

"'But, Master,' Simon answered, 'we worked hard all night and caught nothing.' Nonetheless, Simon obeyed Jesus, for he had grown to trust his master. When he put out his nets again, he caught such a great quantity of fish that their nets began to break.

"'From now on,' Jesus told them, 'you will be fishers of men.'"

Willimond finished his story, holding up one of the nets as if he were about to cast it over Lindlaf. Lindlaf laughed.

"We need this Jesus of yours today, it seems," Lopystre said. They had just finished checking the second weir and had found it nearly empty.

"Perhaps we will do better in the upper weir this day," Willimond said. The others looked at him strangely, and Willimond suddenly wished he hadn't said that.

Together they walked up the river silently and expectantly. But alas, the third weir proved no more fruitful that day than had the first two. So with meager keepings they set about the task of mending and resetting the weirs for the next tide.

Shortly after midday dark storm clouds began to gather overhead. At dusk, which came early, the sky opened up and began to pour forth torrents of rain upon the village of Hwitstan. The rain lasted that night and through the next day. Lopystre and Willimond dutifully braved the rains and checked the weirs—and found them all nearly empty. After some feeble and halfhearted work on the shores, they returned to their house to spend the remainder of the day where it was dry.

Lindlaf spent most of that day in the back room with a bad cough, and Blostma, who had cut her finger on a sharp stick, spent most of the day crying.

The days following were cold and cloudy. The warm spring weather Willimond had enjoyed for his first week in Hwitstan was gone, replaced by the spring rains. The village turned muddy, and people grew less talkative and at times almost hostile. Ulestan and Froda were nowhere to be seen, and Finn gave no request to see Willimond. Time dragged slowly for everyone. The monk, though eager to see Finn once again, did his best to remain patient and keep his good spirits. He continued to work hard beside his three companions and to learn his task. He would wait for God's timing—or he would at least try. But it was not easy. The cool weather made it difficult to enter the water, though it brought with it some good catches of fish as well as some poor ones; days of abundance intermingled with days of poverty.

One day, after more than a week had passed since Willimond's last visit with Finn, one of the weirs was severely damaged. A heavy log floating downstream in the high spring water was thrown against the wall of the weir by the quickly receding tide. In the process of clearing the log away, Lopystre's right hand was broken. Without his help, it took nearly a full week for the other three to repair the damage to the weir. Lopystre, forced to watch from the shoreline, grew angry and frustrated at their slow pace.

All the while the monk wondered what Finn was thinking, when he would be called again, if he would be allowed to remain in Hwitstan, and if he would continue to be fed. Another two weeks would pass after Lopystre's injury before Willimond was called once more to meet with Finn.

●

The warm, dry weather had returned to Friesland, bringing hopes that it would stay for the summer. The village was already looking forward to Summer's Day celebration. Lopystre, though his hand was still bandaged, was again in good spirits. He could not work the weirs as well as he would have liked, but with the added help of Willimond they were able to manage. He strolled down the slope to the river late one morning to find Willimond in the water with Lawyrke and Lindlaf.

"Well, my friend monk," Lopystre said, "it appears as though it is your turn for a rest."

"I do not begrudge you your rest," Willimond responded. "It is better to let your hand heal now so it may serve you better in the years to come."

"I do not disagree. Nonetheless, today I will take your place. You have been called by Finn."

"Now?" Willimond's heart leapt.

"That is the first time the king has spoken to me in such a way," Lopystre said, not hearing Willimond's question. He was so clearly pleased at having been spoken to by Finn that Willimond listened to him without interrupting. "I now know why so many serve him so faithfully," Lopystre continued. "He addressed me as if I were a friend. He asked me about my weirs. He told me of my father and how skilled he had been in making them. He knew much more about me than I ever imagined. How he knows so much, I could not guess. He even asked me about you," Lopystre said to his son, who beamed at that information.

"And me?" Lawyrke asked with his eyes.

"And you too," Lopystre said, turning to his brother.

"He is a good king," Willimond said, then added, "Does he wish to see me now?"

"Immediately."

Willimond grabbed his cloak and hurried toward Finnsburg, stopping only to pick up the parchments from his corner of Lopystre's hut. What would Finn ask him this time? he wondered.

Ulestan and Froda were both standing at the entrance of the great hall when Willimond arrived.

"You have come," Ulestan said in greeting. "That is good. I think you will be happy with what you hear." Both he and Froda were smiling.

Willimond began to step into the hall, but Ulestan placed a hand lightly upon his shoulder. "Finn waits for you atop the tower," he said, pointing up the slope which separated the village from the sea. "He often stands there and looks out to sea."

"When she is lonely for her people," Froda added, "Hildeburh joins him. From there she can look far to the north."

"That is where they like to talk with their friends," Ulestan said as they began the small ascent. Willimond did not miss the significance of that comment, though he said nothing in reply as they walked up the slope to the base of the tower.

Froda led the way up the ladder, and Willimond followed, with Ulestan climbing last. Finn was waiting for them at the top, sword over shoulder and ash staff in hand. Beside him stood Hildeburh. Seeing her in daylight for the first time, Willimond was astonished. Though her womb was, if possible, even larger than before, her beauty in no way seemed diminished. Or if it was, then without child she must have been beyond description.

And Finn was kingly indeed! He towered over the monk—indeed over all in the tower, even over Ulestan who was a strong warrior himself. The king's broad back truly seemed capable of supporting a kingdom!

As Willimond bowed low, Hildeburh looked at him and smiled sweetly.

"Before you stands the flower of Friesland—Hildeburh the fair, daughter of Hoc, the jewel of the Danes," Finn said.

"A jewel of surpassing value," Willimond replied, bowing lower.

"Rise and stand beside us," Finn commanded. As the monk came to his feet, Finn turned to face the sea. As he did, the scar on his neck and shoulder became visible to Willimond for the first time, and he wondered from whence it had come.

"The seas are mighty," Finn said after they had stood silently for a few moments. "If it is as you say and your god created them, he too must be mighty."

Willimond nodded. "He is mighty indeed."

"Whether that is the case or not, I know that the seas are not mine to control. Though I follow the Swan Road now and again, it is only with great reverence and care that I tread upon those paths. No, these mighty waters are not mine to take or to give. Yet," he continued, "there is much upon these shores which I may give or take as a king may."

Finn turned to Willimond and held his gaze until the young monk turned away. As he did, he saw that Ulestan and Froda were both smiling. Hildeburh was as well.

"You would build a 'church' for your god to dwell in?"

"No, my king," Willimond replied. Finn appeared surprised by the answer. "God does not dwell in buildings made by man," the monk explained, "nor does he need us to serve Him and take care of Him. I desire a place not where God can dwell among men, but where men can go and worship God."

Finn lifted his hands in either confusion or amusement. "If this god is so great, can we not worship him anywhere?" Willimond was about to answer yes, but Finn did not give him the opportunity. "But I do not understand the ways of your god as you do. What I do understand is being a king. I will build a church for your god here in Hwitstan." Willimond's eyes lit up with wonder. "You will be a priest for your god here in Friesland."

Willimond dropped again to his knee. "Thank you, my king."

"Perhaps it will not be as grand as your home in Lindisfarne," Finn continued. *It will be far more grand to me*, Willimond thought. "I understand not what a priest does. In that, you will have to instruct me."

"Gladly," Willimond answered.

"But I do understand the need for food. While you serve your god, you will also serve my people by continuing to work the weirs with Lopystre."

Willimond was only slightly disappointed. Though the added labor of working the weirs would take valuable time, he had already grown to enjoy that task. Now he would be like Paul the tentmaker. "In that I am content," he answered. "But you may find that I serve your people best by teaching them about the God."

"That shall be seen," Finn replied. "There is certainly much to be taught."

"May I ask, then, a second favor?"

"Speak it."

"It is the way of God that He has set aside the seventh day of every week for men to worship Him. If I am to be His priest, then I must serve Him on that day by teaching His Word in the church."

"The seventh day shall be yours to do as your god requires. On that day you shall be free from the weirs."

"But whom shall you teach?" Hildeburh asked, not unkindly.

It was the first time Willimond had heard the voice of the queen; strong and yet feminine, it could easily command the wills of many men were she ever so to choose. So startled was he to hear her, in fact, that it took a few moments for the impact of her question to settle on him. Whom was he to teach? Who would listen? God, as of yet, had no servants in Hwitstan save Willimond himself. As Finn had been speaking, so excited was Willimond about the church that he had assumed the king himself would be among those who entered its doors.

"Do you yourselves believe the message I have brought?" the monk finally asked.

Hildeburh said nothing, but Finn shook his head deliberately. "You bring strange and interesting teaching, and I would hear more of it, but—no, I am not ready to accept it now, nor might I ever be."

Willimond's heart dropped at this, but he answered Hildeburh's question nonetheless. "I will teach any and all who come through the doors to seek the words of God, be they many or few, peasant or king. It is up to God to bring whom He chooses."

"So be it," Finn replied. "Ulestan will see to it that the building begins at once. You shall help him in choosing a place. There also shall you have your own dwelling, that you may be close to your god."

"Again I thank you," the monk replied.

"There is one more thing," Finn said a few moments later as Ulestan, Willimond and Froda started to depart. "I have need at times for one who knows letters and writing. I may call upon you. When I do, I may also have more questions about your god."

XX

The Mediator

On the way back to the village they passed Finnlaf, who was running up the hill toward the tower. "Ulestan," he shouted, out of breath from having sprinted from the far side of the village, "there are many men in the village . . . messengers . . . I think they are Franks."

Willimond saw a hot glance pass between Froda and Ulestan. His knowledge of the Franks was small—much less than his knowledge of the Frisians. He knew only a little of the raids on Domburg many years past and of the ambush which had brought about the death of Folcwalda—only what Lopystre had told him. But the response in Ulestan's eyes to this news from Finnlaf told the monk enough: the Franks were still not welcome in Hwitstan.

"Your father is in the tower," Ulestan said. "Tell him what you have told us, and then stay there with your mother."

"How many are there?" Froda asked.

"There were ten or twelve, I think, but I did not count," the prince said. "Aelfer and Beow are talking with them now."

"Good. Go now and tell Finn," Ulestan replied. Then, turning to Froda he said, "Aeltar is across the river where the men are building the new tower. It might be best if you bring word to him to return to Hwitstan."

"It might be best if I stay with you," Froda replied succinctly. It was clear that he had no intentions of leaving Hwitstan for any purpose. "Perhaps our monk may be of service."

Ulestan looked first at Froda and then back at Willimond. "You know where the new tower is?"

"Yonder?" Willimond pointed northeastward across the

mouth of the Hwitstan River to the top of a small hill. Even as he looked, he saw flashes of silver in the sunlight.

"Good. Go at once and bring them the message you have just heard."

Willimond bowed and left immediately. The tide was high, and it was some distance up the river to the small wooden bridge. He ran the entire way, grunting a few inadequate words of explanation to Lopystre as he passed. When he reached the bridge, he paused to catch his breath and then continued back down the opposite side of the river at a slower pace.

By the time Willimond reached Aeltar, he was drenched in sweat and completely winded.

Aeltar stood atop a chest-high log structure, the beginnings of a new tower. "What brings you here?" he shouted a bit more loudly than necessary, but not unkindly.

Willimond bent over and tried to catch his breath. "Ulestan . . ." he began, and then paused again. "Ulestan sent me. There are Franks in Hwitstan."

Aeltar leapt lightly to the ground and grabbed Willimond by the shoulders. "A warband?"

"I think not . . ." he panted. "Ten or twelve."

The workmen paused from their labors and listened to the conversation.

"Ulestan wants me?" Aeltar asked. "What about Finn?"

"Ulestan asked that you return to the village." Willimond's breath was finally returning. "Finn does not yet know, but he will soon."

"Come!" Aeltar commanded him. Willimond followed him around the back of the tower site, where the thane untethered a small black and white horse. Beside his horse three other warriors were sitting casually in the shade watching the villagers' progress on the new tower. They had not heard Willimond's message.

"Franks in Hwitstan," Aeltar said. That was all that was necessary. They had their horses almost at once.

In a single, graceful leap Aeltar was astride his own mount. He reached down, and before Willimond knew it he was on the horse beside the thane. The monk, who was not looking forward to the long walk back, had no objections. Galloping all the way, they were back in the village in less than half the time it had taken him to run to the tower.

When they came through the outer ring of huts into the center of Hwitstan, Willimond saw a large crowd gathered by the door of Finnsburg. A small group—he later counted fourteen—of strangely clad men stood there. They were surrounded by fifty or more armed Frisians, thanes most of them, members of Finn's hearthwerod. But more than a few villagers stood by as well. To the side, fourteen tired horses were being held by other villagers. So the visitors were separated from their horses. Had Willimond known anything about armed conflict, he would have known how great an advantage those horses would have been had the Franks still been on them. Now the Franks looked nervous and afraid, standing in a tight circle facing outward. A few had drawn swords.

"Do we war with the Franks?" Willimond asked Aeltar as he slid off the side of the horse. He knew not that Aeltar himself was from Domburg, the village that had suffered cruelly from Frankish raids.

"They killed and ambushed Folcwalda in a raid," he answered as though it had just happened the week before and as if that clearly answered Willimond's question. Aeltar did not mention what they had done to the son of Ecgwalda, his chieftain.

"When?" Willimond asked.

"Eight years ago," Aeltar said, and then he was pushing his way to the front of the crowd.

Though he could later not remember why he had done so, Willimond followed in Aeltar's wake.

"We would speak with your king," the foremost of the Franks was saying.

Ulestan, Aelfer, Beow and Froda stood in their way, blocking the entrance to Finnsburg. Guthman and Guthric stood a little to the side. All six had their swords drawn. Finn was not in sight. Willimond guessed he was already inside.

"Shall we admit to see our lord the slayers of his kinsman?" Ulestan asked.

"My lord . . ." The man addressed Ulestan as a superior. ". . . we are neither the slayers of your lord, nor do we know of what you speak."

"Are you not Franks?" Ulestan asked.

"We are," he answered, turning first to Froda, then to Beow

and Aelfer, and then back to Ulestan. A deathly silence followed. The Frankish visitor was at a loss for words, and none there were eager to aid him. The circle about them tightened. "Folcwalda was killed many years ago," he finally said. "This we know. But Chlotar is also long since dead. He was not greatly loved among our people. We have a new king. I am Pepyn, a servant of Dagobert."

At the mention of Folcwalda's death—from Frankish lips, no less!—Ulestan grasped his sword more firmly and clenched his teeth. Long-gone memories twitched across his visage like ghosts.

It was Froda who finally answered, "Of the death of Chlotar we know. We do not grieve. Of Dagobert we have heard also, though his name means little. It will take many more years than have already passed before we forget the passing of Folcwalda— or the manner of his passing."

"Good men, if you will but allow us to speak with Finn, per- haps we can speak further of this matter. It may be of great benefit to both of our peoples." Then, unwisely, so Willimond deemed, Pepyn ended with a threat. "If, however, you would pre- fer war with our people, then you have but to slay us and a war you would have."

Another long silence followed. The only sound to be heard was that of the remaining few swords being pulled out of their sheaths.

"This matter is for Finn," Ulestan replied.

Pepyn bowed.

"But unarmed shall you enter into his presence."

"Little do we like that," Pepyn answered, looking around. "Do you ask us to go to our deaths unarmed?"

"Pepyn, servant of Dagobert," Froda said distinctly and slowly, stepping forward and raising the edge of his sword so that it was poised at the level of Pepyn's belly and only a foot away, "if Ulestan asks you to enter our hall unarmed, then you may know that you will leave these doors unharmed. Not at least until you have swords again in your hands shall you be struck down."

Ulestan stood perfectly still.

Willimond's thoughts turned suddenly to God. *Lord*, he prayed silently, his eyes looking to the heavens, *turn these events to Your glory. Spare, in Your grace, the lives of those present.*

"These terms we will accept," Pepyn replied. "May the gods honor you as you honor your words to us."

Fourteen swords and shields were laid at the entrance of Finnsburg, and fourteen Franks entered cautiously. They followed Ulestan, Froda, Aelfer and Beow and were followed by Aeltar, Guthric, Guthman and as many more as counted themselves among Finn's hearthwerod.

Willimond, too, found himself irresistibly drawn inside, though no such right could he claim. He ever after wondered at the wisdom of that decision.

In the center of the hall, on his tall bench beside a cold hearth, Finn sat. His sword lay naked across his knees. His eyes cut the distance to the door as a fast ship with the wind at its back slices through the waves. The rest of the hall was empty save for two thanes who stood as statues upon either side of their king, old but not yet weary, toughened by many scars. Hereric and Edmen they were. The sight of them sent chills down the monk's back as he followed Aeltar into the hall.

Pepyn, followed by his band, approached Finn and bowed very low. "I am Pepyn, servant of Dagobert, humbly seeking your pleasure."

"For what purpose do you travel to Friesland?" Finn asked.

"We come as an embassy from Dagobert to Finn, from the land of the Franks to Friesland. We seek peace."

"Were you seeking peace when you raided our shores and killed our people?" Finn asked.

"Many years past are the days of which you speak," Pepyn said.

"Too early in life was Folcwalda taken from his people," Finn replied, his eyes still fixed sharply upon his guests. Were his glance a sword, the Franks would no longer have been alive.

"And yet we had then a different king. Chlotar is no longer. Dagobert rules now. Of the deeds of Chlotar, Dagobert makes no claim; on behalf of our kingdom he has repented."

"Does his repentance return Folcwalda?"

"No," Pepyn answered, "but it may bring with it peace."

Finn said nothing, but it appeared that his eyes softened somewhat.

"King Finn," Pepyn said, "we have a long tale, but it may be worth hearing. We came not to relive the past, but to speak of peace between us. Perhaps this tale will do much to bring that peace about."

"We will listen," Finn declared. "You may sit as you speak."

The Franks looked nervously about as they took seats on the benches of Finnsburg. Finn's men followed. Willimond found himself sitting beside Aeltar, just a few feet away from Pepyn as he told his tale.

"In the last days of Chlotar's kingship there came to his court one day a Danish ship bearing three lords and their small warband. Of their purpose for coming I know much—more than I desired—for my father was a chieftain and feasted often in the hall of Chlotar. Guthlaf, Hunlaf and Oslaf were the names of these Danes, and their hearts were as wicked as Chlotar's." So closely was every eye watching Pepyn that none saw Ulestan catch his breath at the names of those three. A faint and distant memory began to haunt him, and a look of distaste crossed his face. His brow wrinkled, and his lips curled back. In Aelfer's mind as well was kindled a slow glimmer of recognition.

"Though they little trusted Chlotar," Pepyn continued, "nor he them, they understood each other well in their dark thoughts. 'Come, make war on Folcwalda,' they counseled Chlotar. 'His kingdom grows rich, and there is much land to be plundered.'

"Chlotar was slow to agree, for he could not fathom their purposes, nor was he eager to make new enemies. 'What have I to gain?' he asked.

"'Land and wealth,' they replied. 'Would you have a new and powerful king arising on your very borders?'

"'Little do I fear an attack from these. But neither do I want to waste my own money waging a needless war. There is little enough wealth to be gained in that land.'

"'Of that you may be surprised,' they said.

"'What have you to gain?' Chlotar then asked, beginning to give way to his greed. 'Is not the Frisian queen one of yours?' In that, he spoke of Hildeburh.

"'Not one of ours,' they replied. 'She is the sister of Hnaef, who rules in a place that ought to be ours.' Beyond that remark they made no other hint of what they themselves had to gain from a war between the Franks and Frisians. On and on they talked, and they spoke not with words only, but with gold, promising great wealth to Chlotar if he would but agree. In the end it was by gold that Chlotar was persuaded. Even so, he would not openly go to war with Friesland. His chieftains were strongly opposed and would not consent. Instead, against the wishes of some and without the knowledge of others, he sent a small warband to raid the Frisian shores. When the raids did not provide the wealth the Danish lords had promised, they paid the warband themselves as if the Franks were hired soldiers.

"Of the death of Folcwalda and the defeat of his raiding bands, word eventually reached Chlotar, and he called an end to the raids. The Danish lords never returned. We do not understand the purposes for the actions of these three, nor will we defend the actions of Chlotar. To the end of his days he dealt in treachery and deceit. But do not hold his actions against the Frankish people nor against Dagobert, who rules justly as a king should.

"Of my father," Pepyn concluded, "perhaps he has already received his just reward for his place at the side of Chlotar. They died the same death on the same day. Of that death I will not speak."

Finn listened quietly to the entire tale. When it was over, he looked around him at each of his thanes gathered there. They returned his gaze, but none spoke a word.

In the silence that followed, the Franks grew visibly more nervous. They began to feel for swords that were not there.

A voice broke the silence. "Perhaps your tale is true, perhaps it is not. But it does not change what has happened. By the hands of Franks Folcwalda was slain." The voice was not Finn's. It came from behind him. Edmen's eyes were dark and narrow as he spoke. According to Lopystre's tale, had he not been with Folcwalda at the time of his death? Willimond reflected. And his brother as well? Had not his brother later been killed by the Franks also? Willimond saw many nods from Finn's thanes in response to Edmen's words. "My lord," Edmen said to Finn a few seconds later, "their blood is forfeit."

Pepyn's eyes opened wide. Was it fear or simply dismay that registered in his face? Willimond could not tell. "Have we been led weaponless to the slaughter?" he almost shouted.

"Was Wulfanwod armed when he was struck down?" Edmen returned the shout and drew his sword.

Pepyn rose to his feet. His men followed, looking about with fear. All about them men were holding swords and glaring at them with hostile intent. The Franks tried to form a tight circle, but they had little hope of defense. Nobody moved.

"Ulestan?" Pepyn said, turning to the thane.

Ulestan turned to Finn. "By my word and by your order have their weapons been taken from them."

"Lord," Edmen said, "they have not given justice to others—do they deserve it themselves? But if you desire, we may return to them their swords and then put them to the death. I will gladly strike the first blow."

Finn looked around him again. There were a few mumbles and nods of agreement. Ulestan looked very troubled but said nothing.

"My king . . ." Willimond looked about him and was surprised to find himself speaking. Finn looked sternly at the young monk, who suddenly felt very much out of place. "My king," he continued nonetheless, "he was a wise man who said, 'Conquer your enemies by making them your friends. Otherwise your enemy conquers you, because a conquered enemy is still an enemy.'"

"Are these the words of your god?" Finn asked.

"No." Willimond blushed. "But my God has spoken much about mercy. 'Blessed are the merciful,' He said, 'for they shall themselves receive mercy.'"

"Does your god speak naught of just vengeance?" Edmen's voice rose in anger.

Finn raised his hand to silence his thane, but Willimond was already answering. "Vengeance God claims for Himself. Those who serve Him should seek rather for peace."

"Does a mighty god fear battle so much?" Finn asked.

"It takes greater might to pursue peace than war. Mercy requires more strength than does vengeance. Any man can have war. How many peace?" Willimond spoke with greater boldness than he ever imagined, and yet his knees were trembling so violently he had to hold them with his hands. He expected at any moment to be struck down for saying such things to the king.

"My king," Ulestan said, "the monk speaks wisely."

Nobody was more surprised to hear those words than Willimond. Hope increased in his heart. Perhaps the king would listen to the words of his thane though he would not listen to an insignificant monk.

Finn turned to his thane. "Was it you who brought him in here?"

"No, it was not I," the thane responded. "Yet he is here, and his words might well be heeded."

XXI

A Warning

nce again silence descended on the great hall of Finnsburg like a spring fog in shallow water. The air was thick with tension. The Franks remained knotted in a group, facing death as they looked about them at their enemies. The Frisians held their positions, swords poised, waiting for a word from their king. In the midst of it, for the briefest of moments Pepyn's eyes met Willimond's, and a look of gratitude and understanding passed between them.

What passed through Finn's mind during those next few moments, none knew, nor ever would. His anger and the memory of his father weighed heavily on his heart, as did the words of Edmen. He could not easily forget his father's death at the hands of the Franks. Nor was he wont to listen to their words of accusation against the Danes, his wife's folk. But in that hour the words of a trusted thane and a young monk weighed more heavily upon him than did his feelings. Not lightly could he cast aside the advice of Ulestan the Owl. That wise one had not before failed him. And Finn was just. He was a good king. His word he would not break, nor unrightly would he take life.

When none present thought they could stand to wait even a second longer, Finn finally spoke. "For what purpose have you come?" he asked Pepyn.

When the king spoke those words, something seemed to snap in Edmen, and he sank heavily to the bench. Finn's tone and manner, though still sharp, was less hostile. The decision had been made. The king and treasure-giver had betrayed Edmen, had refused him his right to avenge Folcwalda, to avenge his own brother Eormen. Would his king make peace with his most hated enemies? Edmen's will to fight was gone. For that thane, all hope had vanished.

Pepyn sensed in Finn exactly what Edmen had sensed, but with a different response. Hope returned to that brave Merovingian. He allowed his stance to relax somewhat, though he did not return to his seat, and he answered Finn, "It is as I have said. We desire peace."

"There is no war between us," Finn replied.

"Our ships cannot pass along your shores or stop in your villages. There is no trade between our people save through the hands of others. If we ride to your hall we find speartips and swords pointed at our bellies. This is not peace. Much we could gain in these difficult days from trade between our people. Further, there are other powers to the south that grow stronger each day. Will you face them alone?"

As Folcwalda's reasoning had sounded good to many chieftains during the days he built his kingdom, so too did Pepyn's words sound wise to Finn. On they talked and questioned, speaking of trade and hostile southern empires, of Dagobert and his kingdom and earls. Pepyn spoke, and Finn listened. Finn spoke, and Pepyn listened. Wisely and carefully did the Frank phrase his questions and answers, avoiding any subject which might renew the anger. And so, bit by bit and word by word the tension and hostility slowly dissolved between the nations, though it did not utterly disappear. These two spoke throughout the day and into the evening. In the end much was agreed upon and many bargains struck. Little love was there between the Franks and the thanes of Finn, but by Finn's command they feasted together that night in Finnsburg. A gathering of souls in the hall of a king does much to dissipate ill-will, as does shared food, drink and song.

Yet, though feast was served and wine consumed, though the poet sang, there were three who did not share joy that night. Of all Finn's thanes, earls and retainers, only Edmen and Hereric remained not in the hall for feast and song, but departed from Hwitstan altogether. Before mead was shared and before Daelga sang, Edmen had come silently before the king with Hereric a witness at his side. Without a word he laid the sword of his brother Eormen upon the lap of Finn. No word was necessary. Finn did not miss the significance of the gesture, nor did any other there. By ancient custom, that thane was calling upon the king to avenge his brother. That time-honored tradition was his last hope. By laws more ancient than Friesland itself was the king bound to recognize Edmen's request for repayment of his brother's blood.

One more time did Pepyn's fear return to him and one more time did he reach for a weapon that was not there. Around him, his men stared wide-eyed as Finn received the sword from Edmen. But Finn refused both custom and request. No less did he love his own father than did Edmen his brother, but Finn would not unjustly spill blood or cause feuds. He was a good king. As ones betrayed, Edmen and Hereric left Finnsburg. Never again were either seen in Friesland, nor did tale ever return of their deaths.

Nor for Willimond did the events that followed proceed as well as they had for Pepyn. Though the monk's wise words had been well taken, he had nevertheless entered unsummoned into Finnsburg and had spoken boldly in the king's counsel though he had no such right. To feast with the king was an honor. To be counted among Finn's hearthwerod was a privilege accorded to few. None before had so boldly taken it upon themselves to pursue such rights, and Finn was greatly displeased.

"Much have you been given, and yet you have hazarded it all by seeking what has not been granted and demanding what is not your right," Finn said to him in front of all gathered. "By such acts has many a king lost his throne and many an ambitious thane usurped that which was not his."

When he heard those words Willimond's heart sunk, for in that brief time he had already begun to imagine himself a king's counselor, as Aidan was for Oswald. Now he feared only for his church.

"My word I will not break. You shall have your church. But in this is your punishment set: Not again shall your feet enter this hall, nor shall your voice speak to my ears save only if you are called. On the day that your feet pass through this door or your voice reach my ears unbidden, your reward on that day shall be death."

Heavyhearted did Willimond leave the hall and walk into the dusk of Hwitstan. In one day so much had been gained and so much lost. *In all things*, he told himself again and again, *the hand of God will work. In the building of the church He will work His will. In the punishment from Finn He will work His will as well.*

Not in these words, however, did Willimond find much comfort, true words though they were, but from a single hug from the young Blostma as he walked into Lopystre's house that evening. In that single embrace his heart was lifted far higher than words ever could. And so it was in good spirits that he went to rest that night.

The following day brought the beginning of the building of the church at Hwitstan; no great hall like Finnsburg, but grand nonetheless in the eyes of Willimond. He could not have been more joyful. In but one summer he would have a church of his own. How many years had it taken Aidan in Northumbria before Lindisfarne had been begun? But Lindisfarne was a great abbey. This was but a small chapel. And Willimond was still alone. Hildeburh's question still repeated itself in his ears. Who would come? he wondered.

When told of the news, Lopystre was delighted to hear that Willimond would remain in Hwitstan to help with the weirs. Two extra hands were always welcome—especially with one of his own broken. If Lopystre was also happy to hear that Willimond would soon have a home of his own attached to the church and that the monk would not have to live with him anymore, he said nothing about it. The young monk continued to work with Lopystre as he had been told, but as much as he could he also observed the building of his new church. His early morning time of prayer he at once began to take at the new church site so he could note the progress.

The location for the church he had chosen himself. As Finnsburg was the center of the northern end of the village, the church was to be the center of the southern end of the village. It would be built, to the dismay of a few traders, in the clearing where previously there had been a market of sorts. The church's entrance would face southward, away from the sea, so the cold north winds would not enter as easily.

The wooden foundation grew quickly. Looking at the walls taking shape, Willimond guessed that thirty or more might fit inside. Who those thirty would be, he did not yet know. Every day he prayed for the hearts of the villagers—and particularly for the hearts of his king and queen.

Ulestan visited frequently and also watched as the church took shape. His visits, however, were usually short. "I do not know what I expect," he said to Willimond one morning as the two stood watching four villagers lift a timber onto the west wall.

Willimond looked curiously at Ulestan, his attention diverted from the labor in front of him. "From what?"

"This building. It looks much like any other hall that men might build, save that it is somewhat bigger than most. How is this any different?"

Willimond smiled. That, then, was the reason for Ulestan's visits. Did he expect something magical and mysterious in this simple church? "Only in our hearts is it different. God does not dwell in a building made by men. Nor do we need to be here to speak with God. He hears us always."

"Then why do you build this church, this 'house for God'?" It was the same question Finn had asked many days earlier. But Finn had not given Willimond an opportunity to respond, and he had spent the next many days thinking of how he might have answered.

"Why did Finn build a hall? Why not each of you to your own house?" As he asked this, he felt a twinge of regret that he now was excluded from Finnsburg. None who desired, he told himself, would ever be excluded from *his* hall!

Ulestan seemed surprised and taken aback at the question. "That is the way it has always been! It is good for a king's thanes to gather together in his presence, for his battle-companions to enjoy together the fellowship of the hearth. In so doing, we become one."

"Yes," Willimond answered. "That is much the way it is with God, the great King. He enjoys having His people gathered together. And it is good for the people as well. It makes them one."

Ulestan nodded in understanding. That much of what Willimond said made sense to him: shared fellowship in the hall.

"Now let me ask you this," Willimond said a few moments later, "for I am greatly curious. Naught has been said of the role of the Danes in the death of Folcwalda. Yet Finn seemed to accept the tale told by the Franks."

The jaws of the thane snapped shut, and his face reddened. His fist closed tightly over the hilt of his sword. His head turned sharply to the side, and his neck muscles bulged and strained. "You are correct," he replied, "naught has been said, nor is such ever likely."

"Have I angered you?" Willimond asked quickly, for he did not understand the sudden reaction to his question.

"Not you," Ulestan answered. His anger was directed toward the Danes, though he said it not aloud. Three faces still plagued his memory. Nor could he forget the Danish coins found in the treasure-hoard of the raiders who had killed Folcwalda. He said nothing for a minute or so, and Willimond stood waiting. "Of the Danes, Finn will not speak," he finally answered.

"Why not?"

"Is it not obvious? Who is his wife?"

●

It took less than three weeks to complete the church. It was on the eve of Summer's Day that the first service was held in Hwitstan to worship the One God and Jesus His Son. As the day approached, Willimond eagerly spoke with many villagers, inviting all who wished to come and worship God and to hear His Word proclaimed. How many would listen, he did not know.

When the day came, Willimond arose early. He had spent his first night in his new home, a small room attached to the back of the church. As was his habit, he descended to the river to wash and pray. The sun too had risen early that day, and preparations were already being made for the feast of the following day. At the first light of dawn the monk was startled from his prayers by the squeal of a pig as it was slaughtered for the feast. The second and third squeals did not take him as much by surprise.

At the third hour he returned to the church. The village had already grown busy when he walked back to his new home. More than the usual number of traders were present, and a few of them, those who recognized Willimond as the monk who built his church in the market clearing, made remarks that were not kind. Many of Finn's chieftains had also arrived with their warbands, and those who were not in Finnsburg with the king wandered about the village.

Once back, Willimond did not again venture outside his

doors. His time was spent searching and reading his scrolls, preparing the message he would preach that day. Questions flooded his mind and distracted his preparations. What if only one came? What if only two? What if he was alone? His recent doubts returned. Was he really supposed to be in Hwitstan? But through all that, he managed to focus his thoughts enough to prepare what he would say, if anyone came.

The ninth hour—the appointed time—arrived. Willimond stood atop a low bench in the front of the church hall and waited. He was thankful that the wait was not long.

The ageless poet Daelga was the first through his doors. His hands hanging loosely at his sides, he strode casually and confidently into the small building and sat on one of the benches to Willimond's left. Only the presence of Finn would have surprised Willimond more than that of this poet. *I have not spoken one word to him*, the monk thought. *The Lord has appointed many whom we might never foresee*, he reminded himself.

Ulestan entered next. He followed so closely behind Daelga that Willimond wondered if he had been waiting outside, not wanting to enter alone. He was a marked contrast to Daelga. Ulestan's manner was eager and nervous. His sword was not with him, and his hand kept grasping at his side where it should have been. *No sword—Is this in reverence to the Lord?* the monk wondered. Ulestan sat on a bench near a back corner, as far away from Willimond as he could get, but he leaned forward on the edge of his bench with a look of anticipation.

Froda followed, his sword still at his side. He looked about for Ulestan and took a seat beside him.

To Willimond's joy, Lopystre entered but a minute or two later. He carried Blostma on his shoulder, with Berigyldan a step to his left. Lindlaf followed them, looking curiously about him as he walked.

The last two to enter Willimond only vaguely recognized. It was the older man with the crippled hand and his toothless wife who had brought Willimond his meal the first evening in Hwitstan when he had stayed in the lodging with the traders.

"This, then, is the flock over which the Lord has set me," Willimond whispered softly when it became clear that no more would be following. He smiled broadly. Looking at their faces, it was clear that not one of them knew what to do or what to expect. Each was as ignorant and curious as the rest. "Lord, I thank Thee for these."

He preached his first sermon, telling his appointed flock about the Good Shepherd, Jesus, who had laid down His life for His sheep. So nervous and excited was he that he hardly knew what he said. Nor, perhaps, did all those present hear his words either, for they too were nervous. Yet they were attentive. Willimond finished before he knew he had begun, and dismissed his first church with his blessing. They rose and departed quickly, without a word.

Yet when all had gone, the old man with the crippled hand stepped back into the church. In a choked voice he thanked Willimond. "Once before, when I was very young, I heard of your God. I have not since ceased to hope that one day I would hear more. This day my prayers have been answered." He departed, leaving Willimond in tears.

XXII

That Which Was Broken

These nine, and frequently Lawyrke and his wife as well, returned week after week to hear Willimond preach from the Holy Scriptures. This he did faithfully. Lopystre, Berigyldan, Lindlaf and Blostma were baptized later that summer and joyfully shared with Willimond in the holy breaking of bread. The old man and his wife soon followed.

As word spread and Willimond chanced to meet many others in the village, the small gathering began to grow. At times twenty gathered in the small hall to hear him speak. Many came simply because of Daelga, who was well-liked by all. But though Daelga came each week, he ever left quickly afterward and would not speak with Willimond. Others came because of Ulestan and Froda.

If Ulestan would but be baptized, Willimond thought, *others will surely follow*. But this thought he kept to himself. It was best, he knew, for Ulestan to come to his own decision and to count well the cost of giving his life to God.

As Willimond continued to preach and watch his small congregation grow, he also continued his work on the weirs. With the baptism of Lopystre, a new and greater friendship had grown between the two. Ever and again could be heard the sounds of laughter rising from the river as they labored together joyously. Many of those who came to the small church in those days came perhaps only because they had heard that laughter and wondered in their hearts what caused it.

The sun was still warm and the days still long, though signs of fall had begun to appear, when Willimond was called unexpectedly to return to Finnsburg to speak with Finn. Early one day Ulestan found the monk working the weirs. The two had by this time grown to be close friends and spoke often of many things: of fishing, of wars and kings, of the Angles and Saxons, and most frequently of God. Ulestan had an unending stream of questions, some of which Willimond found quite difficult to answer. In return, Willimond learned much from Ulestan about Friesland and her people, and particularly about Finn and Folcwalda.

"You have been summoned by the king," Ulestan said quietly so that Lopystre and the others would not hear. "The matter is urgent."

Willimond gathered his things quickly and followed Ulestan up the hill toward the village. "Surely Hildeburh has given birth by this time," he asked, for he had not seen the king in some time and desired news before he went to him.

"Do not speak too loudly or frequently of that topic," Ulestan warned in a manner uncharacteristically harsh for the thane. "It is best not to speak of it at all."

"For what reason?" Willimond asked honestly. "I do not understand."

"Some time ago Finn decided it best that if he had a second male heir his enemies should not know of him—that he should be raised quietly."

That, then, was the reason why none spoke of Hildeburh's outward signs of pregnancy, nor would there be any celebration when the child was born. Willimond understood the wisdom of Finn's decision, though he considered it a difficult secret to keep. "And has this male heir been born?"

Ulestan glanced sternly again at Willimond and then nodded in affirmation.

Finnsburg was dark and nearly vacant when they entered. Near the fire, which now burned low, sat two figures. One held a small bundle. A large object lay on the bench between them.

Willimond approached with Ulestan. He had not been in Finnsburg for many weeks and knew not whether this summons brought with it a welcome. Had Finn's heart softened toward him?

His eyes adjusted to the low light. The two seated figures

were indeed Finn and Hildeburh. It was Hildeburh who held the bundle, and what it was the monk knew from intuition almost at once, though it was not until he was halfway across the floor that he recognized the form of a young baby, saw the tiny hand reaching upward toward his mother's face, and heard the soft crying. But Willimond also knew at once that what lay on the bench between Finn and Hildeburh was the reason for his summons. He heard the low moans escaping the prostrate form of Finnlaf before he was able to recognize the young boy's face.

Finn and Hildeburh watched through anguish-filled eyes as the young monk approached, walking through the hall from which he had only recently been banished.

"By Ulestan's counsel have I brought you here," Finn stated. His face was stone. All emotion had been drained.

How much Ulestan has done for me already, Willimond thought. *He still speaks for me.*

Tears streamed down Hildeburh's face as Willimond knelt beside the sick child, her eyes pleading with him as she mechanically rocked her other son. Finnlaf's face was pale. Only his occasional low moaning and the faint rise and fall of his chest gave hint of life. Willimond placed his hand on the boy's forehead. It was burning with fever.

"I know nothing of healing," Willimond said, looking back and forth between Finn and Hildeburh. *What am I to do?* "I am sorry." *For what reason has Ulestan brought me here? No apology will suffice to ease their pain. For what reason has God brought me here?*

Finn turned to Ulestan. "Do you taunt me, my friend?" he accused his thane. "For nothing then have you been accepted back in my presence," he said angrily, turning back toward Willimond. "Go and return not again."

"But your god . . . ?" Hildeburh pleaded as Willimond rose to depart. Finn reached across his son to place a silencing hand on his queen's shoulder. But she would not be silenced. "Ulestan said he is a god of healing . . . that he raises men from the dead."

"God is powerful, but . . ."

"Then speak with him," the queen begged. She ceased the slow rocking of her newborn and pulled him tightly to her bosom. "He must not die."

"Does your god not care for men as you claim?" Finn rose to his feet. He was no longer asking Willimond to leave. He was begging him to stay. "Look upon Finnlaf's face. Does your god care for this? Mercy would you have me show in the name of your god. Does your god himself show mercy?"

"We do not always understand God's ways," Willimond tried to explain. "Pain and suffering do not please Him. But those are the ways of the world. They come from the Devil, not from God." Hollow words spoken to the parents of a dying child, they fell on deaf ears.

"Is payment required?" Finn demanded. "What is the price?" He unwrapped a gold ring from his wrist and tossed it at the feet of Willimond.

The monk was shaking his head. *No!* he shouted silently.

Another and then another ring landed at Willimond's feet, each worth more than Willimond's entire purse.

"No," he whispered.

"Does he require my kingdom? I have nothing else." Finn removed the heavy gold torc from around his neck. It was the torc of the king—Folcwalda's and then Finn's. It landed at Willimond's feet with a heavy thud.

"These things are already God's," Willimond tried to say. "He cannot be bought." He wasn't sure if the words came out.

Finn spun around and faced the far wall. Then he spun again and suddenly his great sword was raised high over his head. Willimond stood dumbfounded and watched in terror as it fell. He saw the end of his life upon him and had no time to prepare for it.

The great war-sword embedded itself deep in a bench beside Ulestan. With the strength of three men Finn tossed the bench aside and it crashed into two others, knocking them over as well.

"I have nothing else," Finn pleaded.

Willimond was weeping, not for himself, but for his king.

Then Finn's eyes settled on something new. He stepped back toward Hildeburh, who looked up at him questioningly. Quickly but gently he reached down and pulled from her hands their second son. She resisted for a moment, but finally let go when she saw the sudden calm sweeping over him—and when she understood he would not be denied.

"Does your god desire my child?" He held the baby out. Willimond's arms came out instinctively, and the king's new son was set into them. "Then he may have one . . . But let him spare the life of Finnlaf."

Willimond knew not what to say. How could he explain to them that one cannot bargain with God as with a trader, that He demands one's life and gives a life back in return?

"Does your god hear me?" Finn cried out. He looked toward the rafters of the great hall he had built. "God, I give you this child. He is yours. Let Willimond your servant take care of him. I ask only that you spare the life of Finnlaf." He was shouting at the ceiling.

There was silence.

Willimond tried to hand the child back to Finn, but the king would not accept him. He placed the child in Hildeburh's arms. Finn pulled the queen to her feet. Willimond looked down again at Finnlaf. The boy's breathing had almost stopped, but the muscles in his arms were twitching. Sweat was bleeding from his forehead.

When the monk looked up, Finn, Hildeburh and Ulestan were gone.

●

Never before had Willimond spent a day and night praying as fervently as he did that day. He prayed for Finn and Hildeburh, for Ulestan, for the village of Hwitstan. He prayed for wisdom. He prayed for the new believers in his church.

And lastly, he prayed for Finnlaf. Fearfully and eagerly he prayed for him. Fearfully, for he did not know if God would answer his prayers. Eagerly, for he desired that He would.

Throughout the night his prayers were lifted up to heaven. On his knees before the fire he prayed. With his hands on the child's fevered head he prayed. Whether on his face on the hard floor or standing with his hands raised to heaven, he prayed.

The sun set on his prayers, and the moon rose with them.

●

Many days' journey to the north, Aidan himself was praying for Willimond. "Lord God, Father in Heaven, great is Your name. As You are with us this evening, may Your presence be felt by Willimond as well. Give him strength in the mission to which You have called him. And as You hear our prayers, hear his as well."

"Your will be done," the other brothers at Lindisfarne joined in.

●

As the dawn was breaking the next morning, Willimond fell asleep on the floor beside Finnlaf. When he awoke, the midday brightness was streaming through the door and Finn was standing over him, casting his shadow on Willimond's face. It took the monk a moment to remember where he was and why he was there. When he did, he sat up quickly. Finnlaf was gone. The torc and rings were gone as well.

"You live still," Finn said.

For how much longer? Willimond wondered as he searched the hall for any sign of the boy. "Where . . ."

"Atop the tower with Hildeburh."

"Alive?"

"He is doing very well, though he was surprised to awake alone in the hall with you. I think he was a bit scared." The king was laughing. It was a joyous sound for Willimond.

"You shall be rewarded greatly. Thankful I am that Ulestan brought you here."

"Do not reward me," Willimond answered. "It was God who healed him. Be thankful to Him."

Finn's eyes dimmed for a moment. "You speak of my bargain."

"No," the monk answered honestly. In truth, he had forgotten about it.

"It will be kept. The child shall be given into your keeping. The giving of his name is up to you. Also, you shall raise him. The child is in the care of your god."

"But . . ."

"But in this I warn you: Never shall you mention who his parents are. This command is for your safety as well as his." Seeing the look of confusion in Willimond's eyes, the king continued, "The wife of Deomaer the jeweler shall be his nurse. In that will you have aid."

Willimond rose to his feet. He was confused. Was this really happening? He followed Finn out the door of the hut. As he emerged, the older man from his church caught sight of him from across the village and came running as fast as he could to where Willimond stood.

"My hand!" he exclaimed, holding it out. Willimond looked closely but saw nothing wrong. What was this man talking about? "It is healed. It is as strong as before it was damaged."

Finn looked curiously at the man and at Willimond, then strode quickly and silently off toward the hill and his waiting wife and son.

The two who remained held each other firmly and rejoiced together.

When Willimond returned to his hut, a young woman whom he had seen but a few times was waiting for him. She held two children in her arms—one her own and the other the monk's new charge. Side by side like young twins, the babies were nursing with all their energy as if it were the only thing worth living for. The woman looked up and smiled joyfully at Willimond as he entered. She didn't care who he was. She had given birth to a child, and that was reason enough for pride and joy!

Three weeks later young Kristinge was baptized along with Ulestan.

PART IV

The Fight at Finnsburg

Oft the wanderer
    Waits for mercy,
For the Father's favor.
    His frame is troubled.
Through the waterway,
    The frost-cold sea,
With hands he must paddle;
    The path of exiles
For a long time he follows.
    His fate is well settled.

    (The Wanderer)

XXIII

The Wanderers

I watched in sorrow as Ulestan, Willimond and Kristinge turned southward and rode slowly out of Hwitstan. Long grey locks of hair hung loosely over the bent back of the once-mighty thane, and wrinkles creased his brow. His formerly proud shoulders sagged heavily, and his right arm dangled limply at his side. He stared despondently at the path ahead. Long had Ulestan lived—and wisely, but it was the weight of his parting and not of his age which burdened him most. No longer was he riding to war with his king as he so often had before, but to lonely exile. Neither shield nor sword did he bear at his side.

Beside Ulestan rode Willimond and Kristinge. Tears flowed freely down the face of the monk and disappeared beneath his robe. His hood was pulled tightly about his head, hiding the streaks of grey which so recently had appeared in his beard and tonsure. Only with great determination did that monk keep his eyes fixed on the road before him.

Painful was the parting of Ulestan and Willimond from their homes, and sad were their farewells. Loath were they to set out on that journey, and much did they leave behind of great value to each. Alas for Ulestan, leaving his king whom he had served so faithfully, leaving his hearth and hall. A wanderer he would be, grey and tired. Alas for Willimond. Long he had labored in Hwitstan, and deeply had he given his heart to his small congregation. Not easily was he persuaded to depart from that place.

Alas too for Kristinge. His, perhaps, was the most grievous parting, for father and mother did he leave behind though he knew it not. Yes, he alone, in the brightness and joy of his youth,

253

bore his head high and rode with great hope and anticipation. He faced the road ahead with eagerness; the world was still before him.

Perhaps it will be that Kristinge's spirit will yet lift the moods and hearts of his companions. May Ulestan and Willimond once more find joy in the Holy One. I do not envy them.

And yet, though grief filled their leaving, I would that I had been with them riding from this place of sorrow. For sorrow will surely be the mark of these days. Alas, it has already marked the days well. But who then would tell the tale? For that reason alone must I remain. Yes, I must stay behind and bear witness, though I do not desire that sad chore. Truly do I wish that I had departed with them.

> From Hwitstan he went,
>   Wise thane Ulestan;
> From hearth, from home,
>   From hall and king.
> Wanders he now,
>   But not alone;
> With God's own man,
>   Monk Willimond.
>
> Who guides them whither?
>   The wind? The Spirit.
> These two did take,
>   Traveling far,
> The long road south.
>   With snow behind,
> Their charge between,
>   The twain ride on.
>
> Not fear nor foe
>   Did forth them drive.
> They did not desire
>   That sorrowful way.
> A task, a trust,
>   On two was laid;
> One sole command
>   The king did give.

By the grace of God,
  The Good One's mercy,
To joy and to peace
  Their path may still lead.
And hope is held
  The third may return;
A king to Friesland,
  Finn's son, Kristinge.

I, Daelga, have served both Finn, son of Folcwalda and Folcwalda, son of Folgar faithfully. If any man finds fault in my service, may my life be as the sand of the sea which washes away with the surf. I write these things down now even as I await the return of Kristinge, son of Finn, rightful king of Friesland.

XXIV

The Danes

In late autumn three Danish warships set sail homeward from the Saxon coast. Their time of raiding was over until the days of spring followed the cold winter. Ninety men and six there were who eagerly pursued the Swan Road seeking their homes. They hoped soon to feast beside the hearth.

In the center of those ships Hnaef sat proudly. Bold in battle and generous to his thanes, the son of Hoc was a good king! Little fault could be found in his reign. To the port side of the Danish king's ship, Hengest sat in a second ship like to the first. No envy did he have for his king's throne. This thane served Hnaef well. Had Hnaef more such thanes as Hengest, and none of the mould of Guthlaf, Oslaf and Hunlaf, much might have been different.

Alas, it was not so. In that third ship sat the three Jutish brothers, haughty and full of conceit. Guthlaf, Oslaf and Hunlaf they were, kin at heart with Heremod. Wicked were their ways and evil their dealings with men. Craftier than Chlotar they were, and no less cruel or ambitious.

"What think you, my brothers?" Hunlaf, the youngest of the three, asked. They spoke among themselves in low whispers so that even their oarsmen could not hear them.

"It is a bold plan," Guthlaf answered, nodding his head slowly.

"I like it little," Oslaf said, casting his glance back and forth between his elder and younger brothers. "Your ambitions rise too high."

"You thought differently when the crown of Friesland was at stake," Hunlaf said.

"We had little to lose then," Oslaf replied. "The Frisian lordlings were too frightened to oppose us openly, and later the Franks did our work for us. But what did it gain?"

"Had we succeeded in killing both Folcwalda and Finn," Guthlaf answered, "we surely could have persuaded Hnaef to give us Hildeburh, and with her the Frisian throne."

"Us?" Oslaf laughed. Guthlaf did not reply.

"By 'us' I believe our honored brother means himself," Hunlaf corrected cynically.

"If we had succeeded, you know you would have shared in the spoils!" Guthlaf's face was growing red.

"'If' is the crucial word," Oslaf reminded them. "We gained nothing for our troubles. Gained? Hah! We squandered valuable coins on the worthless Frankish assassins."

"Not worthless," the youngest said. "They succeeded admirably in killing Folcwalda."

"And to what avail? He would most likely be dead by now anyway."

Guthlaf did not respond, but sat glaring angrily at the hinted accusations of his two younger siblings.

Hunlaf looked from one to the other and then shrugged casually. "Why worry over the past? In the end it cost us little for what we might have gained." He paused for a moment and fingered the bright red silk wrapped around the sheathed blade on his lap. "And now we have much more to gain."

"The Danish throne!" Guthlaf's voice rose, and a few of the sailors around them cast nervous glances at the brothers. Even among their own paid warband few liked these three. Among both Danes and Jutes, there were many who despised them.

"How do you propose to bring about the death of Hnaef?" Oslaf's voice was so low now that he had to repeat the question three times before his brothers heard him.

"It will be a simple thing to start a battle in Hwitstan," Hunlaf answered, fingering the blade of his jeweled scabbard. "You have seen the animosity many hold toward the Danes . . ."

"And us in particular," Oslaf interrupted.

Hunlaf smiled again and shrugged, turning his hands upward in the air. He cared little how many loved or hated him. "Our warband is large. Once a battle begins, it will not easily be ended."

"And Hnaef?" Oslaf whispered, his eyebrows raised.

"If the Frisians do not kill him, I will." The words came easily and with such cold assurance that even Guthlaf looked at his brother in stunned amazement.

"You would do such a thing to your treasure-giver?" Oslaf finally asked.

"Are not the Danes usurpers? Invaders in Jutish land?" Hunlaf answered. "The throne belongs to the Jutes. You ask if I would do this thing? For the Danish throne yes!"

"The Danish throne for whom?" Oslaf pressed. "Or do you too forget that we are three?"

"With the Danish throne in our hands, the Frisian torc will not be far behind," Hunlaf answered, evading the question. "Once we control the Danes, we may give Hildeburh and Friesland to whomever we wish."

"I still count only two thrones," Oslaf persisted.

"I am the youngest," Hunlaf reminded them, "yet still I am willing to wield the knife myself. Should the thrones be given to the eldest two, I shall gladly trust in the generosity of my brothers." His sly smile was enigmatic.

Guthlaf and Oslaf did not reply. Hunlaf waited a moment and then continued, "In the confusion of battle, will the death of our king surprise any? We are never far from Hnaef. It will be but a small thing for a misplaced knife or sword to pierce his back at an opportune time. The blame for this we will easily pass to the Frisians, and it will be that much easier to bring our spears upon them and steal their throne."

"Are you forgetting Hengest?" Oslaf asked. All three knew well that Hengest's kinship to Hnaef was closer than Guthlaf's.

"He is weak. He will pose no threat. We are three; he is but one. Where one falters, three prevail."

"Those words at least are true," Oslaf agreed, and then fell silent. No more was said between the three, but seeds had been planted that would bear the foulest of fruit.

Who now knows if their devised ill could have been avoided or a lesser evil received in its place. It is a paradox: fate, some say, is well settled, but men follow the paths of their choosing. We indeed reap what we have sown: death when we sow vengeance, the sword when we sow violence, but peace when we sow peace.

XXV

Kristinge

inter was quickly approaching Friesland. The first frost had come many weeks ago, and snow had already fallen twice. Though it had not stayed long upon the ground, it was a sure tiding of more to come. Even as Danish ships were sailing homeward with their spoils, the village of Hwitstan was busily preparing for winter. While the women worked repairing the wattle-work in the walls and roofs, the men of Hwitstan were smoking pork and salting herring, preserving them for the winter ahead. Hunters and trappers were taking their last trips before the heavy winter snow made travel more difficult.

Despite the hard work, these were joyful days for many in Hwitstan and throughout Friesland. Craftsmen, traders, fishermen, farmers, thanes and noblemen alike prospered under a good and wise king. Though evil was plotted against them, the people dwelt in peace, and the princes of the land grew in strength and wisdom. In different ways and with different teachers, the sons of Finn learned well.

●

Willimond the monk was working along the river, enjoying one of autumn's last fleeting days of warmth. The air was pleasant and mild, such as it is on but a handful of afternoons late in the fall of each year. The water was chilly, but the monk was still able to work the weirs with his fellow fishermen and weir-keepers. It was the fifteenth fall that had passed since he had come to Hwitstan.

Has it indeed been that long? Willimond found himself thinking. *Two times seven years and one summer I have been in Friesland. It seems like a lifetime . . . or perhaps just a few days.* He laughed aloud.

Lopystre stood in the stream beside Willimond, examining the newly built fifth weir. Like the previous four, it was nearly empty that day. "Is the One speaking to you?" he asked, looking over his shoulder at the monk.

"What?" Willimond brought his thoughts back to the task at hand.

"Clearly you are not laughing at the empty weirs. I thought perhaps God had given you some other reason for your joy."

"So many are they that I could not count the reasons He has given me for joy, good friend," Willimond replied, the smile still bright on his face. "But that was not the reason for my laughter just now."

"Will you enlighten us, or shall we remain forever in the darkness?" Lopystre asked in good humor. The weirs had provided plentifully that fall, so he was not greatly disturbed by one barren day.

"I was remembering that first day when I came to Hwitstan. In some ways it seems like yesterday."

"I, too, remember that day well." The fisherman joined in the laughter. "How odd I thought your robe and hair. But you offered help, and not lightly do I turn away a strong and generous hand."

Willimond rubbed his scalp. He still kept the same tonsure—a thick half-moon shaved from the top of his scalp—but his hair was thinning, and a few faint streaks of grey were appearing around his ears and in his beard. "Generous perhaps but not too strong, I think. Yet there you were, your nets so full that you could hardly pull the fish ashore. Lopystre, Lindlaf and Lawyrke . . ." He stopped suddenly. Two others had just walked up beside him. The older of the two was Lindlaf, who now looked so much like his father once had that Willimond sometimes confused them. The other was Lawerklaf, son of Lawyrke. Lawyrke had drowned six years ago when his foot had caught in a loose net and the tide had pulled him under. Lawerklaf was now almost sixteen years of age, but Willimond was still hesitant to speak about his father in his presence.

"Do not stop," Lawerklaf said. "It brings me joy to hear about my father. The time for grief is past. He has gone to be with the One."

"How true are your words," Willimond said, patting the lad on the head. "And wise for one of your years."

"One of my years, old grey head?" The lad laughed. "Am I so young, or does everyone begin to look young to you now?"

"Not too young . . ." The monk took the jest well. ". . . but young enough for this . . ." His hand dropped quickly from the lad's head to his shoulder, and Lawerklaf was suddenly tumbling backwards into the river. He retained only enough balance to pull Willimond in with him.

As they were helping each other out of the water, young Kristinge came striding down the hill. He looked at his teacher with some amusement.

"Father?" he asked. Though he knew the monk was not his real father, he used the title out of respect and affection. Who his real parents were, he did not know.

Willimond looked up. Seeing Kristinge standing there, he stepped quickly out of the river to greet him. "How are you doing, my son?"

"Well enough," Kristinge answered, hesitating only slightly as he glanced at the other three who stood watching him. They stared at him as men do when they know something fearful or wonderful about you, but are afraid to say what. They well knew he was the prince, though they were not allowed to mention this under penalty of death.

"But . . . ?" Willimond pursued, seeing the look of confusion in the boy's eyes.

"I am having difficulty with this passage," he answered, holding up a scroll. Willimond walked over to him and examined the passage in question, being careful not to get the precious scroll wet. The scroll was among many which the brothers had sent to him from Lindisfarne the year before to celebrate his four-teenth year in Friesland. One of these scrolls replaced that very one which Finn had burned fifteen years earlier to test the young monk. Along with the scrolls, the brothers had sent a heavy new cloak of northern wool.

"It is this word here," Kristinge said pointing.

"Can you read it?"

"*Humilitas*?" Kristinge asked tentatively.

"But you do not know what it means?"

Kristinge shook his head slowly. "You have spoken of it before, but I do not know its full meaning," he confessed.

"Alas, my son," Willimond said, placing his hand on the boy's shoulder, "too few of us do! Come, let us walk as we talk." Taking leave of the other weir-keepers, Willimond and Kristinge started back up the hill, and the monk proceeded to explain *humilitas* to his pupil.

"'Have this attitude in yourself,'" he began, "'which was also in Jesus, the Christ, who, though he himself had the very form of God, did not regard equality with God a thing to hold on to, but laid aside his privileges and took the form of a slave.'"

"The words of Paul," Kristinge responded.

"Yes." Willimond smiled at his pupil's knowledge. "And what is he speaking of?"

"*Humilitas*?"

"*Humilitas*," the monk confirmed. "And what did Paul say about humility?"

Kristinge looked down at the scroll before him and began to read. "'Do nothing from selfishness or . . .'" He paused and thought for a minute. "'. . . or empty conceit, but with humility of mind let each of you regard one another as more important than himself.'"

"Very good. And what does it mean to regard others as more important than yourself?"

Kristinge did not respond, so Willimond continued, "Holy Scripture teaches us that 'Everyone who exalts himself shall be humbled, and he who humbles himself shall be exalted.' Humility is like the ladder of Jacob upon which the angels climbed up and down. We go up the ladder by humbling ourselves and down by praising ourselves. The first step of that ladder—the first step of humility—is to obey all of God's commandments and to never ignore them. To do your own will is to exalt yourself higher than God. To be obedient to God is to acknowledge that He is Lord."

"Are these the teachings of Benedict?" Kristinge asked.

Willimond looked up in sudden surprise. "Yes indeed," he answered. "But where have you heard of Benedict?"

"Since the scrolls arrived, you and Ulestan have often talked of this 'Rule of Benedict.'" Kristinge suddenly turned red and dropped his eyes. "I am sorry . . . I did not mean to be overhearing your conversations."

"You have done no wrong," the monk said gently. "We spoke openly and in your hearing."

"I could not help but hear," Kristinge said, lifting his eyes again when he realized he would not be reprimanded. "You often argued over this rule."

"We did not argue . . ." Willimond began to say. Then he realized that perhaps they had. The letter he had received along with the cloak and scrolls from Lindisfarne had mentioned that Benedict's Rule was now being used in addition to the Columban Rule at the monastery in Lindisfarne. Some of the scrolls the brothers had sent contained the teachings from this new Rule. He had read them with great interest and had shared them with Ulestan as well. Since then he and Ulestan had often disagreed on the merits and faults of the Rule. To the ears of Kristinge, perhaps it had sounded like arguing.

"Yes, that was the teaching of Benedict on humility," Willimond finally said. "But come, let us return to the Holy Scriptures and continue your lesson. Read to me more from the words of Paul."

●

"You are doing well," Willimond said when the lesson ended some time later. Kristinge did not respond. His head was sagging, and his eyes were downcast. Willimond looked at the boy and remembered with empathy the struggles he himself had gone through many years earlier as he learned to read Latin. The task had seemed endless. And yet, though it was difficult he had enjoyed the work. To be able to read the words of God and understand them—there was no greater joy! And now Kristinge had the same desire to learn. No, his desire was greater—it was a passion. *There is a great fire within him*, Willimond thought. *If he could but journey to Luxeuil and study there . . .*

At times Kristinge's desire was almost too great. He was hard on himself, harder on himself even than Willimond, his teacher. "When I was a lad of your age," Willimond said, seeking to encourage his pupil, "I too struggled with the Holy Writings. Apprehending their meaning is no easy task. Yet I think you have learned far more than I had at your age. I was understanding only the writings of the Scriptures, but you have already nearly mastered your own language as well."

"Am I really doing well?" Kristinge asked, his eyes lighting up.

"I could not ask for a better, more devoted student. I wish only that you had a better teacher! Much could you learn in Luxeuil from those more knowledgeable than I, if you could but someday travel there."

"I would not wish to leave you, father."

"No?" Willimond smiled, putting his hand affectionately on the boy's shoulder. "I would not have you leave here either. But there is so much you could learn at Luxeuil . . . And so many places where the One could use your learning. Someday you may need to leave, for God calls His servants to many places."

"Like He called you from Lindisfarne to Hwitstan?"

Though he spoke of it rarely, Willimond still remembered the vision he had seen many years earlier; indeed as if it had happened only the day before. "Yes," he replied, "much like that. Yet His callings come in many different ways at different times to different people. Few receive visions in the night."

"When I am called, I hope it is to Luxeuil, that I may learn more and study from real books," Kristinge said with wonder. Then he asked, "How will I be called when it is time for me to leave?"

"That we shall see. We shall see. But we need not speak of it now. We do not yet know that you shall ever have to leave Hwitstan. There is much to be done in Friesland. In Aalsom, Dronrip, Wijnaldum, Wieuwerd, Ezinge, Beowic and throughout the land are many who have been baptized and desire to learn more about the God they serve . . . And others who have not yet believed but desire to hear . . . And many still who have not heard at all. I have yet to travel as far as Domburg or Wic by Dorestad."

"May I come with you when you travel next?"

"We shall see about that as well," Willimond responded, but

he wondered what the king would think of his son traveling with Willimond to visit churches and preach the gospel. A look of anxiety clouded the monk's face at the thought of crossing the king's wishes. Yet was it not true that Willimond had an even higher King than Finn? And was not Kristinge given into his keeping, and into the service of God—by the word of Finn himself, no less?

After a long pause the monk's expression changed. "I think, my son, that the answer will be 'yes.' It is well time that we journeyed together. Was I not but fourteen when first I accompanied Aidan? But come, there is still much learning to be done, and I will not be traveling again until spring. Tell me, now, about *humilitas*."

"*Humilitas*," Kristinge responded, "humility . . . 'Have this attitude . . .'"

XXVI

The Hunt

Prince Finnlaf descended from Finnweard and strode down the hill into Hwitstan. He crossed the village to where his sturdy black and white horse was tethered on the far side of the pond, stopping on the way to gather a bundle of lances from in front of Finnsburg. He was feeling restless. He knew too well that the winter months were fast approaching, and that he would soon be spending too much time under a roof. His young heart was still unappreciative of long periods of calm and quietude, and so he was bent on enjoying the last of the warm fall days.

In so many ways the prince was the child of his father. Both king and prince were broad-chested, with thick middles and long powerful legs. The prince had Finn's deep-set eyes, round sturdy chin, and strong shoulders, though Finnlaf's shoulders were not as yet marked by scars. In height Finnlaf had surpassed his father by an inch or two, though he was not quite as muscular, especially in the forearms. In personality the prince was even more like the king than in appearance. He was quiet and thoughtful; quick to listen, but not easily persuaded from a path once settled on; slow to anger, but not easily put off once aroused. Only in his blue eyes, his light blond hair, and his love of the woods and countryside did he reveal his mother's blood.

At Finnlaf's side as he crossed the village walked Ulestan. Grey was his hair now, and wrinkles marked his brow, revealing, as Finn was fond of saying of him, "the wisdom hidden beneath." Long that thane had served his king in loyalty and faith, giving to him treasures he had won in battle and seeking no other hearth or treasure-giver. Fifty years and four Ulestan had lived on this earth, surpassing all but a very few; no earl or thane in Hwitstan could equal his days. Despite his years, Ulestan bore himself well and proudly. Perhaps leaner and more wiry and a bit slower than in his youth, he was nonetheless a strong thane. His grip was still firm and his sword sharp. If his strength was lessened somewhat, it was compensated for by greater wisdom and knowledge. Few even of the youngest and strongest thanes dared challenge him in any of the games, and those that did most often lost.

Finn had chosen well when he had called on Ulestan to train his beloved prince in the ways of the sword. There was no better man in all of Friesland for this task than Ulestan the Owl. In his handling of the sword, the prince learned quickly and soon surpassed all in Hwitstan save for the best of Finn's thanes and the mightiest of the clan chieftains. These, too, he would likely soon surpass. Ulestan ensured by his wise teaching that Finnlaf would be neither an enemy to be taken lightly nor a friend without worth or to be easily despised.

And that wise thane was not content simply to instruct the prince in ways of warfare. He knew the danger of a strong hand without wisdom, of a fool who wields a sword too eagerly. For every word which Ulestan gave to the prince about how to fight, he gave two words on how to avoid fighting.

"I do not understand," Finnlaf had said one day, "why we spend hours training with the sword, and yet you tell me again and again that war is to be avoided."

"War is to be passed by if possible," the thane said. "It is an ugly thing. 'Blessed are the peacemakers.'"

"Then why this sword?" the prince asked, holding his blade in front of him.

"If God permits, you will one day be king. It is the duty of a king to protect his people, and it is often the sword itself which buys peace and freedom for his people."

"And so we need to fight."

"Perhaps . . . Or perhaps not. Wise words may accomplish peace at far less cost. Do not needlessly throw away the lives of your people in war when you may find peace in other ways."

"What are these 'other ways' you speak of?"

"They change from time to time and place to place. But if you seek for them, you will often find them. Do not be afraid to defend your peace with the sword, but be not overeager to find war when it is unnecessary."

That conversation had taken place some years ago, but Finnlaf had not forgotten it.

●

Two and twenty years the prince now had behind him, and the time of his training with Ulestan was past. He sat now at the side of his father, and what he learned he learned by doing. Yet Ulestan, though no longer his teacher, was still Finnlaf's friend and advisor. Far and often these two traveled together when Ulestan was not needed at the side of Finn. And frequently did they talk as well. Most often they spoke of Folcwalda, whom Finnlaf had never known. But also they spoke of the God whom Willimond preached and Ulestan served. Finnlaf was ever full of questions.

A wise thane Ulestan was. First Folcwalda, then Finn, and now Finnlaf all relied heavily on his words. Not often did those words fail them.

"Will you accompany me on this hunt?" the prince asked on this day when they reached the far side of the village where their mounts were tethered.

"Only if you will not be dissuaded."

"I will not," the prince answered, patting his horse gently as he began to untie it.

"And you will not bring any others?"

"You already know the answer to that. Gathering my father's thanes to ride with me would take days. And they make so much noise, it is a wonder we ever see game."

"How about Aelfin, son of Aeltar? Does he not ride with you often?"

"Ah, he does. None other, save for you, would I have beside me for a hunt. But he has recently gone to Domburg to visit his father. Word came yesterday that Aeltar is grievously ill and will not last the winter."

"'Tis ill news indeed! I had not heard it. Finn will be grieved."

"He will indeed, for Aeltar is like a brother to him. Though

Finn's hall is almost empty, he sent Aelfin and his warband home with his blessings. He almost went himself to see Aeltar once more."

"Nor is it good news for you," Ulestan continued. "If Aeltar dies, Aelfin will certainly be the new chieftain. Though he still be your thane, he may not ride at your side as often. His place will be in Domburg."

"I had thought of that," Finnlaf nodded somberly. "Yet I would not have another ruling Domburg."

"Nor I," Ulestan responded.

They both stood still for a moment, lost in their own thoughts. Then in one fluid motion Finnlaf swung astride his horse. "Come if you will. I would not delay longer. The track of this mighty boar is already two days old. He will not wait for us forever."

In a moment both were astride their mounts riding toward the river. They crossed at the bridge upstream from the weirs and soon disappeared into the woods to the east. The four weir-keepers looked upstream and watched them pass, then returned to their work.

Three days later, both men began to lose hope for the hunt. Beginning at the edge of the village fields where the boar had been seen, they had ridden in wider and wider circles searching for fresh tracks, but had not come upon anything less than a couple days old.

They were thinking of returning to the village when late in the morning they finally found what they were seeking. "These are recent, by the look," Finnlaf said excitedly as he knelt beside his horse and examined the ground. Fresh boar tracks led through some soft mud beside a little spring. "What think you, good friend?" he asked the thane.

"You are the master tracker, not I," Ulestan responded, but he knelt down beside the prince and examined the tracks himself anyway. "I would agree. They look not more than a few hours old—from sometime last night I would guess. Look too at the size. This is no small boar."

Finnlaf nodded in agreement. "Then let us be off. Perhaps today is the day."

A small game trail wound off through the woods on the other side of the spring, and the tracks disappeared in that direction. Soon two horses were pounding down the path, one after the other. Finnlaf's mount was in the lead, but Ulestan was not far behind. Through a small, dense wood they rode, keeping to the well-worn game trail. Low branches brushed at their faces, forcing the two riders to stay low or be swept off their horses. A few startled birds fluttered out of their way in fright.

They had not gone far when Finnlaf suddenly reined to a halt. His horse responded so suddenly that the prince was almost thrown to the ground. Ulestan, who could not see ahead, rode up alongside Finnlaf to see for himself what prevented their pursuit. A large tree had fallen and now lay at shoulder height across their trail. A thick tangle of branches filled the path below, and a heavy thicket extended into the woods on either side.

"What would you have us do now?" Ulestan asked. He did not relish the thought of trying to clear the trail, nor was he anxious to ride through or around the thicket. In fact, the thane had suggested ending the hunt the day before when they had met with no success.

"Shall we try to jump this tree? I sense that we are near our prey." The prince's face was flush with excitement. His horse, too, was impatient to be on the chase again and tossed his head anxiously.

Ulestan looked at the prince in amusement at his suggestion. "I think that if you try, I will be carrying you back to Hwitstan stretched across my saddle." This was something the thane would never have said to Folcwalda, nor even to Finn, but Finnlaf, though a prince, was many years his younger and had at one time been his pupil. "It would require a mighty leap even from a stag, and that is no deer you are riding."

"Then would you ride back? Would you return to Hwitstan in defeat?" The prince's tone was boastful and challenging, but not unfriendly.

"The chase has carried us far already . . ." Ulestan began, but he could not resist Finnlaf's challenge. "But no . . . We are close now. I can feel it too."

The prince breathed deeply and shifted the grip on his lance. With his other hand he readjusted the bow and quiver which were slung over his shoulder. Then the two remained still for a moment longer, each wondering in his own mind how they might continue the hunt. The thicket stretched far in both directions.

"There is nothing to do but to go around, though I little like the delay," Finnlaf finally said. "I fear we will lose precious ground on our prey. I wonder if he senses that we are close."

In answer to the prince, there came then such a horrifying and unexpected sound—more frightful than the frenzied scream of battle and the clash of swords and as terrifying as the howling of many wolves—that both he and Ulestan were startled out of their seats, trained horsemen though they were. The riders sought to regain their balance while their horses neighed and moved back uneasily, tossing their heads from side to side. When prince and thane finally succeeded at reseating themselves, they looked about expectantly. They well knew what they had heard. It was the growling snort of a boar—a sound heard by many careless hunters seconds before their deaths. The beast was very close at hand. They expected to see it charging at any moment, and they held their lances ready.

They had barely recovered from the first surprise when there was another snort, louder than the first. Ulestan's mount reared, and the thane was almost thrown. At the same time, from right under the horses' hooves the branches of the fallen tree erupted in a flurry and out the other side shot a great boar, straight away from the two hunters. Ulestan, who was busy controlling his mount, did not see it. Finnlaf did. It was a mighty beast indeed. Powerful muscles lined its back, and its fur stood up in a straight row. Its shoulders were enormous. One tusk appeared to be broken, but the other was longer, stronger and sharper than any the prince had ever seen. A moment after he saw the beast, it was gone.

No further discussion was needed. Finnlaf swung sharply to his right and Ulestan to the left, and they were soon riding as fast as they could around the edge of the thicket on opposite sides. They drove their mounts as hard as they dared across the uneven forest ground—over fallen logs, around bushes, and under low branches—keeping as close as they could to the lost trail. Yet though they rode as fast as they could, the thicket was so wide that it took many minutes of fighting through and around it to reach the trail on the other side. Ulestan arrived there first, but Finnlaf was soon on his heels. They paused for a second and listened. In the distance they could still hear the boar racing ahead and letting out occasional growls and snorts. Then they were off in pursuit. The trail widened and the ceiling of branches raised up, allowing them to travel even faster. They gained quickly on the fleeing prey. Finnlaf's faster mount quickly passed Ulestan on his right and galloped a few feet ahead. The thane pounded down the trail behind him.

The trail crested a small hill and dropped again down the far side. The horses stretched their necks; they did not hold back from the chase. At the bottom of the hill the trail opened onto a small meadow. Partway across, Ulestan got his first glimpse of the boar as it ran along the game trail through the tall grass. Both men lowered their lances, gripped them firmly, and pressed on. In a few seconds they were at the spot where they had seen their mighty quarry. But it had now disappeared into the taller grass whipping against their legs. Further, their horses were getting winded and tired, their mouths flecked with foam.

Then, as eight hooves pounded across the meadow and two pairs of eyes peered eagerly ahead hoping for another glimpse of the beast, there suddenly appeared out of the tall grass at their right another creature, tall, tan and graceful. Again taken by surprise, it took a moment for the prince and the thane to adjust their gazes and realize what this new animal was: a mighty stag, larger than any Ulestan had seen in his long life. A second later the stag had leapt across the trail in front of them and bounded off into the grass on their left, where it quickly disappeared—but not before Ulestan had seen its magnificent rack. Both riders wheeled to a halt and looked around. A moment later the stag appeared in the trail a few dozen feet behind them. In complete surprise the two men stared at it blankly for a long moment.

The stag too paused and looked back at them, as much surprised at their appearance as they at his. Yet Ulestan was quick-witted and a renowned hunter. Slowly so as not to frighten the magnificent creature, he set his lance in his saddle and pulled his bow off his shoulder. An arrow slid silently out of the quiver. But before he could notch it, the stag turned its head and disappeared once more, this time back up the trail down which the men had just come.

The still-surprised Ulestan stared after it, his arrow yet in his hand. He looked back at his prince. "Alas!" he cried. "Whither now? Never have I seen such a mighty stag."

"My prey lies ahead, not back," Finnlaf urged impatiently, "and he puts distance between us even now."

"Eight and eight points it must have had," Ulestan breathed in amazement.

"Or more. But come, we hunt boar."

"I cannot turn from such a hunt as this," Ulestan announced, speaking not of the boar, but of the stag.

"Nor I," Finnlaf replied, speaking of the boar. "So let us be off as each sees best. We meet back here when we may." He turned and was gone.

Ulestan watched the prince for only a moment and then rode back up the trail in pursuit of the deer. It did not take him long to see it, waiting just inside the woods across the meadow. When the animal saw the rider, it bounded down the trail again.

Ulestan followed, his bow and arrow held ready in hand. Not yet tired from his pursuit of the boar, he again rode as hard as he could in chase. He asked of his steed an extra gift of speed. The valiant servant responded, and they narrowed the distance. The thane's anticipation grew. He was almost within bowshot.

Yet, if the stag was aware of his danger, he showed no fear. Graceful and smooth was his leaping gait, and no panic overtook him. His mighty rack floated through the air high and proud. Had he tried, the stag might easily have lost his pursuer. A quick turn into the dense thicket and his hunter could not have followed. Yet for some reason he did not stray from the path, though his end surely drew near.

Then, just as Ulestan came within bowshot of his prey, to his dismay he saw ahead the fallen tree which blocked the path. He would be able to go no further, and he had no hunting dogs. If he were forced again to ride the long way, he would surely lose his prey. He kept on hoping for some other possibility. Where would the stag turn? It could not pass through the tree. It too would be trapped. It would undoubtedly enter the thicket by some secret path where Ulestan could not follow. But if it hesitated just a moment, if it slowed or paused just slightly, Ulestan might have opportunity to strike the magnificent beast. He was close enough now. He reined his horse to a halt and notched an arrow to his string.

The stag reached the tree.

Ulestan let an arrow fly.

The feathered shaft soared through the air on mark for its target.

Then the mighty stag did the last thing Ulestan expected. Without breaking his stride, without the slightest moment of hesitation, the great animal leapt. High over the tree he sailed, as gracefully as any hawk in flight. Even as he reached the peak of his leap, the arrow reached the top of its arc and turned downward, where its target had been just a split second before. There, in the middle of the trail beside the fallen tree, stood a young buck. Ulestan saw him for the first time, and saw too where his arrow was flying. The buck looked up in confusion as his father leapt high over his head. Then, a second too late, he turned to see Ulestan. Even as he did so, the arrow fell. The point pierced his shoulder and sank deep into his heart. The young buck staggered a few feet, attempted to escape under the fallen tree, caught its rack on a branch, and fell struggling.

The mighty stag landed safely on the other side, turned around once as if to boast in triumph, and then disappeared.

Ulestan rode forward slowly. For a fleeting moment he considered making the jump himself and pursuing the great stag. But he knew he could not. His heart sank, and his excitement turned to disappointment.

He dismounted and examined, with no sense of success, the kill at his feet. It was a large deer, though no comparison to the one for which the arrow had been meant. Such excellent meat was scarce, he knew, and would be well appreciated back in the village. Yet, that did not console him for the failure of his hunt. Alas, it was too late to do anything about it. Pulling his knife from the sheath at his waist, he ended the buck's misery. Then he began the work of skinning it.

When he arrived back at the meadow in the late afternoon, Finnlaf was waiting for him. The carcass of the boar was strapped to a small, makeshift litter behind his horse.

"I see you have found success!" Ulestan congratulated the prince.

"And you, as well," Finnlaf responded.

"Not as much as it would seem," the thane said, and went on to tell his story.

"'Tis a strange tale indeed," the prince said when Ulestan was finished. "And when you shot the arrow, you did not see the other deer?"

"No, for my eyes were fixed firmly on my target. Ah, what a mighty leap carried him from my sight."

"Mighty indeed if it cleared that fallen tree. But come, let us think no more of it. It has been a long day. Let us rest here for the night and return toward Hwitstan in the morning."

While Ulestan tied their horses to fallen logs, Finnlaf finished skinning the boar. Then they began a fire. That night, beneath a clear, starry sky in the cold evening air of late fall, they feasted well on venison and pork beside a warm blaze . And their horses grazed richly in the lush meadow, rewarded for their hard work that day.

The following morning the two hunters arose early and started on their way back to Hwitstan. They put the venison and pork in heavy cloth bags and slung them over their saddles. The weather was cold enough that the meat would last for a few days before being smoked or eaten. In addition to the meat, Finnlaf also kept the boar's head as a trophy, lest any doubt the size of the boar.

"If we return the way we came and keep up a good pace," the prince announced as they started, "we should be at Finnsburg by sundown tomorrow."

"Then let us proceed with such haste as is necessary."

They began the day in good spirits. Finnlaf was joyful at the success of his hunt, and Ulestan shared in his prince's joy. The air was crisp and cool, pleasant for traveling. They talked idly as they rode, laughing together at shared stories. Though they spoke of eagerness to return to hearth and hall, and neither was wont to needlessly delay the voyage, yet neither were they in a great rush. It was not a day for hurry, and both were enjoying the weather and company, as well as the chance to be away from the village.

They had ridden only as far as the fallen tree when Ulestan suddenly grabbed Finnlaf, riding beside him. Standing in the middle of the trail, just where the other buck had fallen, stood the mighty stag! Ulestan and Finn felt their hearts pound in excitement. The thane had surely not expected this turn of fate.

The great beast raised its rack and looked straight at the

approaching riders. He showed no fear and did not dart away. He made no move to run, even as Ulestan restrung his bow and pulled another arrow from the quiver.

"I believe he is mourning," Finnlaf whispered. The animal looked back and forth between the two riders and the head of his fallen comrade which still lay on the ground beside the tree where Ulestan had skinned it. Only then did the creature move. The great stag lowered its rack and took two steps toward the hunters. Never before in Ulestan's memory had a stag, no matter how great, been so brazen as to charge a hunter. *Does he seek revenge?* the thane wondered. He held his bow still a moment longer in awe and curiosity.

He notched his arrow to the string as the stag began to charge.

Ulestan released his arrow, and it did not miss.

XXVII

Of Finn
and Hildeburh

Many are the choices men and women make, both for good and for ill, whose effect may be felt to the end of their days and beyond. And not by them alone are the echoes of their decisions heard, but by those near and far, and by none more than their sons, daughters, husbands and wives.

As the men and women of Hwitstan returned to their homes late in the day, they saw against the darkening sky a familiar silhouette. Finn stood atop Finnweard gazing across the sea with his queen at his right side. And in his left hand he held his sturdy ash staff. As much as his torc, it was a symbol of his power. Not since the day of his coronation as king, the day of Folcwalda's death, had he been seen without it.

Hildeburh shivered and slipped her left arm around Finn's waist. He pulled her closer with his right. The sun was dropping below the horizon, leaving the western sky a fiery orange. Behind the tower Hwitstan already lay in shadows.

"Twenty and four years it has been—twelve years and twelve," Finn said. He was watching Hildeburh gaze northeastward across the sea toward the land of her father—the land of the Danes. Her thoughts were clearly elsewhere. She had not even seen the sunset. "After so long, do you still miss your home?"

Hildeburh turned toward her husband. She held his eyes with hers and made him listen. "This is my home now. I would not leave." She paused to make sure he had heard her and then continued, "But yes, I do miss my people. My brother especially."

"Then you are content? You would not leave? You do not regret becoming the wife of the Frisian king?"

"Too much time do you spend with your people if you know me so little after so many years," she replied, still looking into his eyes. "Not once have I wished that I were not your wife. Nor would I ever leave Hwitstan—not while you are alive. Yet may I not even think of my family? Of my brother? May I not remember the fields and hills of my youth and still have my heart here with you?"

Finn did not respond. Few in the land of Friesland could rebuke the king—few would even dare—but Hildeburh was one of them.

"And not with you only," she added when she saw that he was silent. "Remember that you are no longer the only reason for my presence here. There are two others at least."

Finn knew of what she spoke, but he asked anyway. "Finnlaf?"

"And Kristinge too, even if he knows it not. Yet, though he does not call me 'mother,' I would watch him grow. I would see him become a man." A tear sparkled in her eye as she spoke.

"Finnlaf is man already," Finn replied proudly, avoiding as was his habit the subject of Kristinge. Since the day his youngest son had been given into the care of Willimond some fifteen years earlier, Finn had never been eager to speak of him. He would not even mention Kristinge's name unless it was Hildeburh who spoke of him first, and even then he grew irritable when they talked of their second son. Of Finnlaf his heir, on the other hand, Finn never tired of speaking. "Have you seen how he rides? How he hunts? How he talks with his thanes? Do you see the respect he has from them? Already they would give their heart to him. Many indeed have sworn their allegiance to his future kingship."

Hildeburh nodded absentmindedly, her thoughts elsewhere once again.

"And well he handles a sword too. He is tall and strong. Almost, even now, could he win the kingdom by the might of his arm. Almost. There are still some who could contest him, but not many. And of those who have the strength to dare, all serve him willingly nonetheless.

"He is wise as well," the king continued after a moment.

"He knows how to gain the trust of men. He is generous and true to his word. Such should a king be!"

"Wise, yes," Hildeburh answered, her thoughts returning to the conversation. "But Kristinge is the wiser. There is more to strength than might in arms and more to wisdom than ruling a kingdom." She expected her husband to object, but he said nothing. For once the smile remained on his face as she spoke to him of their younger son.

"Already he reads and writes . . . and not in our language alone, but in the language of the Empire as well. You speak of swords and spears. Have you seen our other son's love of books and of learning? Willimond says the boy learns faster than he can teach him.

"And the skill in his hands!" the queen continued. She shivered again, this time in excitement and joy. "To hear him play the harp with Daelga is a joy beyond words. Already he makes poems."

"Hymns he calls them," Finn interrupted with some disdain. "They are written for his god."

"Is that so wrong?" Hildeburh answered.

"No." The king smiled again at his wife. "I, too, have heard his voice and his skill at the harp. He is gifted indeed at what he does."

"Yet, you would have him bear a sword instead?"

"No," Finn answered firmly to Hildeburh's surprise. "One prince is surely enough for our family. I would not have them vying for the throne. It is best that he does not know."

Is Kristinge any less a prince because he carries no sword? Hildeburh almost asked, but she thought better of this and remained quiet.

"Truly they have grown up well," Finn said. "No king could ask for more."

"Indeed, they have grown up well," Hildeburh responded. "They have grown up well, for they have been taught well. In Ulestan and Willimond are two wise and trustworthy servants. You could not have chosen better."

"I have not journeyed much these last few years," Finn said, suddenly shifting the topic of conversation. "Yet, little would keep me from doing so now. As you have said, our servants are trustworthy."

Hildeburh did not reply. Her hands went suddenly cold, and another shiver shook her frame. She felt a heavy weight sink to her stomach. Too well she remembered the long seasons when her father and brother were gone, the months when she was left alone with her crazed mother and the old nurse who cared for her. The days had gone on endlessly, waiting for their return. After all those years, her mother had never grown accustomed to being left behind. Had it been loneliness that killed her? Was it going to begin all over again for Hildeburh? Would she become like her mother? *But he is a king*, she reminded herself. *It is his duty. And it was on such a voyage that he met me.*

"I would that I could visit your country once again," Finn continued. "The lands of the Danes—Scyld's fields."

Hildeburh's eyes lit up with sudden hope. Did he mean to visit her brother? Could it be? Would he take her with him?

"Finnlaf is wise among men, and strong. He has many loyal thanes. He could rule well while we were gone."

"'We'? Do you mean this?" Hildeburh asked, her heart bursting with joy within her.

"I think it is time for you to visit once again the land of your youth. Yes, I mean what I say. We shall both go. When the ice melts in the spring, I will gather some loyal thanes and we will travel together to the land of your youth. Come this spring, you will visit the Dane mark and we will see your brother."

Hildeburh leapt into Finn's arms with such enthusiasm that were he not so strong and she so light they might have tumbled right off the tower.

XXVIII

The Gathering of Clouds

Finn and Hildeburh were just preparing to walk back to the village when a distant flash of light caught Finn's attention. At first he thought it might be lightning, but there was no storm and it was the wrong season.

"It is the watchtower," Hildeburh exclaimed before Finn had a chance to say anything. She was right. Low in the eastern horizon a flickering orange flame appeared and disappeared three times. There was a pause, and then it flashed thrice more.

"Three ships? 'Tis late in the fall for a trading party that large." Finn voiced his thought aloud.

"Who do you think it is?" Hildeburh asked nervously as she peered out across Hwitstanwic.

"I know not, but it is best that we be prepared. There are but fifty warriors in Hwitstan tonight, and only eight of my thanes . . ."

"And there are three ships coming." Hildeburh finished the thought. She knew well the size of warbands and the number that might travel in each ship. "There could be sixty armed men aboard."

Finn was thinking that the number might be closer to seventy and five or even eighty, but did not say so. "If it is a warband, there might well be that many," he replied slowly. Leaning over the southern edge of the tower, he shouted down into the gloom below. "Guthric!"

"Yes, my lord, I have seen," the voice of the thane replied out of the darkness.

Finn's thoughts turned immediately to his two most trusted servants and wisest advisors—Finnlaf his son and Ulestan his thane. "Where is Finnlaf?" he asked.

"He has not yet returned from the hunt."

"And Ulestan as well?"

"He is with him, my lord."

Two conflicting thoughts crossed the king's mind. If it came to a battle, he would sorely miss the support and strength at arms of Finnlaf and Ulestan. And yet he was glad they were gone, for if it was indeed an enemy approaching, his son did not share the danger. For as much as he desired his son's strength, he desired more his safety. A heavy burden which had rushed in on him with the sighting of the signal lifted momentarily from his heart.

"Return to Finnsburg at once and gather a warband," he commanded his thane. "Bring all of the thanes and warriors present and escort Hildeburh to a place of safety away from Finnsburg. I will wait for you here."

"As you wish, my lord," Guthric answered. Hildeburh had already begun climbing down. The thane and the queen disappeared down the hill at a brisk pace.

"Where is Guthman?" Finn shouted a moment later.

"He is with the guard at the beach," Guthric replied, his voice carrying from halfway down the hill.

Finn turned to face the sea. The night sky was clear, and the moon, just now appearing in the east, cast a dim light across the water. Under the faint grey sky Finn could see waves glimmering across Hwitstanwic. Thankfully, there was still no sign of the approaching ships. He waited.

Never before had Finn feared battle, though as a wise king he did not seek it or needlessly sacrifice lives. Yet this night a dark foreboding was upon him. He did not wish to find strange warriors upon his beaches. And his hall was nearly empty that night, for Aelfin and his band had just departed. They had returned to Domburg to the side of Aeltar, Aelfin's dying father. Froda was gone as well, and Finn wished deeply for his presence, for he was a close friend and advisor. Why, he wondered, had he let that trusted thane leave him and return to Wic by Dorestad? But he knew the answer even as he silently asked the question. He had not let Froda return. Out of gratitude to his loyal servant he had sent him to Dorestad. Froda's brother Frothwine was vying to be chieftain, a position rightfully his, and he was being opposed by Réadban, an old warrior and clanchief who sought instead to set his young son Radbod upon the throne—Radbod who was barely old enough to carry a sword, no less rule a clan! So Frothwine had called upon Froda to help him. Now Froda was gone, and Ulestan and Finnlaf as well. Perhaps Finn would have been better off if he had killed Réadban many years earlier when he had had the chance. He had caused only trouble within the realm.

So with uncharacteristic anxiety building within him, Finn watched and waited. Long moments passed. His thoughts tossed sea-like between Froda, Finnlaf and Ulestan. He had come to rely upon each heavily. He did not desire to face battle alone. And Hildeburh . . . Was she safe?

More time passed. Perhaps the signal was false. The thought took hold, and his hopes urged it on; perhaps the guards were fooled by the moon's light upon the waters. But deep in his heart he knew this was not true, that the signal was not false. So he continued to wait, hoping soon to hear the sound of his own warband approaching behind him.

A few minutes later Finn saw a faint dark spot on the water. It was moving around the point and into the bay. Or was this too a trick of the moon on the waves? Two more dark spots followed the first. It was indeed three ships! His guards had not been mistaken. The ships approached rapidly and silently across the bay; any noise which their oars might have made splashing in the water was covered by the steady sound of waves breaking on shore. Finn wondered if the guards by the beach had seen the signal. He watched in silence as the unknown ships drew closer. He knew well his duty to his people. If need be, he would give his life to defend the village.

The king finally heard the sound of his own warband coming up the hill behind him, and he breathed a quick sigh in relief. He was soon on the ground beside Guthric.

"How many?" Finn whispered.

"There are thirty of us, my lord," Guthric answered.

Finn's heart sank. Only thirty? But he had known when Guthman had left minutes earlier how many were in the hall that night, and that a warband would not suddenly appear at his command. There was naught to be done. The approaching ships were almost to shore—sixty or more men. Finn started down the beach and his hearthwerod followed.

"Aelfer awaits in the hall with ten more," Guthric continued. "Guthman should have five guards with him on the beach. A messenger has been sent along the coast and may return soon with three guards from the northern watchtower."

"That is fifty by my count," Finn said aloud, though it was directed toward himself. Or fifty less one, he remembered. Aelfer could no longer be counted as a warrior. His leg had been badly crushed by a falling horse during a boar hunt at Summer's Day celebration. He could barely stand on his own.

"That is all that is to be found in Hwitstan this day, my lord," Guthric apologized.

"Well I know that," Finn replied more harshly than he intended. Most of the men in his warband had been sent back to their own chieftains and villages for the winter. Hwitstan was nearly empty.

"I could send to Ezinge," Guthric suggested. "In little more than a day Eofan could return with twenty men."

"Alas, if this is a raiding party that would be too late. We are better to keep the messenger here with sword in hand." The king paused and then went on, "Does Aelfer know the number of boats?"

"He does, my lord. He will do what he may to prepare the village." Guthric added softly, as if he were ashamed to say it, "And yet he himself may not prove to be much aid if it comes to a fight."

Finn ignored the comment. "There is no more we can do. Look, they land even now."

One at a time, each of the three ships slid onto the beach. They were large ships, larger than Finn had guessed, six or even eight feet longer than those used by the Frisians. Thirty warriors they might easily hold, he calculated quickly, and his strange dread deepened. Nor were the ships comforting to look upon. In the faint moonlight the grinning dragon head on the prow of the first was cold and frightening.

The ships began to unload. The men who stepped out were tall and well armed. They were not traders. This was without doubt a warband. Yet no swords were drawn, no spears were raised. Were they planning on attacking? Would they withdraw upon seeing themselves challenged?

Finn arrived with his following just as Guthman and the five guards stepped forward to challenge the intruders. From his stand on the beach, Guthman had not seen the signal from the watchtower. He was as surprised to see Finn and Guthric suddenly appear at his back with thirty armed men as he had been to see the three ships arrive seconds earlier. Nonetheless, though he had seen three ships approach and knew not that his king was coming behind him, he had not left his post. He was a good thane, trustworthy and loyal, prepared to defend the shores of his king with but five swords—prepared, if necessary, to die for his king and people. His hopes were raised when he saw the friendly swords appearing beside him.

"What men come to our shores so well armed and late at night?" Guthman's voice challenged clearly. Finn held back and gave his thane the honor to speak for him.

"This is a strange welcome for a friend," a deep voice answered out of the night. As he spoke, the leader of the unknown warband stepped forward and approached Guthman where he stood in front of his king.

"Hnaef!" Finn shouted when he recognized him.

"My brother," the Danish king replied, and grabbed Finn by the shoulders.

"At strange times do we find you standing upon our shores, and yet you are, as always, welcome." So relieved was Finn to find a friend rather than an enemy appearing armed at his doorstep that his usual formal manner was gone. There would be time for that later beneath the roof of his hall.

"The welcome of Finn is renowned indeed and gladly do I accept it," Hnaef said. Hengest stepped up beside him as he spoke. "Where is my sister?"

"Indeed, this was no welcome," Finn replied solemnly. "Had I known you were coming, a great welcome feast would have been prepared. But we feared the worst. We came to greet you with our swords."

"An unwelcome visit that would have been, and not fitting for the brother of your wife. And I ask again, where is my sister?"

"Ah!" Finn laughed, still expressing his relief. "Even were my wife not the sister of a Danish king, I would not take her to war with me. Her beauty is too great to be spoiled by a spear. She awaits in the hall."

"Then let us proceed there at once," Hnaef said. "It has been long since I have seen her."

"She, too, is anxious to see you," Finn said. Of that he had no doubt.

As the kings were talking, the rest of the Danish party stepped from their ships onto the beach. They now waited for their king's command. A few, seeing the armed Frisians before them, held spears or swords ready at hand. Had the Frisians counted, they would have found ninety and six Danish spear-bearers. Finn's people were outnumbered better than two men to every one.

"Come," Finn said, motioning with his staff toward the hill behind him. With his other hand he still held his shield which Guthric, anticipating battle, had brought to him. His sword Healfwyrhta remained on his back. "Let my welcome be given from hearth and hall. Tonight you shall share Finnsburg with me."

"Does the rest of your warband await you there?" Hnaef asked, looking at the small size of Finn's company.

"But a few," Finn replied. "This is all I have this day. The rest of them have gone to their villages and homes for the winter. They will return in the spring." As soon as he had said this he wished he hadn't, for at that moment Guthlaf, Oslaf and Hunlaf stepped up beside Hnaef and Hengest. Hunlaf the Jute, glancing condescendingly at the small warband before him, laughed in derision at Finn's words.

Finn ignored the laugh. Nodding to Guthric, he turned and started up the hill with Hnaef at his side.

"What brings you to our shores, my friend and brother?" Finn asked as they walked.

"We, too, are returning to our homes for the winter. I took it in my heart to visit my sister."

"Returning from where?" Finn was only mildly curious. His attention was focused on the number of Danes he was leading into his village. *I am leading a warband into my village and hall without so much as a fight*, he thought. He sought in vain for some other option. There was none—or none he might take without losing pride, for he had already welcomed them to his hall.

"Gaining wealth." Hnaef smiled. Finn only half-remembered his question and did not fully hear Hnaef's answer. "The Anglish and Saxon shores are ripe for harvest," the Danish king continued. "They have grown smug and lazy since the Britons were defeated."

This Finn heard, and he did not return the smile. As a king, he had never been one to prosper through raiding and warfare. He did not understand the Danes and their Viking practices.

"They build temples to their god," Hnaef continued, "and they fill them with wealth which they do not protect with the sword. Their gold and silver are quickly and easily won. They build on islands and beside rivers where we may come and go as quickly as we wish."

A memory of his father, dying from wounds inflicted by Frankish raiders, flooded Finn's mind. And he had not forgotten the atrocities done to the people of Domburg, nor the tales of the devastation of Wulfanwod's clan at the hands of the raiders.

"Do you raid and murder even your own people?" Finn asked with sudden animosity.

Hnaef looked back at Finn in surprise. Hunlaf laughed again, more cruelly this time. "Surely you do not take offense at such work?" the Danish king asked. "It is the way of our people. It is no less the way of any people. Wealth comes through war and conquest."

Finn did not respond. He reminded himself silently that it was not the Danes who had killed Folcwalda or raided Domburg, and his sudden anger toward Hnaef dissipated somewhat. Still, he found himself wondering if the temples the Danes had raided had been those of Willimond's folk in Lindisfarne. What would the monk think?

"Come," Finn said finally. "The time for battles is past. You have returned to the comforts of home. Tonight we drink, and tomorrow we will feast." Yet as soon as he had said this, he found himself wanting the Danish king to refuse his hospitality, to turn right then and set sail. He thought of himself feeding the large Danish warband with the precious winter stores of his own people, and he did not cherish the thought.

"We must not tarry," Hnaef replied. "The winter storms will be upon the seas soon, and wives await my men."

Finn breathed a sigh of relief. "Then come, we will at least share the mead cup," he offered more joyfully. "My poet will sing, and our people will share the hall this night."

"It is good!" Hnaef replied.

They reached the top of the hill, passed the now-empty watchtower, and descended into Hwitstan. The warband of Hnaef laughed and jested loudly as they went. They had traveled far that day and looked forward to food, drink and respite from their labors. Proud men they were and feared no ambush. Finn's folk, however, were quieter and more cautious. They talked among themselves in low voices and looked nervously about them at the fearsome Danes whom they were leading into their village.

All was quiet as the two warbands approached Finnsburg. The folk of the village were expecting a battle. Some kept themselves in hiding, while others waited at the edge of the village, ready to flee in case there was a raid. In all of Hwitstan there was no movement. Only three men were visible. Aelfer was one. He stood in the doorway of the hall holding his old battle sword from the days of his health. His courage was not lessened by the crutch supporting his shoulder. Flanking him on either side were two guards carrying long spears. Sothfreond and Treowine they were, of Aelfer's tribe. Treowine was the husband of Aelfer's sister, and Sothfreond was his cousin. Though they were not thanes of Finn, both were faithful friends and comrades of Aelfer, and they were loyal as well to their king. In the faint light they could not identify Finn among those approaching. Yet, they held their ground as good warriors. These three also were willing to die defending their king and hall.

In the shadows within the hall, four more Frisians hid silently. Another four waited just around the corner, listening for a command.

When the leaders of the approaching company drew near, Sothfreond and Treowine stepped forward and lowered their spears—three facing more than a hundred. Aelfer stayed where he was, leaning on his crutch. "Who comes before the hall of the High King, Finn of Friesland? Make yourselves known to us," he demanded.

"Well done, faithful servant," Finn replied. "It is I, the king himself."

Aelfer breathed a sigh of relief, but he did not move aside

from the doorway. He was looking at the large warhost moving behind his king. "Do they come in peace?" he asked.

"In peace," Finn replied. "Tonight we share the mead cup with Hnaef, son of Hoc, king of the Danes and with the thanes of his warhost."

"Hnaef!" a voice burst out. Hildeburh, who had stayed within the hall against Finn's wishes, rushed past Aelfer and threw her arms around her brother. They greeted one another joyfully. There was no person alive whom Hildeburh desired to see more than her brother, nor any folk more than her own, the Danes. She was jubilant. It was a happy reunion, and it took a few moments before anything else was accomplished.

Then one by one as the villagers recognized the voices of their king and queen and heard no sounds of battle, their fear left them. The bolder and more curious of them peered out from their homes at the scene in front of Finnsburg.

"Tonight there will be fellowship in the hall, and we will drink to the reunion of brother and sister," Finn proclaimed, and the entire band both of Frisians and Danes streamed into Finnsburg behind their kings. There would be no battle that night.

Yet the joy which Hildeburh felt at seeing her brother, and the relief which Finn felt at finding a friend where he had feared an enemy, was not shared by all those in Hwitstan. At least one of Finn's servants felt instead pain and humiliation. As soon as the king had entered the hall, Aelfer collapsed in exhaustion. His job was done, but he had received no thanks or honor. Near the back of the hall, away from any seat of glory, he lay upon the floor and watched as the two warbands entered the hall in high moods. The pain that he had been holding back shot up his leg like a well-kindled fire, and he nearly lost consciousness. Since his knee and hip had been badly crushed, it was difficult for him to even stand. Yet for his king he had stood this night. He had sought faithfully to defend his hall. And Finn, in his relief, had not even taken thought for him. He had not noticed Aelfer's suffering—the suffering of his loyal servant. But Hunlaf did take notice, and he sought to use it to his advantage. With a sudden vicious movement, the Jute kicked Finn's thane in his wounded thigh as he passed. Pain cut through Aelfer like a knife. He winced sharply in agony, and only by the strength of his will did he not allow himself to cry out.

Sothfreond and Treowine looked up in surprise to see Hunlaf sneering down at their friend. Then, as quickly as he had done the deed, the Jute was gone, as if nothing had happened. The warriors had no time even to draw their weapons. Yet Aelfer knew it was no accident. So also did his two comrades who sat beside him. Anger burned fiercely in their hearts.

But if any others besides those four were aware of what had transpired, they said naught of it, thinking it better not to interfere. Soon Frisian and Dane alike were on benches around the hearth in the hall of the great king.

●

"Tonight there shall be song," Finn announced some time later, after all had been seated and the drink had been passed among those gathered. Hildeburh and Hnaef stopped speaking with each other for a moment and listened. "We shall have a story from Daelga. Summon the poet."

With harp in hand, Daelga answered the summons moments later. A poet he was; a scop and not a thane. He was no member of the king's hearthwerod. Yet into Finn's presence he could go; in the hall of Finnsburg he could sit and sing at feasts. And he was fed well. He was richly rewarded for his work—if work it could be called, for from youth to old age he had always loved what he did. He had not been far away when Finn had called.

"What does the king desire?" Daelga asked, bowing low.

Finn looked at Hildeburh and Hnaef and then back at Daelga. "In honor of this night, we shall have a song of the Danes."

"So shall it be," said Daelga humbly. For humble he was in spirit, though oft his station led him to act otherwise. He once more bowed low to the two kings and to the queen, and then began to search his mind for a suitable song. Not often did Daelga have trouble thinking of one, though that night he did. As his eyes wandered to and fro seeking some inspiration, they fell upon Hunlaf. The Jute returned his gaze with pure hatred. Daelga stumbled backward as if struck. That face looked familiar to him, but from where? Dark braided hair, bound lavishly in bright silks; eyes that pierced like a poisoned dart . . . Daelga turned away quickly, but the venom of that glance had already poisoned his thoughts and mood.

Was it fate or prophecy or chance that next moved his voice? He was afterward never sure.

Daelga was distraught by Hunlaf, whose wickedness he perceived. Before he was aware of what he was doing, the tale of Heremod came pouring from his mouth. *What foolishness!* he thought. *This is not a tale to honor the Danes!* But it was too late. His voice was lifted in song; his mouth had begun to sing of its own accord; his fingers strummed the harp without his will. And so Daelga sang the tale of Heremod, the son of Ecgwela. He sang loudly and did not conceal the wickedness of that Danish king.

With proud and haughty heart, Heremod had killed his own table-companions, his shoulder-comrades, his very own kinsmen, and by evil deeds had secured his crown. And his wickedness bloated him like a salty herring in wintertime. With each passing day the wicked Dane had grown more bloodthirsty until finally his thanes rebelled against him. Then Heremod came to the end of his strength and courage, and in cowardice he fled to the land of the Jutes.

At the hands of the Jutes, Heremod sought refuge but found it not. The Jutes put him to death for his wicked deeds. They killed him in his sleep and sent his body back to his people.

Daelga did not stop until the tale was finished. He told all of it.

> *"Then came to an end*
> *The evil of Heremod,*
> *Strength, glory, fame,*
> *Folly and pride.*
> *Surging sorrows*
> *Had stricken him too long.*
> *To his nobles and thanes,*
> *To his folk he had become*
> *A burden far too great.*
> *Crime had taken him.*

> *By the Jutes sent away,*
> *No sanctuary given.*
> *His trust was betrayed.*
> *Death he found instead."*

All this Daelga sang for a Danish warband, for a Danish king!

When he finished, there was silence—an angry, dead silence. Every Dane in the hall was glaring at him furiously—every Dane save for one. That one was Hildeburh. She alone watched him not in anger, but in curiosity and compassion. Daelga cast his eyes downward in shame, and in amazement at his own audacity. He was sweating profusely. His hands were shaking.

Still there was silence in the hall.

Finn, my king, he wanted to shout, *say something*. But Finn did not speak. *Command me. Accuse me. Forgive me*. Silence. *Speak!* The silence was overwhelming. Surely the Frisians were aware of the offense, but they would do nothing. Where was Ulestan?

Daelga could stand the silence no more. Was he a coward? He did not know. He was a poet and not a warrior.

In an effort to appease his angered audience, he picked up his harp once more. He controlled his shaking hands and began to play. He sang of Scyld, the mightiest of the Danes, and of the glory of his deeds, and he added many new verses of praise for that great one. When he finished, he did not wait for a response, but picked up his harp and fled from the hall.

"I think this worm of a poet has spoken well in singing of Heremod," Hunlaf whispered to his brothers as soon as Daelga had left. Guthlaf and Oslaf looked at him blankly. "How much easier our task now if we kill Hnaef in his sleep," Hunlaf explained. "When our warband awakes to find him dead with a knife in his back, it will be but an easy thing to blame this deed on Finn."

"Would you have war this very night?" Oslaf asked.

"Have we not two men for every one of theirs? The fight will be quickly and easily won, and the two kingdoms will be ours!"

XXIX

The Storm Breaks

innlaf and Ulestan returned to Hwitstan early the following morning, winded and tired from hard riding. They too had spotted the signal fire, but from many miles away. Fearing the worst they had pressed on, hoping to return home that very night. Yet they had finally been forced to stop for fear of becoming lost, crippling their horses on unseen roots, or being caught in the neck by low dark branches. When the blackness under the forest canopy had become complete and they could no longer see the trail ahead of them, they had reined to a halt. Their fears made them restless and they slept little, arising at the first hint of dawn. Then they were once again riding hard. Their fears were multiplied by a night of sleeplessness and anxiety.

The village of Hwitstan was quiet as they dismounted at the door of the great hall. There had been no guards in Finnweard, and none at the door of Finnsburg either. They glanced around at the surrounding fields. No farmers were to be seen. Was it too early? . . . Or had something happened? A deathly gloom hung about the place and settled on the two riders. Finnlaf looked briefly at Ulestan. Curiosity mingled with fear filled his gaze. Ulestan's returning glance showed the same emotions. They delayed no longer. The prince strode briskly through the door of Finnsburg with the thane at his side.

What he saw when he entered took him by surprise: Bodies filled the hall. There were at least one hundred of them, strewn about haphazardly on benches or the hard ground. Some of them he knew. Others were strange to him—foreigners, northlanders.

"Danes," Ulestan said disdainfully, looking at the device of a dragon on a nearby shield. They picked their way across the hall, stepping carefully among the bodies, looking for Finn.

Finn lay beside the hearth with his thanes in a circle about him. His left arm hung limply at his side, but his right still clutched his sword. The gold torc of kingship was about his neck, and his staff leaned against a bench beside him. Hnaef lay on the other side of the hearth, which now held but a few smouldering embers. Hengest and his other thanes were beside him, as were many of his earls and the mightiest of his warriors.

Three pairs of eyes watched Finnlaf and Ulestan closely as they proceeded across the room. One had just drawn a knife but resheathed it quickly. "He will be the first to die for his interference," Hunlaf breathed to his brothers.

"Father!" Finnlaf said, rushing to kneel beside the king.

Finn sat up slowly, looking rather dazed. "Finnlaf, my son, you return . . . And none too early. How fared you on the hunt?"

"It is over," the prince answered. A dread had been upon him from the moment he entered the silent village. A flood of relief came over him when he found his father alive.

"Did you find success?" the king asked. "Did fate look kindly upon you?"

"You must ask your thane," Finnlaf responded with a knowing glance at Ulestan.

Finn looked at Ulestan as well.

"Far beyond what we expected, my lord," the thane replied proudly, and he told the story of their hunt to the waking king. As he spoke, the other men in the hall slowly began to awake as well. Those close enough to hear listened to Ulestan's tale with interest. When the thane was finished, he gestured around the room and asked, "And now, do you not have a tale for us? For I perceive that our host has increased somewhat."

At that moment Hnaef, who was now fully awake, rose to his feet and spoke for the first time that morning. "Ulestan, trusted companion of the Frisian kings, the owl, wise in counsel . . . I had hoped I might see you again. Few indeed are the thanes who have offered such noble service as you—though I, indeed, am blessed with some—and fewer still are the kings who deserve such service, though there are none more worthy than Finn."

As the Danish king spoke words of praise for Ulestan and

Finn, Hunlaf's jealousy and hatred burned all the more toward them, and he determined in his heart to see to their end.

Ulestan bowed his head humbly. "It is a great honor to once again share hearth and hall with the renowned brother of my queen." But Finnlaf was already on his feet and hurrying to the side of Hnaef.

"My uncle," he cried with delight, and they held one another firmly. Through the years a great bond had grown between them—a bond as thick as their shared blood which no mark could erase. Oft they had hunted one with the other whenever their travels brought them together. They were of kindred spirit, these two.

"Come, Finnlaf, and show me the head of this great boar," Hnaef said as he released his nephew from his grasp.

So began the celebration of that day, and it lasted until sunset. Though he held back the greater part of his winter stores, still it was no small quantity of food and mead that was brought forth by Finn to accompany the supply of pork and venison so recently provided. The two warbands feasted, laughed and sported while villagers looked on. And there was song as well. Though Daelga did not appear that day, young Kristinge, with the approval of Willimond, brought forth his harp and sang in the place of the old poet, who was in hiding. There was no lack of mirth or recreation.

Yet joy is ever the enemy of evil, and evil the enemy of joy. Throughout the day, while others feasted and gamed, the hearts of Guthlaf, Oslaf and Hunlaf brooded and plotted, and the brothers grumbled and complained at every opportunity. "Who is this whelp of a poet?" Hunlaf asked. "We were better off with the old one."

Oslaf wondered as well. He looked hard at Kristinge, and for a brief moment there was a faint glimmer of recognition in his mind. Had he seen Finnlaf and Kristinge side by side, perhaps he would have guessed the truth. Yet, whether it was the God of Kristinge who acted in his behalf or not, the eyes of Oslaf were quickly closed and the glimmer of recognition faded, and thus the lineage of Kristinge was not revealed to these evildoers. Had the truth not been hidden, the pupil of Willimond would not have lived the night, and the evil of that day would have been far greater.

Even so, the evil plots of the brothers had already been planted, and they began to grow and fester. All day they taunted the young prince Finnlaf. And though the prince showed great patience and responded not in kind, yet many were the Frisians whose tempers rose in their prince's defense. Their hatred burned toward the Jutes and toward the Danes as well, for among the Frisian clans many did not distinguish between those northern tribes. Of all this, neither Finn nor Hnaef were aware, for the brothers were careful not to speak rudely or reveal themselves in front of their king. Yet evil words are not quickly turned aside, and if they find ears, they will play their role until the end.

"Come," Hnaef said to Finn as the sun was setting. "Tomorrow my people must leave to sail home or we shall be stranded here for the winter. I fear your stores would not last for such a great company. We must return to the hall and sleep. Morning will arrive all too early."

"Wisely spoken, good king," Finn replied. He too had taken thought of his winter stores of food. So the word was soon given by the two kings, and their hearthwerods were once more gathered beneath the roof of the hall.

When all were gathered on benches by the hearth, Finn spoke to Hnaef, one king to another. "For fifty half-years there has been peace between Dane and Frisian, between the Honor-Scyldings and Folcwalda's people. By the gods may there be fifty more! Good is the king of the Danes. None may be found better than Hnaef, son of Hoc. You work truth and right for your folk and are a strong guardian of the land. In strength you govern steadily. As in the past, I shall be a friend to you. If ever warriors and thanes you need, we will be at your side. If rulers rise against you, or chieftains fail to pay tribute, one hundred Frisian shields and swords will stand with you. Be faithful, good friend, to your people and to ours. Turn not to wickedness and your descendants will rule long after you."

Hnaef replied with words of praise to his brother-in-law. "Far across the seas have stories of your deeds carried. None are likely to come against you in war. Valiant and strong are you and your thanes. Well you are protected by spear and sword against nations across the earth. Yet, if ever a day comes when men rise against you, Danish ships shall sail at your call. Short will be the distance across the Swan Road if ever you be at need."

Then Hnaef, the son of Hoc turned to Finnlaf, his nephew, and said more words of caution and praise, so loudly that all in the hall could clearly hear them. "Have no care for pride, great warrior, nor imitate the deeds of Niphad. Good is the flesh that has sprung from our blood, and long may it rule if you treat your thanes well. Be generous in the giving of rings, and break not your vows and promises. No greater boar hunter have I known in all my days. Keep your ash sharpened."

Honorable was that Danish king, and truly were his words meant. Alas, but Hnaef's thanes were less good and did not honor the promises of their king.

When Hnaef had finished, Hildeburh rose also and addressed her brother with imploring words, seeking his support for the day when her son would seek the crown. Placing a golden cup in his hands, she spoke thus: "Drink health from the cup, good brother. Carry spear and shield with strength, and prosper with great riches. Be good in counsel, and make yourself known. And should your days last longer than those of Finn, be kind to your nephew. Give him good counsel, and support him with the strength of your arm. Be true to one another as to your thanes, and the peace may last a hundred half-years and more. Remember, too, that when comes the day to pass your crown, pass with it your love for our people. Forget not your sister and kin in Friesland." She bowed low to her husband and brother, then departed from the hall.

Throughout the speeches Aelfer sat in the smoky shadows near the back wall. He had moved little during the day and had taken no part in the celebration. Only when his concerned companions had brought him food had he eaten.

"What troubles you, my friend?" Treowine asked him after Hildeburh had finished her speech. Sothfreond stood by, listening. His heart felt the same concern for Aelfer as did Treowine's.

"The injury pains me this day," Aelfer answered, and in that he did not lie. While attempting to stand on his wounded leg to guard the door of Finnsburg, he had done some further injury to the damaged knee and hip, and his pain had grown throughout the day. But the full truth he withheld because of his pride. He would not speak of the greater injury. The kick he had received from Hunlaf had hurt him to the core of his spirit, mind and soul. As a younger man, healthy and uninjured, he could have defended himself. His honor would not have been so easily attacked, nor would the honor of his king. Yet now he was dependent on others. He had lain on the floor, wounded and kicked by a Jutish dog, and his king had not even noticed. Though Aelfer had served Finn longer than any other thane save Ulestan alone, Finn had said nothing in praise of his servant. No rings had been given to adorn his neck. No swords, shields or helmets taken in battle were bestowed on him. His life he had given in service to Finn, and what was his reward? He sat in the back of the hall with the dogs who waited for scraps! Finn did not even notice him. Was this the end and value of Aelfer's life and of his life's service? Or had he, in this last attempt at service to his king, failed? Yes, he thought, he had failed. "I would be better off dead," he muttered softly. "At least in death and burial Finn would honor me."

Suddenly the High King was calling out for Aelfer!

To hear his name called by Finn came as a great surprise to Aelfer. The king, in the excitement and confusion of Hnaef's arrival, had indeed forgotten about his trustworthy thane. Nor had he remembered him the following day. Because of Aelfer's injury, Finn had ceased to rely on him. Though he was still welcome beside the hearth, he was no longer as useful in service as he once had been. Finn was a king of action and of deed, of great and mighty plans. The chief tools of those plans were his thanes. To such an extent was Finn's mind filled with his purposes that those who were not part of them found little place in his thought. This was true even of his son Kristinge. In this, perhaps, fault could be found with that king, that he gave not the honor to Aelfer that he might have given to a thane who had died in battle. Aelfer was right—he would have received more honor had he died.

Yet now the thought of this thane who had served the king so faithfully, even in injury, came to Finn's mind. So, removing from about his wrist a gold ring with which to reward him, he called for his servant Aelfer.

Surprised by the summons, Aelfer stood awkwardly and stumbled forward. Treowine rose quickly to his feet and supported his friend. Together they made their way toward their king, Aelfer leaning on the shoulder of Treowine.

Hunlaf, who sat beside Hnaef, caught the eye of a servant, a hired member of his warband who sat on a bench between Finn and Aelfer. The servant understood the glance, for he had received instructions that very afternoon.

As Aelfer approached, the sharpened tip of a spear suddenly appeared at the ankle of his good leg. Too late Treowine saw it. The blade cut into Aelfer's ankle, and he fell. The corner of the bench caught his head, and he never received his reward.

Treowine's sword was already sliding free of its sheath when his friend crashed painfully against the bench. Even as Aelfer breathed his last, Treowine's sword pierced the neck of the Dane who had done the cruel deed.

Before the two kings were even on their feet, two bodies lay slumped to the floor. And before they could speak a word of peace or restraint, there was a second Danish spear lifting toward Treowine's back. But Treowine was too quick. He spun and knocked the spear aside with his next sword swing, and with the following another Dane fell to the floor dead. Sothfreond was at Treowine's side in a moment.

At once every man in the hall rose to his feet in surprise. So quickly did all this happen that those farthest away were staring in numb disbelief, still not quite sure what had transpired. But those closer had seen, and their swords and spears were already drawn.

In but the briefest of moments a battle had begun within Finnsburg.

Finn and Hnaef exchanged anguished looks. Blades were in hand, their tried and true battle-hardened weapons, but they would not use them against each other. Their earlier pledge they would not break. Yet, neither were they prepared for what was taking place. For the first time, those wise and quick-thinking kings knew not what to do. And second by second as they delayed their action, the battle spread around the hall. Frisian swords were raised against Danish spears, and in the close quarters many had already fallen. Only a few held back from battle. Beside Finn stood Finnlaf, Ulestan, Guthman and Guthric. They awaited their king's command, as good thanes should. Beside Hnaef were Hengest, Guthlaf, Oslaf and Hunlaf. Hengest alone of those four sought eagerly to obey his king. The other three grinned at the success of their plan and did not seek to hide their glee. Had any seen the looks of satisfaction on their faces, they would have known well who had caused the battle. But no one noticed, for their eyes were focused elsewhere.

The two kings held each other's gaze a moment longer as each gauged the other's intentions. All the while the heat of battle was increasing. The words spread earlier that day by the Jutish brothers had done their work. Lines were set, and the Frisians did not hesitate to vent their anger. Men found comrades and shoulder-companions and turned their attention upon their foes. In those dangerously close confines, a fierce battle was being fought. And as Finn and Hnaef looked again upon the hall, one thing was clear to both. The Frisians, though greatly outnumbered, were carrying the day. The superior numbers of the Danes availed them little, for in the close crowded hall there was no room to form battle lines or plan tactics. Weapons could hardly be swung without striking companion as well as foe. The Spear-Danes were accustomed to open spaces, to raids and quick attacks, to striking from beyond the reach of an enemy, and not for fighting indoors. The Frisians were making quick work with their swords. And they were fighting in their own hall, defending their own land and king. Many had wives and children living within Hwitstan itself. With every ounce of their strength they fought. Five Frisian warriors had already fallen, but more than thrice as many Danes would not see their homes again. The surviving Danes were fighting defensively, but were quickly losing the only advantage they had.

A silent decision was reached by Finn and Hnaef. It passed between them without words.

"Cease!" Finn shouted. But his voice could not be heard. The din of shield upon shield and the screams of those injured was too great. "Cease!" he shouted again with all his might. Again it was to no avail. How could his men obey? The fighting was too close; there was no place to retreat. More than a few were down with brutal knife wounds, hard inflicted. And once down, they were trampled by friend and enemy alike. To lower a weapon if your enemy did not would mean death.

Finn saw at once that words alone would not suffice to bring an end to the battle. Grabbing the shield which lay beside him and holding tightly to his sword, he approached the center of the conflict. At a word from Hnaef, Hengest went with him. The two had some hope which one alone would not have to bring an end to the battle, for the Danes would not strike Hengest, nor the Frisians Finn. When men saw them approaching and not exchanging blows, they lowered their weapons. One by one spears and swords were silenced. The plan began to work. Yet so great was the crowd and confusion and so fierce the fighting that progress was slow. Many still fought, and more good warriors fell each moment. Finn and Hengest continued on fervently.

Seeing that the desire of their king to end the battle was finding success, Guthman and Guthric moved to the other side of the hall and did what they could. Far from the side of Finnlaf and Ulestan they went, not knowing where they would most be needed.

Then came the opportunity for which Hunlaf had waited. He saw his moment arrive, and he performed the most wicked of deeds yet done in his lifetime. In later days when the tale was told, no Dane or Jute would have cause to be proud. Hunlaf took a step backward and stood behind the others. A knife slid free from the sheath hidden beneath his richly decorated cloak. His brothers saw him and, knowing his plans, stepped backward also, beginning to draw their swords as they did so.

●

Ulestan and Finnlaf noted the progress of Finn and Hengest, and that the fighting was slowly coming to an end around them. But it was taking too long. Many already lay dead and dying, and more were still falling. Cuthwald the Bold had been pierced through by a Danish spear. His brother Cuthric had fallen avenging him. Hrethmond and Hrethric would not again see their home. Long they had served Finn. The loyal Aeshere felt the knife's edge pierce his side too deeply. It was an ill happening that brought about the end of so many mighty warriors. And the prince and thane also saw that Guthric and Guthman were meeting with no success on the other side of the hall where they sought to end the fighting. Because they were both Frisians, the Danes saw them as two more enemies. In this way rather than halting the fight, Guthric and Guthman were drawn into it. Ulestan and Finnlaf held back, fearing they also would make matters worse if they tried to intercede. They stood a few paces away from the Danish king, watching and hoping that no more good thanes would die needlessly. *Why does Hnaef not send his thanes to the aid of Guthric and Guthman?* Ulestan wondered.

For a time Hnaef considered allowing the battle to continue. Never had that king lost in open warfare, and his pride was great. The Danes would win easily, he thought. Many treasures he could then take home from Finnsburg, for Friesland had become richer than he imagined. Nor would he be breaking his bond with Finn, for he had not himself lifted his sword nor ordered the battle. Had not Finn's own thane begun the fight? If Finn and Hengest brought the battle to an end, so be it, but he was not eager to aid them. But slowly his outlook changed. His own folk were falling. Faster than he thought possible, his mighty warband was being decimated. He could wait no longer. He would send Guthlaf, Oslaf and Hunlaf to the aid of the Frisian thanes.

●

The knife in Hunlaf's hand was not his own, but one previously stolen from a Frisian guard. His own dagger, richly jeweled and decorated, still hung at his side for all to see. Hunlaf gripped the stolen knife firmly and stepped forward. Long ago his heart had been hardened, and too many wicked deeds had he already done to be dissuaded from one more. In one swift motion the knife in his hand plunged deeply into the back of his king and pierced his heart.

Finnlaf, hearing a sudden movement, turned to see the act. He watched his uncle's eyes widen in shock and pain; he watched too as the Danish king's hands clutched futilely at the air behind him, as he took a half-step forward, stumbled, and fell in anguish, unable even to turn and face his killer. Finnlaf alone, amidst the turmoil and confusion in the hall, witnessed his uncle's death. He alone saw the killer. Not even Hnaef, in his last moments, guessed who had betrayed him.

With sudden swiftness Finnlaf's sword leapt free of its sheath. "Betrayer," he spat.

"Now you too must die," Hunlaf growled at Finnlaf with a sneer.

●

Out of the corner of his eye Ulestan saw Hnaef fall. The sudden motion surprised him, and he ducked an imaginary blow. Then he turned to see Finnlaf standing alone, with sword drawn, facing the three Jutes. Nor did that brave prince retreat. His pride was great, and he had loved his uncle. The rage filling his heart gave him the strength of two. Then Ulestan's own blade swung up in reflex as a blow was directed at his head from the sword of Guthlaf. It struck him with the force of pure hatred, and he stumbled backward. At the same time two swords came down on Finnlaf. How the prince managed to avoid both blows without a shield, Ulestan could not tell. Somehow Finnlaf spun safely away to his right, placing Oslaf between himself and Hunlaf so that he only had to face one of them at a time.

Well done, Ulestan thought with relief and pride. It was the first time he had seen his former pupil in battle. *He thinks quickly and wisely. I have trained him well. May it be well enough.* Then he was blocking another blow from Guthlaf. He staggered backward again. Guthlaf made no delay, but cut upward, aiming at Ulestan's exposed arm. Ulestan barely turned the thrust aside. Then came a hard swing at his head. Again Ulestan raised his sword to block it, and again he staggered under the force of the blow. Unable to bring his sword back down in time, he leapt over a swipe at his legs that would have separated ankle from knee. The fight had just begun and already he felt tired. His age was telling. If he were to defeat the Jute, he must do it soon. Yet he could not return even one blow. Guthlaf was well-trained, a veteran of many battles, and he was taller and stronger. Ulestan had not recovered his balance from Guthlaf's initial assault, so furious had it been. Nor was he giving his full attention to his opponent as he ought to do, for he was concerned for his prince.

Finnlaf, however, was faring well—better than Ulestan. Miraculously, he was holding his own against two strong enemies and had an upper hand on one. He was successfully keeping Oslaf between himself and Hunlaf, and was bearing down ferociously on the closer of them, raining a great many blows with both strength and speed. Fear showed plainly on the face of Oslaf, who was clearly overmatched by the prince. And Hunlaf was growing more and more frustrated and impatient, continuously finding himself unable to get at Finnlaf. Yet Hunlaf's presence alone kept his brother alive. So hard was Finnlaf working to keep Oslaf between himself and Hunlaf that he could not deliver the fatal blow. Whenever he was nearly in position to strike, he would have to move away suddenly to avoid Hunlaf. Help must come to him soon or he would not prevail.

But from where could help come? Finn and Hengest had finally brought the fighting to an end, only to turn and find that Finnlaf and Ulestan were giving battle to Guthlaf, Oslaf and Hunlaf. A look of horror appeared on Finn's face. His own son was fighting for his life within the doors of the king's own hall! Why? He had not yet seen the body of Hnaef who lay in his own blood. He knew not of the treachery of Hunlaf. The center of the hall had become a stage, and the High King was looking on, trying to understand the meaning of the drama, trying to guess the end. He liked not what he saw. As fast as they could, Finn and Hengest began to move back toward the hearth where the prince and thanes were fighting. At the same time, Guthric and Guthman were returning from the other side.

Of all this, Ulestan was only vaguely aware. He suddenly found himself fighting Guthlaf behind Finnlaf's back. How had that happened? Had it been his own carelessness? Finnlaf was too occupied with his own opponents; he did not know he was surrounded. But Guthlaf knew. Ulestan must not allow him a free moment, or the prince would receive the blow.

Then Hunlaf made a mistake. Growing impatient with Finnlaf's tactics, and seeing suddenly that the Frisian prince had nowhere to back up, he made a sudden lunge forward around his brother's right shoulder. The prince was ready. He stepped deftly to his own right, parrying as he did a blow from Oslaf, and then brought his sword back down on Hunlaf's exposed neck as the Jute lunged past. Hunlaf fell like a stone. Oslaf stepped backward in horrified surprise.

Having won one victory already, Finnlaf turned to face Oslaf. He did not see the Jute behind him. Guthlaf took advantage of Ulestan's distraction and fatigue. He took a sudden step backward out of Ulestan's reach and, spinning on his foot, hurled a two-handed blow at the prince's exposed neck.

"Finnlaf!" Ulestan shouted and dove forward to try to block

the blow. He was too far away and too late. Finnlaf heard the shout and stepped aside as quickly as he could. The blow, aimed at his neck, cut into his right shoulder, nearly severing the arm. His sword clattered to the floor, a sound that all heard but none more clearly than Finn, who was still many strides away.

Something hard—perhaps Guthlaf's elbow, or the hilt of his sword—crashed into Ulestan's shoulder a second later. The bone shattered, and pain exploded through his body. But he did not faint. The pain sharpened his senses, and he became all too aware of the moments that followed. He picked up his head and watched as Guthlaf raised his sword over the body of the fallen prince. The Jute was ignoring the Frisian thane now, and Ulestan was close enough to help. His face was just a few feet away from Finnlaf. With all his might he struggled to raise his sword to defend his prince and friend, but could not. There was no strength in his shattered shoulder. No help could he give the son of his treasure-giver.

In the sight of all, the blade of Guthlaf swung freely down upon the wounded prince. For a moment the eyes of Ulestan and Finnlaf met. Mercifully, the prince's eyes closed as his head rolled free of his body.

XXX

The Grief of
Hildeburh

Though Guthlaf surely wished that it might, his blade did not fall next upon Ulestan. Ulestan lay there, no more able to defend himself than he had the prince, expecting a death blow to come at any moment. But when he looked up, instead of Guthlaf he saw Guthric and Guthman standing over him in his defense. The two Jutes held their ground a few feet away. Oslaf was looking down in sadness at the bodies beneath him, but Guthlaf looked neither down nor to the side. If he felt any grief, he did not show it. He grinned wickedly at the approaching Frisians and held his blade in front of him, challenging them to battle. Guthman and Guthric accepted the challenge. They approached with a smouldering fierceness that burned brighter than the hottest flame.

Throughout the hall men readied themselves to fight to death. Those who had lain down their swords and spears picked them up again. There was a brief moment of silence—silence as close to death as Ulestan would ever wish to be.

And from that silence burst forth the most beautiful and terrible sound Ulestan had ever heard. It ripped the very fabric of the air—a high, piercing note that resounded through the hall, shaking it to its foundations. Was this a call to arms? A wail of grief? It seemed to the thane as he lay there in a swoon that he had heard that sound before. On and on that single note blew, and all other sounds ceased. Then, for the second time in his life, in the midst of battle Ulestan sank into unconsciousness.

●

Just before Finnlaf was struck down by Guthlaf, Finn and Hengest had succeeded in bringing an end to the fighting. Bodies, mostly those of Danes, lay strewn about the floor in puddles of blood. Many still groaned in the final agonies of death. Yet, miraculously the swords and spears had been stilled by those two valiant men. But when the Danes turned to see their king lying dead on the floor, and the Frisians to see their prince struck down before their eyes, a bitter hatred filled the hearts of each for the other. For never was a prince more beloved to his people than was Finnlaf, son of Finn, son of Folcwalda. Nor had the Danes ever known a king whom they honored so highly as Hnaef, save for Scyld himself. Little hope was there, were the fighting to begin again, for it to cease before one host or the other was completely destroyed.

Yet, as the warbands were once again raising their swords and girding their hearts and minds for a final battle, Finn lifted his great horn to his lips and blew the mightiest blast which ever had been blown on that horn. Whether he was calling his men to war, or whether it was in grief over his son, he himself might not have known at the time. Yet, when the note had been blown and the horn was silent, all eyes were upon that king. For a moment only men waited for some word or action. And for that brief time outside of time, Finn's thoughts were turned away from the dead son beside his own hearth to the memory of that same son in days past—and to the son who still lived. And where thoughts of hatred and revenge might have filled his heart over the loss of Finnlaf, there was instead a moment of peace. Or was it simply emptiness?

"Come," he said to Hengest. His tone of command could not be refused. "Cease!" he commanded to his people again.

"The prince is dead," a Frisian voice shouted out.

"The king is dead," shouted a Dane. "Such treachery and treason cannot be ignored."

"There will be a time for war," Finn said again, holding his sword about him and rising to his full height. "There will be war when your kings command it. It has not been commanded."

"We listen not to the Frisian king," a voice shouted out, though no spears were raised.

Hengest looked about him. His eyes were filled with doubt and confusion. He looked first upon his fallen king, and then upon Guthlaf and Oslaf who stood before him lusting for blood and hating him as much as they had hated Hnaef and Finnlaf. Finally he looked upon Finn, who stood beside him in strength and silence.

"Danes, people of Hnaef," he addressed them slowly, "listen to me. Do not raise your weapons. Let there first be a time of council."

The Danes listened. The hall was silent as Finn and Hengest walked slowly the few remaining steps back to the hearth. Both avoided looking at the bodies lying on the floor. Guthman and Guthric followed Finn, and Guthlaf and Oslaf followed Hengest.

But before either Finn or Hengest could speak, Guthlaf's voice was heard. "They have killed Hnaef. There is a Frisian knife in his back. We need no other reason for war. We must lead our people against these . . ."

"I am king now," Hengest said, interrupting him. The jaws of both Guthlaf and Oslaf dropped. "If you will oppose me, then oppose me now, for our nation will not face the Frisians a divided people."

Guthlaf clamped his mouth shut and narrowed his eyes. *So this one is not so easily dealt with*, he thought. *Yet there will be time.*

"On whom rests the blood of our king?" Hengest said, turning to Finn.

"Ask me not of the blood of your king. Ask me of the blood of my son."

"It was Finnlaf who killed Hnaef," Guthlaf said. "Blood for blood did we repay him."

"That is a lie, my lord," Guthric said.

"Did you see?" Finn asked with eager interest.

Guthric lowered his head. "No." Then he raised his eyes again and continued, "Yet, Finnlaf loved his uncle. That was plain to all."

"May not ambition destroy even love, if love there truly was?" Guthlaf asked.

"May it not?" Finn answered, accusing the Jute with his

glance. "If ambition may destroy bonds of blood, then surely it may destroy weaker bonds."

"Blood for blood," Hengest said. His voice rose as he repeated that phrase. "Blood for blood. Our king lies dead in your hall after you offered us your hospitality. There must be an answer made!"

"An answer has been made. Beside your king lies Finnlaf. Blood for blood . . . the death has been paid. Do you require more? No greater payment could I make than my own son." From neck to foot, every muscle on Finn's body was poised and ready for release. His voice held more than a hint of angry challenge. His determination for peace was fading fast. If Hengest desired more, Finn would surely give it to him. *More blood? You shall have to cut it from my very heart!*

"Truly you speak," Hengest replied, refusing the challenge. "Blood has been paid for blood, grief for grief. Justice has been given by the gods themselves."

"My lord, you cannot say this," Guthlaf pleaded. "They cannot be released from this crime or the Danes will never find peace again. Her enemies will be about her like swarming bees!"

Guthlaf's voice was lost to the new king. As Hengest's blood cooled, so did his head. And he was wiser and more cunning than either Guthlaf or Finn knew. Looking about him, he saw the bodies of the fallen Danes scattered about the hall. He saw as well the looks of fierce determination in the eyes of the Frisians. The situation before him was not a question of blood for blood or grief for grief. There could be no victory, he knew. Were he to chose to fight, not one Dane would sail home for the winter. For even if the battle were won by the Danes within, the hall would surely be burned to the ground from without—and every Dane with it. They could not this day fight the Frisians and win. If they were to avenge Hnaef, it would be another day upon a different battlefield.

And Hengest also knew that Finn's words were true. Finn's own son had indeed died. Had not the dead been avenged already?

Yet, Hengest was still a Dane, a Spear-Dane mighty in battle. In this he listened to Guthlaf. Though he knew well that no retribution was in fact owed, he must demand it nonetheless or risk the pride of his people—and perhaps his new kingship as well. And so he spoke haughty words of judgment to the already injured Frisian king, thus further sealing the fate of both peoples.

"As you have taken away our treasure-giver, so you shall become our treasure-giver yourself," Hengest began. To Finn alone he now spoke, proclaiming the doom of the Frisians. "No more in hearth or hall shall Hnaef, son of Hoc give rings to his thanes. No more shall he pour mead for his hearthwerod. This burden is now upon you. A new hall shall you build for the Danes, as great as this in which we now sit. For a year and a month you shall feed our warband, and treasures shall you give no less rich than those which you give to your own thanes."

"And if we refuse?" Finn asked, his eyes once again narrowing.

"We shall return in the spring," Hengest replied. "If this hall is not built, Hwitstan shall flow red with the blood of your people. No longer will it called Hwitstan, but Swatbaeth, 'the bloody bath.'" In this did Hengest prove an able king, wise in the ways of war. For knowing he could not win a victory that day, he gained escape for his people and, further, offered it cloaked as mercy, as if it were a gift he were giving. Even as he spoke, he knew well that whether his terms were accepted or not, he could return in the springtime with a far greater host.

Whether or not Finn perceived Hengest's thoughts mattered not. He was ill-disposed to accept those terms. His son lay dead upon the hard floor, and the reality of that death was making itself known to the king with each passing moment.

Had one more word been spoken, one sword raised, or one step taken, there surely would have been more battle that day, and even Finn could not have stopped it. His sword would have brought the vengeance he now desired. But the hall was silent, and Finn remembered his words of peace to Hnaef. Also, his warband was still outnumbered. He would not bring about a battle within his own hall. But neither would he bow to Hengest's terms. After a moment he replied, "We shall await you in the spring." The words were spoken slowly and fiercely; there was little doubt as to their intent.

When Finn had spoken, men of both warbands girded once more for battle, fearing the worst. They did not misinterpret his tone or fail to miss his hostility.

And so Finn stood there facing Hengest, wavering on the

verge of renewing the battle, and Hengest, though he knew fear, did not back down from his demands. But at that moment, before either could act or speak again, there came bursting into the hall Hildeburh of the Danes, the Queen of Friesland, her face white with fear and her eyes panic-stricken. And all thoughts of battle died away. She alone of all those gathered there on that dark day was loved by both Dane and Frisian alike. None would harm her. From across the village where she had spent the remainder of the evening talking with Willimond and Kristinge, she had heard Finn's battle horn. As had most of the villagers, she had come running. She paused briefly at the door to listen for sounds of battle. Hearing none, she entered.

The sight that met Hildeburh did not lessen her fear. Bodies were strewn across the hall. Blood lay thick upon the floor. Men she knew, both Danes and Frisians, lay slain beside her. The moans of the dying could still be heard. And in the dim light of fire and lamp, she could not see her husband. She froze where she was, unable to move forward. What had happened? Where was Finn? Her panic grew. When Finn turned to meet her and caught her eye, she breathed a sigh of relief and started toward him. Her relief ended when she saw the look on his face. He held out a hand for her to stop, but she would not. As she ran to him, Frisian and Dane alike parted before her.

No greater grief has ever been known by any woman than the grief known by Hildeburh that day. At the feet of her husband both her brother and son lay broken, victims of tragic violence. Finnlaf's head lay a few feet away from his body. She could not even bear to look at him. But she, unlike the others, noted that her brother yet breathed. She went to him at once. Only then did the others understand that Hnaef still lived.

"Hnaef . . ." Hildeburh wept. When he heard her voice, he opened his eyes. Hildeburh grabbed her brother's hand. The dying Danish king tried to speak. Guthlaf and Oslaf looked at each other in fear at what he would say. Both held their swords ready, expecting now for the Danes to suddenly become their enemies. But Hnaef could not speak, and the effort was his last. Even had he guessed who his assassins were, he could not now reveal them. His eyes closed again, and his hand fell free of his sister's. Hildeburh fainted.

Only two of the Danish ships sailed home for the winter. The third held the bodies of Hnaef and Finnlaf. With their swords and treasures laid across their chests, they were placed in the great ship of Hnaef upon a mound of wood. High was the funeral pyre of these two, and long did it burn.

Yet longer still did Hildeburh weep. Great is the sadness of watching a parent die. Greater still that of a brother. But no greater grief is known to any but to stand at the funeral of a child. All these sorrows did Hildeburh know, nor would they soon pass over, as did those of Weland and Beaduhilde.

> *Proud, he, our prince, passed now to death;*
> > *Felled by his foes, was Finnlaf slain.*
> *In battle buried by blade of traitors,*
> > *A Dane's blade, his kin's, whose king he avenged.*
> *In Hwitstan's hall, by hearth and beam,*
> > *Fell brave Finnlaf, Finn's worthy son.*
>
> *His battle he won, his uncle avenged;*
> > *He slew Hunlaf, that hated Jute.*
> *Yet three were they, all thanes of night,*
> > *Hunlaf kinslayer, Guthlaf and Oslaf.*
> *His enemies three and Finnlaf but one,*
> > *A blade to his back, fell the good one, slain.*
>
> *Not boar nor buck nor bear shall he hunt.*
> > *The mighty one's bow will bend no more.*
> *No crown shall he wear, no kingship for him,*
> > *Of Hildeburh, Finn, and Folcwalda, kin.*
> *To Hwitstan's hall, to hearth and to beam,*
> > *To men and to mead no more shall come.*
>
> *That dark day fell not he alone,*
> > *But with that prince proud thanes too many:*
> *Hrethmond, Hrethric, hearth companions,*
> > *Spears-Danes did slay, sent to the grave;*
> *Cuthric and Cuthwald cut down too soon,*
> > *Aelfer and Aeshere abandoned not their king.*

317

Proud he, our prince, passed now to death.
    Felled by his foes, was Finnlaf slain.
Great is our grief! Was good, whom was lost.
    For Hwitstan, alas! Long shall we mourn.

Not until long after the Danes had departed did Daelga sing that song, for hateful to him was the sight of them, nor would they have abided those words. Yet he sings now for any who would hear:

Let the truth be known
    Lest the lies of the hateful brothers be heard by many
And the name of the brave one be slandered—
    He who was our prince!

XXXI

The Coming of Winter

inter was long and quiet in Hwitstan that year, and elsewhere in Friesland as well. Word of Finnlaf's death was quickly spread throughout the land, and many voices were lifted in mourning. Many there were who loved him, both thanes and commoners alike. He was a good prince. Long and quiet was that winter in Hwitstan, and dark and cold as well.

•

In the weeks that followed the death of Finnlaf, a violent storm silently brewed in Finnsburg and in the heart of the High King. Finn carried his grief and anger like a sword, striking out at all who were near, even at those he loved most dearly. The great restraint which he had shown in Hwitstan on that evil night was gone, replaced by rage. *Why did I not finished the battle then?* That question plagued him. *Why did I not avenge my son?* Now the Danes were gone. He had allowed to escape those who killed his son. So the anger which he had withheld from the Danes was turned unfairly upon his own people, as if they were to blame for his loss. Finn's heart began to sour, to decay like leaves beneath the winter's snow. He spoke little during those days, and when he did it was with harsh and hostile words. His manner became dark and sullen, and he ceased to give treasure in his hall. He became a different king altogether than the Finn who for so long had ruled Friesland. Thus Finnsburg became an unhappy hall, and all of Hwitstan suffered.

It is a great sorrow that many lesser men lost their love for Finn during those days, remembering him only as he became and not how he had been. They had seen their king put low by the words of Hengest, and they did not forget. Nor did Finn work to regain their love or to redeem himself in their eyes. Instead he did the opposite. Many were they who suffered the brutal lash of his tongue. Not the least of these was Ulestan. It seemed to many that the king blamed that faithful thane for the death of his son. Though he did not say so openly, what few words he spoke to Ulestan held an accusing tone. As sly hints and cold remarks are often more harshly borne than open accusation, Ulestan bore the most brutal of Finn's assaults and the worst of his rage. Nor did that brave thane need punishment or accusation, for he could not have been brought any lower than his own spirit had already taken him. So deeply did he love the prince that he took upon himself the full blame for not preventing his death. Finn's harsh words seemed to the thane just.

In those days of trial and despair, Ulestan went often to visit Willimond, seeking comfort and wise words. He who had faced death time and again, who had shown more strength than entire armies, wept upon the shoulder of the monk. "Twice I have fallen," he confessed. "Once at the side of Folcwalda and once at the side of Finnlaf. Now both lie dead. Alas, I would that I had taken the fated blade upon my own neck." And from that day forth Ulestan never again lifted a sword. The hilt of the weapon which had first struck Finnlaf and brought him down had also smashed Ulestan's shoulder. His right arm now dangled limply and uselessly at his side. He was so humbled by his injury and defeat that he refused even to bear a sword in his sheath. "I am no longer a fit thane for my king," he cried.

So Ulestan visited the monk often, and often did he spend time alone in the church of Willimond's God. Yet nothing the monk could say would raise the spirits of that brave one. Though Willimond tried his hardest, Ulestan was beyond his reach. This caused the monk great grief, for Ulestan was dear to him—a friend as close as a brother—and he pained to see the man's spirits so low. Day after day Willimond sought to comfort him, and day after day he failed. Ulestan would not be comforted. He would hear no words, but turned his thoughts instead to self-pity and self-blame.

Yet in the worst of times, some small joy was found for the thane, and this came from an unexpected source. As many years before he had done for Willimond, Lopystre once again opened his home to one who needed it. And as Willimond had once held the weir-keeper's daughter in his arms, so now Ulestan held his granddaughter, the child of Lyndlaf. In those moments some joy returned to the joyless one. There is much healing in the eyes of a child. Praise the Mighty One—He provided comfort for His servant Ulestan. Perhaps this fragile thread was all which kept the thane from sinking into more despair and darkness than a soul can tolerate.

For others, though not for Ulestan, the words of Willimond did provide great comfort. Many were the families and children of thanes lost in that battle. Aelfer never rose again, his neck broken against a mead bench where once he had sat to receive treasure. Aeshere, Hrethmond and Hrethalf, proud and loyal thanes all, did not live to see that winter, nor did the brothers Cuthric or Cuthwald, who also were pierced by Danish spears and knives. Hearing that the teaching might ease their pain, many came to the small church for the first time that winter. Mightily blessed was the tongue of that monk to bring healing, and great is the power of the Holy One to heal.

Kristinge, too, proved a comfort to many. With each passing day his voice grew more powerful and captivating. There was healing in his songs—perhaps even more than in the sermons of the monk. Kristinge had the gift of Orpheus, some said. And as he grew in knowledge and wisdom, and as his love of books and Scripture increased as well, so too did his love of poem and verse. Hymns and songs he composed for the Lord, and many were those who listened eagerly. As Daelga made and sang great tales of heroes, the student of Willimond put the Word of God to verse.

"The Spirit has given this one the gift of song," Daelga said quietly to Willimond one day. Daelga too had been baptized into the Holy Faith, and his words had great meaning.

"Truly He has," the monk replied. "Truly He has."

XXXII

The Redemption of Hildeburh

ildeburh was among those in the village of Hwitstan who began to come often to the small church. Whether she came to hear the words of Willimond or the voice of Kristinge, only she knew. She would not speak of Kristinge to any but Finn and Willimond. Even to the monk she spoke only of "your servant" and not of "my son." Silently at first, she would come and sit close to the back of the church and would leave shortly after Willimond's sermon was over.

Yet one cold day she did not leave. When all the others had returned to their homes, she sat alone in the back of the hall. She remained perfectly still with her hands folded across her lap and her eyes turned downward.

Tears sprang to Willimond's eyes as he watched her sitting there. *What great grief this woman knows! How can she bear it?* She made no move to talk to him, or even to acknowledge him. *Dare I speak with her?* he wondered. What could he say?

After a long time the monk finally spoke. "What troubles you, my queen?" He could think of no other words to bridge the river of her silence; yet, as soon as his words were spoken they seemed trite and callous. *Is there anyone who does not know what is troubling her?* he thought.

To Willimond's surprise, a look of great relief came across Hildeburh's face. "Many times over the years have I desired to hear more about your God," she answered him in a soft voice, "but my husband wished otherwise."

"Many times have I desired to tell you," the monk answered, and he took a seat beside her.

"Now more than ever do I yearn to know the One you serve."

"And He yearns to make Himself known. You need only ask."

Hildeburh started to speak, but hesitated.

"Do you still fear what Finn will say?" Willimond asked, seeing her sudden look of anguish.

A tear rolled from her eye. "I wish that Finn cared what I did. But he does not. He cares for little but for the Danes to return."

"Will he build the hall?" the monk asked cautiously.

"He will not."

"Then there will be battle." His voice trailed off, and he did not finish. *And Hwitstan will be burned. My church will be burned.*

"He wishes his son avenged," the queen replied, lifting her eyes and holding Willimond's gaze. Though her words did not say so, her eyes did: she was pleading for help. "He wishes he had never halted the battle. He wishes he had died in place of his son. He wishes . . . He does not even speak to me, save in words of anger about my family of Danes."

"What may I do?" Willimond asked, wishing more than anything that he could answer whatever her request might be.

"Why did your God allow my son to die?"

Never had Willimond a more difficult question to answer, and it was made no easier for having caught him unprepared. Why indeed had God allowed the prince to perish? What answer could he give? How could he answer when he knew not the answer himself?

"I do not know," he whispered.

"Does He have a reason?" the queen asked again.

"For all things there is a reason," the monk answered.

"Then your God takes pleasure in the pain and suffering of men?"

Willimond winced at this question. "No pleasure does God take in the pain and suffering of any."

"Then why does He allow it? Why do such things happen?"

"There is no easy answer . . ." He hesitated.

"But there is an answer?" Tears were streaming down

Hildeburh's face as she asked this. "For if there is, I desire to know. If your God really does care about us, then I would know Him."

"God cares deeply for you, and even now He seeks to comfort you. You need but ask."

"And the answer to my question?"

"May I ask you a question first?"

Hildeburh nodded.

"You loved your son greatly."

Hildeburh bit her lip and nodded again.

"Yet still you allowed him to make his own choices—even if they brought about suffering—his own suffering." Willimond waited for the queen to respond, but she could not. She began to tremble. The monk went on, "So too does God allow us to make our own choices, even if they bring about suffering. To serve God freely, we must also have the freedom to turn away from Him. It is true with Finn's thanes as well. Those who are most dear to him are those who have chosen freely to serve him, not those under obligation."

As the monk spoke, he looked into the eyes of his queen and doing so found that he deeply loved her—not as a man to a wife, but as a servant to his master. Such strength and sorrow filled her eyes! Even in her grief her beauty was surpassing. Why indeed had God allowed this one to suffer? Yet even her pain had brought about some good. Was it not this very suffering which had brought her to Him, which had caused in her a desire to know the One God?

Willimond continued his answer as best as he could. "And there is an enemy, the Evil One. He delights in pain and suffering—in wicked deeds."

"Is this Evil One more powerful than your God?"

"No," Willimond replied. "And yet God allows the Evil One, too, to freely rebel. And He allows us to choose freely whom we will serve. To those who serve Him, He promises peace."

"I would have this peace."

"Would you serve God? Would you place your life in His hands? Would you acknowledge that you need Him?"

"I would," replied the queen, and as she spoke those words, from somewhere in her heart there arose a true joy, a knowledge of peace in the midst of pain and sorrow. Her grief did not disappear, but a hand reached down and held the burden of it for her. She felt . . . she felt Grace.

That very day, as a cold wind blew from the north, she was baptized in the icy pond.

After the baptism of Hildeburh came a lifting of her spirit. She came often afterwards to the church of Willimond and talked frequently with the monk, learning much about the God she now served. Though sorrow still filled her heart, her joy became even greater. She became a source of light in Hwitstan, a candle in a dark room. Where she went, men and women smiled, and hurts healed.

But she was only one.

XXXIII

The Return of Finn

If Finn saw Hildeburh's baptism or noticed a change in her heart, he did not say. His mood did not change, or if it did it was for the worse. One by one loyal thanes left Finnsburg and returned to their homes, unable to sleep beneath such a joyless roof. Soon only two remained: Guthric and Guthman.

One day the king and his two faithful thanes were standing atop Finnweard looking across the icy harbor. Hwitstan was knee-deep in snow, and the dark clouds were threatening to drop more.

"Messengers have been sent, my lord," Guthric said to his king.

"And no reply?" Finn asked.

"None yet, my lord," the thane answered.

"May they all be damned," the king shouted as he pounded his fist on the low railing.

"Give them time," Guthman said. "Spring is still far off."

"Do they rebel against me? Do they question my kingship?"

"They do not question you, my lord. But travel is not easy. The greater lords are a long way off. Our messengers have not even returned from Domburg or Wic by Dorestad. Perhaps they have not even arrived there yet."

"Yet spring will come, and with it will come Danish ships. We must be ready. We must have a great warhost, for surely they will land with many ships."

"When spring comes, you will have a great warhost behind you," Guthric assured the king.

The king did not respond. He pulled his cloak more tightly about him and lapsed into a sullen silence.

Guthric waited a few moments and then nodded at Guthman. Guthman quickly disappeared into the village. He would speak to those thanes and earls who still remained in Hwitstan—the members of Finn's hearthwerod. There must be some who would still sleep in the hall.

Yet there were none to be found. Thanes and warriors who were once loyal had returned to their homes and villages. Nor would any words from Guthric or Guthman convince them otherwise. Some complained of Finn's silence, others of his temper. Some mentioned there was no gift giving, others said naught. And in the eyes of them all, whether spoken or unspoken, there was a fear of the coming Danish warhost. The warriors had a vision of Finnsburg burning, and none wished to be in the hall when this came to pass. Nor were there any brave words from their king to fill them with courage as there had been in the past.

Finnsburg had become a quiet and sullen place, and none noticed it more than the king himself. "Where are these cowards?" the king demanded that night. He found himself nearly alone in his great hall when the sun set. He was again accompanied only by Guthric and Guthman. Void of mead and mighty warriors, the hall seemed dark and cold. Even Ulestan had long since been driven out by angry words from Finn. He alone, of all those who had departed, had not left from fear or disloyalty, but from shame.

"My king," Guthman said, almost pleading, "if you would but fill them with brave words! Call them back to the hall. Your people would come."

"Does a king plead for people to serve him?"

If we three are here alone, surely we will fall to the Danes, thought the thane, but he said nothing. If he must fall alone at the side of his king, he would do it. Yet, he felt compelled to try to awaken the king's understanding. "My lord, if I may . . . it is you who have made this hall a place of death! No treasure-giving has there been. No mead has flowed into the cups of your servants."

"Death?" Finn shouted, rising to his feet. In an instant he held his great battle sword Healfwyrhta above his head. Guthric placed his hand on his own sword, but Guthman did not flinch. With head bowed, he remained before his king. Finn slowly sat down again. A tear fell from his eyes. "Would you, too, turn away from me?"

"Never, my lord," Guthman replied.

"Treasure-giving? My hearthwerod demands treasure. Freely have I given to all who served. Generously have rings been granted to my thanes. Nor have the mead cups of any ever run dry. Do my people so quickly forget?"

"No, my king," Guthric said, "they do not. That is why I say again, speak bold words to them. Call them back to the hall. Go among your people. They love you still."

"That I will not do," the king replied. "I will not plead. Alone will I fight the Danes and avenge my son if I must." With such conviction and force did he say these words that Guthric and Guthman afterwards remained quiet.

So for many nights Finnsburg sat empty. The proud hall which had once been filled with song and celebration, feast and fellowship was barren. And Finn grew more sullen by the day.

●

Yet, as time passed and the winter moved slowly on, Hildeburh seemed to grow stronger. No explanation was there for her peace save that she had felt the touch of comfort from her new Father. It was that very peace that gave her the strength to return to Willimond once again.

"You must speak to God for me," she said to the monk. She had gone to visit him late in the afternoon on a bitter cold day when but a very few ventured outside.

"Of what?" Willimond replied. Ulestan was present as well and sat listening to the conversation, but he said nothing. His thoughts were still wrapped in gloom. Though he had rejoiced for a time at the news of Hildeburh's receiving of the Christ as her Lord, his joy had not returned to him.

"You must speak to God about Finn," Hildeburh pleaded. "He will not even leave his hall. I sit alone all day waiting for him, but he does not come to me. He believes his thanes have abandoned him, and . . ." She hesitated. "And I fear he is right. So low are his spirits that few may tolerate being around him. There is already talk of another king. I would comfort him as God has comforted me, but he will not be comforted."

"What may I do?" the monk asked, perplexed. "I may not even speak to him unbidden. He will not call for me."

"No," Hildeburh replied, "but you may speak to God. Have you not been teaching us that we must call upon God as our helper?"

"Yes. Each of us must call upon God. You may as well as I."

"But God listens to you."

"He listens to all of us," the monk insisted.

Hildeburh hesitated. For a moment a look of bewilderment crossed her face. Then she spoke again, though more softly. "Once before you have prayed to God, and He brought healing to my family. Finnlaf lay on the bed of death, and God rescued him. Now Finn suffers a more grievous illness. He is in need of healing. Speak to God for me," she pleaded. "He will listen to you."

How could the monk refuse? Nor did he want to. Yet, what could he promise? He knew not what God's answer would be.

"The words you read yesterday . . ." Hildeburh said hopefully.

Willimond looked at her in surprise. So she did listen to his teaching! "'And the prayer offered in faith will restore the one who is unwell . . .'" He repeated the words.

"I have faith," she affirmed. "Yet it is you who must pray."

The monk smiled and nodded. Had her faith already surpassed his? "Then you shall join me in prayer."

Together these two knelt in supplication, the one for his king and the other for her husband. Fervently did they bring their requests before their Lord—Willimond with words and Hildeburh in her heart. All afternoon they interceded for Finn who did not believe; they sought healing on his behalf.

And even while Willimond and Hildeburh knelt in prayer interceding with God, or perhaps because they did so, Guthman and Guthric were interceding as well, not with God but with the people. From door to door did they go, seeking out hale warriors and thanes that they might restore them to their king. Many bold words were spoken to those who had once sat on the benches of Finnsburg: "I remember well when we drank mead together and feasted in the hall of our king. Brave words did we speak to serve him in need. Rings did he give us in plenty, rings which many of us bear to this day—rings and treasures alike. No suffering did any of us have at his hand. Not like Heremod was Finn. No treachery did he commit at our expense. Helmets, shields and hard swords did he give us—good weapons of old. And we pledged to use these in his service. He counted us brave and courageous. We slept in his hall. Now the day has come that our liege lord needs us. Shall he alone suffer pain and fall in battle? He needs the strength of good fighters. Let us go to him. Or will you walk foreverafter in shame, wanderers bereft of king and gift-giver?"

Few indeed could give answer these two, for their words had great effect. Many looked away in shame, but not one was unmoved.

●

Finn did not leave the hall that night, nor all the next day. Hildeburh's spirits once again sank low. *The God has not heard us or does not care*, she thought. Guthman and Guthric, too, thought their words had been in vain. And for a time Willimond wondered the same thing. Yet, he did not cease to pray. Together with Kristinge, they lifted their voices to the High Throne all that day and the next and the next after it. Nor did that monk break his fast during that time.

And His God heard him.

At dusk on the third day, the great battle horn of Finn was once more heard in Hwitstan. Nobody saw him leave Finnsburg save for Guthman and Guthric, who followed him wondering what was to happen. Finn arrived at Finnweard and told his faithful thanes to await him below.

Expecting some dreadful thing to happen, they obeyed nonetheless.

When the horn was sounded, men and women all across the village could not help but lift up their eyes and look upon the hill. Some, thinking the Danes had arrived, grabbed a few bundles of prized possessions and prepared to flee. But others found their hearts lifted with sudden excitement and courage, and they ran out seeking to aid their king. These were chiefly those touched by the words of Guthman and Guthric. Three days they had had to think over the thanes' words, and the courage and loyalty latent within them was aroused once more.

For a brief moment Willimond thought he had heard the trumpet of the Lord, and he looked to the skies waiting to be taken Home. It was said in later days that that horn blast was heard as far as Ezinge and that no greater sound was ever winded from that horn save for that which the king blew on the day of his death.

But Guthman, Guthric and Hildeburh knew what the horn blast meant. For all three had hoped that their real king would someday return, the king they knew—that Finn's courage and hope would come back to him. When they heard that warhorn sound, their hearts leapt in joy, for they knew the day had come. Each hoped or prayed that the day had come soon enough.

When the sound gave way to silence, and the cautious had been convinced that there were no Danish spears coming over the hill, the entire village went out to meet their king. It was a glorious sight. Finn came striding down the hill flanked by Guthman and Guthric and met his people at the door of Finnsburg.

Before he could say a word, Hildeburh came running to him and threw her arms around her king and husband. He did not refuse the embrace. With eyes closed, the king and queen held each other for a long time in front of their subjects.

Two miracles were worked that day—one in the heart of the king, and one in the hearts of his people. For as the king and queen embraced, Guthman and Guthric knelt before them and laid their swords before their sovereign. When Finn looked up, his entire people were kneeling before him in the deep snow. One by one his thanes and warriors came forth and laid their swords and shields at his feet. At first each approached in shame. But the eyes of the king spoke forgiveness, and the thanes quickly regained their joy. Soon there were twenty and five swords at the feet of Finn and as many thanes and warriors kneeling beside them.

It was a small company to go against the powerful Spear-Danes, but the king did not begrudge it.

"Sorrow not, wise warriors," the king began. "It is better for a man to avenge his friends than to mourn much. Too long have

I grieved. The time for sorrow has passed. Many are the brave deeds of this company. Many are the brave deeds still to be done."

"For hearth and hall!" Guthric shouted.

"For hearth and hall!" Finn's hearthwerod joined in.

"For hearth and hall!" the villagers repeated. Though many had never seen the inside of Finnsburg, they nonetheless loved their king.

"For king and for throne!" Guthric shouted more loudly. The cheer was repeated by all.

"Tonight there shall be feasting in Hwitstan," the king shouted loudly enough for the entire village to hear. Standing so that the last golden rays of the evening sun fell upon his face, he lifted his sword.

XXXIV

The Restoration of Ulestan

Indeed the feasting in Hwitstan that night was nearly the equal of any Summer's Day celebration. Once more the flame burned brightly in Finnsburg as it had so often before. Yet, not all saw the flame or felt its heat.

Of all Finn's thanes who were present that day, Ulestan alone did not join the celebration. Nor had he laid his sword at Finn's feet as had the other thanes, for Ulestan no longer bore a blade. Instead he sat alone beneath the roof of the church. Deeply did he wish to be taken once more into his king's trust, but he did not feel worthy. As sounds of the celebration rose, Ulestan sank deeper into his own gloom.

"You are a fool!" Willimond shouted.

Startled, Ulestan jumped up in surprise. He turned and saw the monk standing at the entrance of the church, looking in at him. How long had Willimond been there? Ulestan wondered. How long had he himself been there? He wondered that too, but it did not matter to him anymore. He turned around and sunk again to his knees, ignoring the monk.

"You are a fool," Willimond repeated. "I pitied you once, but I pity you no more."

Ulestan did not turn to face the monk. He did not see the tears in Willimond's eyes, belying his harsh words.

"You, once a mighty warrior, are but a child," the monk went on. He would never have dreamed that he would one day speak to a mighty thane as he was now speaking to Ulestan. But in his life he had done many things of which he had never before dreamed, and so he continued, "You are a warrior no more."

Ulestan was stung. Willimond was his friend—his only friend. Yet now . . . He reached up with his good hand and massaged his crippled shoulder.

"No, not because of your injury," the monk went on, struggling to sound firm and not to let out his tears. What he was doing brought him no joy. "Many men have suffered worse and not abandoned their king as you now have. It is your heart that has failed you, not your shoulder. I need not pity you, for you pity yourself enough for both of us. What do you hope to accomplish by it? Who are you punishing?"

His words were finding their mark. Tears came to Ulestan's eyes.

"Do you think God will not forgive you? You know well that He does, that He has already. It is you who will not forgive yourself. You prefer to wallow like a fish caught in a net. But you are unlike a fish, for at least a fish in a weir struggles. You will not even do that. You have given up. Ulestan the Wise? No. You are Ulestan the Fool. Why? Because you are proud, and in your pride you reject the greatest gift God has given you—forgiveness. You choose instead despair. And you pretend you are serving the king still. You are twice a fool."

Willimond's voice softened suddenly. "And yet even to a fool I would speak further." Coming up behind Ulestan, he laid a hand on his friend's good shoulder. Ulestan winced as if struck. "Turn and accept that which has been offered. Do you not know? 'There is no punishment for those in Christ Jesus.' Accept God's forgiveness. Then you will learn to forgive yourself. Serve Him still. Do you not know that it is God's strength which makes you strong, and not your own? Too long have you trusted in yourself. It is time to trust in Him. The proud He will humble, but the humble He will lift up. Look no longer upon yourself, for there you will find rage, ruin and despair. Turn your eyes to Him and find instead hope."

The monk fell silent. For a long time he stood there in his church with his hands upon his friend's shoulder. Ulestan did not move. Had he even heard? Would he listen? Willimond did not know. He had tried his best. There was no more he could do. As the sun was setting, he turned and walked from the church.

●

Through the setting of the sun and the rising and setting of the moon, the thane did not move from his place. Like a statue of one praying, he sat in silence and darkness. He made no sound when Willimond came in and threw a wool cloak over his shoulders. Only the breath from his nostrils gave testimony to the life within him.

Not until the sun was beginning to rise the following morning did Ulestan move from his vigil. Like a tree that had been cut down, he fell upon his face and began to weep. They were tears of sorrow at first, but as his words came before the High Throne and were heard by the One he served, his tears turned to joy. No forgiveness had he received from Finn, nor would he ever receive any from Finnlaf, but he knew and accepted the forgiveness of his God, and with this came peace.

●

Weeks later Finn and Hildeburh sat beside the hearth under Finnsburg's high roof. The low winter sun of late afternoon streamed in through the west-facing door. Willimond and Ulestan, the monk and the thane, stood before the king and queen. Though a fire burned brightly in the hearth beside them, their hearts were wrapped in a deathly chill.

"You must leave Hwitstan within a fortnight." The words came from Finn.

The words took Willimond completely by surprise. For a moment he started blankly, as if he had either not heard or not understood. "Why, my king?" he finally protested. Ulestan said nothing, his eyes cast on the floor in front of him.

"You must take Kristinge far from here. He will not be safe anywhere in Friesland."

Willimond was bewildered. This command came as a complete surprise to him. He had no desire to leave the church he had worked so hard to begin and nurture. "Kristinge's parentage is secret. Why is he not safe?"

"Are all eyes in the village blind? Though the people are

silent, do you think they do not know? And his resemblance cannot be mistaken by any who look closely." The pride in Finn's eyes was unmistakable as he said this.

"None of your people would harm him, and surely the Danes do not know."

"Perhaps the Danes do not know—yet . . ."

"Nor will they," pleaded Willimond. "The people of Hwitstan would not tell them."

Finn smiled sadly. "Would they not? How about others? From Domburg? From Ezinge? From Wic by Dorestad?"

"Your people are loyal . . . They would not betray you." Though Willimond spoke these words primarily to sway the decision of Finn, he sincerely believed them true.

"I wish that I could believe you . . ."

Please, Lord God, let me stay! the monk prayed silently.

"But I cannot. Alas, there are too many ambitious earls and chieftains. Do you think with Finnlaf dead and me as well as . . ." Finn did not finish the sentence. "If I fall, there are those who would not hesitate to kill Kristinge to bring kingship to themselves or their sons. And who would defend him? He has no thanes. He is too young—too weak."

Throughout the conversation Hildeburh had remained silent. Her eyes looked back and forth between Willimond and Ulestan. However, when Finn spoke of his own death so openly, a look of sudden horror filled her eyes. She stared aghast at her husband. Still she did not speak.

But Willimond saw her look and turned to her for help. "Hildeburh, will you not speak for me? Why must we be made to leave?"

"Are you so certain about your death?" the queen whispered to her husband. Once again tears filled her eyes.

Finn did not answer her. He rose so quickly to his feet that Willimond involuntarily took a step backward. "You have my son. Will you turn my wife from me as well?"

At this, Ulestan's eyes came off the floor. All three stared at the king in surprise. But no one had any response for him. For a long moment nobody stirred, and Willimond began to fear for his life.

"No . . . Those words were not deserved." Finn sighed and sat down. "By my decision was Kristinge given into your keeping,

and willingly did you take him. Thus I say to you again: his safety
is your burden. You must leave Hwitstan at once."

The command was firm, and Willimond knew it. But still he
persisted. "Why must we leave at once?"

"Spring approaches. The Danes will return. Do you think
there will be no battle? Do you think they will come seeking
peace? The words of the wise do not lie: 'Most often, after the fall
of prince or king, the deadly spear rests but a little while though
the bride is good.'"

"But where will we go? Would you have us return to
Lindisfarne?" At that thought the heart of the monk was tem-
porarily lifted. Almost would he be willing to go if he could see
his home again.

"No," Finn replied, removing even that hope from the
monk's thoughts. "You must turn south. Once spring comes, the
seas will not be safe for Frisian ships. Nor could any coastland
harbor a Frisian prince safely. Even now the Danes raid the
Anglish and Saxon shores freely. Your monasteries make easy tar-
gets."

Hildeburh's eyes were wide-open now. She was staring at
her husband in undisguised fright. "Are you so intent upon your
own death?"

Finn did not answer her, but instead asked her his own
question. "Will you not go with them?"

"I will not! I will be at your side even to death!" Hildeburh
responded.

"I would have you safe . . ."

"Then you must find peace."

"I cannot! It is your son as well whose body was taken by
fire. Would you have him unavenged?"

"And it was my brother who died beside him. Would you
add my husband to the pyre?"

Now Ulestan and Willimond stared in amazement at
Hildeburh, for none other would ever have dared to speak to Finn
in such a way. "If I must," he whispered so quietly that only his
wife heard him. She turned and walked away before her tears
could be seen.

"To the south you must go," Finn continued when
Hildeburh had left. "You have often spoken of Luxeuil. Could
you not find a haven there?"

"But what of my people here?"

"If your god is who you say, then he may take care of them."

Willimond fell silent. He could think of nothing else to say. But a voice broke the silence. It belonged to Ulestan. "And what of me?" he asked, looking for the first time into Finn's eyes.

"You will go with them. This son you will protect with your life!"

"That I will do," the thane replied and nodded his head in acknowledgment.

As Willimond looked hard at his friend, he thought he noticed a slight change. For the first time in many weeks Ulestan was standing upright to his full stature. Though one hand still dangled limply from his injured shoulder and arm, the other was clenched in determination. His eyes gleamed with a hint of pride. *Is this exile a punishment or a gift?* the monk wondered. *Is Finn being cruel? Or wiser than I imagined?* And even as he wondered this, he perceived the truth. Ulestan was not being given an insult, but a trust, a chance to redeem himself. And with that opportunity, new courage flowed into the thane. For though he had finally acknowledged God's forgiveness, he had still not been able to forgive himself for his failure to protect Finnlaf. Nor could he face Finn. A burden too great for words had rested upon his shoulder, but now that weight was being lifted. Finn had restored his trust in him—he had restored Ulestan's trust in himself. It was not exile to which Ulestan was being sent. He was being given the charge to protect Finn's other son, his only son. The king would not have done this if Ulestan was utterly rejected in his sight.

Finn paused and let his words settle. They were having the effect on Ulestan which he had hoped they would have. He continued, "There is one thing more." From the clarity and tone of Finn's voice and the sternness in his glance Willimond knew that this was more important than anything he had yet said.

"You must both promise me this," the king commanded. "Upon the sword and staff of the king you must swear, and upon your Holy Writings: When Kristinge is older, you must tell him who he is. You may wait until he is more mature and wiser, but he must someday know." There and then he made Kristinge and Ulestan kneel before him and lay their hands upon the sword and staff.

Together, under Finn's compulsion, Ulestan and Willimond

made the pledge according to the king's wishes. Then they turned and left the hall. And as Willimond walked away, the impact of what Finn had commanded struck him. Kristinge must someday know. Would Finn have his son return? To be king? To give up his service of God?

Or would the kingship of Friesland be the greatest possible service Kristinge could ever render to God?

XXXV

Many Partings

Explaining to Kristinge the reason for their sudden departure from Hwitstan was both more difficult and far easier than Willimond had imagined. It was more difficult because he could not tell him the true reason for their leaving, and yet he would not lie to him. But it proved easier as well, for when he told Kristinge they would be traveling to Luxeuil, Kristinge leapt with joy! Long had he dreamed of going there, ever since Willimond had first told him of that great monastery and place of learning.

The day of departure came upon them, and with many tears the monk preached his last sermon to his people. Ulestan slept for the last time on a bench beside his king, restored to his place within the hall and beside the hearth. Many were the gifts given to these two for their long voyage. To Ulestan were given countless precious rings, both gold and silver. All were crafted by the hand of Deomaer himself, who had grown to a place of high esteem for the works of his hands. Throughout the north Friesland was praised for the beauty of her rings and pendants, and many were the kings who sent apprentices to study under the master jeweler there. But the last gift Ulestan received was the greatest of all. Ulestan would take no weapon from his king, though many mighty ones were offered. Not again would that thane bear a sword. So in place of a sword Finn gave his thane his own staff, the great ash with golden boar's head which had so long been at his side. Many folk wondered at that gift, for they had never seen Finn without his staff. Tears welled in the eyes of both giver and receiver when that gift was given.

To Willimond was given a gold cup from which to drink the

Communion which he had sought on many occasions, with no avail, to explain to Finn. Though Finn understood not the purpose of the Communion feast, he understood well its importance to Willimond, and so blessed him with a worthy gift at their parting. To Willimond also were given by the people of his congregation cloaks, scarfs, boots and many other items made for him by their own hands. So much did he love his people and they him that these simple presents were worth more to him than countless priceless jewels.

The whole village watched in sorrow as Ulestan, Kristinge and Willimond turned southward and rode slowly out of Hwitstan. And oft, both on that day and since, have many wished that they had been with them.

> From Hwitstan he went,
>> Wise thane Ulestan;
> From hearth, from home,
>> From hall and king
> Wanders he now,
>> But not alone;
> With God's own man,
>> Monk Willimond.
>
> Who guides them whither?
>> The wind? The Spirit.
> These two did take,
>> Traveling far,
> The long road south.
>> With snow behind,
> Their charge between,
>> The twain ride on.
>
> Not fear nor foe
>> Did forth them drive.
> They did not desire
>> That sorrowful way.
> A task, a trust,
>> On two was laid;
> One sole command
>> The king did give.

By the grace of God,
The Good One's mercy,
To joy and to peace
Their path may still lead.
And hope is held
The third may return;
A king to Friesland,
Finn's son, Kristinge.

And so these three passed from Hwitstan and eventually out of Friesland. Great sadness filled the hearts of all who knew them. And when they were gone, the spirits of those who remained were once again sorely dampened. For many were they who knew Kristinge as Finn's son, and these wondered at the danger out of which the king would send his own prince. Would he require their lives but spare that of his son?

●

Even as this lonely company rode southward out of sight, a great warband was made ready in the north. For the son of Hunlaf received from his uncles his father's blade, Battle-bright. His uncles placed it in his hands and urged him to go before Hengest, demanding that his father be avenged. Laying that blade on the lap of Hengest, Hunlaf's son reminded the new king of their custom: that blood be paid for blood and that a father's death be avenged. Hengest thought to himself of Hnaef's death and of the wrongs done them at the hands of the Frisians—or so he thought, for he knew not of the treachery of Hunlaf and his brothers. Thus was he easily persuaded by the counsel of Guthlaf and Oslaf. A warband was made ready to return to the south when weather once more would allow them to sail.

●

And as winter waned and spring approached, hearts were lowered further in Hwitstan. For Finn, passing as was his wont around the village, would speak to his people and tell them of the return of his warband—of the coming of his thanes, earls, chieftains and warriors. Hwitstan, he promised, would once again be the throne of Friesland. Yet, no warriors came. And neither Guthman nor Guthric could hide their despair. For with each passing day, and with every flake of snow to melt and flow down the river to the sea, the day of the Danes' coming approached. And still there was no warband to defend against them. Messengers returned from their errands alone.

Finn's chieftains were denying their aid, though not in so many words. "I have need of many men this spring," said some, complaining of raiders and outlaws from which their people needed protection. "I can spare but a few," said others, who would send but a token number to the aid of their king. So Finn's warband grew slowly and sporadically. As March approached, there were but seventy and five armed men sleeping in Finnsburg.

Finn did not despair. Again he sent out messengers. This time he charged them with greater urgency and made threats against some of his chieftains. Still there was little response. Only from Aelfin, son of Aeltar in Domburg, and from Froda in Dorestad, the farthest away of any of the Frisian chieftains, did there come considerable aid. Froda arrived with twenty warriors and bad news. His brother had lost the throne to the upstart Radbod the Young, and Radbod would not send any help to the king. So Froda had left with all who would follow him and had come to serve the king. He was a good thane, and Finn did not fail to show his gratitude.

Aelfin, who grieved Finnlaf's death as much as any save Finn and Hildeburh, sent what help he could. Though he himself came not, a warband under his command arrived on horseback late one evening, its leader bearing the pierced coin of Domburg's chieftain. Twenty and five sword-bearers, all mounted, joined Finn's host, and twenty more without mounts came by ship. Finn's warband swelled to a little over one hundred and forty.

Day by day now the watchmen scanned the harbors for the Danish ships, even as they watched and waited for more Frisian warriors to arrive. But Hildeburh remained in her home. She would not show her face to any save Finn. "Pay the blood money," she pleaded more than once. "Make amends. I would not have my husband joining my son and brother in death."

But Finn would not pay the slayers of his son.

"Lay aside your pride," she asked again.

He would not. And whenever Finn joined others after speaking with Hildeburh, his face revealed the pain and anguish in her heart. He would not speak to another of what passed between them, but it was plain that Hildeburh desired, more than anything else, peace between their peoples.

●

The Danes came as they had promised. Fifteen ships and nearly five hundred men landed on the shores of Hwitstanwic. And with less than two hundred did Finn go down to meet them. Yet he still would not turn. He would not sue for peace, nor would he abandon battle to wait until his strength was restored.

Battle was indeed given that day—the Battle of Hwitstan. Swords met swords, and shields received spear points. Many hearty men lost their lives, and many others were given their death wounds. It would be a long song were the tale of this battle told in full, for valiant deeds and many were done by the people of Friesland, and the deeds of Finn surpassed them all. With Guthric on his right and Guthman on his left, he faced the host of Hengest.

Long did Daelga and Hildeburh watch the battle unfold below them. From atop Finnweard, where so often she had stood beside Finn, Hildeburh took her place without him. Side by side she and the poet saw brave companions fall.

"Alas," Daelga said aloud, "if I could hold a sword and were not a poet, I would fight at his side, that valiant king."

"But to what purpose?" Hildeburh asked. Though her voice was filled with grief and anguish, her meaning was clear.

Daelga was surprised at her words. "That I could share in his glory," he answered. "He is a good king. I would serve him to the last."

"Is there glory in this? I see none." Her question was sincere, though bitterness sharpened her tongue.

Daelga did not respond.

"Evil is triumphing," Hildeburh continued when the poet was silent. "And to what purpose? Because of pride."

Once more words came unbidden to Daelga's mouth. They were the words not of tale nor lay, but of the psalmist. For as a poet, Daelga was touched by the beauty of the Psalms read by Willimond, and many had found a place in his heart, and now they came pouring forth from his mouth:

> "'Why dost Thou stand far off, O God?
>> Why dost thou hide thine eyes in times of strife?
> In pride do the wicked pursue the burdened;
>> Let them be caught in the schemes
>> which they have plotted.
> The wicked man boasts of his heart's desire,
>> And the greedy man curses and rejects the Lord.
> The wicked, in the pride of his being, does not seek Him.
>> He believes there is no God.
> The wicked man's ways are strong and mighty;
>> Thy justice is too high and out of his sight;
>> He snorts at his adversaries.
> Why dost thou stand far off, O God?
>> Why dost thou hide thine eyes in times of strife?'"

When he had finished, Daelga said no more. Hildeburh did not respond. Knowing in their own hearts the grief once known by that psalmist, and having no answers to his questions, they fell silent. Their eyes returned to the battle before them.

The Frisian host had dwindled to but two dozen. And though many more Danes lay dead than the number of Frisians who had fallen, there were many of Hengest's host who still stood. Finn's warband was now more greatly outnumbered than when the battle had begun. The king fought on, though his companions continued to fall. If his hope had vanished, it did not show in the strength or swiftness of his blade.

In the end there were but three: Finn, Guthric and Beowlaf, son of Beow. Guthman had fallen to Hunlaf's son, struck down by the very blade which Hunlaf had borne. Yet, with him on that long journey Guthman took Guthlaf and Oslaf both. Guthric avenged his brother upon Hunlaf's son, but it cost him his shield arm, which now hung shattered and useless. With his right arm he swung his sword valiantly and protected his king.

Only then, when the end had drawn near, did Hildeburh turn away from the fight. She could watch no longer, but turned her face away from the sea and closed her eyes.

So softly that her voice could barely be heard over the din of the shouting Danes and the clash of those few swords which fought on, she spoke. "Why does God allow defeat? I do not know. There is little comfort in that question. And yet this I know, friend Daelga. Defeat is not final. Joy is final. Kristinge lives on. Ulestan lives. Willimond lives. Through the defeat God's servants have been scattered, that is true. And yet to where? To bring his Word elsewhere. Even I, lowly servant that I am, will be scattered."

Daelga turned away from the battle and questioned her with his eyes.

She felt his gaze upon her, though she returned it not. "Do you think my people will leave me here? They will not. Nor will they slay me. I will be taken as if prisoner back to the land of my birth. And when I go I will bring the Word which Willimond brought to me. To those who killed my husband and brother, I will preach. If they will listen not to the death of one, perhaps they will listen to the death of three." She paused and gathered strength. "'If I fly on the wings of the dawn, if I make my home in the farthest part of the sea, even there God's hand will lead me, and God's right hand will take hold of me . . .'" Then that good queen was silent.

From whence came her strength? Daelga did not know. Or perhaps he did. For only One is able to give such strength. Truly she was a great queen, and no equal did she have upon the face of the earth. The poet turned back to the battle. Rarely did he lack for words as he did then. His eyes returned to the fight before him and found Finn. The king still stood, with his two faithful thanes, Beowlaf and Guthric, beside him.

Daelga watched until the end, which was not long in coming.

The Frisian king was worn and tired. His spirit was spent. At the hand of Hengest, Finn fell at last. His death was mercifully short. Beowlaf and Guthric, faithful to the end, refused mercy and soon joined their king whom they had served in life.

The Battle of Hwitstan was finished. The king and his thanes lay dead.

So also died Guthlaf and Oslaf, who went to join their brother. Their wicked deeds had borne their fruit, though they would not earn the reward they desired from them.

The village of Hwitstan was then raided and plundered. Frisian treasure was taken by the hands of the Danes. And the great hall of Finnsburg, which had known much glory in her few years, was burned low. The villagers fled to the forests and fields. Many were hunted down and killed. Others watched the smoke rise and wept for what was lost. Those who escaped the Danish sword had nowhere to go.

Daelga the poet, who had served Folgar, Folcwalda, and Finn, and had known Finnlaf in the days of his youth, was let live until his life's days met their end. Not by the kindness of the Danes was he shown mercy, but because Hildeburh sued for it and would not be denied. In that, if in no other event of that day, was the hand of God shown to him.

Against her will, Hildeburh was taken back to the land of the Danes—the land of cruel spears. She was not wrong. She knew her people well and understood that they would not leave her in Friesland. But with her went the power of the Spirit of God, already undeniably strong in one whose faith was so young.

And on that very day that Finnsburg was burned, the journey of Ulestan, Willimond and Kristinge came to an end. Far to the south the weary travelers arrived at the gates of Luxeuil. Riding over a low hill, they spotted ahead the solid stone walls of the monastery surrounded by its barns, small vineyards and freshly tilled gardens.

A pair of monks working a field off to their right greeted them warmly as they approached. "Welcome in the name of our Lord," one of them called out, straightening his back and letting his hoe rest for a moment.

"From whence do you come and what do you seek?" the other asked in a friendly manner.

"We are pilgrims traveling from the northlands, seeking shelter and . . ." Willimond began to answer, and then paused. He looked at his two companions. What were they seeking? he wondered.

"And?" the second monk pursued.

Ulestan's eyes were tired and vacant, but Kristinge's, despite his fatigue, were open and alert with fresh excitement. Long he had wanted to come to Luxeuil, and now he was there. What would it be like?

"We are pilgrims," Willimond repeated. He could see that they were studying his robe which, though worn and tattered, was similar to their own. He let his hood fall to reveal his greying tonsure. "We would study here, if you would have us."

"Food and shelter we will gladly give, and would not turn weary travelers away," the first monk replied. "If you would study here . . . Well, you must speak to the abbot. Ride on. You will be met at the gate."

Willimond, Ulestan and Kristinge obeyed and once more spurred their mounts onward. "We are almost there," the monk sighed. "God has indeed blessed us."

"Has He?" Ulestan asked. "Sorrow, death and fatigue I feel, and not blessing."

"Do you not know that He has?" the monk replied. "God has not once called me from my home but, no matter how hard the parting, I have not found Him to doubly bless me wherever He would lead me. If I have learned anything, it is this."

"And you would gladly leave behind all that you labored for?" Ulestan demanded. "I did not it so. I would have died at the side of my king."

A tear fell from Willimond's face, and he turned away from his friend. "I grieve," he answered slowly. "Yet I also rejoice, for many have heard the Word and believed. That is something that can never be taken away from them, in life or in death. A work was accomplished which will last through eternity."

Simultaneously both of their glances turned upon the back of Kristinge, who in his eagerness to finally reach their destination had ridden a few paces ahead of his companions. The eyes of the young prince scanned the monastery walls for signs of life.

The monk from Lindisfarne pulled close to the thane and stopped short, grabbing the other's mount. "You serve a Heavenly King now, and greater is He than all earthly monarchs. But even your earthly king may you now serve better than ever before."

Ulestan returned a questioning glance. A glimmer of hope appeared in his eyes.

Matthew T. Dickerson

"Even in human tragedy may our Lord bring about His own glory. Do you not see? Finn himself has said it. He who rides with us is a future king, the son of Finn, son of Folcwalda. It is Finn's wish that he return and take the throne. Look at him. He has the courage of Finn—if not his strength, and the foresight of Folcwalda. And he will have within him the wisdom of the living God. A godly king upon the throne of Friesland! What greater task could we set ourselves to? What more could you wish for your people? How could you bring more honor to Finn?"

Kristinge stopped and looked back impatiently. He was too far ahead to have heard them. Willimond and Ulestan spurred their tired mounts and quickly caught up with the lad. The three of them approached the gate together. It opened, and out stepped a tall man with a broad grin and curly brown hair.

"Peace, weary travelers," the abbot said.

"Peace," Ulestan replied, his journey finally over.

●

And now are all gone and Daelga left alone; left alone to tell of the great sorrow of that time.

It is said by the wise that amid the tales of sorrow and ruin in the darkest of days, there are yet some of joy, and under death's darkness a Light that endures. I would that I knew such a tale, for little joy is there in the telling of this one: the telling of the fall of Finn the strong, and of the grief of Hildeburh the fair. Yet perhaps there is joy to be found by some even in the hearing of this tale, though that joy be mingled with grief. May the Holy One show such Light to His servants, even as He showed the way to Ulestan, Willimond and Kristinge and safely guided their feet onward.